A *Maid*

FOR ALL SEASONS

VOLUME 3

A  Maid
FOR ALL SEASONS

VOLUME 3

Education at Red Blossom College

by
Devlin O'Neill

Venus
Garden City, New York

Published by Venus Book Club, 401 Franklin Avenue, Garden City, New York 11530.

Book design by Christos Peterson

ISBN: 1-58288-175-8

Printed in the United States of America

Chapter 1

A COLD WIND

THE LAW OFFICE conference room smelled of musty paper, furniture polish, and sorrow. Snow flurried outside while the attorney read the will. When he finished, Lisa raised her head from the firm pillow of Beth's arm, picked up her copy and handed it to Michael. He stacked her papers with his and dropped them into a briefcase, then stood and shook the lawyer's hand. The man nodded.

"Good day, Mr. Swayne . . . ladies." He bowed to Beth and Lisa. "I am truly sorry for your loss."

He cleared his throat, rounded the table and went out the door. Michael pulled a white handkerchief from his inside coat pocket. Lisa took it and dabbed her tears.

Michael Swayne, a real estate broker in the small Midwest town, hired Lisa as his maid right after she graduated high school. He stood six-one in his British-made wingtips, had a full head of gray hair, and, although over fifty-five, refused to join AARP because, he said, retired people bored him. The middle-class values of his native England were deeply ingrained, and he never faltered in his duty toward his employees in matters of discipline.

Beth Trelawny, Mr. Swayne's executive assistant and only other employee, was the high end of thirty-something. She had long auburn hair, usually braided French-style during the business day, and stood six feet tall in her office pumps. Her eight years with Michael resulted in a fierce loyalty, both in and out of the workplace, even when, or perhaps especially when, he demonstrated his disciplinary zeal.

The top of Lisa Carlson's head came almost even with Beth's

shoulder when they stood side by side. She turned twenty-one the previous July, but her height, her short, pointy nose, wide-set blue eyes and a tendency to roll out her lower lip made her appear younger. Waiters always asked for ID when she ordered wine with dinner. She lived in a cozy bedroom at Mr. Swayne's house, even after her duties as his maid were sharply curtailed when he sent her to college for a business degree.

Lisa's attachment to Mr. Swayne could not have been firmer, and not only because of his generosity. She relied on his strength, his business acumen, and his ability to remain calm and unflustered, even when she behaved foolishly and he brought the matter to her attention. Ms. Trelawny corrected her as well, on occasion, but Beth displayed more emotion than did Michael.

"Thanks." Lisa clutched soft, folded linen.

Michael sat and patted her knee. "Are you all right, my dear?"

"Yeah, um . . . I didn't mean to fall apart . . . again."

Beth hugged her. "We understand. You're still upset from Darcy's funeral and this only made things worse."

Lisa nodded and looked at Michael. "But why did she leave the stores to *me?* I'm not even related to her."

He took a deep breath. "Ms. Weller took the long view, I think. She knew you loved the shops, perhaps more than her relations do, and since there was enough in her estate to satisfy the family, what with the house and the business insurance, she must have decided to. . . ."

"But Michael, I . . . I can't run them the way *she* did."

"Of course not, honey." Beth pulled the girl to her feet and smoothed her hair. "That's what *in trust for* means. We'll handle things until you're ready to take over."

Michael raised an eyebrow. "Or you could sell them outright, as the attorney suggested."

Lisa gasped and new tears welled in her eyes.

Beth glared at him. "If Darcy wanted them sold she would've left them to her brat niece."

"She put half her *life* into Lola's, Michael."

He sighed and hugged her. "I know. I shouldn't have mentioned it, and I'll do whatever I can to help you. Shall we go home?"

She nodded and took his hand. "Can you drop me at my dad's house? Greg said he'd meet me there when he got done with his final."

"Certainly."

They walked through the reception area and rode the elevator down to the basement garage. Mr. Swayne opened the front passenger door for Lisa while Beth got into the back seat of the Mercedes. Lisa buckled her shoulder harness and looked at Michael.

"If . . . if I really own the stores . . . that means I can hire whoever I want?"

"Well yes, but. . . ." He pursed his lips and glanced at Beth in the rearview mirror as he backed the car.

Beth sighed. "What he means is . . . it has to be a good *business* decision . . . and you need to clear it with the trustees."

Lisa nodded. "And that's you guys . . . so I can hire Greg? Darcy said she'd make him a manager as soon as he graduated, and he'll graduate in a couple of weeks, so can I? Huh?"

"Are you sure you want your boyfriend working for you, honey?"

"Why not?" Lisa turned and scowled at Beth. "You work for *your* boyfriend, so why can't I . . . ?"

"Excuse me?" Michael smirked, gunned the sedan up the ramp and stopped at the sidewalk. "When did I become Ms. Trelawny's *boyfriend*? Or has she another employer that I am unaware of?"

Lisa nudged a strand of hair behind her ear. "I uh . . . I just meant, um. . . ."

He winked and smiled. "It's all right, Lisa. Only we must think things through before we jump in with both feet."

She scowled. "*Geeze*, Michael, I thought you were mad at me."

The Mercedes slipped into the light traffic. "I never am angry with you, my dear . . . not even when you do silly things. But we are now responsible for a five-million-dollar business and almost a hundred employees, so we have to learn to discuss decisions rationally."

"I *know*, but Darcy *promised* Greg that job and it wouldn't be fair if we didn't. . . ."

Beth leaned forward and rubbed Lisa's shoulder. "We'll talk about it later, OK?"

"But what am I supposed to tell Greg? I mean, they're selling Darcy's house and he won't even have a place to *live*. What's he supposed to *do*?"

"Honey, it'll be all right. Greg's a big boy and he can. . . ."

"He can just go to hell for all *you* care. Damn it, I *own* Lola's . . . the lawyer *said* so . . . and I can do whatever I want, so just take me *home*."

Lisa turned to the window and wept. Beth settled back, took a deep breath and looked at Michael. He nodded. Tires slithered on the snow-wet street as he punched the accelerator and twisted the wheel. The black sedan hugged asphalt as it veered left in front of an oncoming truck and shot through a yellow light.

He glanced at his young maid while he drove toward the house on the hill. Twice he opened his mouth, then sighed and shut it. Lisa sobbed into her fists and kicked the door panel. Beth clutched the shoulder harness as they sped along.

The garage door rolled up when Michael thumbed a contact on the dashboard. He stopped and switched off the engine. Lisa whimpered, looked up, and then jerked around.

"You said you'd take me *home*."

Michael frowned, raised the steering wheel and released his safety harness. "And I *will* do . . . but not in your present condition, young lady. I refuse to inflict your emotional distress on your father and sister, not to mention Greg. Now get out of the car and go to your room." He turned his head. "Beth, would you, please?"

The woman nodded. "I'll take care of her."

Lisa stomped the floorboard. "I want to go home *now*."

"You *are* home, missy." Beth got out and yanked open the front door. The harness slithered across Lisa's breasts when the woman thumbed the buckle. "Come on . . . you heard the boss. Go to your room."

"But I don't *want* to . . . for crying out *loud*, Beth!" Lisa swiped tears and then squealed when the woman pulled her out of the car.

"I *said*, go to your room!"

"OK!" Lisa complained when Beth tugged off her overcoat in the kitchen, then complained more as the woman helped her along with sharp smacks to the seat of her woolen skirt. She opened the door to Lisa's room and pushed her toward the dresser.

"Why are you being so *mean*, Beth?"

"You'll *think* mean in a minute. Why are *you* acting like a spoiled brat?"

"I'm *not*."

Beth snatched a handful of Kleenex from a box on the dresser. Lisa grunted when her bottom thumped the cushioned stool and squinted as Beth wiped away tears. The woman sighed.

"So . . . you've owned a chain of boutiques for what? An hour? And already you're acting like a poor little rich girl. What's the idea talking to Michael that way?"

Lisa glared and blew her nose. "What's the idea smacking my *butt* all the way through the house? Damn it, I'm not a little *girl* anymore."

"And that's another thing . . . where did all the hell and damn come from? You know Michael hates cussing. What's gotten *into* you?"

"*Nothing*, I . . . I want. . . ." New tears welled in her eyes. "I want to go home."

Beth blinked back a tear and bent to hug the girl. "I know, honey. That's where we should be after somebody dies . . . someone we love . . . but you can't go to your dad's house until we straighten out a few things."

Lisa wrapped her arms around Beth's neck. "But what about Greg? He . . . he said he'd meet me there."

"It's only eleven o'clock and his last exam isn't until one, so we have plenty of time."

"OK . . . but I'm really worried about him. I mean, what's he gonna *do* now that Darcy's gone?"

Beth smiled. "That's what we need to talk about."

"Yeah but . . . I mean . . . OK." Lisa sighed. "He said he'd help me with my make-up classes. I know you guys are disappointed I didn't finish the semester."

"I think even Darcy would understand that you weren't up to it . . . after the accident."

Michael leaned against the doorframe. "Feeling better, my dear?"

Lisa pouted at him. "Michael, I really . . . I want to. . . ." She grunted and jerked to her feet. "Mr. Swayne, Greg gets that job *now*."

Beth turned and shook her head. "Nice timing, Mr. Swayne."

He raised an eyebrow and nodded. "So I see. Lisa, could we discuss this?"

Fire burned in her light-blue eyes. "You can discuss it all you *want* . . . but the bottom line is, Greg gets a manager job!"

"Oh, bloody hell." Beth stepped away from the girl.

Michael shot her a steely glance and then looked at Lisa. "The bottom line, young lady, is that you do *not* talk to me in that manner. I appreciate the stress you have endured over the past few weeks, but I *won't* tolerate such impertinence."

Lisa backed toward the bed as long-dormant butterflies flapped in her tummy. Michael took a deep breath and slipped off a gray Pierre Cardin suit coat. Beth caught it when he tossed it away, and Lisa gasped as he held out a hand.

"Sir, I . . . I didn't *mean* to . . . Michael? I'm sorry! You're not gonna . . . no, *please?*"

Her heart throbbed beneath firm breasts, and taut nipples burned against a pink satin bra when he took her arm, turned, and sat on the bed. She squealed when he drew her across his thighs, and the butterflies in her tummy bounced like super-balls.

"It has been some time since I've had to correct you . . . far *too* long, it seems. Stop kicking, Lisa . . . you know what happens when you misbehave."

"But I don't *wanna* get spanked . . . I'm too *big* to get spanked, damn it!"

Michael scowled to hide a smile. Beth shook her head as he lifted the girl's skirt to expose pink satin panties. The soft cloth puckered across a deep, narrow divide in her round bottom, and plump under curve peeked beneath the leg bands. Lisa yelped when he swatted the tender flesh just above her thighs.

"*What* did you say, young lady?"

Lisa sniffled and jammed her elbows into the quilt. "I can't believe you'd *do* this to me, Michael. It's not fair! After all we've *been* through? I mean, geeze! Ow!"

A sharp clap echoed and warm sting prickled her cheeks.

"Hush!" His hand rested on her satiny behind for a moment, then he thumbed the panties down. "What I can't believe is that you would do this to *me*."

"Michael, no!" She reached back to grab her underwear.

"Take your hand away this *instant*, Lisa."

She clasped her fists beneath her chin and quivered as he squeezed bare mounds. "Please sir, I. . . ."

"I said *hush*. You have screeched, pouted, demanded, and generally acted like a spoiled child ever since we left the attorney's office and I have had *enough*."

"I'm sorry and I won't do it anymore so please don't spank me *owee*!"

His palm smacked again and crisp heat swept across tender, naked flesh. Quick, hard swats followed, and shameful tears burned Lisa's eyes. She kicked and squirmed, but he held her waist in an iron grip and rained hot spanks on her bottom. Beth's incisors teased lower lip as she watched Lisa's white behind turn pink, then coral, then red under Michael's hand. The girl wailed, squealed, and then shrieked.

Michael gritted his teeth while his palm stung, burned and then went numb. Lisa shuddered as he scooped her up to cradle her in his arms. Tears scalded his neck and heat from her bottom warmed his thighs.

"Shh . . . it's all right, Lisa. You were a bad girl and I had to spank you very hard . . . but it's quite all right now."

She wiped her nose on a blouse sleeve and sobbed. "I . . . I . . . I'm *sorry*, Michael. Do . . . do you forgive me?"

"Of course I do. But you must promise to listen to me . . . and to Beth . . . when we try to help you."

Lisa nodded and glanced at the woman. Beth sat on the bed and stroked Lisa's hair.

"Are you through being a brat, honey?"

Michael frowned. "Beth!"

"OK, OK . . . I forgive you, too . . . but you had that coming. No more Gloria Vanderbilt?"

The girl wrinkled her nose and looked at Michael. He smiled.

"Another poor little rich girl. You really should read her book, now that you're in a similar predicament."

"Did . . . did she get spanked?"

Beth laughed. Michael shook his head.

"No . . . and that's why I think you will come through this situation in better shape than she did."

Lisa opened her mouth but Michael covered it with his lips. Beth sighed.

"I'll get the cold cream."

She went into the bathroom and grabbed a jar. Michael patted Lisa's back and twisted her around to lie across his lap. She moaned, clenched her rear cheeks, and then wriggled her tummy an inch forward so that her bottom lifted and rounded over his thighs. Michael took a deep breath as the smooth, shadowy cleft widened. Beth smirked and handed him the jar. He coughed and nodded.

"Thank you, Ms. . . . um . . . Beth."

"No problem, Mr. um Michael."

Beth winked and sat on the bedside as Michael scooped cool slickness with his fingers and stroked white cream over tight, red flesh. He massaged relief into her sore cheeks while Beth held her hand. Lisa sighed and squirmed as she clutched Beth's fingers. Michael dipped more cream and rubbed it along the tender crease at the base of Lisa's bottom. She gasped and parted her thighs. His fingertips touched hot wetness, slipped inside, and found the tiny, fiery node between slick lower lips.

Moist electric sparks shot up Lisa's spine, danced between her ears and exploded behind closed eyelids. Smooth tremors shook her belly, moved down her legs, and then up through her breasts. She squealed and lifted her hips. Michael caressed the puckered vent between her cheeks with his thumb while his middle finger stroked circles around her clitoris. Syrupy fire bathed her from crown to heel, and magnificent shock waves jolted her soul. Lisa screeched, twisted around, and collapsed into his arms.

He smiled as she moaned, gathered her up and put her on the bed, then kissed her and left the room. Beth helped her out of her damp clothes and into a fleecy sweat suit, then went to find Michael.

Chapter 2

FRIENDLY SKIES

RAINWATER PUDDLED THE tarmac around the DC-10's tires. It sat at the LAX gate while a cold steady rain such as Los Angeles hadn't seen in eighteen months fell from a gray February sky.

Professor Dylan Travis gritted his teeth and hoped he wouldn't be called for a body search. He shook his head while the gate agents frisked a twelve-year-old boy and two grandmotherly women for deadly weapons. His jaws ached but he didn't snarl at the woman who took his ticket, then sat at the front of the first cabin. The flight attendant brought him a Glenlivet and a glass of water while the rest of the passengers shuffled in. She smiled as she scritched the top off the bottle, and then backed against the bulkhead next to his leg when four gangly teenagers jostled past. The woman nodded to them as they leered and heaved their bin-hog carry-ons through the aisle.

Dylan poured scotch and glanced at her. "You're usually on the Boston plane, aren't you?"

She nodded and smiled but didn't look at him as more passengers trooped by. "Hi! Go right on back! Oops! You OK? We can check that bag if you want. All right. Hi! Welcome aboard!"

He sipped and let the malt warm his mouth before he swallowed. The attendant's knee rubbed his while she greeted passengers. He sat alone in the first row on the starboard side. His eyes closed and he leaned back. The attendant went to seat two more first-cabin passengers, but returned after a minute and again he felt her leg. He opened his eyes when the couple one row back and across the aisle asked for gin and tonics. Her bottom stretched gray trousers as she leaned over to serve the drinks. She straightened and turned to wink at him.

When all passengers had boarded, the woman secured the door and then puttered in a cabinet. She pantomimed the buckle-and-oxygen-mask routine while another attendant recited the safety script over the PA, and then strapped into a jump seat beside the cockpit door. Engines screamed, relaxed, screamed again, and the jet rolled. Dylan finished his scotch just as the plane roared into the sky. He guzzled water to make his ears pop. They reached altitude and the attendant brought another plastic bottle.

"Are you OK, Professor?"

He nodded and stretched his jaw. "Yes, thank you. How's Jack doing with the new job?"

She frowned. "My boyfriend's name is Jim and you know that perfectly well."

Metal scratched plastic when he twisted the bottle cap. Dylan grinned.

"Oh yeah. Jim . . . and you're Candy. I remember."

She growled, snatched the bottle from his hand and poured amber fluid into his glass. "I could cut you off, you know."

He gasped. "Sandy! I *said* Sandy, honest! And you have two Siamese cats named Oscar and Felix, but one of them has a problem with his. . . ."

Sandy batted his nose with a fingertip and laughed. "Just hush, Professor. I won't cut you off *yet*. Now be a good boy and quit teasing me while I get some work done."

"Whatever you say, ma'am, just don't. . . ."

She put a finger across his lips and Dylan smiled.

"I said to quit it, mister. You are *such* a pain in the butt."

He kissed her finger. "I could rub it out for you."

"What?"

"The pain in your butt."

Sandy winked. "I bet you could . . . but I have a job to do. I'll be back in a few. . . ."

"Miss! Could I get a drink?"

The male half of the gin and tonic couple shook his glass at

Sandy. She smiled a very professional smile and went to him. There were only five passengers in first-class. Sandy took care of their needs in short order and then helped in the main cabin.

Dylan sighed, sipped whisky, pushed his chair back and drowsed. Somewhere over the high desert, the plane lurched and he awakened. Sandy clattered in the galley and he caught glimpses of her bottom as she bent to reach lower compartments. He cleared his throat, waited a dozen seconds and then moaned. Her head popped around the bulkhead. She glared at him and then smiled.

"You're pretty noisy, Professor."

He grinned and held up his glass. "And *you* are derelict in your duties, Miss."

She rolled her eyes. "Yes, *sir*. Would you care for another Glenlivet, sir? It would be my pleasure to bring you another, sir . . . if you can prove you're not getting schnockered, sir."

His jaw dropped and he set the glass on the console. He twisted around to look at the couple across the aisle, who dozed in their chairs, then leaned over to see the two women fast asleep in the rear seats. Sandy grinned when he scowled and crooked his finger. She opened a drawer and took out a bottle, then bit her lip as her back thumped the bulkhead in front of him. He pushed the button to set his seatback in the full upright and locked position.

"You need your fanny smacked, don't you?"

Sandy pouted. "No, sir. Not right now, sir." She glanced at the cockpit door and then looked at Dylan. "But I told Jim what you said . . . and you know what? I spent seventeen hundred dollars on clothes at Saks and he *spanked* me."

Dylan chuckled and took the bottle. "Did it help?"

She grinned. "Uh huh . . . and he only made me take back half of the clothes . . . but *geeze* did I get wet."

He smiled and poured. "I told you, didn't I?"

"Yeah." She glanced around the cabin, turned to look into the galley and then settled her bottom on his chair arm. "Did I read your ticket right? New York and then Hamburg?"

Cool warmth drizzled his throat as he sipped. "I'm going to see my sister."

She scowled. "Why didn't you just take an over-the-pole flight from LAX?"

"I could have . . . but I need time to think. I think better on airplanes."

Sandy grinned. "No, you *drink* better on airplanes."

"Are you *asking* for a spanking, young lady?"

"Are you offering?"

"No, and don't tempt me. You're way too cute for your own good."

"Thanks." She glanced at the other passengers. "Your sister lives in Hamburg?"

He nodded. "She married a friend of mine who lived there . . . but he died . . . in a plane crash a couple of years ago."

"That's awful! Is she OK?"

"As OK as she can be, I guess. The daughter took it pretty hard, though."

"How old is her daughter?"

"*His* daughter . . . her mother died of leukemia when she was just a baby."

"Poor thing . . . no wonder she took it so hard."

Dylan took a deep breath and another sip. "It's been kind of rough on her, and she's been kind of rough on my sister."

"What do you mean?"

"Well, my sister is only twelve years older than the girl . . . which was fine as long as Gerhard was around. I mean, he never intended for Fel to be a mother to Teresa . . . which is OK because she's not really the motherly type."

"Bullshit. *All* women are the motherly type if they get a chance."

He smiled. "If you say so . . . but Fel always said that about herself."

"What's her name? *Fell?*"

"Felicia . . . a family name from her mother's side. I wasn't too crazy about it, but Dad would have named her Throatwarbler Mangrove if Carly told him to. Fel's mother was pretty and young and spoiled rotten . . . but Dad worshipped her."

Sandy laughed, took his empty bottle and brought him another from the drawer. "So Felicia is your half-sister?"

"Uh huh. She was a late-life surprise for my dad . . . well, for all of us. She was an adorable baby, though . . . and it was hilarious watching Dad show her off to his buddies. They all had grandkids, and he strutted around with this little doll in his arms and his chest stuck out like, 'Hey! Look what I did!'"

"I'll bet . . . so is he still around?"

Dylan shook his head. "He passed about a year ago . . . in a nursing home. Carly . . . Fel's mom . . . hooked up with a musician in Venice Beach and they ran off to New York when Felicia was in kindergarten. Dad never really recovered from the divorce."

"That's *terrible*."

"I told you she was spoiled."

Sandy pouted and shook her head. "What about *your* mom?"

"She's quite well, thank you. Lives in Seattle with her third husband . . . or is it her fourth? I've lost track."

"I doubt *that*, Professor. But back to your sister . . . it sounds like you've got one orphan trying to raise another."

"That's pretty much the case. Teresa's nineteen now and it seems the older she gets, the worse she acts."

"What . . . like drugs and stuff?"

"No, I would have spotted that . . . she just doesn't *do* anything . . . skips school, blows off homework, sits at the computer and plays in chat rooms all day."

"And now Uncle Dylan is going all the way to Germany to straighten out his little brat niece?"

He squinted at her and smirked. "Possibly. I'm going to Germany to talk her into coming here. It took me almost six months to set everything up, and six months before that to convince Fel she needed to come back to the States."

"So your niece . . . Teresa? She needs convincing, too?"

"She's not too thrilled about leaving her friends . . . but she always wanted to live in America, so I think I can persuade her."

"The change will do her good, if nothing else. Will she go to school here?"

"Two schools, in fact. University and an adjunct college."

"What? Like a language school?"

Dylan nodded. "In a way, but more than that. She started speaking English when she was four . . . so she could talk to me when I came to visit . . . and she's fluent in Italian and Spanish. Not so hot in French, she says . . . but knows all the dirty words."

Sandy laughed. "I had six quarters of French in college and I can barely order off a menu anymore."

"That's because you don't use it. It's different in Europe."

"Yeah, I know. So what's this school *for* . . . if not to teach her English?"

"It's to teach her *better* English . . . and to improve her behavior."

The woman raised her eyebrows. "Improve it how?"

"Through individual attention, strong leadership, and discipline."

"Oh yeah? If there's a school like that in LA I should tell my sister about it. *Her* darling little brats are about one curfew violation short of some serious D home time."

Dylan chuckled and sipped. "You mentioned them. Courtney and . . . Justine, was it?"

"Courtney and Jasmine . . . yeah. So what's the name of this school?"

"Red Blossom College . . . but it's not in LA . . . and it doesn't accept minors."

"Well *that* sucks. How come you're sending your niece away to school after you bring her back here?"

"I'm not. The university and the college are both in the same town . . . which is where I'm moving."

"What? You're leaving LA? What am I supposed to do on the LA to Boston flight without you to annoy me?"

Dylan squeezed her thigh and smiled while Sandy folded her arms and glared.

"I'll still fly to Boston . . . but either out of Omaha or Des Moines."

She gasped. "What are *you* going to do in flyover land, Professor?"

He shrugged. "Same as always . . . teach, write . . . search for universal truth in an ever-changing culture."

"Oh yeah right . . . business as usual." She laughed. "Are you talking about that little town where you go on your sabbaticals?"

"That's the one . . . very peaceful place. My father used to stay at the cottage when he needed to escape the rat race, and I did the same after I started teaching."

"Seems like a long way to go just to get away. Why buy a house there?"

"We didn't . . . his aunt left it to Dad, so it's mine and my sister's now. Nice people . . . easy to make friends there . . . even did some tutoring when I stayed for any length of time."

"Always the professor, huh?" Sandy's left eye squinched almost shut. "So . . . this college? With the discipline and everything? Sounds like something *you* would invent."

Dylan nodded and raised his glass. "Red Blossom College at Red Blossom Cottage."

Sandy chuckled. "I should have known. But what are you going to *do* to that girl? Will she be the only one at the school?"

"Of course not. I already have seven applicants . . . all college age . . . and I had the cottage completely remodeled."

"Wait a minute . . . you mean the same kind of discipline we've been talking about on the red-eye flights to Boston for the past couple of years? The kind that gets my undies damp just *thinking* about?"

Dylan sighed. "Young lady, the state of your underwear is certainly no concern of. . . ."

"But you *told* me . . . in so many words . . . that I ought to. . . ."

"Hush, girl."

She scowled. "OK . . . sir."

"As I was saying, . . . *your* reaction to a certain type of stimulus is very different from that of a woman fifteen years younger than you . . . so there is really no comparison . . . even though the stimulus may be similar in nature."

Dylan frowned, and then smiled as Sandy leaned over to whisper in his ear.

"If you take the girl's panties down to spank her, you can *bet* her reaction will be similar in nature."

He grabbed Sandy's arm and kissed her cheek. "But I *am* the professor . . . and well versed in the disciplinary arts . . . so you will have to take it on faith that I know what I'm doing."

The woman giggled and shrugged off his hand. "I will *not* take it on faith. I want full reports, with details, as soon as they happen."

"Oh, *do* you now? And how do you propose I relay these reports to you?"

"There's always e-mail . . . but I'd rather you just tell me."

Dylan shook his head. "You're never home and I refuse to tell stories to an answering machine."

"Then how about . . . when you decide which airport you're going to use as your base, I'll try to get my Boston route changed."

He smiled. "I certainly can do that. Now. Is there anything to eat?"

Sandy grinned, picked up the empty bottle and backed into the galley.

Chapter 3

A LESSON FROM HISTORY

TERESA STOOD ON the mat just inside the History building door and stamped snow off her boots while she watched Uncle Dylan's face. He looked straight ahead as he untied the belt of his long leather coat, then slipped it off and draped it over his arm. Her heart thumped like a jackhammer beneath her breasts as she unzipped her jacket.

Sometimes it was hard for Teresa to remember why she loved him, especially when he shifted into professor mode. She ran quivery fingers through shoulder-length, light brown hair as he led her to the lift. Teresa was five feet six inches tall and weighed a bit over 120 pounds. She had a round, cherubic face, and bright green eyes.

They rode in silence to the fourth floor. Teresa blinked and chewed a fingertip. She wanted to say something, anything, but Uncle Dylan had his stern look on and the words caught in her throat. The lift doors opened and they walked across the hall. Black letters on the half-glassed office door read "Henry H. Bender." Teresa leaned back when he reached for the latch.

"Uh-Uncle Dylan?"

"What, Teresa?"

"*Please?*"

He frowned. "Please what?"

"Please do not make me go in. He . . . he said he wants to see *you* . . . not me."

"Stop being ridiculous and come along."

Teresa whimpered and he took her hand. A blonde woman at the desk looked up and smiled when they entered the anteroom. She was early twenty-something with light-blue eyes, an upturned nose, and a smug tilt to her chin. A pink tongue-tip caressed full lips as she leaned forward to inspect the cut of Dylan's American suit.

"Good day, sir." She grinned when he smiled. "May I help you?"

Dylan handed her his card. "We have an appointment with Professor Bender at two o'clock."

The woman nodded and clicked the computer mouse, then watched Dylan as the schedule popped onto the screen. "Certainly, Professor Travis. One minute, please."

She took a handset from the console and pressed a button. Teresa turned away when the young woman looked at her. Dylan put his hands on her shoulders and slid the fluffy ski jacket down her arms. Butterflies danced in her tummy when his hip brushed the seat of her snug jeans. He hung their coats on pegs by the door. The woman cleared her throat and put the receiver down.

"Go right in, sir."

"Thank you. Wait here, Teresa."

"But, do I have to . . . ?"

"*Wait.*" His tone made her tremble.

Dylan opened the inner door. Professor Bender stood and held out a hand. His face had a scholar's pallor; pale blue eyes glimmered beneath thick brows; stringy white hair fringed his bare head. He stood two inches shorter than Dylan, had a long, thin nose above a small mouth, and a pointed chin. Teresa bit her lip as the door shut.

"You may sit over there while you still can," the receptionist said in English.

Teresa gaped when the woman winked. "*What?*"

"If you want to sit over there, it's quite all right."

"That is *not* what you said."

The woman smirked and turned to the keyboard. Teresa huffed and crossed her arms as she sat in a side chair. She squirmed on the padded seat and glared at the woman's back. A murmur of conversation came from behind the office door. Teresa could tell who spoke, but not what was said. Itchy warmth tantalized her bottom beneath cotton underpants and brushed denim jeans. She crossed and uncrossed her ankles as she struggled to hear. The receptionist got up and leaned over to open the lower drawer in a cherrywood credenza. Her short woolen skirt rode up slender thighs and exposed the gusset of cream-colored silk panties. Two light pink stripes spanned plump fleshy crescents, just where the cheeks joined the thighs. Teresa covered a gasp with her palm and the woman turned.

"Excuse me?"

"I did not say anything."

"Oh? I thought you spoke."

Teresa frowned and stared at the wall. Four black and white photos hung just above her line of sight and she stood to see them. Young men in rowing uniforms grinned for the camera as they leaned on their oars. Small Union Jacks hung from a cable stretched between two poles. She thought she recognized a very young Professor Bender and bent for a closer look. Pants seam snugged between round cheeks and she shut her eyes as manic butterflies returned to her tummy. Behind her eyelids she saw clearly her own bottom, when Uncle Dylan spanked it only two days before.

⁂

Teresa squealed like a little girl when he stopped his rented BMW in the driveway. She always squealed when Uncle Dylan came to visit, though she promised herself she wouldn't. His blue eyes sparkled when he stepped through the door, hugged and kissed her, and she grinned when he dug a stuffed bear from his bag and gave it to her. Wrapped with red satin ribbon around the bear's tummy was the new CD by her favorite LA boy band, the one she had downloaded two songs from on the pirate site.

Dylan hugged his sister while Teresa hugged the bear, and she was surprised when Felicia said she could go listen to her CD. She logged on to a chat room while she played with her soft new toy and let the silky smooth boy-harmonies caress her ears. It felt so wonderful and she was so happy with her uncle's present, but then she remembered the trouble at school and realized her stepmother might tell him about it, so she said goodbye to her friends and shut off the stereo.

Felicia and Dylan sat at the kitchen table. She sipped red wine from a goblet and he had a big glass with just a little brown liquor in it. They looked up when she peeked around the doorjamb.

"Hi, sweetie . . . come in." Dylan pushed back his chair and held out his arms.

Teresa pouted as she trudged toward him. She whimpered when he took her hands and pulled her onto his lap.

"I . . . um . . . thank you for the disk, Uncle Dylan."

"You're more than welcome. Fel told me how much you like that group." He hugged her and then cupped her chin. "Are you OK?"

She huffed and looked at her stepmother. "What *else* have you been telling him?"

Felicia shook her head. She was almost as tall as Dylan, and nearly as wide at the shoulders, but lighter of complexion. Her hair was brown, just a shade darker than Teresa's, and she had Dylan's bright blue eyes, full lips and ready smile. She tried to smile at that moment but failed.

"I uh . . . I only said that you were having a few problems at university."

Teresa gasped and wriggled, but Dylan held her close. "Felicia, it is merely *nothing*. You must not trouble Uncle Dylan with these matters, and also it is none of his business."

Dylan shook his head and kissed Teresa's cheek. "I'm afraid it *is* my business, sweetie . . . so why don't you tell me about it?"

"I will not and you cannot *make* me because I am an adult now and I need my space so leave me *alone*."

"You need *something*, that's for sure."

He took a deep breath and Teresa shuddered when his arm muscles tensed. She pushed against his hard chest with both hands but he scooped her up and carried her into the living room. Her calves scissored and plush bunny slippers sailed off her feet. He sat on the sofa, turned her across his lap and grabbed a handful of thick cotton gym pants. They slid off her pert behind when he tugged, and Teresa screeched as he thumbed boy-leg briefs down to bare her bottom.

"Hush that squawking. Your manners have become absolutely atrocious, young lady. How *dare* you yell at Felicia, or at *me*, for that matter?"

Teresa kicked, twisted and reached back to cover her shameful nakedness, but Dylan tightened his grip on her waist, grabbed her right wrist and swatted hard. Fiery sting lanced through her cheeks and she yelped. He slapped again and she squealed.

"Naiee! Uncle Dylan! You must *not* . . . you *cannot* . . . *no!*"

On and on he spanked, and higher and higher the flames leapt in her soft behind while he scolded in his smooth, even baritone. She wriggled and wailed but knew it was no use. Uncle Dylan was there to punish her, and awful as that was, at least he was there. Tears wetted the sofa cushion as she pushed up her hips to accept his sharp, nasty, cleansing spanks.

When it was over, she quivered and sobbed while he cuddled her. His neck smelled of musky citrus and his hand felt like rich velour as he rubbed her sore bottom. He told her that he would talk to the professor who gave her so many problems, and she yielded with only a token protest.

Professor Bender's door opened and Teresa gritted her teeth as she turned away from the photos. Dylan held the stapled pages of her assignment in his hand.

"Come in, please."

She glared at the odious document as she shuffled toward the inner sanctum and ignored the receptionist's grin. The door clicked shut. There were two heavy wooden chairs in front of the desk. She trembled as Dylan made her sit in one and then sat beside her in the other. Oaken chair arms cooled her sweaty palms and she stared at the desktop. Scarcely three feet away, at the far edge of the desk, very near the professor's right elbow, lay a thin rattan cane, its brown tip pointed straight at her heart. Professor Bender took her paper from Dylan and then cleared his throat.

"Hello, Teresa."

"Good day, sir," she whispered.

"I have told your uncle of my concerns regarding your conduct. Since I spoke to you about the matter earlier, I'd like to hear your thoughts."

She stared at the cane as if it were a serpent that might strike at any moment. Dylan cleared his throat.

"Teresa?"

"What?" She jerked toward him.

"We want to know how *you* see the matter. What do *you* think we ought to do about your conduct? And I would appreciate it if you'd stop daydreaming."

"I ... I'm sorry, Uncle Dylan, I only. . . ." She sobbed and grabbed his jacket sleeve with both hands.

"What on *earth*?"

"Do not let him cane me, Uncle Dylan, *please*?"

"Teresa, for heaven's sake."

"I ... I *know* I was being lazy and I should not have downloaded that story as my assignment . . . but I did not claim it was *mine*."

Professor Bender leaned back and shook his head. "Teresa, this isn't the nineteenth century. I doubt if anyone has counted the laws, policies, and regulations that forbid my *touching* a student, let alone *caning* one . . . and while I'm gratified to see that you have taken to heart the research you did into historic disciplinary practices, you must realize that this little stick is merely a toy . . . a souvenir given me by a student with a rather fanciful imagination."

Teresa took a deep, shuddery breath. "Yes, sir, I ... I understand." She released her stranglehold on Uncle Dylan's jacket and twined her fingers in her lap. "I . . . I will do better, Professor. I will use the research to write my own papers from now on." She looked at Dylan. "OK?"

He smiled. "Yes, but there's the matter of your inattention in class."

Bender slid a sheet from the stack on his desk. "As well as your quiz performance. For instance . . . when I asked who instigated the Munich Putsch, you said Kaiser Wilhelm." Teresa blushed and the professor sighed. "When I asked where Archduke Ferdinand was assassinated, you said in Sacramento. All told, you got three correct out of twenty . . . and I *gave* you one of those."

Dylan frowned. "What was that, Professor?"

"I asked for the capital of West Germany and she said there *is* no West Germany."

Teresa shrugged and looked at Dylan. "I thought it was a trick question."

He shook his head. "Teresa, do you want to fail this class?"

Tears welled in her eyes. "No, I . . . I *want* to do better, honestly, I only . . . need to concentrate."

"What can I do to help?"

She fluttered moist eyelashes and smiled. "Have patience with me? Like you always do?"

"I do, don't I?" He sighed, sat back, and then smiled at the man across the desk. "I see what you mean, Professor. I do feel rather wrapped around someone's little finger."

Teresa sat bolt upright and gaped. "Uncle Dylan, that is not *truth*. I never said that I would wrap. . . ."

Professor Bender picked the cane two inches off the desktop and slapped it against oak veneer. "Be quiet, girl."

Dylan stood, turned, set his fists on his hips and glared.

"Uncle Dylan, do not *look* at me like this! You are scaring me."

"The professor can't punish you for your idleness, except by failing you . . . and *that* is unacceptable. But he has offered me an alternative."

Her jaw clenched and butterflies raced through her tummy. "I do not know what you mean."

"I think you *do*, Teresa. Starting now, and until the end of the term, your history assignments will be your first priority. Before I go home, I will proofread the essay you write to replace the drivel you downloaded, and then I will check the rest of your assignments by e-mail."

She sighed with relief and nodded. "Yes, Uncle Dylan. I shall work very hard to make up for this error in judgment."

His lips twisted in a half smile. "Indeed you *shall*, young lady . . . so you get used to how hard you will work at your new school in America."

"What? But I did not say I will go to America! How can you merely . . . ?"

"Hush, Teresa." He held up a hand, the thumb and forefinger extended an inch apart. "You are *this* close to being dismissed from university and since I can't fly to Germany every time you get into trouble, you *will* go . . . to where I can instruct you properly."

"But . . . but Uncle Dylan!" A hot tear rolled down her cheek. "You . . . you said we would talk about this. You cannot take me from my *home*."

He shook his head. "I'm taking you *to* your home . . . and we will finish this discussion later. Right now I want to know one thing."

"Whuh . . . what?"

"Did you even *read* that paper you handed in?"

She blinked, nodded and smudged dampness from her eyes. The web site was called Victorian Schoolgirls, and contained stories and essays, a few well written, most very bad, all pure fantasy. They claimed to depict the nineteenth-century British education system, but the imbedded graphics, with a few line-drawn exceptions, were of models old enough to have schoolgirl daughters of their own. Teresa knew the essay she copied was not authentic, but the overall tone of the piece was cold, pedantic and very much in line with the attitude of the era toward the efficacy of corporal discipline.

"Yeh-yes, Uncle Dylan."

"Do you recall *why* those girls were sent to the Dean's study to be punished?"

Teresa tried to swallow the lump in her throat but it wouldn't go down past the flock of furious butterflies. "They . . . they did not pay attention in class." The words came out in a hoarse croak.

Professor Bender nodded. "And they wasted their time on matters of no consequence. Does that sound familiar, Teresa?"

She jumped to her feet and threw her arms around Dylan's neck. "I'm sorry," she whispered to his ear. "I will be good from now on, and . . . you perhaps should spank me a *little* when we go home . . . but not *hard* because you already. . . . ."

He held her close. "I'm not going to spank you when we go home."

A smile lit her face as she let go of his neck and looked up. "Thank you, Uncle Dylan." Deep furrows creased his brow. Her jaw dropped and her heart skipped a beat. "No . . . you . . . you cannot mean that you will. . . ."

His eyes blazed. "Professor Bender has expended a great deal of time and energy on you, young lady, and he deserves to see justice done."

"*No!*"

"Unfasten your jeans." Dylan grasped her shoulders and held her at arm's length. "*Now*, Teresa."

"But Uncle . . . you cannot *do* this." Fiery redness bathed her face as she glanced at Bender. "He . . . he will see my . . . my *underwear*."

"That is the *least* of your worries . . . now do as I told you, Teresa Luisa."

She whimpered and held onto the button fly of her pants with both hands. Teresa Luisa! The childish in-trouble name echoed in her head and she stomped a foot.

"You *cannot* treat me like a three-year-old!"

"I would *never* spank a three-year-old. Lower your jeans and I won't tell you again."

"Oh *God* . . . please don't do this to me!"

His glare burned into her soul and she grunted as she turned away from the desk. Fingers fumbled the top button at her waist. Dylan grunted and led her to a hard, armless chair next to the wall, sat in it, and pushed her hands away. She shut her eyes and clasped her fists at her chin. He flipped the buttons open and pushed her pants halfway down her thighs. Teresa wailed as he draped her across his lap. Shoe leather squeaked when Bender stood and walked around behind her. She sobbed and looked over her shoulder at the amused smirk on the man's thin lips.

"Uncle Dylan, don't let him *watch*."

"The professor has five daughters, so this is nothing he hasn't seen."

"But that does not . . . no not my panties!"

Teresa wriggled, twisted and grabbed, but Dylan held her wrist and slid white cotton briefs down her bottom. She sobbed and pale cheeks flushed pink with shame. He shifted his feet and raised his arm. Rear muscles clenched and she yelped when his hand smacked across her deep cleft. She barely felt the sting for the flood of embarrassment that rushed up her neck and into her face. Twenty quick, sharp spanks landed on her tender behind and hot tears stung her eyes. The door-latch clicked and Teresa and Dylan jerked toward it.

"Aha!" Professor Bender grabbed the receptionist by her ear. "I warned you about peeking at keyholes, my girl."

"Nah! Ow! Please, I . . . I *wasn't* . . . I . . . I was looking for a file, that's all!" She grimaced as he pulled her into the room and shut the door.

"The file cabinet is on the other side of the room, Elena."

"Yeah but I . . . oh geeze!"

Teresa reached back to cover her bare, pink fanny, but Dylan nudged her hand away and concealed her nakedness with his forearm while he looked at Bender. The man shrugged an apology as he led Elena between the two armchairs.

"Since you can't seem to mind your business outside, young lady . . . I'll just give you some business to attend to in here."

Dylan covered his mouth and coughed. "Professor, I don't think. . . ."

Elena howled when the professor bent her over the desk. "Daddy, *please*."

The sting in Teresa's behind turned to rosy warmth beneath her uncle's protective arm as Elena's skirt rose to display skimpy panties and the marks on her bottom. The girl squealed and kicked.

"Be *still*." Bender put a hand on her back and turned to Dylan. "I'm sorry, Professor Travis . . . this won't take a moment."

He reached over and picked up the cane. Elena slapped the desk-top.

"Daddy, *no*! Mom switched me this morning and it still stings!"

"You should have thought of that before you put your nose where it doesn't belong."

"*Daddy!*"

"Stop this nonsense or your mother will switch you again when we get home."

She scowled at her father, then sniffled and reached out to grab the far edge of the desk. Soft whimpers, like a kitten's whine, squeaked from her throat as she pushed her hips back. Silky knickers slid further into the cleft as her bottom rounded.

"I . . . I'm *sorry*, Daddy. Not too hard, *please?*"

Teresa bit her lip and twisted her neck to look at Dylan. His eyebrows arched and he let her slide backward to kneel beside him. He patted her tingly rear cheeks and she leaned into his side. Bender flipped his daughter's skirt out of the way and pulled down her panties. Twenty faded pink stripes marred the pale orbs. Bender shook his head, tucked the cane under his left arm, and rubbed a tender cheek.

"Why did your mother have to switch you, Elena?"

"She didn't *have* to, she just . . . ow! Daddy!"

Bender shook sting from his palm. "None of your sauce, girl. Why did she switch you?"

Elena pouted. "Be . . . because I didn't get up in time to help with breakfast this morning . . . and it really, really *hurts*."

"As well it should. You know better than to shirk your duties." He swished the rattan through the air and Elena flinched. "If you keep still and behave yourself I'll try not to overlap the cuts."

"But *Daddy*."

"Be *quiet*, Elena . . . and push your bottom out farther."

She wailed and slid backward. Teresa blushed and Dylan took a deep breath as Elena's deep cleft opened. Plump, pink lips, veiled by crinkly, light-brown hair, appeared at the base of the cheeks. Teresa cupped a hand over her mouth to cover a grin when her uncle squirmed on the chair and parted his knees. She felt Dylan's glare before she looked up and saw it, so she raised her eyebrows to appear innocent. He frowned and shook his left index finger at her nose.

Bender lifted the cane. It swished, thipped, and Elena screeched. A pale, straight line, bordered in red, appeared at the top of her cleft, centered between two faded switch marks.

"Daddy, not so hard!"

"Hush, girl . . . and stay in position. Three more."

"Naaaiiieee!"

Another fresh stripe glowed between two older ones at the center of her bottom and tears dripped onto the desk. Dylan shifted his feet while Teresa clenched her jaw. The cane whished and cracked again. Elena's scream came from deep inside, and she stamped her feet and sobbed. Air whiffed between Bender's lips as he patted his daughter's back. The final cut flicked just above the lines Teresa had seen in the outer office. The heat from Elena's bottom burned in Teresa's cheeks and she clutched a handful of Dylan's trouser leg. Bender nodded, put down the cane and took hold of his daughter's arm.

"Get up, Elena."

She straightened her back, then leaned against her father's chest. He hugged her and rubbed the sore, streaked behind. She moaned for a few seconds and then looked up.

"I . . . I'm sorry, Daddy," she whispered.

"It's all right now. Go stand in the corner like a good girl."

Her heel clicked the floor. "But Daddy!"

"Elena Maria!"

He smacked her right cheek, not quite as hard as he would swat a puppy away from a favorite shoe, but she yelped and covered her bottom with both hands.

"OK! Geeze!"

The professor kissed her forehead and pushed her toward the corner behind the desk. Medium-heeled pumps wobbled as she limped to the wall.

"Skirt up, Elena . . . you know the rules."

She snorted and gathered pleated wool at her waist. Long, bare legs twitched and she whimpered as her panties slid down and bunched at her ankles. Bender turned, leaned against the desk, and smiled.

"My apologies once more, Professor Travis. Do continue."

Dylan nodded, glanced at Teresa, and then pulled her across his lap. She pouted, planted her palms on the floor, but said nothing as he rested a hand on her bare behind. A warm hardness pressed her left hip and she gasped at the tingle between her thighs. Dylan wriggled backward and cleared his throat.

"Thank you, Professor Bender . . . but I see that your little stick is more than a souvenir."

Bushy white eyebrows arched as he glanced at the cane. "Perhaps . . . but it *was* given me by a student . . . my wife's younger sister . . . who does have the most fanciful imagination. In fact, she and a friend wrote the piece Teresa turned in as her assignment."

Dylan's jaw dropped. "Your sister-in-law is Ponsonby Hopkirk?"

"Half of him . . . more or less."

"Quite, *quite* fantastic."

Bender smirked. "She refuses to divulge the identity of her co-author, but I suspect several of my colleagues in England. Still . . . the cane *is* only for family. Both my wife's sisters live with us, along with my daughters, and I gave up long ago trying to maintain order in a house full of Anglo-Saxon . . . and stubbornly Saxon . . . females with my hand or a hairbrush. A stick gets to the seat of the problem in short order." He glanced at his daughter's bare red behind and then looked at Dylan. "Would you care to try it, sir?"

Teresa gasped. "Uncle Dylan, *no*."

"Hush." He patted her bottom and shook his head. "Thanks anyway, Professor . . . not until I'm sure she needs more than my hand to straighten her out. I have all the time in the world to teach her."

Bender shrugged and crossed his arms. "As you wish. Please proceed."

Teresa moaned when she felt Dylan's thigh muscles tighten beneath her tummy. Elena peered over her shoulder, held up her skirt with one hand and rubbed fresh stripes with the other while she admired Dylan's broad shoulders and hard jawline. His arm rose high and Teresa held her breath. Sharp, quick sting lanced through tender cheeks, and she gasped but kept her arms straight.

At least it's not the cane . . . at least it's not the cane, she chanted to herself as she counted the spanks.

Ten. Twenty. Thirty. She squealed as waves of heat flowed over her bottom, and tried to focus on Elena's tormented behind but turned away when the girl grinned. Forty. Fifty. Blue jeans slid to her ankles when she kicked, and her panties drooped past her knees. She sobbed when Uncle Dylan pushed her to her feet, stood, and hugged her. Fire reddened her cheeks, fore and aft, as she wept into his chest, and salty sorrow drenched his tie. He helped her trudge the thousand miles to the corner and didn't let her trip on the denim and damp cotton that bunched at her ankles. Elena winked as Teresa groaned.

Dylan looked at Bender and pointed an open hand at his niece's sore behind. "A bit more time consuming but just as effective, don't you think?"

Bushy eyebrows twitched and Bender nodded. "Quite so, yes. I wish I could indulge the luxury but time is an issue. Of course, one must always worry about lasting marks with the rod."

"That would be a concern for me as well."

The man smiled. "I practiced on a pillow. I found that if I stop short and let the inertia of the cane carry the stroke, it stings like the very dickens but does no real damage."

"You show admirable restraint, sir."

"I must, sir. I love my family more than life itself."

"Yes, I can see that."

Bender cleared his throat. "Elena? Straighten your clothes and come here."

The girl dropped her skirt, stooped to pull up her panties, and then skipped into her father's arms. He kissed her forehead and thumbed a stray blonde wisp from her eye.

"Are there any more appointments this afternoon, my dear?"

"I don't think so, Daddy."

"Then perhaps we will shut early and stop at the wine bar on the way home."

She kissed him quick on the mouth and grinned. "OK. Can we buy a bottle of that merlot Mom likes?"

He chuckled. "A peace offering?" She nodded. "That's a fine idea. Now run along and wash your face."

Elena held out a hand to Dylan. "Nice to meet you, sir. Sorry for the interruption."

He smiled, squeezed the hand, and bowed. She turned to grin at Teresa as she went out and shut the door. Professor Bender sighed.

"Don't get the wrong idea. Elena is merely filling in while my secretary is on holiday and I pay her from my own pocket. I prefer that arrangement to the graduate students they usually send me for temporary help. She is the eldest but I'm training all my girls to step in at the office when the need arises."

"I see."

"Yes . . . well . . . Teresa?"

"Sir?"

"If you have your uncle's permission, you may come out of the corner."

She pouted and looked over her shoulder. "Uncle Dylan?"

He nodded and she yanked up her clothes.

⊙⊬

BMW tires crunched new snow on the Autobahn and whiteness swirled around the car. Dylan turned the wipers on high and leaned forward, his eyes wide. Teresa rested on her hip and held onto his thigh. Hard muscles shifted as he worked the gas and brake pedals to nudge the sedan through the storm.

"Can we stop at the wine bar too, Uncle Dylan?"

"*May* we . . . ?"

Teresa huffed. "*May* we stop there?"

"No, sweetie, the roads are too messy . . . and besides, you have homework to do."

She flinched as she sat up on her achy bottom, folded her arms and stared straight ahead. "You are being very mean. My behind is most hurtful and you will not even let me have a glass of wine to numb the pain."

Knuckles whitened as he clutched the steering wheel and he took a deep breath. Teresa bit a fingertip and looked at him out of the corner of her eye.

"Uncle Dylan? I'm sorry, I. . . ."

"Hush and let me concentrate."

His eyes flickered and the car slithered down a ramp. He turned right and headed for the house. Teresa bit her lip when he set the brake and got out. The passenger door jerked open and he reached for her hand.

"You are not mad at me, are you, Uncle Dylan?"

Teresa yelped when he pulled her out.

"The very idea!" He swatted the back of her jeans. "Acting like a brat after I went to so much trouble to get you off the hook with Bender."

"I'm *sorry*, Uncle Dylan, I didn't *mean* to. . . ."

"Hush!"

Felicia peered through the window, waved to them and opened the side door. "Dylan, get *in* here."

She grabbed Teresa and dragged her inside. Dylan shut the door and snapped the lock.

"Fel, what's wrong?"

The kettle hissed as she lifted it from the stove. "There's a blizzard warning. I guess you didn't hear it."

"No . . . but I *thought* the weather was worse than usual. Are you all right?"

She nodded and poured steamy water into thick mugs. "I was worried, that's all. Do you want hot chocolate?"

Teresa sat at the kitchen table. Dylan smiled, opened a cabinet, and drizzled Scotch over his cocoa. Felicia stirred the cup and looked at him. He winked.

"I think now is the time . . . ask her, Fel."

"OK." She took a mug and turned to her stepdaughter. "Honey? Do you . . . wouldn't you like to go to America? Just for a while?"

Teresa squirmed on the kitchen chair. Chocolaty warmth tingled her nostrils as Felicia set the cocoa in front of her, and a different sort of warmth tingled beneath her jeans. She pouted, took three puffy breaths, and wrapped her fingers around the cup. Dylan looked at her, his brows arched, his eyes like wet sapphires. Teresa sipped and shrugged.

"Can I have my own phone line for the computer?"

Dylan nodded. "You *may* have anything you want . . . within reason . . . as long as you behave yourself."

She grimaced and then smiled when he winked. "Then I *shall* live in America . . . for a time . . . so long as you promise not to treat me as a three-year-old."

He laughed. "That I would *never* do."

Felicia squeaked when Dylan grabbed her shoulders and kissed her cheek. Teresa giggled when they both leaned over to hug her.

Chapter 4

IN LOCO PARENTIS

BETH BURROWED FROM beneath the blanket, snuggled Michael's bare arm and stared at his calm, handsome face. His eyelids fluttered, opened, and he smiled. She kissed his smile and then pouted.

"You're an ogre, you know? A nasty, evil, British ogre . . . and that hairbrush wasn't *even* necessary."

He frowned. "Young lady, if you are laboring under the delusion that I am too weakened by our bout of wanton sex to smack your impertinent behind . . . you had better disabuse yourself of the notion."

"Cor', don't we talk posh, then!"

She squealed when he twisted around and lay on top of her. His damp manhood rubbed her wet vagina and she moaned. Michael glared into her eyes.

"*What* have I told you about that 'Liza Doolittle accent? Hmm?"

"Uh . . . that it turns you on?"

He laughed, rolled onto his back and took her with him. "Nonsense . . . you only do it to annoy, because you know it teases."

Beth chuckled and straddled his hips. "You can't be *that* annoyed . . . if you're quoting Lewis Carroll."

"Paraphrasing, rather."

"Oh, don't be finicky . . . my butt's *still* sore. Can I have some more cold cream?"

"*May* I . . . ?"

"Michael!" She covered his lips with her mouth and their tongues met. After half a minute she sighed, rested her chin on his chest and looked at him. "It really *is* sore. You haven't spanked me that hard in a long time."

He folded the pillows under his neck to raise his head, then stretched his arms to cup Beth's warm, red bottom. Plump cheeks quivered as he caressed.

"I *am* sorry, my dear. I didn't mean to swat you so severely over such a trivial. . . ."

She gasped. "What's the matter with you? Where'd all this *mea culpa* crap come from?"

"Well, I only . . . I suppose I've been. . . ."

"It's Lisa . . . isn't it?" He nodded. "Yeah . . . I don't know what to do about her either. She bounces back and forth between spoiled brat and pitiful sobbing waif and it's driving us both crazy."

"Indeed . . . I'm afraid we are too close to her not to be affected. I slapped her bum a quick dozen yesterday . . . on her *panties*, mind you . . . when I found her surfing the Internet instead of studying . . . and she spent the whole afternoon locked in her room."

Beth sighed. "I know . . . I got the gory details on the phone last night. She said she was going to quit school and move in with her dad."

"*What?*"

"Don't worry . . . she changed her mind after we talked a while."

"Over a few swats on the behind? For heaven's sake, Beth."

She put a finger to his lips and shook her head. "It wasn't the swats . . . she's just having a bad time since Darcy died. Anything could have set her off."

He nodded. "Darcy exerted the same sort of control over the girl that I used to have, and now that she's gone. . . ."

"*Used* to have? What are you talking about? Lisa loves you more than anyone in the world."

"Yes, and therein lies the rub . . . because try as I will, I can't help but return the emotion."

"What's wrong with that? She *needs* a lot of love right now."

"I quite agree . . . but she *also* needs someone to take her firmly in hand and guide her."

"Uh huh . . . I still don't see any *rub*."

Michael sighed, pushed Beth onto her side and turned to face her. "Do you recall, some years ago, when I advised you . . . *told* you . . . not to invest so heavily in a certain stock?"

Beth frowned. "Yes . . . and blistered my ass with a belt when I did it anyway. Still haven't figured out how you knew all the dot-coms were going to tank."

"That isn't the point, Beth. You refused to listen to reason because *I* told you."

"But Michael I . . . I *usually* take your advice, it's just. . . ."

He smirked and pressed two fingers to her mouth. "You sound *exactly* like Lisa."

"Nuh *uh!*" She pouted and blinked, and Michael laughed.

"But you knew that if I became cross with you over the matter . . . and even if I did, as you say, blister your ass . . . that we would wind up in bed . . . or at the least I would give you a bit of that sort of comfort whilst I applied the cold cream."

She sighed and wrapped an arm around his neck. "As I recall, you screwed my brains out *after* you got me off with your fingers."

He scowled but his eyes twinkled in the dimness. "Young lady, I do not screw *anyone's*. . . ."

"Oh hush." She kissed him and then licked her lips. "You can punish me for bad language later. I still don't understand what this has to do with Lisa. You don't take *her* to bed after you spank her . . . unless there's something I don't know about."

Michael shook his head. "I'm afraid once was enough."

Beth's eyebrows arched. "That time in Mexico?"

"Yes . . . not to mention the numerous occasions she has, um, gotten off . . . with my collusion, witting or not . . . while she lay half-naked across my lap. I believe our intimacy, Lisa's and mine, has compromised my authority. She thinks of me as her friend and lover now . . . more than her employer."

"Oh Christ . . . so what do we *do?* Send her to Dad and see if *he* can straighten her out?"

He sighed. "It's not out of the question . . . but we still are trustees of the shops, so we can't back away from her entirely."

"Of course we can't . . . she's practically family and. . . ."

"Then let me ask you this . . . what has happened to cause the change in Lisa?"

"What do you mean *what*? Darcy's car wreck, obviously."

"Exactly . . . but more disturbing to Lisa even than Darcy's death is Darcy's *absence*. Darcy was a strong, steadying influence on Lisa, but an *outside* influence . . . apart from her home life."

"Yeah right. Her life with Darcy couldn't have been *that* much different when it came to discipline. Darcy was as good with her fingers as you or me, after she paddled a girl's heinie."

Michael smiled. "Oh *was* she, now?"

Beth pinched his arm and grinned. "Yes, but I won't go there . . . not right now, anyway. It sounded like you were going to make a point . . . before you got all distracted by salacious thoughts. Ow! Michael!" She pouted and rubbed sharp new sting from her bottom.

He kissed her and then helped her rub. "I do indeed have a point, and if you'll stop interrupting I'll get to it."

"OK . . . but I want cold cream afterwards." She sighed as he lay back and cuddled her beneath his arm.

"You remember Dylan Travis, don't you?"

Beth chuckled. "How could I forget? You guys got drunk on Guinness and champagne when you were in grad school and went around to all the sorority houses asking if any of the girls needed to be paddled."

Michael scowled and hugged her shoulders. "Why is it that's the *only* thing about the man you ever seem to recall? That happened over thirty years ago . . . and didn't you promise never to tell that story again?"

She blinked at him. "In public . . . I said I'd never tell it in *public* again . . . and I only said *that* so you'd quit whacking me with the paddle. It's a *great* story." Beth grinned and then whimpered when he squeezed her bottom. "Michael!"

"Hush . . . you scandalized half the Chamber of Commerce when you told it to our whole table at the awards dinner."

"But I was so *bored* . . . and I doubt if anybody believed it. Anyway, so what about Travis?"

"He's had their family cottage renovated and a new room added."

"I know . . . I saw the file on your desk. It was sweet of you to give the job to Lisa's father."

Michael shook his head. "Sweet had nothing to do with it . . . he is very good at what he does and Dylan's instructions were quite explicit. I needed to do nothing at all . . . except inspect the job when Jack called me."

Beth frowned. "That's your point? Jack Carlson, professional contractor for twenty-five years, can remodel a house?"

"No, the point is . . . the *reason* Dylan wanted it remodeled . . . it seems he has founded a college . . . a college for young ladies, in fact."

"Oh *please*." Beth giggled and smoothed a knuckle along Michael's jaw. "And he wants you to teach at the college . . . or does he need a resident disciplinarian? Ouch! Michael! *Stop* that." She turned her head when he tried to kiss her. "No . . . not if you're gonna keep slapping my butt."

He cupped her chin and she sniffed, but then offered her lips. Michael covered them with his mouth and then patted her bottom as he leaned back.

"Would you like a glass of wine, my dear?"

"Mm hmm . . . that would be nice."

"Splendid. Will you bring me a small whisky while you're down there?"

Beth sputtered, swatted his arm, and stuck out her tongue, then rolled off the bed. She wrapped his long, terrycloth robe around her shoulders, scuffed bare feet into his Deerfoam slippers and switched on the overhead light as she went out the door. His irritated shout and unlikely threat echoed behind her as she trotted through the hall and down the stairs.

She frowned at a Chablis bottle in the refrigerator, then took a merlot from the cabinet, dug out a corkscrew and opened it. Deep purple splashed when she filled a goblet to the rim. She slurped a mouthful off the top and then carried the glass into the back hallway. Lisa's bedroom door squeaked and Beth bit her lip as she pushed it.

The girl lay on her side, her face toward the window, her blonde hair a sleep-tousled mess. Half her white bottom glowed in the spill from the hall light. Beth set the glass on the dresser, gently tugged

Lisa's flannel nightshirt over the bare cheeks and then tucked a heavy quilt around her shoulders. Lisa wriggled, puffed, and muttered incomprehensible syllables. Beth smiled, leaned over, and kissed the girl's forehead, then took her wine and shut the door behind her.

Smooth, brown malt slid into a crystal lowball glass when she stopped at the sideboard in the living room. She carried the drinks upstairs and leaned against the bedroom doorjamb. Michael had the pillow mashed to his eyes. Beth snorted and switched off the light.

"You're as spoiled as Lisa is." She sat on the bedside and put the glasses on the nightstand.

He lifted his head and blinked. "Hm?"

"You could of got up and turned the light out, you know."

"I didn't turn it *on*, you know." Michael picked up the whisky and raised it in salute before he took a sip and smiled. "Thank you, my dear. Just what the doctor ordered."

She grinned. "I spit in it."

"Really? That's probably why it tastes so good."

"Michael!" Beth growled, dropped the robe and slippers, and lifted the quilt. He smiled and inched backward so she could wriggle in beside him. "I didn't really . . . but I should have . . . making me go out in the cold like that. What kind of gentleman are you, anyway?"

"An old and exhausted one, it seems." He kissed her lips and peat-fired malt wrinkled her nose. "Did you check on Lisa?"

"Uh huh." She smiled. "She's just fine . . . Poppa."

Michael scowled, then exhaled as he grinned. "You're a wonderful mother, my dear."

"All right, enough." Beth chuckled and twisted around to get the wine. She cuddled closer to him and sighed. "So what about Dylan and this school thing?"

"It's all to do with his niece, apparently. He's bringing her here from Germany in a few months and. . . ."

"His *niece*?"

"Yes . . . why?"

"Is she *really* his niece . . . or is this some California thing?" She gasped when he yanked the covers away and raised his arm over her bare behind. "OK, OK . . . put your hand down . . . *slowly* . . . please?"

"Very well . . . but *do* try to behave." He patted her warm cheeks and then covered them with the quilt. "She *is* his niece . . . by marriage. His sister is the girl's stepmother, but she's had similar problems to Lisa's and he hopes to help her sort them out over here."

"His *sister's* got problems like Lisa's?"

He clicked his tongue, drained the whisky, and set the glass on the nightstand. "No . . . the niece has. Her father died in a plane crash and she took it quite badly . . . understandable, I expect, but Dylan feels it's time for her to move on. In any case, she will go to university here . . . and also to this college for, um . . . remedial training."

Beth grinned. "Will I get my fanny whacked if I guess what *kind* of um, remedial training she'll get at this college?"

Michael smiled and Beth moaned when he squeezed her bottom. "The same kind Lisa needs."

"Yeah, like Lisa would go for *that*." Beth turned to put her glass beside his. "Some guy she doesn't even know has your permission to smack her butt, and she's supposed to jump at the chance to go to his school?"

He sighed. "I suppose we must convince her that it's in her own best interest to accept our proposal."

"Uh huh . . . like how? What can she learn from Dylan . . . besides the fact that he's just as handy with a paddle as you are?"

"I'm not entirely sure that he is." Michael smiled and hugged Beth to his chest. "Apart from a few unsubstantiated rumors, I've only his word in the matter . . . but his specialties are English literature and composition . . . subjects with which Lisa could use more than a little help."

"She can learn *that* stuff at the university."

Michael leaned back and rubbed his chin. "True . . . but she wouldn't get the sort of personalized attention Dylan offers."

"That won't mean a thing to her and you know it." Beth leaned up on her elbow and stared into his eyes. "You're just blowing smoke, Michael. There's something you aren't telling me. What is it? Huh? What?"

He chuckled. "Has Greg found a job yet?"

"You know he hasn't and that's part of the reason Lisa's been so

. . . wait a minute. You're going to bribe her with a job for Greg?"

"*Bribe* is such a distasteful word. Let's say we will reward her . . . and him as well, I suppose . . . for her compliance."

"But where can we put him? There aren't any management openings and probably won't be for. . . ."

"There's the shop downtown."

"For Christ's sake, Michael, that's *Sharon's*. Are you going to fire Darcy's niece? Lisa would never sit still for it and I don't think Greg would either."

"Probably not . . . but if she resigned. . . ." He shrugged and then coughed when Beth slapped his chest.

"All *right*, mister . . . out with it. You already talked to Sharon, didn't you?" He nodded. "And . . . ?"

"And as soon as Darcy's house clears escrow, she will take her Corvette and her tidy little bundle and open her own store in Omaha."

Beth screeched and slapped again. "You are the biggest rat on the face of the . . . Michael, no! *Michael!*"

He laughed as he pulled Beth's squirmy, naked body across his lap. Sharp claps echoed through the bedroom, punctuated by Beth's yelps, curses, vows of revenge, and finally, promises to be good if only he would stop spanking so hard. She moaned and rubbed her swollen behind as he reached for the cold cream jar, then smiled when she felt his stiffness beneath her belly.

Chapter 5

PIZZA AND BEER

LISA SAT ON the sofa in Michael's office and glared out the window at the wet March snowflakes that fell like white raindrops. She wore her black uniform for the first time since Darcy's death. The fact that Michael asked her to wear it made her nervous, but the stiff, familiar cotton comforted and protected her like a shell while he told her about the college she was to attend, and why he wanted to send her there. Beth sat next to her and Michael looked at her from the armchair.

"I know you think it's unfair, Lisa, but. . . ."

"Yes I *do*, Michael." She grunted and stamped the carpet. "I'm doing OK at school so why . . . ?"

"Lisa! Don't interrupt." He scowled and Lisa nibbled a fingertip. "That's *exactly* the sort of thing I'm on about . . . all these scenes and tantrums have *got* to stop . . . and the additional tutoring in composition certainly will do you no harm."

She whimpered and looked at Beth. "My writing isn't *that* bad, is it?"

"Talk to the boss, honey."

"Are *you* on his side?"

"No, I'm on *your* side . . . and I think this is what you need to do."

"But geeze! I mean . . . I hardly do any work around the house as it *is* . . . and now you want me to go to another class?"

"It's only one day a week, and Professor Travis's schedule is flexible." He smiled. "As is mine . . . so you needn't worry about your duties here."

"I know but . . . how can you afford to pay me when I don't *do* anything?"

Michael leaned forward. "I consider your salary an investment in the future of my business . . . whether you ever dust another bookend. Now . . . do we have a deal?"

Lisa folded her arms and leaned back. "And Greg gets the job?" He nodded. "But what if I can't stand this Travis guy? What if he's a complete jerk and . . . and I have a tantrum or something . . . and he kicks me out of his stupid school?"

"That's enough of that, young lady." Michael sighed and rubbed his forehead. "All right . . . Greg has the job, regardless of your performance at Red Blossom College . . . so long as *his* performance is up to standards. As to Professor Travis, you must form your own opinion . . . but he *has* taught at university for many years, and I don't believe you would deliberately throw away a learning opportunity."

"Yeah well . . . OK. I'll *try* it but. . . ." Lisa scowled at a wirebound booklet on the coffee table. "Is he *serious* about the stuff in there?"

Beth picked it up and thumbed it. "The college handbook? Well, you know how cute you are in a school uniform." She grinned and Lisa sneered. "Other than that . . . it's all common sense, honey."

"Uh huh, right . . . common sense from like a hundred years ago. There's junk in there about smoking and dress codes and . . . *curfews*, for crying out loud! If I blow my nose the wrong way, I'll get my butt smacked."

Michael smiled and shook his head. "Professor Travis is a reasonable man and an old friend . . . he would never harm you, any more than I would . . . and you always seem to benefit from *my* discipline."

"Then why *don't* you?"

Lisa sobbed and leaned on Beth's shoulder. Michael stood and rounded the coffee table to sit beside her. She turned and pressed her face into his chest while he patted her back and shushed her.

"There . . . it's all right. We've been all through that . . . and you know why I want you to go."

She swallowed and nodded. "I guess so . . . but it's not *my* fault if I, um . . . don't mind it that much when you spank me."

Beth rolled her eyes and Michael glared at her.

"Yes, well . . . then we're agreed? Would you like to tell Greg about the job?"

"Yeah, but. . . ." Lisa looked up and fisted a tear from her eye.

"What?"

"I . . . I got your tie all wet."

He thumbed the strip of silk and shrugged, then looked into the girl's eyes. They pleaded with him and he forced a scowl.

"Indeed you *did*, young lady. Now it shall have to be cleaned . . . and that's quite annoying. What have you to say for yourself?"

"I'm sorry?"

Beth stifled a laugh and slid to the end of the sofa as Michael moved to the center and tossed Lisa across his lap. Petticoats rustled when he raised her skirts. White cotton briefs hugged her round bottom, framed by dark stockings and black garters. Michael took a deep breath, smiled, and caressed the smooth mounds. Her fresh scent filled his nostrils and quickened his pulse. Tingly warmth radiated from her demure underpants and flowed up his arm.

"I believe we'll have these right *off* so I can chastise you properly."

Lisa gasped and trembled. "Please, sir, not all the way off."

Excited butterflies awakened in Lisa's tummy as Beth grinned and unsnapped garter tabs. Michael tugged the panties down while Lisa squealed weak protests and bent her knees so he could pull them over her feet. She whimpered when his palm clapped her behind. Beth chewed a fingertip and watched the soft, pale bottom turn pink.

Greg's jaw dropped when Lisa told him the news at the restaurant that evening, then he grinned and raised a foamy glass. She smiled and clinked his heavy mug with her own. He leaned back and drained the beer, gasped, and wiped his lips on a sleeve.

"*Geeze*, Greg . . . you're gonna kill yourself."

"Then I'll die a happy man." He turned, belched and blushed as he covered his mouth with a napkin. "Sorry."

Lisa giggled. "You want another one?"

He nodded, waved at the waitress, and then took Lisa's hand. "I can't *believe* it."

"You think I'd lie about something like that?"

"No, I . . . well, you know." He winked. "Anyway, I'd never accuse my boss of lying. How smart would that be?"

She pouted. "You, um . . . you don't need to call me *boss*, OK?"

"Hey, I was only. . . ." Lisa sipped beer and frowned. "What's the matter?"

"Nothing."

"Oh, man . . . I didn't *mean* anything by it."

Lisa shook her head. "No really . . . it's OK."

The waitress picked up Greg's empty and he held up a finger. She nodded and turned away.

He sighed. "So, um . . . when do I start?"

"Two or three weeks . . . maybe sooner . . . depends on Sharon. She could pack it in tomorrow, from what Beth says."

"Escrow doesn't close until mid-April."

"I know, but I think she'll quit before then."

"Uh huh." He nodded thanks when the waitress set a mug in front of him. "Hey, I forgot to tell you . . . I rented an apartment."

Lisa gasped. "You *forgot?*"

"Well yeah . . . when you dropped *your* bombshell." He grinned as she squeezed his hand. "So, you want to see it?"

"You already moved in?"

"Sort of . . . I took some stuff over yesterday." He leaned back as the waitress slid a hot, bubbly pizza between them.

"So? What's it like?"

He scooped a hot slice onto Lisa's plate and licked his fingers. "Well, it's almost a one-bedroom . . . kind of a glorified studio . . . not too far from the store, either . . . and it's got a bed and some kitchen chairs."

"No table?"

"A coffee table . . . but no sofa." He winked. "But now that I've got a job, thanks to you, I can afford furniture *and* rent."

Lisa tried to pick up the pizza but it burned her fingertips. She frowned and reached for a fork.

"What do you mean . . . thanks to me? Darcy *promised* you that job."

"Uh huh." Greg chewed and swallowed. "And you didn't put any pressure on Mr. Swayne, did you?"

"Well um. . . ." A blush colored her cheeks and she concentrated on the pizza.

He laughed. "Yeah, that's what I thought. Hope you didn't push him *too* hard."

She blew on a bite and shrugged. "So . . . can we go see the apartment when we're finished?"

"Sure, if you want . . . but I warn you . . . it's not much to look at."

"That's OK . . . as long as it's got a bed."

Greg coughed, pounded his chest, and then grinned at her.

He pushed the door open and flipped on an overhead light. A single bulb in a dusty glass globe lit the kitchenette/living room. The walk-in closet and bath opened on the opposite wall, and on the right, through a wide archway, was an alcove with a bay window. A double bed and three suitcases nearly filled the space. A tattered pink sheet covered the center of the window, and stained roll-blinds that might once have been white hung askew over the side panes. Greg threw his woolen jacket over a chair and opened the ancient refrigerator.

"You want a Coke or a beer or something?" Lisa shook her head. He twisted the top off a Miller Lite bottle and puffed his cheeks. "Told you it wasn't much."

Lisa wrinkled her nose. "Smells like they painted, though."

"Uh huh . . . and cleaned the oven." He pointed the bottle at the bed. "Oh, um . . . the sheets and blankets? I . . . borrowed those from Darcy's house. I'll return them before the sale."

"Don't worry about it . . . there's so much stuff nobody'll miss them." She walked to the alcove, tested the mattress, and then sat. "This is nice."

"You think?" He followed and sat beside her. "I haven't slept on it yet . . . but it's a lot squishier than the one I'm used to."

She leaned into him. "Greg?"

"Hmm?"

"Can . . . can we sleep here tonight?"

He set the bottle on the floor and hugged her. She lifted her chin and he kissed her hard, then soft, then leaned back and sighed. "I'd like that a lot."

"OK . . . well, um. . . ."

Greg smiled. "Kinda weird, huh?"

"What?"

"Not having to worry whether Dar . . . anybody's going to catch us fooling around." Lisa nodded and turned away to hide her tears. "Hey, come on . . . don't do that. Darcy wanted us to be together . . . even if she did blister our butts when she thought we were paying more attention to each other than to our jobs."

"I know, but. . . ."

"Yeah, I miss her, too. So, um . . . do you want to wait until I get the place fixed up? I mean . . . it's not the most romantic. . . ."

"No, Greg."

Lisa swiped moisture from her face, twisted out of her ski jacket, threw it to the floor and wrenched a heavy sweater over her head. He smiled and grabbed her hands.

"Hey, slow down. I want to peel the tomato."

"You wanna *what?*"

He grinned when she giggled. "It's a line from a Liza Minnelli movie . . . it means. . . ."

"I know what it *means*, Greg!" She got up and stood between his knees. "It means you think I'm red and plump . . . and could use a little salt."

"No, you're plenty salty. . . ." His knuckles brushed soft, sensitive breasts as he unbuttoned her blouse. "But there *are* certain parts that might be considered plump . . . all the *right* parts . . . the cute and sexy parts . . . and I've seen one of those parts get kinda red sometimes."

She sighed when he stood and pushed the sleeves down her arms. Cotton broadcloth fluttered in a heap to the hardwood floor.

"Not any redder than *yours* . . . Gregory."

"Hey! No fair using my in-trouble name . . . and I don't think guys *can* be tomatoes." He gasped when she reached around to squeeze his butt.

"No . . . more like apples." Lisa grinned. "Red and crunchy."

"Mmmm . . . you do know how to flatter a guy."

"So you better not get all flabby . . . with this cushy new job."

He kissed her while his fingers struggled with bra hooks. "No chance . . . I'll stay crunchy so my new boss won't lose interest."

Lisa huffed. "I told you not to call me . . . what *is* it with guys and bra straps, anyway?" She scowled and reached back to unfasten it.

"Must be genetic."

"Yeah well, knock off that *boss* stuff or. . . ."

"You'll paddle me?" He tossed the bra onto the bed and hugged her.

"Nuh uh . . . that's why I can't be your boss." Her nipples tingled as she hugged his chest. "If Darcy's not here to paddle you . . . you won't *get* paddled, that's all."

He sighed and raised her chin to kiss her. "Then I guess I'll have to find somebody else to use it on."

"Use what on?"

"Darcy's paddle . . . she told me to get it out of the house if . . . if anything happened . . . because it might be embarrassing when. . . ."

"Greg! The lawyer told you not to take anything."

"What about the sheets and blankets?"

"Yeah well . . . you *borrowed* those . . . and anyway. . . ."

"Then I guess I stole her collection of, uh . . . literature."

Small, bare breasts quivered when she stamped her foot. "*What* collection of literature?"

He scowled. "Thirty-some novels, a few dozen magazines, and about twenty videos. I've got the list if you want to check it. Oh . . . and three butt plugs, assorted sizes . . . and a couple of dildos . . . one with a harness."

"Oh, my God!" Lisa whimpered, shook her head and hugged him.

"You didn't want *those* in the estate sale, did you, boss?"

"No, I guess . . . *what* did you say?"

"Uh oh." He clapped a hand to his mouth. "I forgot . . . not supposed to say that word."

"Why are you being such a . . . a *brat*?"

Greg chuckled and hugged her tighter. "I *can't* be a brat . . . brats get paddled . . . or at least spanked."

"Yes they *do* and . . . Greg? No! Greg!"

He scooped her in his arms, then sat on the bed and draped her over his lap. She squealed and wriggled as he reached beneath her tummy to unsnap her denim trousers.

"There *is* a brat in this apartment . . . and if it's not me . . . then it's gotta be you."

"Let me go, you . . . you beast!"

Lisa kicked and giggled while he tugged her pants down, and then sighed as he patted the white, microfiber bikini panties that covered half her firm, round fanny.

"All righty, then . . . I'm a beast . . . now I know where I stand . . . or sit, as the case may be."

"Greg . . . Gregory! You let me up this instant!"

"Oooh!" He laughed and squeezed her bottom. "There's that in-trouble name again . . . the one that oughta send chills down my spine when my *boss* uses it . . . but actually it's quite warm in here . . . so I'd better pull your panties down before you suffocate."

"That's the silliest . . . Greg don't!"

Her heart pounded and she took quick breaths as he bared her bottom, bunched the soft underwear at the base of her cheeks, and then leaned down to kiss the tight mounds.

"Hmm . . . looks like somebody smacked your sweet little heinie already."

She jerked her head and stared over her shoulder. "What do you mean? It's not red."

"No . . . just its usual gorgeous pink." He grinned, slicked fingertips across the smooth skin, and held them to her nose. "But if that's not Pond's Cold Cream, I'll lick every bit of it off."

"Oh *geeze*." Lisa pouted.

"Beth? Mr. Swayne? Your other boyfriend?"

"What other . . . Greg! It was Michael, OK? Now let me *go*."

"As *if*." He slapped her fanny a dozen times, just hard enough to sting, and then rubbed while she sighed. "Did he spank you because you got in his face about the job?"

"No . . . and it's none of your business, so let go."

"Nope . . . I have you right where I want you, so settle down."

"But I don't want to *ouch*! That hurts!"

He kissed the hot handprint and then rubbed again. "So why did he spank you?"

"Why are *you* spanking me?"

"Because I like to . . . and because you do too."

"Well?" She grinned and then yelped when he swatted again. "Not so *hard*."

"Mmm . . . speaking of hard. . . ." She whimpered as he pushed her off his lap and tugged at the front of his jeans. He frowned when Lisa snickered. "You know it's rude to laugh at a man's . . . reaction."

"Not as rude as *having* that reaction to spanking my innocent fanny." She pulled him to his feet and grabbed his belt buckle.

Greg wrinkled his nose. "Which innocent fanny is that?"

"The only one I got and it is *too* innocent . . . so can I peel the apple?"

Zipper teeth scritched and Greg moaned. "*God* yes."

Lisa licked her lips and reached inside his pants. "You can always tell if an apple is fresh by how hard the stem is."

He coughed and swallowed. "Yeah? Then I guess I'm about as fresh as they come."

"Uh huh . . . I think *so*."

Clothes, boots, and socks scattered to the floor. Naked, Greg knelt to open a suitcase, dumped out a toiletry bag, and rummaged in the pile. Lisa shivered, pulled back the covers and crawled into bed. He jammed a strip of condoms and a small tube under the pillow and climbed beneath the quilt. She turned on her side and their arms and legs twined in a tangled embrace, his stiffness hot against her tummy. He cupped her tingly bottom in both hands and she moaned. They kissed, and their tongues danced a passionate tango while hard nipples burned like hot nails against his chest.

He parted her cheeks and caressed the smooth cleft. Lisa gasped, wriggled upward, and rubbed her moist vagina along his erection. Electric heat sparked her clitoris. A fingertip nudged her tender rear dimple and she squealed as red waves rippled up her spine. The finger pushed, insinuated, teased, and then plunged inside, past the springy circle and deep into hot, quivery tightness. Red waves turned purple and strobed behind her eyelids. She tugged his neck and whispered in his ear.

"Please?" The word graveled in a dry throat.

She whimpered when his finger abandoned her bottom. Greg swallowed hard, ripped open a foil packet with his teeth, and groaned as Lisa took the condom and rolled it over his hard shaft. She uncapped the tube and squirted lubricant into her palm. He gasped when she wrapped him in her fingers.

"Careful, Lisa."

"Yeah." She smiled and loosened her grip. "You too, OK?"

He kissed her lips and she rolled over. "Always."

His left arm slid beneath her ribs. She clasped his hand to her breast and pushed her hips into him. He reached down and guided the fat, mushroom tip between warm, pillowy cheeks. Lisa took long ragged breaths, then arched her back and squealed as the slick, spongy knob popped into her tightness. Sweet pain flowed like hot wine through her bottom while Greg held her in his arms and kissed her ear.

"Are you OK?"

"Uh . . . uh huh . . . it's fine . . . go on."

Hardness inched inside and pushed quivery heat into her vagina. His right hand roamed over her belly as the left squeezed her breast. She moaned when his finger found her slit, caressed for a moment, and dipped into pink wetness. He pressed forward and Lisa shuddered.

"Oh . . . oh *God* . . . right *there*."

He panted, grinned, and drew slow, tingly circles around her clitoris with a fingertip. His erection filled her while he teased shivery sparks from the tiny bud at the center of her being. She reached back to grasp his buttock and pulled him closer. Soft cheeks heated his belly and Greg moaned as he buried his sword to the hilt in her velvety sheath. His fingertip stroked the bud's tip and the crisis boiled within. Lisa panted and trembled as liquid lightning flashed through her vagina. Reflex tremors tightened her muscles and gripped his penis like a smooth, pulsing vise.

She wailed out her orgasm and thrashed in his arms. Greg gasped and hugged her while he willed back his own climax. Lisa groaned and wiped her mouth, then squealed when he rolled her forward and lay on top of her.

"Guh . . . Greg? What are you doing? Oh my *God*."

He held her hands above her head and kissed her neck. "I'm making love to your innocent fanny."

"But I can't *move*." She twisted her arms and legs but he held tight.

"Why would you want to?"

"I . . . I just feel so . . . *helpless*."

"Not helpless, Lisa . . . completely protected."

"Yeah but . . . oooh . . . Greg!"

He raised his hips and his penis slid halfway out, and then slowly plunged into her depths. Slippery friction reignited the embers between her thighs. Lisa relaxed and surrendered to his need, his desire, his protection. He lifted again, and plunged again, quicker and quicker. Her anus throbbed with delicious ache. Greg panted, mad with exquisite pleasure, delirious beneath a tidal wave of passion. Both screamed when the wave crashed, and his passion pumped into her.

Minutes ticked by and neither moved. Lisa moaned when he rolled off, and whimpered as his warm, soft penis slipped out, then wriggled over to clutch his arm.

"God, that was *wonderful*."

"You're telling *me*." He kissed her, then leaned back and wiped sweat from his face. "I didn't hurt you, did I?"

"Of course not . . . sorta surprised me, though."

He smiled. "Didn't know I was such a take-charge kinda guy, huh?"

"Sure I did . . . I was surprised it took you so long to *show* me." She giggled when he grabbed her, and then squealed when he swatted her tender behind.

"I'll show you a lot more often from now on."

"Mmmm . . . then I better get used to it, huh?"

"You got that right." He kissed her lips, long and soft, then patted her bottom. "I gotta go to the john."

"Oh *that's* romantic." She grinned and backed away when he raised his hand. "Yes, sir . . . whatever you say, sir."

"You're a little imp, aren't you?"

"Uh huh . . . that's something *you're* gonna have to get used to."

"I'll manage." He winked. "You want anything while I'm up?"

"Did you say you've got Coke?"

"Sure . . . um . . . if we're going to stay the night, you'd better call Mr. Swayne."

She sneered. "Like he *cares* where I am. He's already sending me to that stupid. . . ." Lisa stopped and bit her lip.

Greg frowned and leaned on his elbow. "Sending you where?"

"*Nothing* . . . never mind . . . go to the bathroom."

"I thought something was bothering you. Why are you mad at him?"

"I'm not, OK? Just *go*."

"Yeah sure." He grunted. "But I'll be back."

Lisa suppressed a giggle at his Schwarzenegger delivery. She huddled beneath the covers and listened to his water splash, then to the refrigerator door's click and slam. He handed her a plastic cup of fizzy cola, picked up his beer, scooted under the covers, and propped himself against the worn and chipped laminate headboard.

"So? What's up with Mr. Swayne?"

"I *told* you . . . nothing."

"Knock it off, Lisa. It's got something to do with me, doesn't it? With the job?"

"No, just. . . ." She slurped soda and wriggled into his side. "Just *hold* me, OK?"

He hugged her and kissed her forehead. "I think I have a right to know."

"*God*, you're annoying."

"What happened to *Yes, sir, whatever you say, sir?*"

His arm snaked beneath the sheet and hovered over her bottom. Rear cheeks clenched and she whimpered.

"OK! I . . . I have to go to a stupid extra English class. I didn't want to tell you . . . but that's the trade-off for you getting the job."

He scowled and twisted to look into her eyes. "I get the job 'cause you go to a class? *That's* pretty weird . . . and why English? Yours isn't *that* bad . . . apart from your tendency to write in sentence fragments."

"No but . . . Michael thinks I need more discipline."

"You? You're the most disciplined girl in the Midwest!"

She shook her head. "I used to be . . . but since Darcy died . . . don't you remember? Two weeks ago? When I . . . ?"

"Hey! We said we wouldn't talk about that . . . you apologized for going off on me . . . and that's it."

"I know, but . . . you didn't *discipline* me . . . and I was being a total brat."

"Of *course* I didn't, because I could tell you were still upset from. . . ." He sighed and then grimaced as he sipped warm beer. "OK . . . I kinda see Michael's point . . . but what kind of class is going to put you back on track . . . assuming you need to be?"

Lisa told him about Professor Travis, Red Blossom College, the school handbook, the uniforms, the rules, regulations, and penalties. Greg listened, eyes wide, mouth open, and then drained his bottle to the foamy dregs.

"Penalties, huh?"

"Uh huh . . . Darcy called them sanctions."

"Doesn't matter what he calls them . . . they're gonna sting." He took a deep breath and let it out. "So . . . you agreed to that? For me?"

"Yeah but . . . see?" Lisa pouted. "*That's* why I didn't tell you . . . 'cause you'd think it's a big deal . . . and you owe me or something."

"Well *duh*, Lisa!" He squeezed her hard and kissed her lips. "Like I didn't already owe you for making me the happiest man on the planet just for going to bed with me."

"Mmmm . . . I like that." She sighed and licked his tongue.

"But promise you'll let me do one thing."

She frowned and rolled over to set her cup on the floor. "No you can *not* come to class and watch me get paddled . . . geeze!"

He chuckled. "That wasn't what I was going to ask . . . but if this reform school thing turns out to be like that. . . ."

"It's *not* a. . . ."

"Yeah, whatever . . . but if you *do* happen to get your adorable fanny paddled, I um . . . I want you to call me so I can take care of it . . . that's all."

Lisa stared at his chest and rubbed a taut nipple with her thumb. "The way you did tonight?" He nodded. "You *know* I'll call you . . . but I think it defeats the purpose of this extra discipline I'm supposed to get if you're *too* nice to it . . . afterward."

"Probably but. . . ." He squirmed as her thumb pad shot quivers through his ribs and down his loins. "I guess I could *scold* you the whole time I'm being nice to your bottom."

She leaned over to lick the hard, masculine node. "That might work . . . as long as you don't scold me in that icky Terminator voice."

He snarled, deep and raspy, as he grabbed her with both hands. "Get over my lap if you want to live."

Lisa screeched and laughed as he threw her across his thighs and swatted her tender, satisfied bottom.

Chapter 6

RED BLOSSOM COTTAGE

DYLAN SHUT OFF the engine and lifted the wheel, then held the door while he squeezed from the car and sidestepped out of the narrow garage. Weeds grew between cracks in the driveway and he frowned as he turned toward the front of the house. A bird had left its calling card on the number painted atop a six-foot brick gatepost. He picked up a fallen leaf and rubbed away the dropping. The spiked iron fence around the front garden gleamed with fresh black enamel, and a flag-stoned lane wound between clumps of honeysuckle and hibiscus toward the cottage. He pushed open the gate and dropped the soiled leaf into the ground cover. His Italian wingtips clicked the stones as he walked to the door, but the clicks were muffled in the foliage and lost under a chorus of bird song. Thick, moist ivy clung to the cottage's stucco walls and fifty-foot willows shaded the front and both sides. He slotted a key into the latch and twisted.

The odor of new paint failed to cover the smell of old books. Ceiling-high cases lined both sides of the entry hall and he ran his fingers along tattered spines. He turned right into the parlor, now the study, opened Venetian blinds to let in the morning sun and set his briefcase on the desk next to a blue iMac. The computer sang a chord when he thumbed a contact, then it flickered and booted up. Dylan sat in the ancient oak roll-chair and leaned back.

He mouse-clicked and read a file.

"Name: Peterson, Ashley L.

Age: 19.

Home address: Laguna Hills, Calif.

Parents: Peterson, Fallon J., Cecelia L. née Martin (sister of Patrick T. Martin. Resumed Peterson following third failed marriage).

Marital status: Divorced.

Contact: Mother.

Financials, general: Cecelia's father funded trust for Ashley; Cecelia manages portfolio based on three substantial divorce settlements.

Issues, immediate: Received HS diploma despite discipline problems that included detention at OC juvenile center: disorderly conduct, vandalism, giving false information. Enrolled at J.C.; low grades and overnight disappearances; citation for possession of alcohol.

Issues, long-term: lived with mother following divorce from natural father, age 5, minimal contact with father thereafter; first stepfather, age 8, Alfred Perlmutter, international banker; second stepfather, age 14, Calvin 'Clete' Boyard, sports agent and promoter. Mother's third marriage lasted 10 months.

Notes: Cecelia called 6 times seeking help.

Student contacts: Talked to Ashley at home; she brushed off the idea of 'living in the boondocks.' Two days later she came home drunk at 3 am. Cecilia said she would send Ashley to aunt and uncle in Lompoc and transfer guardianship and trust fund control to them. Ashley begged Cecelia to call me instead. Spoke to Ashley on the phone and said I would allow her on a trial basis but only if she accepted punishment for drinking. She hung up on me then called back 10 minutes later. Cecelia brought her to the house and I spanked Ashley bare while Cecelia observed, then reviewed rulebook with her."

Dylan sighed and clicked another file, then opened the desk drawer and took a key from beneath a pile of German coins. He unlocked a cabinet and smiled when the cork popped from a bottle of twelve-year-old malt. Peat fire and sea salt tingled his nose as he poured a healthy slosh into a crystal lowball glass. He settled back, inhaled warm fumes, and read the screen.

"Name: Dahlgren, Britney M.

Age: 19.

Home address: Mission Viejo, Calif.

Parents: Martin, Patrick T. (brother of Cecelia Martin Peterson), Dahlgren, Veronica S.

Marital status: Divorced/widowed. (Father missing on sailboat and presumed dead. Mother kept maiden/professional stage name and changed child's name following father's disappearance.)

Contact: Mother.

Financials, general: Patrick's father funded trust for Britney; Cecelia Peterson manages Veronica's portfolio, based on Patrick's insurance settlement and bequests from his father's estate.

Issues, immediate: discipline problems following HS graduation and enrollment at J.C.; only one issue in HS, 3-day ISS for alleged cheating on exam; recent DUI reduced to reckless driving; attorney's fee and court costs: $8,695; overnight disappearances in company with Ashley Peterson.

Issues, long-term: when Britney was 9, mother married Georges VanderPlatz, TV makeup artist and long-time friend of the family. A year after the wedding, VanderPlatz arrested in North Hollywood for soliciting sex from underage male in a police sting; following the arrest and subsequent divorce, Britney underwent weekly psych therapy for six months, owing to her close relationship with VanderPlatz; mother hired Conchita Cabazon, naturalized Salvadoran, as housekeeper/nanny when Britney was 11.

Notes: Veronica heard about RBC from Cecelia and called me. Conchita left them following Britney's HS graduation and returned to El Salvador to care for ailing father. Britney began to act out thereafter.

Student contacts: Visited Dahlgren home twice: first evening, Britney called an hour past appointment time and said she forgot. Second visit, Britney passive-aggressive after talking with Ashley about RBC. Counseled Veronica that Britney would not be a good fit, at which point Veronica verbally and physically attacked me. Realized her intent, took her across my lap and spanked the seat of her shorts. Britney ran to her room and refused to come out until Veronica threatened her with the aunt and uncle in Lompoc. Britney relented and came downstairs, where I spanked her bare in Veronica's presence. She apologized and agreed to attend RBC."

Smooth malt tickled his palate as Dylan sipped and closed the file. He stood, stretched and gazed out the window, then sat and opened another icon.

"Nillson, Sonja K.; Nillson, Birgid J. (twins)

Age: 18.

Home address: Rochester, Minn.

Parents: Christina Nillson, MD.

Marital status. Never married. Adopted girls at birth in Sweden. Biological mother is Christina's 2nd cousin. Father unknown. Twins born when mother was 14; Christina was 31 and in residence at Uppsala hospital. Biological mother found dead of drug overdose in Amsterdam hotel five years later.

Contact: Mother.

Financials, general: Trust fund for girls from biological grandfather, to be settled at age 30; mother has good income and substantial portfolio.

Issues, immediate: Sexually active since early teens; no pregnancies or STDs. Christina took job at rural hospital near Hamburg when girls were 7; accepted position at Mayo Clinic hospital last year. Girls enrolled at university in Minnesota, but grades and deportment abysmal; numerous nights out past curfew, suspected marijuana use, probable sex. Both evince passive-aggressive sullenness typical of early teens when confronted about activities. Grounding, privileges revoked.

Issues, long-term: Strong bond w/mother; dependence borders on neurosis; Christina spanked them both from age 7 to age 14; stopped when girls grew taller than her. Arrested emotional development in both, with overt sexuality as compensation device.

Notes: Christina met Felicia through Gerhard. He directed the girls' trust fund in Hamburg until his death; she kept in contact with Fel following move to Rochester; Christina called me when Fel told her about RBC.

Student contacts: Stopped in Minneapolis in May. Christina and girls drove to hotel for the afternoon. At lunch, girls refused to answer simple questions. When both went to the lavatory, made Christina wait while I followed. Found them on the lawn smoking cigarettes. Hauled them to restaurant desk, told maitre d' to tell Dr. Nillson where to find us then took girls to the room. They threatened to call police; made them stand in the corner until Christina arrived then searched them. They ditched the cigarette pack, but smelled of smoke. Christina gave 15-minute lecture on the evils of tobacco then hugged the girls while they apologized. Told them that wasn't the end of the matter and took Christina aside. She agreed so I gave them a short lecture then spanked them bare. Ordered sandwiches and conversation much livelier, but girls were not happy when I explained college philosophy. Only agreed to the move when Christina said that the alternative was to be grounded until they graduated from university."

Dylan chuckled, finished the scotch, and wondered how Christina, the forthright and honest Swede, had managed to utter such an unlikely threat with a straight face. He shook his head and clicked on Lisa Carlson's file, then turned when the doorbell rang. Blinds clattered when he leaned over to look out the window.

A petite blonde stood on the porch. Her plaid, pleated skirt hung just above smooth kneecaps. A fresh, white blouse glowed in the June sunlight and a maroon-and-silver rep tie, knotted in a perfect half-Windsor, swayed to and fro in the divide between small, round breasts as she chewed a fingertip and twisted her waist in small arcs. The padded strap of a leather satchel looped over her shoulder. Dylan took a mint from the bowl on the desk and tongued it as he walked through the hall.

"Hello, Lisa." He smiled and opened the door wide.

"Professor Travis?"

"Yes . . . please come in."

"OK . . . um, thanks."

"May I take your bag?"

"Sure . . . thank you, sir."

"Why don't we talk in the kitchen? Would you like something to drink?"

"No thanks. I'm fine. Sir."

He pointed to a chair, set her satchel on the counter, and nodded as she sat. "Where did you park, Lisa?"

"Huh? Oh . . . I took the bus."

"I see. Then you *must* be thirsty. Buses are as bad as airplanes for dehydration." Dylan opened the refrigerator and stepped back. "See anything you like?"

Lisa's eyes widened as she stared at the shelves, packed tight with bottles and cans of all sizes. The lower bins were full of red, yellow, and orange fruit.

"Um . . . is that Pepsi Twist?"

"Yes . . . with sugar or without?"

"With, please."

He grabbed the soda and a half-liter of water and shut the door. Lisa smiled when he set the bottles on the table and opened a cabinet.

"Glass?"

"No, thanks." She twisted off the cap and sipped tangy sweetness.

Dylan sat in a chair next to her. "I appreciate your coming early today, Lisa." He leaned back and opened the water.

"No problem, Professor."

"Still . . . it was good of you to make the effort. I've met the other girls and it didn't seem right that I hadn't met you . . . the only local in the group."

"Yes sir, I um . . . I didn't mean to. . . ."

"You didn't *mean* to be disrespectful? When you missed our appointments at Mr. Swayne's house? Is that what you didn't mean, Lisa?"

She squirmed her bottom on the hard chair. "But I *called* so you know what happened, and . . . and anyway, Michael . . . um . . . Mr. Swayne must of already told you my whole life story, so why do you need to . . . ?"

"Stop it, Lisa." He sighed and tipped the water bottle between his lips. "As a matter of fact, I do know a great deal about you . . . but that isn't the same as knowing *you*. What I'd like to find out now . . . is whether you thought anyone would believe that your boyfriend's car broke down both times we were scheduled to have lunch."

"But it *did* . . . so I had to go. . . ."

"And I also need to know why a girl as obviously intelligent as you couldn't come up with a more original excuse the second time."

He chuckled and winked. Lisa gasped and leaned back.

"She told you, didn't she?"

"Hmm? Who told me what?"

"Beth . . . told you what she did when I bailed the second time."

Dylan shook his head. "I haven't spoken to Ms. Trelawny . . . but I gather from your tone that there were consequences of your actions . . . or inaction, I suppose."

Lisa sighed and shrugged. "She wasn't real happy with me . . . neither of them were."

"Neither of them *was* . . . neither is a singular pronoun."

"Huh?"

"Never mind . . . we'll cover that later. Then I have Ms. Trelawny to thank for your early arrival?"

"Yeah . . . um . . . yes, sir. I told her you called and she kind of insisted."

"I see. May I venture a guess as to why you didn't want to meet me for lunch?" Another shrug. "It isn't that you're afraid of me . . . is it, Lisa? Or that I know too much about you . . . it's the fact that you know too much about *me* . . . and the way I deal with a young lady's discipline issues . . . and that's not something you felt comfortable discussing in the company of your friends and co-workers. Is that fairly close to the truth?"

She gulped soda. "I guess. I know I've been a real bi . . . brat, lately . . . and I *sure* didn't want to hear about it at lunch." She pouted and leaned on her elbows. "Did Michael tell you he wanted me to see a shrink . . . some kinda grief counselor? I *hate* doctors. I hate even going for a checkup."

"That's *not* a healthy attitude, young lady."

"Yeah . . . that's what everybody tells me." She coughed and wiped her eye.

Dylan held out his hand and Lisa took it. "One tried and true therapy for grief is hard work . . . and that's what I expect of you here. You don't know me but you know *of* me . . . and perhaps you have heard that I can be strict. So I want you to realize how very high my expectations are . . . and how very sorry you will be if you fail to live up to them."

"I . . . I know . . . sir, and . . . I read the handbook."

He nodded. "What did Ms. Trelawny do? When you ditched the second lunch appointment?"

Lisa tried to pull her hand away but he held it. "Um, that's . . . uh. . . ."

"None of my business? On the contrary, young lady . . . it *is* my business, and I expect an answer." Lisa whimpered and looked away from Dylan's hard stare. "Well?"

"OK! She . . . *spanked* me, OK?"

"With her hand? On your bare bottom?"

"What?"

"You heard me."

"*Yes* . . . geeze!"

"And did she make you feel better afterward?"

She pushed her chair backward and twisted to her feet but Dylan stood and grabbed both her arms.

"Lisa! I asked you a question."

"Oh, God . . . yes! She . . . she . . . oh *shit*."

Dylan suppressed a smile and pinched the top of Lisa's ear between his thumb and forefinger. She squealed and stomped the floor.

"Quit stamping your little doe hoof, Lisa . . . if you read the handbook you know profanity isn't allowed here."

"But I . . . ow! *Geeze*, Professor, that hurts!"

He let go of her ear and thrust his right hand beneath her armpit. Loafer soles barely touched the floor as he propelled her down the hallway to the thirty-by-fifteen-foot classroom at the back of the cottage.

Light filtered through the closed Venetian blinds that covered four windows on the far side. A wide green chalkboard was bolted to the right-hand wall, behind a huge oak desk. The desktop gleamed with polish, bare except for a crook-handled rattan cane. Eight student tables, each with a straight-backed chair, faced the teacher's desk in rows of two. Carved graffiti covered the antique tabletops, and they glowed with a deep coat of varnish. Lisa screeched when her eyes focused on the cane.

"Hush, girl. You know better than to use that word, and I'm sure Mr. Swayne wouldn't condone. . . ."

"But not a *cane* . . . not for saying sh . . . that!"

"Oh, for pity's sake . . . that's not for you." Dylan smirked as he bent Lisa over the desk, her nose an inch from the hard, yellow stick. "At least not yet. But you *do* need your backside paddled, young lady . . . so keep still while I get it."

She pushed up on her arms. "Get what?"

"The paddle, of course . . . and I said to keep still."

"But I don't *want* to. . . ."

"Not another word, Lisa Marie."

The horrid in-trouble name from a man she hardly knew hit her like a slap on the jaw and she gaped as he opened a desk drawer. Fiery butterflies darted in her tummy while she clenched her fists and chewed a thumb knuckle. Warm tingles bathed her bottom, safe for the moment inside its shelter of cotton and light wool. She gazed at Dylan's eyes. They were blue like Michael's, but brighter, sharper, more distant. He stood a couple of inches shorter than Michael, and his shoulders weren't quite as wide, or his fingers as long and grace-ful. His hair was dark brown, flecked with gray at the temples, and his nose had a slight leftward bend, as if it had been broken and not set correctly.

Dylan reached into the drawer and removed the paddle. It was two feet long and five inches wide, with a six-by-three-inch handle, made of ash wood, rounded at the edges, and polished to a bright, blonde sheen. He twirled it in his hand. Scarlet letters on both faces read *RBC*.

"Please Professor, I . . . I didn't *mean* to. . . ."

"What did I just say, Lisa?"

She bit her lip, leaned forward, and pressed her forehead to the desktop. His heels clicked hardwood and echoed in her ears. Satin lin-ing whished when he yanked up her skirt. Lisa tapped a loafer toe on the floor as tender cheeks clenched beneath tight cotton briefs. Dylan thumbed elastic, bent, and skimmed the underwear down. A desperate, kittenish squeal escaped her throat as cool air caressed bare flesh. His left hand pressed her back as she wriggled.

"Be *still*, Lisa . . . you've been bad and your bottom must pay for it."

"No please? I'm *sorry*, OK?"

He smiled and patted her cheeks with the board, then held it two feet from her squirmy behind. "Twenty for the vulgar language . . . and forty for blowing off our lunch appointments."

"No*owee*!"

The paddle landed, flicked back, and swatted again. Harsh, wooden sting zipped through her buttocks and burst like a grenade in her ears. She grunted, squalled, kicked, and pounded the desktop with her fists while Dylan held her down and spanked the quivery pink behind. Lisa fought back tears, and then sighed when he stopped and rubbed soreness with his knuckles.

"That was twenty, Lisa . . . now you'll have your forty."

"Oh God please noooo!"

Wood cracked and brimstone scalded her petite fanny. Over and over the nasty paddle burned, and higher and higher into the upper octaves reached her squeals. Dylan leaned forward and clamped her waist in his left forearm while he swatted the girl's bottom. Her shoes flew off and landed on the floor. When red turned to crimson he relented and shortened his stroke, but clapped quick and sharp.

A salty puddle glistened on the desktop. Lisa sobbed and wiped the back of a hand across her face as Dylan lifted her. The skirt fell to cover her shame and she leaned into his hard chest while he hugged her. Fire covered her from toenail to forehead, and she rubbed the outraged source with both palms. Soft skirt lining soothed the horrific sting, but only a little.

"It's all right now, Lisa. Go to the bathroom and compose yourself."

"Uh . . . uh . . . OK. Whuh . . . where?"

Dylan turned and pointed, then wrapped her in his arm and helped her to a door next to the desk. Behind the door was a small cloakroom with a window on the left side, rows of hooks and pegs on the right, and another door opposite. He opened that and flicked a wall switch to illuminate a bathroom bigger than Lisa's bedroom. Blue and white tiles on the floor and walls sparkled in the light of a dozen frosted globes mounted to the ceiling and along the top of a wide mirror. There were two basins beneath the mirror, and a stall shower, a toilet, and a bidet.

"The other girls will be here in about twenty minutes. The lotion is over there if you need it." Dylan smiled and squeezed her arm.

Lisa nodded and he shut the door. She yanked up her skirt and twisted her neck to examine the bright paddle-rash on her bottom.

"*God*, he's worse than Darcy," she muttered, then blinked back a tear as she rummaged in wide, built-in shelves.

She grabbed a plastic bottle then smiled at the boxes of tampons, bags of feminine napkins, Q-tips, toothbrushes, cotton puffs, makeup swatches, and a dozen other items no man she knew would think to keep in his bathroom. Her heart pounded when she leaned over to look in the bottom shelf.

Tall, slender boxes of Summer's Eve douche ranged side by side with squat Fleet enema containers. Next to the boxes was a plump blue syringe with a fluted three-inch tip. Beside that lay a coiled, clear tube, a soft rubber bag, and five nozzles. There were two pink ones no bigger than her little finger; another, short and black and not quite as big as her thumb; the next was white and as long and a bit wider than her middle finger, with a hole in its rounded end and rows of smaller holes along its sides. A tremulous twinge shuddered her anus and she flinched at the reminder of the nasty sting in her behind.

She went to the basin counter, tucked her skirt into its waistband, and turned to look at her reflection while she smoothed on lotion. The sting abated as she rubbed, and she trembled as she slipped a hand around to touch the sweet tingle between her lower lips, then gasped and looked at her watch.

"Oh geeze!"

Dylan sat in the study and sipped water while he added notes to Lisa's file. The doorbell chimed and he smiled as he greeted the Nillson twins.

"Did you have any trouble finding the cottage, girls?"

"No, sir . . . it was a piece of pie."

"I think you mean piece of cake, Sonja . . . but that's all right."

She smiled. "Piece of cake, then."

"Would you like something to drink?" The girls nodded. "I'll show you the kitchen."

Lisa tiptoed into the classroom. The paddle had disappeared, but there was a smudge of wetness on the desktop, next to the cane. She slipped into her loafers and used her sleeve to polish tears from the oak, careful not to touch the horrid rattan stick. The doorbell rang again, and she sat at a table near the window and leaned back in the chair.

Dylan's voice echoed down the hall as he welcomed the cousins from California. The Swedish twins shuffled through the door, nodded to Lisa, and dropped their satchels on the tables in the third row. Half their tanned thighs were exposed below plaid skirts; thin white blouses clung to high, firm breasts and did nothing to conceal their bras; neckties with loose overhand knots circled slender necks. Hair a shade blonder than Lisa's hung down their necks in ponytails held by bright, frilled elastics. They frowned as they looked about the room, then put down their pop bottles and sat.

"Hi. I'm Lisa."

"My name is Birgid and that is Sonja. We are from Minnesota."

Lisa chuckled. "You're putting me on, right?" The girls looked at each other and shrugged. "That accent . . . I mean . . . you sound like those Sven and Ole jokes I hear from my aunt in Bemidji."

The girls blinked, shrugged again, and turned when Dylan led two more students through the door.

"If everyone will have a seat we'll get started." He smiled, handed Lisa her soda bottle and satchel, and then stood in front of the oak desk. "First of all, there is no eating or drinking during class." The girls frowned. "But since this is a get-acquainted session rather than an official class . . . feel free."

The California cousins rolled their eyes, sat in the back row and opened Diet Cokes. They weren't as tall as the Swedes, but just as slender. Honey-blonde hair with irregular platinum streaks fell to their shoulders in crimp-curled, studied disarray. Their eyelids were shadowed in blue and pink, and their full lips shone with burgundy gloss outlined in black. Open blouse cuffs covered their hands and ties draped the collars in a single half hitch. Dylan smiled and continued.

"Before I show you around the cottage . . . a brief tour, granted, but you'll need to know where things are . . . we'll introduce ourselves. I want you to say your name . . . where you are from . . . and what you hope to achieve while you're here . . . *here* meaning both this class and the university." The girls squirmed and glanced at each other. "My name is Dylan Travis and I'm from Los Angeles, California. You may call me Professor Travis, or Professor, or simply *sir*. I've had several nicknames amongst my students over the years, which I ignore even when I hear them. What I hope to achieve here . . . is to guide you to more effective study habits . . . and a more enlightened and mature approach to life in general." He turned to Lisa and nodded.

She swallowed, licked her lips and cleared her throat. "I'm Lisa Carlson and, um . . . I'm from right here . . . in town . . . lived here all my life and, uh . . . I hope to achieve better English, um, skills . . . and get a business degree from the university."

"Thank you, Lisa." He nodded again.

"I am Birgid Nillson, from Rochester, USA." She glanced at Lisa. "And also from Hamburg, Germany, and Uppsala, Sweden. I will also like to improve the English skill, and to take the certificate from university."

Dylan smiled. "In what area of study, Birgid?"

"Perhaps chemistry or biology . . . I am not sure of this."

"Excellent . . . thank you."

"I am Sonja Nillson . . . also from Minnesota, Germany, and Uppsala . . . but I will like to study computers at university."

"And what do you hope to get out of this class, Sonja?"

"Oh yes . . . to improve the English skill as well."

Ashley grunted and her heels clacked the floor. "If the *parrots* are all done . . . what I'*d* like is to get out of this class without getting my ass whacked . . . *sir*."

Dylan gazed at her, eyes steady, expressionless. "And your name is?"

The girl sneered. "Ashley Peterson . . . and I'm from Orange County . . . oh . . . and *I wanna improve my English skills*," she concluded in a mocking whine.

"I see. Did I understand you to say you intend to bring a donkey to school, Ashley?"

"Huh?"

He crossed his arms and leaned back. "You mentioned an *ass*. I didn't think to address the subject in the handbook . . . but no livestock is allowed in the classroom."

Lisa smiled and the twins giggled. Ashley snarled.

"I meant my *butt* . . . like you didn't know . . . and anyway, what is it with you and girls' *asses*, huh?"

"That's enough, Ashley."

"Are you some kinda perv? Do you get your rocks off . . . ?"

Ashley gasped and her face paled as Dylan stalked toward her. He grabbed her arm and she cringed when he yanked her from the chair.

"Since subtlety is wasted on you, young lady. . . ." He pushed her to the front of the class while she squealed. "And because you are determined to make an issue of the matter, I will demonstrate . . . yet again . . . what it *is* with me and that part of a girl's anatomy."

"Let me go, you son of a *owitch*!"

Dylan swatted the rear of Ashley's skirt and lifted her arm to keep her off-balance while he rolled his chair to the front of the desk, then sat and dragged her across his knees.

"First of all . . . the word you used is a vulgar term for the buttocks . . . and the handbook clearly states that vulgar, profane or abusive language is not permitted, and violations are penalized."

Ashley's wail drowned most of his statement. She kicked, wriggled and batted his leg with her fists, but he snugged her waist tight under his left arm and turned up her skirt.

"Let me go! You can't *do* this to me!"

"You know I *can* . . . because I *have* . . . and on your bare *heinie*."

He tugged down pink bikini panties. Ashley's angry, embarrassed screech quavered as she glanced at the Swedish twins' amused faces. She kicked harder and screamed louder, more in shame than pain, when Dylan clapped her rounded cheeks and left a warm pink smudge on both crowns.

"OK, OK . . . I'm *sorry* . . . now let me *go*."

"When the lesson is over, Ashley . . . not before."

"No! Ow! Shit!"

She turned her head to hide the tears that puddled in her eyes, and whimpered while he rained sharp, quick slaps over her wriggly bottom. Dylan shook his head.

"The lesson won't even *begin*. . . ." He raised his arm high. "Until you stop! That! Language!" Ashley yelped as he punctuated each word with a harsh swat to the base of her cheeks. "You asked me what it is with me and a girl's bottom . . . so I'll *tell* you." She yelped when he swatted again. "Nature, in Her wisdom, provided a nerve-ending rich target so I can administer carefully regulated *painful* reminders to a girl that she does *not* call her professor a pervert! Or generally act like a defiant! Spoiled! Smart-mouthed! Little! Brat!"

"Ow! Ouch! Eek! Eeesh! Owee! Okaaay!"

Dylan flexed his fingers as sharp clacks and Ashley's shouts echoed in his ears. He tested the warmth in her red bottom with his wrist and loosened his grip on her waist.

"Now, Ashley . . . the handbook very specifically states . . . and we went over this at home, if you recall . . . that white cotton underpants are required at all times. Isn't that so? Ashley?"

She sniffed, knuckled away a tear and stared at the floor. "Yeah."

"Yeah . . . *sir*, Ashley." His quick slap drew another yelp.

"Jesus *Christ* . . . yeah, *sir* . . . OK?"

"Then why are you not *wearing* white cotton underpants?"

"I . . . I forgot."

A blush, more shameful than the sting in her behind, crept up her neck as she whined the childish excuse. Dylan lifted her onto her feet and stood her in front of him. She stared at the chalkboard and the skirt dropped to hide her humiliated cheeks from the other girls. He leaned back, opened a drawer to pluck tissue from a box, then pressed it into her damp palm and turned her around.

"Get your handbook, Ashley."

"I . . . it's at the apartment."

He sighed. "You know you're supposed to bring it to class, young lady."

"I forg . . . I . . . yeah. Sir."

"Will someone lend Ashley a handbook, please?" Satchels rustled and Dylan took a step forward. "Thank you, Birgid." Ashley's arm trembled as she took the book from him. "Remove your underpants and put them on the desk."

She gaped at him for a second and her jaw quivered. "Whuh . . . *why?*"

"Because I *said* to. Do you intend to make an issue of *this* as well?"

"No but . . . *Christ*, Professor, that's *way* . . . ow! Stop hitting me!"

He held her arm as she backed away. "Then stop using profanity . . . and do what I told you . . . now."

"OK, *OK*, shi . . . *geeze!*"

The tiny pink panties clung at her thigh tops. Ashley stared at the floor while she reached under her skirt to nudge them down her legs. She whimpered when the roll of silk and cotton fell onto her loafers.

Dylan tapped the desktop. "Right here, Ashley."

She whimpered, lifted her feet and reached down. Her lips curled in disgust as she slapped the garment on polished oak.

"There . . . *happy?*"

"Watch your tone of voice, young lady."

"But it's just so. . . ." She hissed and twisted the handbook in nervous fingers.

"Go stand in the corner."

Her eyes widened and she struggled against his steely grip. "You've *got* to be kidding."

"I never kid in matters of discipline . . . do what I told you. Stand right over there and read the section on proper school attire."

"Oh, for Christ's . . . crap's . . . for crying out *loud*, I'm not six years old!"

"Then stop behaving as if you *were*. Into the corner . . . now, Ashley . . . or should I begin the lesson again?"

"*No.*" She wriggled and he let go of her arm.

New tears sprang to her eyes as she shuffled over to stand between the end of the chalkboard and the edge of a casement window. She felt, more than heard, his footsteps behind her and whirled to look at him.

"Face the corner and lift your skirt."

"What? Are you crazy? *No!*"

"Hush, girl . . . I don't like to make an example of you . . . but you gave me no choice."

"Professor, *please*, I . . . I'm *sorry* . . . don't make me. . . ."

"Shh."

Warm, hard fingers raised her skirt, and smooth, cool serge caressed hot, tender cheeks when, for the briefest moment, while he tucked skirt hem into skirt waist, Dylan's pleated trousers brushed her sore bottom. She moaned and leaned her forehead against the wall. He stepped back and fiery blush heated Ashley's face as she felt every eye in the room on her bare, disgraceful behind.

"Oh *God*," she whispered.

He turned, pulled the chair to its place behind the desk, and then cleared his throat. "Where were we? Britney, I believe you were next."

She coughed, licked her lips and sat up straight. "I'm uh . . . Britney Dahlgren and . . . I live in Mission Viejo, and . . . I wanna take film classes at the university . . . and maybe go to the UCLA film school later."

Dylan sat on the edge of the desk. "A laudable ambition, Britney . . . now." He made eye contact with each of the four girls. "Has everyone read the college handbook?" They all nodded and he turned again to Britney. "That's excellent . . . then I'd like you to reread the page with the diagram that shows how to put a proper knot in your tie. Any questions?"

Birgid raised a hand. "Professor . . . this woman who comes to our apartment each night?"

"Ms. Scott . . . what about her?"

"It is only. . . ." She glanced at her sister. "Is she *spying* on us?"

"Not spying, Birgid . . . watching over you. It's my job to keep you safe while you're here . . . and Ms. Scott assists me in that way."

"Yes, but . . . she has a key . . . so that she will come in whenever she *wishes*."

He nodded. "To see that you're all right . . . and to make sure you're where you're *supposed* to be."

Sonja huffed. "But we are too old to be having a . . . a. . . ." She looked at Birgid. "*Barnvakt?*"

"Child-watcher? No . . . *baby-sitter*."

"Yes, baby-sitter . . . we are *adults*. Do you not trust us?"

"Trust is earned, Sonja." He shrugged. "If you would prefer a campus dormitory I can arrange it . . . but while you stay in the apartment, Ms. Scott will continue to visit."

"We do not *wish* to live at a dormitory, Professor! This apartment is nice . . . but we do not feel *free*."

Dylan smiled. "Free to do what, Sonja? Stay out until dawn? Throw parties every night?" Sonja scowled and shook her head. "As long as you behave, Ms. Scott will limit her visits to right around curfew. But if you pull any tricks . . . or I find you've gone out after she leaves . . . she will begin random, unannounced inspections . . . and then you will *truly* feel watched. Britney?"

"Huh? Sir?"

"Do you or Ashley have a problem with your . . . guardian?"

"Um . . . not really. Jill's OK . . . and we sorta figured you'd keep an eye on us."

The twins looked at each other, and Lisa glanced over her shoulder at Britney. The girl twisted her lips in a quick sneer and Lisa nodded. She turned when Dylan cleared his throat.

"All right, then . . . we'll move on. Ashley?"

The girl snorted and resisted the impulse to look at him. "What? Sir."

"Lower your skirt and come here."

Cool acetate soothed warm ache when she yanked the garment over her bottom. Long seconds ticked by as she stared straight ahead, into the nasty corner . . . the corner he made her stand in, half naked and totally humiliated while he nattered about bed checks. Ashley felt their eyes, all their eyes, on her, and she wanted to sink into the floor rather than face their amused, sympathetic looks. A thousand years passed, and then she moaned when shoes clicked hardwood. She sighed as he rubbed her shoulders.

"It's all right, Ashley." Dylan's smooth baritone resonated in her head and she swiveled into his arms. "You're a good girl and I'm not mad at you."

"Yeah well . . . maybe I'm mad at *you*."

"Come along now."

His nonresponse to her remark took her aback and she quivered as he led her to the bathroom. He flicked the light switch and pulled a vanity stool from beneath the basin counter. Ashley whimpered but didn't struggle as he sat and pulled her across his lap. A plastic bottle soughed and lotion dribbled into his palm.

"No . . . don't," she whispered when he pushed up the skirt.

"Stop whining, girl."

There was no harshness in his tone, and Ashley planted her palms and toes on the tiles while he slicked cool creaminess over prickly heat. She sighed as welcome relief soothed the hurt in her bottom and her mind.

Lisa grunted, stood, and ignored the other girls' stares as she tip-toed to the door and peeked around the jamb, then shook her head and returned to her seat. Britney leaned forward.

"Um . . . Lisa? Right?"

She turned. "Yeah?"

"What's he *doing* in there?"

"Putting lotion on her butt."

"Well *that* sucks . . . he didn't do that when he. . . ."

Lisa smirked. "When he spanked you?" Britney nodded. "What did you do?"

"Nothing heinous . . . just came home a little loaded is all."

"It doesn't take much, that's for sure."

"So what did you do?"

"Nothing heinous. I didn't think so, anyway . . . so, um . . . he's got somebody checking up on you guys?"

"Yeah, some old lady . . . forties or fifties, I guess."

"And you're OK with that, or . . . ?"

"What was I *supposed* to say? One sore ass in the family is plenty

... and I guess it's the price we pay for not having to live in a dorm. Besides. . . ." She grinned. "Me and Ash know how to work around curfews."

"Uh huh . . . but this is a real small town . . . so that lady may not be the *only* one keeping an eye on you."

"Yeah, maybe . . . so where do *you* live?"

"With my. . . ."

Lisa turned when Dylan entered, followed by a red-faced but calmer Ashley.

"All right, girls . . . let's have a look at the physical plant."

He showed them the bathroom, its facilities and supplies, and Lisa bit her lip while she waited for somebody to look into the lower shelf. No one did, although the girls giggled when Sonja turned the knob to start the fountain in the bidet. They followed him to the hallway and watched as Dylan pointed out the classic books, then went into the study. Deep shelves lined paneled walls and on them ranged pictures, trophies, and mementos of his father's life. He opened a corner cabinet next to a short, plush sofa across from the desk and rummaged through a pile of plastic packets, then turned to Ashley.

"Size six, I believe."

She scoffed. "Four . . . I'm a. . . ."

"Perhaps you'll prefer them a bit loose today . . . don't you think?"

Birgid grinned. "You have also panties for the students?"

Dylan nodded. "How's your Latin, Birgid?"

"A little, Professor . . . you will teach us more?"

"Only two words . . . *semper paratus*."

The girl frowned at the ceiling while she translated through two languages. "Always . . . prepared?"

"That's probably correct . . . but Coast Guard tradition insists it means *always ready*. So I try to be ready for anything . . . the unfortunate accident . . . the untimely demise of a washing machine at your apartment building." He looked at Ashley and she pouted. "Or a girl who. . . ."

"*OK*, Professor . . . I got it . . . but I really like those pink ones."

"Then you may wear them anytime you like . . . *away* from college."

Lisa huffed and stepped back when he wrapped an arm around Ashley and led her to the door, then across the hall and into a bedroom with a queen-sized four-poster, a bureau, an armchair, and a nightstand. Another door, next to a high, narrow, multishelved secretary's desk, opened into a second, much smaller bath.

"This is cozy," Lisa muttered.

He glanced at her and pointed to the secretary. "That's the first-aid station."

Lisa walked over to open drawers and shelf covers. Boxes of bandages and plasters, tubes of unguent, ointment, and emollient, cans of powders, jars of salve, and bottles of disinfectant filled every nook and cranny.

Sonja gasped "We have no such first-aid station in our home, Professor."

"Nor do you need such, Sonja . . . but I have a lot of people to care for . . . so I want to be ready if anyone gets hurt."

Britney sniffed. "You're the only one who hurts anybody."

Lisa gasped and Ashley whimpered. The twins bit their lips and stepped back. Dylan rubbed his forehead.

"Why don't you have a look at the back yard and I'll bring your assignments for next week? You can go out through the door in the kitchen."

The girls grabbed more soda as they passed the refrigerator and went outside. A white gazebo, its sides shaded by trellised honeysuckle vines, sat beneath two oaks in the center of the lawn. Ashley opened a Diet Coke and glared at her cousin.

"That shot wasn't necessary."

"He *did* hurt you." Britney perched on the low wall at the opposite side of the gazebo from Ashley.

"Yeah, but you don't gotta get him pissed off at *you*."

"Hey, it's not like I went *after* him."

"Oh right . . . like *I* did, huh?"

"Well you *did*. How come, Ash? I mean, you told me he already . . . did you think he wouldn't do that again?"

"No! I don't *know* . . . maybe . . . but he was just so . . . *I'm all that* . . . up there with his professor face on, all in control and everything. It made me mad and I kinda lost it."

Britney snickered. "You didn't *lose* it . . . you wanted to find out how far you could push him."

Ashley rubbed the back of her skirt. "Not real far, huh? So at least we know he wasn't kidding."

"I did not have reason to think he *was* kidding." Birgid snorted. "And it is most cruel that he will beat you in so public a place."

Lisa frowned. "Not just her . . . *us* . . . everybody signed his stupid contract or we wouldn't be here."

"That contract's a piece of crap . . . it wouldn't stand up in court." Ashley smirked. "But . . . it's either this or Mike and Gloria."

"Oh God!" Britney rolled her eyes. "They're like . . . *mediaeval*."

Sonja gaped. "Who are these persons?"

"Uncle Mike and Aunt Gloria." Ashley puffed her cheeks. "They live in Lompoc, which is like the end of the world. He's a prison guard and she stays home and sews all day with some religious station blasting from every radio in the house."

Britney nodded. "And they pray for like five minutes before every meal . . . even breakfast."

"I would find this tiresome, as well."

Ashley nodded. "So what did *your* olds threaten if you didn't do reform school?"

Birgid and Sonja looked at each other and blinked. Lisa chuckled.

"She means your parents . . . what was the nasty alternative to *this* place?"

"Oh!" Birgid nodded. "Our mother says we will be grounded until we graduate university." Lisa gasped and Birgid laughed. "We did not believe she will do this . . . but merely to say it tells us she is very angry and perhaps we should agree."

"Besides. . . ." Sonja grinned. "It is warmer here in the winters."

"But you oughta be *used* to the cold." Lisa winked. "If you're really from Sweden."

"We *are* being from Sweden . . . but to be used to the cold is not the same as to enjoy it."

"Yeah, well . . . *we're* gonna freeze our asses off, this far from

OC." Ashley yelped when she leaned her bottom against the wall. "If Professor Crabapple doesn't smack 'em off first."

Lisa grimaced. "We can do better than *Crabapple* . . . um . . . Travis . . . traveler . . . tracker. . . ." She grinned and snapped her fingers. "*Travesty* . . . Professor Travesty! I bet that's what his other students call him."

"No doubt." Britney sighed. "And what's up with that stick on his desk?"

"If he's anything like my boss. . . ." Lisa stopped and bit her lip when everyone looked at her. "I um . . . I think it's just to scare us."

Britney scowled. "You *think*? So what's your boss like?"

"Anyway um. . . ." Lisa cleared her throat. "The handbook says spanking and paddling . . . nothing about caning."

"So what about your . . . ?"

The side door slammed and they turned. Dylan smiled as he strode toward the gazebo.

"Here we are . . . your assignments for next week." He handed out colored folders while the girls frowned. "The instructions are explicit, but if you do have questions I want you to call me. All right?"

The girls chewed their lips and read printed sheets. Ashley moaned.

"This looks like a lot of work . . . Professor."

"It is. I don't want you to be bored and have to look for mischief to get into." He glanced at his watch. "The bus will be here in about twenty minutes, so you should get ready to go."

They trudged into the cottage and Lisa went to the bathroom. She grumbled while she sat on the toilet, then returned to the classroom and pretended to struggle with a satchel strap while Dylan said goodbye to the other girls at the front door. He walked in, his head cocked to one side.

"Problem, Lisa?"

"Yeah, um . . . sorta."

"May I help?"

He reached for the buckle but Lisa stamped her foot.

"You coulda helped earlier, you know."

"What?"

"I mean *geeze* . . . you paddled me purple and . . . and you . . . you gave whatzername . . . Ashley . . . a little baby spanking . . . then you put lotion on her butt and . . . and *that's* what!"

"So I managed to create envy amongst my pupils already . . . this may be a record for me."

"It's not *envy* . . . I just want you to be *fair*."

He reached for her hand but she folded her arms. "All right, Lisa . . . first of all, there wasn't time for the sort of aftercare you apparently think you're entitled to, and secondly, you should be grateful that I made a public example of Ashley instead of you. And most importantly, I refuse to give you any false impression of my intentions regarding your discipline."

Lisa snorted. "So you're gonna blister my fanny whenever you feel like it and then just make me go sit down?"

"No . . . there will likely be corner time as well." She grunted and clenched her fists. "Stop that, Lisa! Give me your hands . . . now." Her lower lip trembled as he took hold of moist fingers. "I always try to be fair, but you must understand the constraints on *my* behavior. Corporal punishment needn't be brutal to be effective, but it also can't be a reward. Do you see?"

"Well yeah but . . . you paddled me so *hard* and all I wanted. . . ."

"All you wanted was for me to complete the lesson by showing you that it's all right . . . the punishment is over and we can get on with other things . . . and normally that's what I *would* do, as I did with Ashley." Lisa looked into his eyes and he smiled. "But this is a learning experience for both of us . . . and until I know you better, I won't risk a gesture of comfort being misconstrued as a reward for bad conduct. So you'll have to get by with only a hug this time."

She sniffled and squeezed his chest when he wrapped his arms around her. "You, um . . . *usually* . . . make girls feel better after you, um. . . ."

He patted her bottom and nodded. "A *little* better, Lisa . . . only a little."

"Yeah OK." Lisa wrinkled her nose and looked up. "So, um . . . Michael told you about me? About . . . you know. . . ."

"Let's say he was quite candid in our discussions and leave it at that, shall we?"

"Oh *God* . . . so you think I'm a. . . ."

"Shh. I'll tell you what I think of you after I get to know you. May I expect the same from you?"

Lisa smirked. "Yes, sir. I shouldn't of made such a big deal out of it, but I kinda felt. . . ."

"It's all right, Lisa . . . I understand." He let go of her and checked the time. "You've missed the bus, it seems, but there's another in an hour . . . or I could give you a ride if you want to wait a bit longer."

"No, that's OK. I'll call Greg to come get me." She bit her lip and dug a cell phone from her bag. "If his car's running."

Dylan chuckled. "All right . . . then you may wait in the study if you'd like. I'd enjoy the company while I write lesson plans."

"Sure . . . I'll be there in a minute."

He smiled and walked down the hall. She sat on the desk and watched him go. Quick tingles swept over her bottom like summer rain as she thumbed a speed key.

"Hi, it's me . . . you wanna take a long lunch and make your boss's sore, paddled bottom feel better?"

She giggled when Greg gasped and dropped the phone.

Chapter 7

A NEW SCHOOL

FELICIA FORGOT TO check their passports until the week before the flight. The documents had expired and bureaucratic red tape delayed their departure from Germany by three weeks. The postponement gave Teresa time to think, and to fret. Every picture on the wall, every piece of furniture, every texture and odor in the house held memories of her mother and father. It pained her to sit at the dining table, and she would never go into her Papa's bedroom. Yet she wanted to stay, to suffer the hurtful reminders, to prove how much she loved them. Her last-minute refusal to leave shocked Felicia and prompted a stern phone call from Dylan. He cajoled, scolded, pleaded, and finally threatened to fly to Hamburg, drag her to the plane, and spank her all the way to America. She was sure, or almost, that he would do no such thing, but he sounded so angry she agreed and began to pack. Felicia sighed with relief and helped her.

They arrived at the Des Moines airport in late June, and it was Teresa's turn to be relieved. Dylan said nothing, and did nothing, about her stubborn tantrum, only hugged and kissed her, and then drove for over an hour on flat, straight roads through green fields that stretched to the horizon. They carried their bags into the two-bedroom apartment at the opposite end of Main Street from Dylan's, but when Teresa and Felicia saw the tasteless, utilitarian furniture, they both whined. Dylan reminded them it was rented and would be replaced as they found suitable pieces, and they apologized.

The next day, Teresa sulked while she unpacked in the austere bedroom, then brightened when Dylan took her and Felicia to the mall and let Teresa loose in a lingerie store with his credit card. A large bag stuffed with expensive underwear in hand, she managed to be cheerful while she shopped for simple plaid skirts, unadorned white blouses, and plain, sensible loafers.

The following Wednesday, after lunch, she got off the bus and glanced at the paper with the cottage's address printed on it, then walked half a block along a shady street. The number painted atop a brick gatepost matched the paper. She pushed open the gate and went to the door, started to press the bell, then stopped, dropped her leather satchel, and brushed specks of lint from her crisp, white blouse. A maroon and silver tie hung, badly knotted, from her throat. She squeezed it tighter to hide it under the collar. Her plaid, pleated skirt rustled as she smoothed it front and back, then took a deep breath and rang the bell. The door swung open on silent hinges and she frowned. A girl stood in the entryway.

She was shorter than Teresa by four inches, and a blonde ponytail accentuated the youthfulness of a clear, scrubbed complexion. Her clothes were identical to Teresa's except for a variation in the skirt's plaid. A perfect half-Windsor held her tie in place.

"Hi, Teresa . . . I'm Lisa . . . come on in."

"Where is Professor Travis?"

"He had a meeting and thought it might go late so he asked me to show you around." Lisa shut the door and Teresa followed her to the classroom. "You can put your stuff anywhere . . . it's just us today." She pointed. "The bathroom is through there."

Teresa nodded and set her bag on a table. "You are also a student?"

"No . . . I just get off on playing schoolgirl." Lisa laughed when Teresa's mouth fell open. "Of *course* I'm a student."

"But . . . you seem so. . . ."

"Much older?"

"You are *older*?"

"Older than you . . . don't let my baby face fool you." She winked.

"Oh! But it is not this . . . only your English . . . it is so colloquial. Why will you need such a school as this?"

Lisa smirked. "Colloquial doesn't work in business letters and stuff . . . that's what my boss says, anyway. I'm just here until my college grades get better."

"You also go to university?"

"Well, yeah . . . same one you do . . . or will, when summer session starts. What year will you be?"

"I am not certain. I completed the placement exam by post, but do not know yet the results."

"I'm a sophomore, technically, but I'll be a junior as soon as I finish up some incompletes."

Teresa blinked and twitched her lip. "I am not understanding a great deal of this." She glanced to the side. "The WC is in there?"

"Uh huh . . . the professor oughta be here pretty soon so you better hurry."

"All right."

Teresa glanced at the chalkboard behind the instructor's desk. Next to it, on a peg at eye level, hung a crook-handled rattan stick. Her heart pounded and she clenched her fingers as she went into the bathroom. She gazed at the bright lights while she sat on the toilet, then washed her hands with rose-scented soap, dried them on a fluffy hand towel, and went back to the classroom. Lisa sat in the back row, her brown penny loafers propped on a table.

"Better?"

"Yes. Thank you." Teresa sat in the chair where she left her satchel and swiveled around. "Lisa?"

"Hm?"

"You are staying in one of the flats Uncle Dylan . . . Professor Travis has rented?"

"I wish . . . those are for the out-of-town students . . . um . . . the *other* out-of-town students. You live with your stepmom, right? I live with my boss." Teresa gasped. Lisa wrinkled her nose. "I didn't mean *that* . . . I stay at his house . . . I *work* there."

Teresa blinked. "You are a . . . domestic?"

"The word is *maid* . . . yeah . . . I'm a maid . . . and I own a whole chain of boutiques."

"Oh, I see." Teresa rolled her eyes. "You must have a *very* busy schedule."

"It's *true*, and you don't gotta be sarcastic . . . the stores are in trust." Lisa folded her arms and glared. "Aren't you a trust brat, too?"

Teresa's jaw dropped. "I have never heard this phrase and it is *most* insulting. Who is telling you this, in any case?"

"Nobody *told* me. *All* the girls here are trust brats . . . never have to work, but their trustee says they gotta at least learn grammar so they don't sound like morons when they complain to Neiman Marcus." Lisa sneered. "So . . . what? Is Uncle Dylan your trustee?"

"That is none of your concern and . . . and you are most impolite to ask."

"Yeah?" Lisa shoes clomped hardwood as she stood. "That's just typical, snotty, trust-brat attitude. I know . . . because Michael made me go to this stupid school for acting exactly the same way, so get *over* yourself."

Teresa rose, clenched her fists and took two steps toward Lisa. "I am *not* snotty, and you do not tell me what to do!"

"Don't think you can tell *me* what to do, either, just 'cause you're his *niece*."

"Oh, then I suppose you are his teacher's *pet* . . . his yellow-haired lap dog!"

"Teresa!"

She gasped and twirled. Dylan stalked in, his eyes ablaze. Lisa moaned and fell into her chair. Teresa whimpered, stepped backward, and sat down hard. His briefcase clunked the desktop and he glanced from one girl to the other.

"Well?"

Long, horrible, silent seconds ticked by. Teresa hugged her tummy to quell the nasty butterflies that dashed about inside. Lisa's lips trembled as she struggled to form words.

"Sorry . . . sir."

"I should think *so* . . . come here, both of you." He rounded the desk, shrugged off his suit coat and hung it on the chair back, then sat and shook his head. Neither girl moved. "Don't make me say it again."

Loafers scraped hardwood as Teresa and Lisa shuffled, jelly-kneed, toward him. They stared at the desktop and jerked in opposite

directions when their elbows touched. Dylan studied their red faces
for a dozen seconds and then leaned forward.

"Lisa?"

She coughed and covered her mouth. "Sir?"

"Is there any point in my asking who started this?"

The girl shook her head. "It . . . just kinda *happened* . . . sir."

"Teresa?"

"Yes, Unc . . . sir?"

"Is Lisa to blame for your shouting match?"

"She . . . and then I. . . ." She knuckled an incipient tear from her
eye. "No, sir, I . . . I was shouting as well as she . . . and I also am
sorry."

"I see . . . then it was *no* one's fault that you would have torn one
another's hair out if I hadn't come in when I did . . . is that correct?"

"But we *wouldn't* of. . . ."

"*No*, Uncle Dylan, it was only. . . ."

"Hush . . . did you read the handbook, girls?" Two heads bobbed.
"The section on fighting?"

They nodded harder and glanced at each other. Teresa looked at
him.

"But we were not *fighting*, Uncle . . . Professor . . . merely. . . ."

He raised a hand. "Fighting includes verbal assaults . . . and I
heard a few of *those* when I opened the front door."

Lisa gasped. "Nuh *uh*! I never called her *anything*, Professor, but
she called me a lap dog and . . . and that's kinda like *bitch*, isn't it?"

Teresa squealed and glared at her. "And you think that *snotty* is a
word of kindness, you. . . ."

"Enough!" Dylan opened a drawer, took the paddle and stalked
toward them. "Bend over the desk."

"No *please?*"

Two voices melded in appeal as the girls backed away. Four
tremulous hands clutched wool-covered bottoms. Dylan clamped the
board beneath his arm and grabbed their wrists.

"I said . . . over the desk."

Jelly knees turned to shaving cream as he dragged them forward.
Teresa sobbed and Lisa grunted when he pushed on their backs. The

girls bent at the waist, and round behinds clenched beneath wool and cotton. Dylan set the paddle down and scowled as he lifted skirts and tucked them into waistbands. Teresa kicked the floor.

"Uncle *Dylan* . . . this is not fair!"

"Quiet, Teresa. You know better than to act that way . . . both of you do . . . and I'm going to paddle both your bare fannies so you remember that you are young ladies and not street hooligans."

Teresa slapped the desktop and twisted. "Not *bare* . . . not in front of *her*!" Elbows clunked oak when he pressed on her shoulder.

"Don't argue with me, young lady. Your naughty bottom won't be bare in front of anyone except me. Lisa is right beside you and *her* naughty bottom will be exactly as bare and just as painful . . . so keep still."

He leaned over to thumb white cotton panties down. Lisa groaned and chewed a knuckle. Teresa squealed and covered her eyes with both hands as cool, moist air bathed naked, vulnerable flesh. Warm cotton bunched at thigh tops and Dylan picked up the paddle. He patted Teresa's back with his palm, did the same to Lisa and then stood, feet apart, with his left thigh at the desk's edge, and gazed at two perfect-peach bottoms.

Lisa's plump mounds shifted as she twisted her ankles. Teresa's cheeks, a bit wider, higher set and more rounded at the crests, dimpled along the hipbones. Smooth, deep valleys divided both behinds, and Dylan sighed as he stretched his right arm, ignored fretful, whiney pleas, and clapped the center of Teresa's fanny with a two-foot stroke.

She yelped and reached back to rub. Dylan barked a stern *no* and smacked Lisa just as hard. Back and forth between their soft bottoms he swatted while he scolded and told them not to cover themselves, until they squirmed so much he leaned over and pressed his forearm into their backs to steady them for the final quick dozen.

Ash wood clattered when he dropped the board onto the desk. Teresa sobbed and Lisa wept when he lifted and wrapped them in strong arms. They clasped paddle-stung cheeks while he whispered smooth syllables that failed to register over the painful shriek in their ears. The shriek diminished when he kissed their foreheads, turned them loose, and leaned against the desk.

"No more of this nonsense then . . . hmm?"

Lisa wagged her head. "No, sir."

"No, Uncle . . . Professor . . . um, Travis . . . sir."

He smiled. "I know it's hard for you, Teresa . . . Uncle Dylan at home . . . Professor at school . . . but you'll get used to it. Lisa?"

She gulped. "Sir?"

"Have you learned your lesson?"

"*God* yeah . . . I mean . . . yes, sir."

"All right then . . . go get some lotion and I'll make you feel a *little* better."

"Any kind I want?" He nodded. "OK." She thumbed her panties and then stopped when he frowned. "All *right* . . . geeze!"

Her bare red cheeks, framed by furled plaid wool and rolled white cotton, jiggled as she strode to the bathroom. She stood on tiptoe to move bottles, tubes, and vials until she found what she wanted, then frowned at the red reflection in the mirror and went back to the classroom.

Teresa pouted and sniffled when Lisa left. Dylan opened a drawer and offered her a box of Kleenex. She snatched two while she glared at him, then wiped her eyes and blew her nose.

"Why must you tell *her* to get the lotion, Uncle Dylan?"

"Because she knows where it is . . . and why are you angry with *me* when you know how naughty *you* were?"

"I was *not* naughty and . . . and besides . . . she is your favorite, isn't she?"

"Don't be ridiculous, sweetie."

He sighed and reached for her, but Teresa turned away just as Lisa walked out the cloakroom door.

"I found this the other day, Professor . . . it smells really good and feels wonderful . . . and it's Bvlgari . . . but I don't know what this means." She handed him the tube and he smiled.

"Petits et Mamans? Infants and mothers. Ms. Scott helped me stock the shelves and she's big on yard sales . . . probably a shower gift that never was opened. Shall we?"

Lisa smiled and took a step back as he circled the desk and sat in his chair. He arched his eyebrows and held up his arms. Teresa frowned at Lisa, then looked at Dylan.

"What?"

"Don't you want lotion on your bottom?"

"Um . . . yes . . . only. . . ."

Dylan shook his head. "I won't wait while you find your own special lotion in the bathroom . . . come here this instant, Teresa, or go stand in the corner now."

Pouty breath fluttered her lips as she stumbled to his side. He smiled, draped her across his lap, snugged her waist into his stomach, and reached a hand toward Lisa. She scowled when she clasped his warm fingers.

"Um . . . Professor?"

"Hm? Come along, Lisa . . . right over my knees . . . there."

"I um . . . it's not like I'm ungrateful or anything. . . ."

Smooth, beige fluid trickled into his palm when he upended the tube. Sweet flowers tickled their noses as he spread light, smooth ointment over red, achy bottoms. The girls sighed and wriggled beneath his palm, and each ignored the other's bare hip as it pressed against her.

"But what, Lisa?"

"That . . . that feels good, Professor, but . . . um . . . you were only kidding about the corner, right?"

He smiled, dribbled more lotion onto his fingers and slicked them into Lisa's cleft. She quivered and he gave her a light squeeze, and then massaged Teresa's firm behind.

"Why would you think *that*, Lisa?"

Both girls turned to look at him, looked at each other, then back at him.

"*No!*"

The word echoed in a perfect harmonic third against the high ceiling, and the cacophony of pleas and complaints that followed made Dylan blink, shudder and grasp squirmy waists hard.

"Lisa! Teresa! Stop that right *now*."

"But *Professor*. . . ."

"Uncle Dylan, you *cannot*. . . ."

"I said *hush*. I *could* have put you in the corner *without* any lotion, and this is the thanks I get. Now up . . . both of you. Lisa . . . by the window . . . Teresa, next to the cloakroom door."

Horrid, nasty butterflies, drawn by the scent of Bvlgari flowers and childish shame, careened through pitiful tummies as the girls slogged toward their corners. They stared straight ahead and felt Dylan's eyes on their sore, slippery bottoms. Lisa muttered and stamped a loafer while Teresa clenched her fists and puffed wordless expletives at her uncle and his barbaric discipline. Dylan replaced the cap on the lotion and stood.

"Fifteen minutes, girls."

"What?"

"Uncle *Dylan*."

They turned to pout at him but he shook his head.

"I *said* fifteen minutes . . . that's how long it will take to unpack the car. If you had been good girls you might have helped . . . but naughty girls with spanked bottoms and bad attitudes are of no use to me . . . so you will stand there until I've finished. Do you understand? Lisa?"

"Geeze, Professor, I. . . ."

"Lisa Marie!"

"OK! Yeah! Sir!"

"Teresa?"

Her heart throbbed and a hoarse *yes* burned her throat. The floor shook when Dylan tramped out, and the walls shivered when he slammed the front door. Lisa rubbed her bottom with both hands. Teresa did the same and peered over her left shoulder.

"I hope you are pleased with this trouble you have caused."

"*I* caused? *You* started it."

"I did *not* . . . you said I am a trust brat."

"I *asked* if you were a trust brat . . . and you went *off* on me!"

"Ha! Then why did you not tell *him* that I caused the fight?"

"Don't you know *anything*? He's just like my dad. When I got in fights with my sister he'd blame *both* of us regardless . . . so why didn't *you*?"

"Be . . . because I am more polite than you and . . . and in any case, you are a terrible person and have made my uncle angry with me."

"*Your uncle, your uncle*," Lisa chanted in a whine. "How a nice guy like Dylan could have a niece as nasty as you I'll *never* understand."

"*What* did you say?"

"You heard me . . . you're just a. . . ."

The front door opened, closed, and the girls stared at the corners while Dylan piled grocery bags onto the kitchen table. After a minute he went out again. Teresa yanked up her panties and dragged her skirt from its waistband as she glared at Lisa.

"How *dare* you call him by his given name?"

"I'll call him anything I *want* . . . you . . . you. . . ." Lisa sneered and tugged underpants and skirt to cover her bottom.

"What? I am a *what*?"

"I don't think medical science has a *name* for what you are . . . but if they've got any in a test tube there's a big *biohazard* sticker on it."

Teresa snarled and took two steps. "Oh *yes*? And how hazardous is this chemical you pour on your mousy hair to turn it such an awful shade of yellow?"

"I *don't* . . . but nothing in the world could be as toxic than that perfume you bathed in. What *is* that . . . *Eau de Garbage*?"

They stood toe-to-toe, fists clenched, hearts pounding. Knuckles rapped window glass and they gasped as they turned. Dylan glared through the pane, his face a bronzed thundercloud, his jaw muscles aquiver, his lips a thin, angry line beneath flared nostrils.

Lisa groaned and furled her skirt as she ran to her corner. Teresa's shaky fingers clutched wool and cotton while she scurried to hers. The kitchen door slammed like the crack of doom and the girls whimpered. Crisp footfalls echoed through the hallway and stopped at the classroom door. Dylan's reproachful glare bored into their backs.

"What in the name of all that's reasonable is *wrong* with you two?"

Panic clutched Teresa's bosom like a fist and she glanced at the plea in Lisa's eyes. She took a deep breath and looked at him.

"We . . . we were merely apologizing, Uncle Dylan."

His left eye twitched and he crossed his arms. "Oh, *really?*"

"Um . . . yeah." Lisa turned and nodded. "We . . . we just wanted to shake hands and be friends . . . before you got back and um. . . ."

"And it is most uh . . . unmannerly to shake hands when one's bum is naked so we. . . ."

"We were gonna go back in the corner, Professor . . . with our uh . . . bums . . . naked . . . just like you told us. Sir."

"Yes, sir . . . that is correct, so you see we. . . ."

"Not another word, *either* of you." Dylan loosened his tie and snaked it from beneath the stiff collar. He tossed it onto the desk and fisted his hips as he shook his head. "How thick do you think those window panes are? How thick do you think *I* am? Into the bathroom, both of you."

The girls grimaced as they looked at each other and napalm butterflies burst in their tummies. Lisa coughed and licked dry lips.

"You're not gonna paddle us again, are you? Sir? Professor?"

"Herr Professor Uncle, my behind is already so sore that. . . ."

"*Move.*"

Fear gripped their hearts and they took short, shallow breaths, stared at the floor and stumbled through the cloakroom. Dylan's fiery eyes followed them, and then he grunted at the sound of a knock on the front door. He turned and took a step, but stopped when it opened.

"Hello! Anyone here?"

"In the classroom, Jill," he shouted.

A slender woman with grayish brown hair, cut short around a pleasant face, carried two paper bags into the room and smiled at Dylan.

"Hi! I found a bunch of ring binders and pencils and stuff at a garage sale for practically nothing so I . . . what's wrong?"

Dylan frowned. "I'm not sure . . . irritable schoolgirl syndrome . . . culture shock . . . sibling rivalry . . . or all of the above . . . almost to the point of mayhem."

Lisa and Teresa gaped as they stood by the bathroom door and listened. Jill set her bags down.

"Anything I can do?"

"Probably . . . come on."

He rolled his sleeves to the elbow and Jill followed him into the bathroom. The girls backed to the opposite wall and yanked their skirts down when he entered and pointed.

"Ms. Scott . . . Lisa Carlson and Teresa Wagner . . . girls, Ms. Scott."

Teresa swallowed hard. "Huh . . . how do you do?"

"Um, hi." Lisa grimaced when the woman smiled.

"Hello." She looked at Dylan. "They're polite, anyway."

"Yes, and they lied their polite little heads off about three minutes ago."

"No, we only . . . !"

"Professor, it wasn't such a . . . !"

"Hush, girls!"

Jill frowned and shook her head. "Not having a good day, are we? So you're gonna spank them?"

"Already tried that." Dylan took a deep breath. "Show her your behinds."

"Professor!"

"Uncle Dylan!"

"Turn around so Ms. Scott can see your naughty bottoms or I *will* get the paddle."

They sputtered, stamped and slid skirts up their hips. Humiliated tears burned their eyes when they twisted about and felt Jill's gaze on slick red flesh.

"Jesus, Dylan . . . what did you use on them . . . a fence post?"

"That's enough from *you*, young lady. I thought you wanted to help."

Lisa blinked and looked a question at Teresa.

"Yes, sir . . . sorry, sir." Jill's smirk belied her docile tone. "So what *are* you going to do?"

"Wash the fibs and the jealousy and the general wickedness out of them."

Jill stared when he stooped to rummage in the lower shelf, and then clucked her tongue as she looked at the girls. Dylan stood and dumped rubber and plastic items on the basin counter.

"Take off all of your clothes, girls."

The dreadful words, spoken in his soft, matter-of-fact tone, burned their ears like hot coals and they pressed their backs to the wall.

"Uh . . . Uncle Dylan? You are not *serious*, are you?"

"You're *kidding*, right?"

"Does it *look* like I'm kidding? Go on . . . undress."

"But *Professor*, you can't just . . . I won't *let* you . . . for Christ's sakes, Dylan, come *on* . . . that's horrible!"

He stalked across the room and Lisa quivered when he cupped her chin and looked into her eyes. "Watch your language, Lisa Marie. You agreed to accept my discipline when you came here . . . but if you'd rather not, we'll forget the whole thing and you may leave."

"I . . . I may?"

"Yes . . . and I'll give you a few hours to tell Mr. Swayne why you are no longer enrolled at RBC before I call him."

"*No*! He'll be furious!"

"I doubt that . . . disappointed, perhaps."

"But that's even worse!"

"Especially when he finds out you were to be punished for lying. What does Mr. Swayne think of liars?"

The girl trembled and leaned into Dylan's arms. He patted her back and then lifted her chin once more.

"What are you going to do, Lisa?"

She snorted and swiped an errant tear with her fist. "Oh shit! I . . . I mean *shoot*! OK!"

Teresa stood on quivery legs, mere inches from her weepy-eyed rival. The girl looked so pitiable and sounded so weak that Teresa almost smiled as she made the most awful decision of her life. She glanced at the enema equipment, took a deep breath, tugged the knot down and yanked the tie over her head, and had her blouse undone before Lisa's shaky fingers opened the first button.

Dylan took a step back, turned to his niece and gaped, then shut his mouth and nodded. "Good girl, Teresa."

Blood pounded in her ears. "Th-thank you, Uncle . . . Professor . . . but . . . you will not hurt me, will you?"

"Of course not, sweetie." Lisa glared and pulled off her blouse as Dylan leaned over and kissed Teresa's forehead. "An enema isn't *about* pain." He looked at Lisa and held out a hand. She grimaced as she gave him her blouse and tie. "Thank you. Jill? Would you take their clothes, please? And lay some towels on the floor?"

"Sure."

Jill draped ties and blouses over her arm. The girls pouted at her, and then glared at each other as they rolled panties to the floor and unzipped skirts. Water splashed in the basin and Dylan tested it with his fingers while he watched them in the mirror.

Teresa cupped a hand over her sex and grunted as she slipped off her loafers. She bent to remove her anklets and suppressed a whimper when warm lightning coursed through damp lower lips. Lisa squinted at her as she lifted her feet to remove her socks. They picked up the clothing and gave it to Jill, then hugged themselves and looked away from each other.

Both wore white brassieres with lace trim above the cups. Rosy flesh peeked through the lace and deep cleavage separated healthy mounds, but Teresa's were two sizes larger than Lisa's. Jill pointed at their chests and opened her mouth, then sighed and turned to Dylan.

"Bras too, Professor?"

"Hm? I did *say*. . . ." He peered at Jill in the mirror and then looked over his shoulder. "Just one more thing for them to . . . no, that's all right . . . not really the area that concerns me."

The woman winked at him as she hung clothes on towel hooks and dropped shoes and socks to the floor beneath. He filled the blue, six-inch bulb with warm water, emptied it into a pink bag, and then refilled it and sprinkled a few drops of peppermint soap into both containers. Jill spread fluffy white towels by his feet then stood and leaned toward his ear.

"You sure you know what you're doing?"

"Of course . . . as you very well *know*, young lady," he whispered.

"Yeah, *technically* . . . and quit calling me young lady . . . I'm old enough to be your. . . ."

"Big sister?" He smiled and fitted the clear hose to the bag. "You don't have to stay if you don't want."

"And miss the master at work?"

"Stay then . . . but keep the sarcasm to yourself, Ms. Scott."

She wrinkled her nose and shook a tube of K-Y Jelly from its box. Dylan measured the bulb's fluted tip against the other nozzles, chose the white one, and secured it to the end of the clear hose.

Awful, squirmy images swirled in Teresa's mind; images of her own behind, Dylan's hand on it while his bright eyes inspected her inmost secrets. She leaned sore cheeks against the tiled wall, grateful for its cool comfort, and looked at Lisa. The girl pouted but gazed with steady eyes at Dylan and Jill and their horrific preparations. Teresa huffed at the thought of Dylan's hand on her nasty bottom, touching it while he inserted the nozzle in her rude little hole. She wondered if Lisa would weep again, from the shame and discomfort, and Teresa vowed to be braver than the American girl, no matter what.

Lisa took deep breaths through her nose to quell the butterflies in her tummy and the tingly ache between her thighs. The unfairness of the situation galled her, that there should be an audience when Dylan touched her sensitive bottom so intimately. Her eyes shifted and her lips flickered in a quick sneer as she glanced at the niece, the stupid niece who thought she was so cool when she mistook Lisa's nervousness for fear and got all courageous to show her up. She looked at Jill, whispering to Dylan, and said a silent *thanks* that the woman had somehow convinced him not to let the German girl flaunt her big boobs. Not that she thought Dylan cared about breasts, any more than Michael did, but it was nice to have one less thing to worry about.

Dylan hung the pink bag from a ceramic wall hook and turned around. Jill sidestepped and watched as he held out both arms. Teresa gasped and Lisa shuddered, and they trudged toward him. His fingers cooled their sweaty palms.

"All right, girls . . . I'll show you what will go into your bottoms . . . so there's no question of fairness." He let go of their hands and picked up the syringe and the hose nozzle. Fiery blush burned their necks. "The white one is a bit thicker than the one on the syringe, but there's an equal amount of soapy water in the bag and the bulb. Now . . . if you want to make an issue of this, I'll ask Ms. Scott to go to the store for another bag and nozzle, and you may stand in your corners until she returns." Both girls shook their heads. "Very well then . . . on all fours, on the towels."

Teresa opened her mouth, then shut it and kept her legs together as she squatted. Her bottom gaped and cool air caressed the tender cleft. She stifled a whimper, clenched her cheeks and leaned forward to rest on her palms. Hard tiles stung her knees, even through the thick towels. A bare hip, moist with perspiration, touched Teresa's thigh and then moved away.

"'Scuse me," Lisa whispered.

"That is all. . . ."

"Heads right down, girls . . . and spread your legs so your kneecaps aren't flat on the floor."

Lisa huffed and parted her thighs, then wriggled and squirmed away from Teresa. The towels wrinkled and bunched, and Dylan knelt to straighten the terrycloth and position the round bottoms.

"Put your head *down*, Lisa, and quit wriggling . . . it won't kill either of you if your feet are touching while I tend to you."

"But *geeze*, Professor!"

"*Enough*, Lisa. Teresa, quit glaring and leave your foot right where it is."

"Yes, sir." She pouted at the towel and concentrated on the unwanted contact to mask the horrendous shame that inundated her soul.

Dylan stood and yanked a latex glove from the box on the counter. He tugged it onto his right hand and leaned over to inspect the deep, amber valleys and the tiny rosebuds within. Jill smirked, opened the K-Y tube and dripped clear slipperiness onto his fingers. He nodded and rested his right knee on the tile, put a gentle palm on Lisa's back and anointed her anus.

"Eww!"

"Steady, Lisa . . . you know this is necessary."

"Yeah but . . . are you gonna put your finger in?"

"Yes, so hold still."

"OK. I just want to be ready."

"That's a good girl . . . there."

He thrust inside to the second knuckle, then pulled out an inch and twisted his wrist as he pushed back in. Lisa mewed like a kitten and bit her thumb as waves of guilty, squirmy pleasure swept through her tummy and tingled her bosom. The slippery finger warmed, caressed, and tantalized for the briefest of moments, but long enough to ignite a shivery spark between her thighs and moisten her lower lips. She grunted to cover a happy squeak when he withdrew his finger.

Jill put on a glove and looked at him, her eyebrows arched. Dylan pointed to the white nozzle. She nodded and held it above the sink while she squeezed jelly and slathered it over the soft plastic. He took it from her with his gloved hand, and then spread Lisa's cheeks with the thumb and middle finger of his other hand. She panted and curled her toes as the blunt tip nudged her tightness. It slipped inside like an old friend and Lisa whimpered as she pushed backward.

"Oooh . . . oweee! Tha . . . that's far *enough*, OK?"

Dylan arched his eyebrows. "Can you hold it there for me, Lisa?"

"Huh? Yeah . . . I *guess* so."

"All right . . . I won't start the water yet. Teresa?"

"What? Um . . . sir?"

"Are you ready?"

She took a deep breath and sneered at Lisa. "Yes, Professor."

"Good."

Latex snapped when he dragged off his glove and tossed it into the trash can beneath the basin. Jill handed him another and he winked as he stood and pulled it on. He took a half step to the right, knelt again, and reached out so Jill could trickle lubricant on his fingers. Teresa gritted her teeth and turned her head so Lisa couldn't see her face, then sighed when Dylan patted her back with his bare hand.

"Push down a little so your bottom opens more, all right?"

"But it is *already*. . . ." She grunted. "Yes, sir."

Teresa bowed her back and squeezed her eyelids tight to block the image from her mind's eye. Still she saw her own cheeks spread wide so Dylan and that woman could observe the shameful opening at its center and the plump lips beneath. Her valiant vow forgotten, she squealed when he dabbed warm slickness on the tight vent.

"Shh . . . it's all right, sweetie. Just relax."

Anger and humiliation burned from forehead to thighs as she nodded and blinked back tears. His fingertip pressed sphincter ring and she gulped air.

"I . . . I am *trying*, Uncle Dylan, but it is so . . . *eek!*"

Hard slickness crept into her bottom and she shuddered. There was no pain, not even the discomfort Dr. Richter caused when the gynecologist probed Teresa's rectum, but blue-white sparks flickered in her vagina, swirled up her breasts, and burst behind her eyelids. The awful, nasty, wonderful finger slid forward, retreated, twisted, while damp, erotic scenes flashed through her mind like a fast-motion video.

"That's good, Teresa."

She whimpered when the finger departed, then bit her lip and gazed over her shoulder. Uncle Dylan's face blurred so she wiped her eyes and looked again. He smiled at her and held out his gloved hand to Jill, who put the syringe into it. The black, fluted tip glistened with jelly, and the blue bulb glowed like neon.

"Uh . . . Uncle . . . sir, I. . . ."

"What is it, sweetie?"

His voice caressed her ears and she swallowed hard.

"I am ready, sir."

He nodded, squeezed her hip with his left hand, and then stretched her bottom wide. Calf muscles tensed and she struggled not to kick as nasty, horrible plastic touched the tender dimple. She clenched delicate muscle but the tip slid through, like an arrowhead into a plum, and impaled her. With dreadful slowness, he pushed the nozzle forward while she pressed her nose to the towel. Her universe shrank to include only the few cubic centimeters between her cheeks. Water dripped inside and the wail from her own throat startled her.

"I know it's icky but you're OK, aren't you?"

"Yuh . . . yes . . . of course. I am fine. Sir."

She glanced at Lisa, and then looked away from the amused smirk on the girl's lips.

"All right, then . . . relax your tummy muscles while I let the water into your bottom holes."

Lisa scowled. "Geeze, embarrass us a little *more*, why don't you?"

Dylan glared at her, then shook his head and flicked the valve on the plastic hose. Lisa quivered as gravity drove warm soapiness down and in. He squeezed the syringe with slow, steady pressure and Teresa gasped at the flood of wet heat. Jill's cotton blouse rustled as she knelt to rub Teresa's tummy.

"It's OK . . . don't fight it. Um . . . Dylan?" Jill nodded at Lisa.

"Hmm? Oh . . . yes." He reached his left arm around and massaged Lisa's belly as he clenched the blue bulb in his right hand. "Sort of like patting your head and. . . ."

"Don't *say* it." Jill scowled and shook her head.

He sighed. "Are you OK, Lisa?"

"Yeah . . . yes, sir . . . the rubbing helps. Are you about done?"

"Very soon . . . but I would like to know if you two are learning anything from this."

"Well, sure. I won't fight with her ever again, swear to God. Oof! Um . . . how much is *in* that thing, anyway?"

"Teresa?"

"Suh . . . sir?"

"Does your tummy hurt?"

"Yes . . . a little . . . but I am all right. Sir."

"Are you learning your lesson?"

She nodded. "Very much, Professor, sir. I will ignore her taunts until forever."

"I see. Lisa? Will you ignore her taunts forever?"

"Yeah . . . no problem."

"That's what I thought. All right, girls . . . I'm going to take the nozzles out so lift your shoulders and put your legs together so you can hold the water in."

"Yes, sir."

"OK."

He shut off the hose valve, pulled the syringe and the nozzle out and dropped them into the basin. The girls pushed up, closed their legs and clamped against the pressure. Jill gaped as Dylan took a box from the shelf and ripped open two super-absorbent tampons. He put on a fresh glove and poured K-Y over the plastic applicators. Lisa stared at him.

"Um, sir? Can . . . may I go to the bathroom now?"

"Not yet, Lisa. This will help you hold the enema while we have a talk."

A desperate wail scratched Teresa's throat. "You already have punished me more than . . . than is *reasonable* . . . how *can* you . . . ?"

His icy glare froze her jaw muscles and she jammed a knuckle between her lips while soapy water gurgled deep inside.

"Put your heads back down, girls . . . now."

"Jesus *Christ*, Dylan, this isn't *even*. . . ."

"Lisa Marie, *hush* . . . and do what I told you before I get angry."

Frustrated tears dripped as Lisa leaned forward. Teresa groaned, clenched her cheeks, and pressed her forehead to the towel. Dylan looked at Jill. She sneered and knelt on the opposite side of the girls. He nodded and she reached over to spread Lisa's cheeks.

"*No!* Professor!"

"I said to *hush*."

Slick plastic slid inside and he pressed the tampon home. The applicator clinked when it hit the waste can. Teresa yelped as Jill opened her bottom and the little cylinder slipped in. She felt the tiny string that clung to her cleft and shuddered at the indignity. Jill let go of her cheeks and backed away. Teresa rolled onto her side, glared and sputtered as Dylan stood.

"Why will you *do* this to us?"

Lisa wriggled around and leaned against Teresa's arm. "Are you crazy or *what*? We don't *deserve* this."

Dylan folded his arms, looked at Jill, and then smiled. "Half an hour ago you two were ready to go to war . . . for what reasons I can only imagine. Stand up, both of you."

The girls stared at him, then grimaced at each other. Jill reached down to help them but Dylan shook his head and she stopped. Lisa whimpered and twisted onto her knees. Teresa glared at him and folded her legs. Lisa groaned and reached for the countertop, pulled herself up, and held out a hand. Teresa took it, squirmed to her feet and they turned to scowl at Dylan. Lisa quivered and clutched her tummy. Teresa grabbed her arm and held the girl tight at her side.

"What *now*, Herr Professor?"

"I want you to bend Lisa over the basin and spank her, Teresa."

"*No!*"

The two-note chord echoed around the room and Dylan sighed.

"Don't tell me *no*, girls. You've been *aching* to hit each other all afternoon . . . now's your chance."

"But Uncle, we. . . ."

"Professor, we. . . ."

"Quiet! Lisa . . . after Teresa spanks you, you will spank her. I can't be fairer than that."

"Oh *God*."

Lisa twisted, leaned over, pressed both palms on the counter and looked back. Teresa grunted and fisted her hips.

"I . . . I do not *wish* to hit her, Uncle Dylan."

"I didn't ask if you wished to . . . I told you to *do* it."

"But *why*?"

"Because you hate her . . . and she hates *you*. You've both behaved like spiteful six-year-olds with a new puppy ever since you met and I want that out of your systems . . . *now*."

"I . . . I do *not* hate her."

Dylan smirked. "Then you've done a good job of *acting* like you do. Are you fibbing to me again?"

Remorseful tears sprang to Teresa's eyes. "Nuh . . . *no*, sir, I . . . I truly do *not* want to hit her . . . or for us to be enemies any longer."

"Don't tell me . . . tell her."

Teresa nodded and looked at Lisa. The girl straightened and attempted a tight smile.

"Me neither, Teresa. You wanna start over?"

"Yes . . . I would like that." Teresa held out a hand, but Lisa shook her head.

"We better hug . . . but not too hard 'cause I'm about to bust."

"OK . . . a small hug and we will begin over."

The girls embraced. Damp flesh stuck together and squished when they parted. Jill rolled her eyes at Dylan.

"All done, Professor?"

"I certainly hope so." He grabbed fresh towels and covered the girls' shoulders. "Come on, Teresa . . . you may use the front bath."

"Yes . . . all right . . . only I don't think I can walk without. . . ." She stared at the floor and held her tummy while she clenched her cheeks.

He smiled, wrapped long arms around her back and thighs, and picked her up. She moaned as he strode down the hall and through the bedroom.

Lisa sighed and sat on the toilet when Jill left and shut the door. She reached back, found the string, then tugged and grimaced when the tampon slid out. Nasty water gushed and Lisa held her breath as she sprayed canned deodorant. Tummy muscles trembled and relaxed, and she wondered why Dylan didn't carry her to the other bathroom, since she was smaller than Teresa. She gasped, flushed the toilet, and muttered.

"That's what got you *into* this, so knock it *off.*"

While she drained, she debated whether to tell Greg about her experience. He would be sympathetic and gentle, but would he be turned on? Would she? Lisa giggled at the obvious answer, and slipped a finger between damp lower lips to comfort herself after the terrible ordeal.

Teresa leaned forward to keep her sore bottom off the seat. She scowled at the floor while her fingers searched for the string. The tampon fell into the bowl, followed by horrid, sudsy foam. Tissue rustled when she unrolled a handful and blew her nose. The ache in her belly abated as water flowed. She flushed and pressed the top of the aerosol Uncle Dylan left next to the toilet. Anger welled in her bosom when she thought of him. He had been so cruel, but then kissed her before he left the bathroom. She would never forgive him for such embarrassment, to spank her bottom so hard and then to open and inspect it, and put nasty, awful things into it while that woman watched. His finger was the worst, worse even than the tampon, because it was so personal, so intimate, and so soon gone.

A bright, delicious image of Dylan's finger inside her, invading, stroking, caressing, glowed in her mind and drove all thought of the

American girl, the paddle, the naked humiliation, out of her mind and sparked an ember at the apex of her thighs. Slick moisture bathed a fingertip as she caressed her tight, hot clitoris. Clouds of fire billowed around her as she climbed the summit, and then exploded in a shower of steamy, shuddery hail. She gasped and trembled while she toweled off the moisture that covered her from head to foot.

❧

Jill sat on the study sofa and smirked at Dylan.

"I don't *believe* you. You're gonna give them homework after *that?*"

He slipped printed sheets into a folder. "This *was* supposed to be a class."

"Uh huh . . . think they learned anything?"

"I hope so. They taught *me* something, anyway."

"What?"

"That I'd better watch those two like a hawk. Even while they were at each others throats, Teresa lied to keep them out of trouble and Lisa played along like they'd rehearsed it."

The woman chuckled. "Looks like the beginning of a beautiful friendship."

"Oh *that's* helpful, Mr. Rick."

Jill grinned. "I did notice the *I*'s changed to *we*'s there at the end."

Dylan nodded. "That's what I was hoping for . . . nothing like shared suffering to overcome petty jealousies."

"Maybe so . . . you're the discipline expert."

He collected pages from the printer. "Yes . . . but I underestimated Lisa's attachment potential."

"You mean her libido?"

"Exactly."

"That's one horny little girl, and you're such a cute old. . . ."

"Jill! I got it, OK?"

She stood and patted his back. "I'll check on Lisa and get Teresa's clothes for her."

Dylan sighed and squeezed her hand. "Thanks. I wasn't too tough on them, was I?"

Jill shrugged. "Maybe you should ask *them*."

He scowled, yanked on her arm and kissed her lips. "Go be use-
ful somewhere else."

"Don't even think it, Dylan!"

She dodged the slap he aimed at the seat of her jeans, and laughed
as she trotted down the hallway.

Chapter 8

NO SMOKING

TERESA SETTLED INTO her new home over the next few days. Dylan drove her to campus to complete the enrollment process and they stopped for coffee at a sidewalk café by the student union building. She tapped the foam atop her latte with a spoon and looked at him.

"Uncle Dylan?"

"Hm?"

"Did . . . what did you tell Felicia?"

"About what, sweetie?"

"The . . . the other day . . . at the cottage. Me and Lisa."

"Nothing at all. Why? Did you want me to tell her?"

Teresa snorted and sipped. "Of course not."

Dylan smiled and squeezed her arm. "What goes on at school is between me and my students, OK?"

"Yes, but . . . what about Ms. Scott? Who is she, anyway?"

"Someone who also won't tell anyone."

"How can you *know* this? Who *is* she?"

"A friend I've known for a long time . . . the first friend I had in this town, as a matter of fact."

"Are you lovers?"

"Teresa!"

"Well? She acts very . . . familiar with you."

He sipped espresso and squinted. "All right . . . I think *lovers* overstates the case . . . but I suppose we have been . . . intimate." Dylan grinned at Teresa's open-mouthed stare. "Did I tell you she's a vampire?"

"Uncle Dylan . . . what are you *talking* about? There is no such thing as. . . ."

"Sure there is . . . they work for the Red Cross and suck blood with needles and tubes. And they just love me because I'm O negative, which is their favorite flavor."

Teresa grimaced and swatted his hand. "That is not funny, Uncle Dylan. So you met her at the blood bank?" He nodded. "And *this* is what you mean by intimate? That she puts a needle in your arm?"

"That's how it started, yes. But you might have noticed she's kind of a smart aleck." Teresa nodded. "I was here on my first sabbatical, writing a book . . . um, twenty-three years ago . . . and it was time to give blood so I. . . ."

"What do you mean, *time* to give blood?"

"I donate every couple of months . . . whenever they call me. Anyway, I went over to the high school, and there was Jill. She gave me grief from the minute I walked in the door."

"But *why?* I think these people should be *grateful* that you will donate."

"They are . . . but they also kid around . . . to help people relax. She teased me more than most of her donors and. . . ."

"Why?"

Dylan shrugged. "She told me later it was because I looked like I needed it, and I've never gotten a clearer answer from her . . . but I flinched a little when she stuck the needle in, and she said, *oh, poor baby*, and gave me this smart-alecky pout . . . so I told her I was going to smack her fanny as soon as the bag was full."

"Oh my *God*. You spanked a Red Cross nurse?"

He laughed. "No . . . but I did take her to dinner."

"And then to bed?"

"Teresa!"

"Well?"

"Let's just say. . . ." He stared at the faded green umbrella above them for a few seconds. "That what I did to you and Lisa the other day wasn't unfamiliar ground for Ms. Scott."

Teresa gasped. "You gave her an *enema*? Uncle Dylan!"

"Now you're being nosy, young lady. But rest assured we can

trust her not to say anything to anyone about what she sees or hears at the college."

"But, Uncle Dylan, you cannot merely. . . ."

"Hush and drink your coffee."

❧

Brakes squeaked as the bus stopped at the corner. Teresa got off, hunched her shoulder into the satchel strap and walked toward the cottage. The warm aroma of honeysuckle made her smile. A fat man in baggy shorts and a damp T-shirt sprayed water on his garden and waved to her from across the street. She waved back as she pushed through the gate. The front door was unlatched so she went in and shut it behind her. The hallway smelled of furniture oil and old pages. Teresa smiled when she heard giggles from the classroom.

"Hi, Lisa." She dropped her satchel on a table.

"Hi, Teresa."

Two girls sat in the back row. Long, white-blonde hair hung down their necks in ponytails. They looked at Teresa and then at Lisa.

"You will introduce the new girl?"

"Oh, um . . . yeah. This is Teresa . . . that's Sonja and Birgid."

"Hi."

"Hello. I have heard you are being from Hamburg."

"Yes, until most recently."

The other twin smiled. "We have lived nearby to Hamburg, but now in Rochester, USA."

Teresa saw a small mole on an earlobe and nodded to its owner. "You are Sonja?"

"*Nej*. I am Birgid."

"Hello, Birgid." She shook the girl's hand and looked at the other sister. "Hello, Sonja."

The twins laughed as Sonja clasped Lisa's fingers. "You are the professor's niece?"

Teresa grimaced and looked at Lisa. "That is not important . . . I am merely a student, just as you are."

"This will be fine for us, I think."

Sonja nodded to her sister and Birgid smiled.

"We will go to the beach at the lake after this class. Will you like to go also?"

"I . . . I must study for university."

Lisa scowled. "Summer session doesn't start until next week. Come on . . . it might be fun."

Teresa shook her head. "I do not have a swimming suit."

Birgid giggled. "Also we do not . . . it is to the nude beach we go."

"I do not think I should. . . ."

The front door opened and shut. The girls scrabbled for paper and pens as Dylan walked into the classroom.

"Good morning." Four voices chorused a reply. "Ashley and Britney won't be joining us today, I'm afraid."

"Aww." Lisa bit her lip when he glared at her.

He set his briefcase on the desk. "I have your assignments graded."

Throats cleared and feet shuffled as bottoms squirmed in hard chairs. Dylan coughed into his hand.

"Birgid?"

"Yes, sir?"

"Are you and Sonja supposed to sit together?"

The sisters frowned at each other. Sonja nudged Birgid's shoulder with her palm. Birgid sighed and picked up her satchel.

"No, sir."

Chair legs scraped hardwood as she moved to the table in front of Teresa.

"Thank you, Birgid."

He pulled a folder from his briefcase and handed out stapled pages. "I want you to take a few minutes and read the comments. Your essays were good, with minor exceptions, so you need to pay close attention to my notes. All right?"

Throats cleared and papers rattled while Dylan jotted in his calendar. The room grew still. Teresa's fingers trembled as she read his red scribbles. He glanced at his watch, looked up and smiled.

"Any questions, girls?" Birgid raised a hand. "Yes?"

"Sir, I am . . . I have worked very hard on this and I do not think it is correct that I shall have a C."

"Oh, really? How long did you work on it?"

She pouted. "For hours and hours."

Dylan shook his head. "Did I not ask for a three-thousand-word essay?"

"Yes, sir."

"And how many did you write?"

"Over *five* thousand . . . the computer is telling me so." Birgid curled out her lower lip.

"I asked for *three* thousand because I want you to learn how to say what you mean with fewer words."

"But, Professor, I did as you have *told* me. I am using the diverted pyramid, and . . . and the transpositional sentences . . . and. . . ."

He held up a hand. Birgid cupped her chin in both palms, clomped her elbows on the worktable and scowled.

"It's all right, Birgid. You used the *inverted* pyramid and *transitional* sentences quite well, but. . . ."

"Then why are you . . . ?"

"Don't interrupt, Birgid." He leaned forward and she whimpered. "I want you to rewrite the essay and tell me in three thousand words or less exactly what you told me in five thousand. Can you do that?"

"I . . . I do not know."

"I want you to try, anyway. That's your assignment for next week."

Birgid sighed. "All right, Professor. I will try."

"Good girl. Anyone else? Lisa?" She shook her head and Dylan raised his right eyebrow. "No complaints?"

"Umm . . . it's just that. . . ." She bit her lip for a second. "A *minus*? I worked really, really hard on this."

"I know, but you shouldn't introduce a new argument in your final paragraph. Other than that, it was a very good paper."

Lisa puffed her cheeks. "OK . . . thanks."

"Sonja? No? Teresa?" She smiled, glanced at Lisa, and shook her head. He turned to the chalkboard. "Very well, then. Let's diagram some sentences."

Dylan ignored their moans as he rose, took a thick paperback from his briefcase and grabbed a shaft of fresh, white chalk from the tray.

"That's quite enough of that, girls. Teresa, come up here, please. I brought an Elizabeth George novel which has some nice long ones in it."

An hour later everyone in the classroom, Dylan included, felt half asleep. Birgid slapped chalk dust from her hands and looked at him. He scanned the three-clause sentence she had dissected, and then looked at the clock.

"Good. Let's take a twenty-minute break."

He backed out of the way as Birgid ran to the door, the other girls close behind. Sonja and Birgid giggled as they opened the refrigerator and grabbed a plastic bottle of Diet Pepsi apiece, and then clattered out the side door. Lisa took a bottle of Mountain Dew and stepped back while Teresa peered inside.

"So, what'd you get on your paper?"

"I um . . . an A." Teresa picked up a Diet Coke, turned to Lisa and frowned as she twisted off the cap.

Lisa shut the refrigerator, tipped the green bottle to her lips and swallowed. "Yeah? Good job."

"You . . . you should have had an A also, except for the error."

"Listen . . . you don't have to do that . . . I really *am* over it. Aren't you?"

Teresa sighed. "Yes . . . truly. But I was afraid that my higher mark might . . . upset you and . . . and spoil our truce."

"No way! Not after last week. Now, if you got an A and I got a *B*, I'd have to kick your butt."

"What?" Lisa winked and Teresa shook her head. "You are kidding with me?"

"Well, duh! I mean . . . besides the fact that you could kick *my* butt, I'm not gonna let a little thing like grades get me . . . *us* . . . in trouble again. *Verstehen?*"

"Oh *ja*." Teresa chuckled. "That was very good . . . except there should be more *shh* on the s."

"OK, I'll work on it."

"So . . . um . . . who are Ashley and Britney?"

Lisa shrugged. "A couple of California girls. You'll meet them eventually."

"Why did you show such distaste for them? Are they so awful?"

"Not really . . . but they've got kind of an attitude . . . like if it isn't California, it's not worth mentioning." She sighed and frowned. "You think Professor Uncle noticed my attitude?"

Teresa grinned. "I must say yes, because he gave you his stern-mode overdrive look."

Lisa smiled and raised her bottle. "That's about what it was . . . knocks a girl flat on her fanny from twenty feet away." Teresa giggled and they toasted with high-caffeine soda. "Let's get some fresh air."

They ambled into the back yard. Birgid and Sonja sat on the gazebo railing and Teresa and Lisa climbed the shallow stairs to sit beside them. Birgid turned her back to the house and dug a cigarette box from the waistband of her skirt. Teresa clapped a hand to her mouth and looked at Lisa. The girl frowned and shook her head.

"Not *here* . . . take 'em to the vineyard."

Birgid laughed. "Of course!"

Sonja followed her down the steps and they disappeared between thick bushes at the back of the garden. Lisa sighed.

"Idiots."

Teresa frowned. "There is a vineyard?"

"Just a trellis with some vines, but it's kinda nice. You want to go look?"

"Sure."

Lisa led the way through a swelter of red blossoms. The wall at the rear of the lot was gray cinderblock, covered halfway up with green moss. A newer pink granite fence ran the property line with the house next door, but an error in the survey left an opening where the two walls should have met. The girls turned sideways and squeezed into the back yard of the house behind the school. Six oak four-by-fours, their sides crusted and blackened with age, supported a lattice of pine two-by-fours and one-by-ones. The bases of the oaken beams were buried in the clay, but the weight of accumulated growth pushed the arbor against the block wall. Lisa ducked and Teresa followed her through a cascade of green and brown into a dark, cool cavern that smelled like old wine.

"This is the vineyard. Here . . . try some." Lisa twisted off a bunch and tugged half a dozen small grapes into her palm.

Teresa took them and smiled as they snapped between her teeth like marbles filled with warm jam. "Mmm . . . very sweet."

"Uh huh. Watch out for the seeds."

They spat pips onto the bare, damp clay. Birgid held out a tan and white box.

"You will have a cigarette, Teresa?"

"No thank you. I do not smoke."

"Oh, go ahead." Lisa reached for the pack. "I don't either but it's fun to flick."

"*Flick?*"

"Sure . . . like this."

Lisa held the filter to her lips and leaned toward Birgid. A red plastic lighter clicked and flamed. Her nose scrunched as Lisa puffed a glow at the cigarette's tip, then yanked it from her mouth and waved at the cloud of smoke as she turned away. Her head tilted back, her eyelids lowered, and she looked at Teresa. She cupped her right elbow in her left palm and held the cigarette between the index and middle fingers of her right hand, the wrist bent back. She flicked her thumbnail on the filter and a tiny wisp of ash floated away.

"Vy don't you see vot ze boys in ze back room vill have, dahling?"

Teresa laughed. "I do not think Marlene Dietrich's accent was as bad as *that*."

"You *sink* not?" Lisa arched her eyebrows and then giggled. "That's the way my friend Beth does it."

"Beth also, um, *flicks?*"

"Yeah . . . when we've had a few drinks we play *femme fatale*."

Birgid shook her head. "This is *most* strange, I think. You are sure you do not want one, Teresa?"

She bit her lip and her hand shook as she reached into the pack. The lighter flashed and she tried not to inhale, but a ribbon of smoke flowed down her throat. She coughed, sputtered, and turned away, and the Marlboro clung to her fingers. Lisa laughed and patted her back.

"You're not gonna die on me, are you?"

Teresa shook her head, took a deep breath, and then mirrored Lisa's Marlene Dietrich. They posed, flicked, and strutted, with exaggerated hip swings, around the arbor while they tried to look solemn and sultry. Birgid grinned.

"Teresa, you *must* come to the beach. We think you will be a fun person."

"No, I really cannot."

Sonja winked. "Colton perhaps shall be there."

"Who is Colton?"

The twins looked at each other and giggled.

"He is a fireman and *such* a hunk."

"Yes, and such *muscles*." Sonja grinned and rolled her eyes.

"And such a long penis, you cannot imagine."

Birgid dropped her cigarette butt and lit another. Sonja did the same, then nodded as she blew a cloud of smoke.

"Last week we are at the beach and we see Colton is sitting alone."

"So we take our towels and lie in the sand in front of him."

"And then open wide our legs."

"So he must see our vaginal parts."

"And discover if he will respond to such a sight as this."

Teresa blushed, put the filter to her lips, then gasped and jerked it away. "So . . . so did he?"

Birgid giggled. "When we are looking at him, he is looking away."

Sonja laughed. "And crossing his ankles and pulling up his knees. . . ."

"So we cannot *see* that his penis is. . . ."

Vines rustled and light flooded the cavern.

"Police! Freeze!" The girls screeched and backed away as a uniformed officer pushed inside. "I said, *freeze*. What are you doing in here?" No one spoke. The officer pointed the flashlight at Teresa's face. "You. What's your name?"

"T . . . Teresa Wagner."

The officer nodded. "All right, Teresa Wagner. What are you *doing* here?"

"We . . . we are merely taking a break from our class."

"Is your class in Mr. Grabowski's back yard?"

"No, we . . . we go to the school . . . the college . . . on the other side of the wall."

"Oh yeah? Professor Travis sent you *here* to have a smoke break?"

Teresa's jaw dropped. The officer shook her head and clicked a microphone attached to her collar. She turned away, talked to her partner in the squad car, then turned back and scanned their faces with the light. Four nervous tongues licked tremulous lips. The woman pulled a notebook from her breast pocket and wrote their names as the girls stammered them.

"All right . . . let's go see the Professor."

"Please *no*." Birgid clasped her hands beneath her chin. "We will leave here and never return again. You . . . you do not need to go *with* us."

The woman smiled. "My car's over there."

"But we really. . . ."

"You're beginning to annoy me . . . Birgid, right?"

"Y-yes, madam."

"Don't call me madam . . . I have a *real* job. Now pick up those butts." The officer followed them through the gap and across the lawn, pushed them into the kitchen and cupped a hand to her mouth. "Professor!"

Dylan jerked from his chair in the study, ran down the hall, and skidded to a stop by the kitchen door. "What's wrong?" He blinked. "Kate?"

She grinned. "Hi, Professor. These yours?"

He smiled and then frowned. "I'm not sure. What have they done?"

Kate took out her notebook. "Trespass . . . agricultural pilferage . . . littering . . . breach of the peace. A smoking offense if they're under eighteen."

"They're over eighteen but they know it's against the rules. I'm sorry, Kate."

She grinned a wicked, crooked grin. "Should I run them in or do you want to *discuss* it with them?"

"You know a discussion is in order." He turned. "All of you, into the classroom."

Lisa groaned. "But Professor, we didn't *mean* to. . . ."

"Now!"

The girls glanced at each other as they trudged out the door. Kate and Dylan followed, slowly, and smiled as they chatted. Four nervous bottoms wriggled on hard chairs as the girls watched them. Dylan glared when he entered the classroom.

"Stand up." Feet shuffled and four anxious faces turned to him. His lips compressed to a thin line. "The officer has good reason to take you to the station, where you will be booked, fingerprinted, and very possibly spend the night in jail. Does anyone have something to say about that?"

Sonja gasped. "No Professor, *please*."

Birgid whimpered. "Please *no*, Professor."

Lisa moaned. "*God*, please no."

Teresa whined. "Uncle Dylan, for God's sake!"

Kate smirked and leaned against the doorframe. Dylan turned to her.

"Officer, I believe they would rather not go with you. What shall we do?"

The woman folded her arms at her chest. "The law is the law, Professor . . . but that's a lot of paperwork. Maybe *you* can think of something."

He sighed as he looked at his pupils, then back at Kate. "I suppose I *could* mete out a suitable form of justice . . . and save you the paperwork."

Kate's lip trembled as she suppressed a smile. "I'd sure appreciate that."

Dylan nodded. "What about it, girls? Either go in handcuffs with the officer or take your punishment like grown-up young ladies."

Lisa grimaced. "My dad and Michael *both* will skin me alive if I get arrested."

Birgid wiped a tear. "Also for us, Professor."

Sonja nodded and bit her lip. "Our mother will be *most* angry if this happens."

He looked at Teresa. She dropped into her seat, crossed her arms on the tabletop and hid her face, and Dylan turned to Kate.

"Shall I proceed, then?"

Her left eyelid twitched. "As long as you're not talking about a hundred lines of Latin. Sir."

His forehead wrinkled. "I see your facetious streak hasn't diminished over the last ten years."

Kate shrugged. "Got worse, if anything. Go ahead, Professor."

He shook his head and held out a hand. "All right, girls. I want the cigarettes first. Birgid?"

"S-sir?"

"Let me have them."

Her fingers trembled as she fished in her waistband and bumped two tables as she stumbled toward him. He took the box and opened it.

"The lighter as well." She whimpered and dug deep to find it, then dropped it into the pack along with two mashed butts. He looked at Sonja. "Were you smoking?"

"I . . . yes, sir."

"Did you pick up your trash?"

"Yes . . . yes, sir."

Sonja uncurled her right hand to show him two flattened filters. "Bring it here."

She walked over and scraped damp cellulose, ash, and loose tobacco into the box. He took the four remaining Marlboros, crushed them in his fist, and put them back inside.

"Tell me what kind of medicine your mother practices."

The girls looked at each other. Birgid licked dry lips.

"Cardiology," she whispered.

"And what do cardiologists hate more than anything, Birgid?"

"Uh . . . cholesterol and . . . and tobacco."

"Indeed . . . a point she made the *last* time I caught you smoking. Now go to the desk, raise your skirts, and lower your panties."

The sisters wailed. Teresa jerked her head up and stared. Birgid clasped her hands at her chin.

"*Please*, sir, if . . . if we are taking this punishment, you will not tell the mother?"

Dylan scowled. "That has nothing to do with the spanking you're about to receive, so do what I told you."

Sonja whimpered and glanced at Kate. "This is too . . . too . . . *skräckinjagande!*"

"English *always*, Sonja."

"It . . . it is *horrifying* and . . . and shameful!"

"You *should* be ashamed. Now go on . . . and no backtalk."

The twins whimpered as they walked to the wide desk and fumbled with their clothes. Dylan looked at Lisa. She glared at the floor and chewed her lip.

"Ms. Carlson?"

She sniffled and pouted as she focused wet blue eyes on him. "I . . . I was just *flicking*, Professor, so you don't gotta. . . ."

"Lisa, do you have something for me?"

She grunted and went to deposit two snuffed cigarettes into the box. Teresa bit a fingertip and her nose wrinkled at the smell of tobacco smoke on her hand. Lisa stalked to the desk. Teresa's face paled as Lisa lifted her skirt and looked over her shoulder. Dylan sighed.

"Teresa?"

She swallowed hard. "Unc . . . sir, I . . . oh *God*."

"What, Teresa? Were *you* smoking?"

"No! I mean . . . not *really*, but. . . ." Sonja, Birgid and Lisa stared at her. Their bare bottoms quivered above rolled panties while their eyes accused. She took a deep breath. "I . . . I was merely *flicking* and . . . Lisa picked up the cigarette when I dropped it."

"I see. Go join your classmates."

Lisa winked when Teresa stepped to the desk and raised her skirt. Kate stood by the doorway and smirked. Teresa blushed as cool air raised goose bumps on tender thighs. She looked at Dylan and opened her mouth, then shut it and pushed her panties down.

Dylan nodded as he surveyed his pupils. The twins' identical behinds, round at the summits but with boy-slim hips, had light, even tans. Lisa's bottom, round and deeply cleft, glowed pinkish white. Teresa's rear was pert and round, a shade darker than Lisa's, and a bit wider than the other girls'. He turned to Kate.

"What was it again? Trespass, pilferage, and. . . ."

She dug out her notebook. "Littering and breach of the peace."

"Breach of the peace?"

"Well sure . . . Mr. Grabowski's peace, anyway. He thought his grapevines were on fire so he called 911."

Dylan sighed and walked around the desk. The girls stared as he opened a drawer and drew out the paddle.

"All right, then . . . ten on each charge."

Birgid squeaked. "That is being *forty*."

"Indeed . . . and few enough for scaring a nice old man. We'll discuss the cigarettes after I've taken care of your *legal* problems."

"But Professor!" Sonja pouted when Dylan glared at her.

"That's *enough*. Bend over, all of you."

The paddle twirled, loose in his grip, as he stepped behind them. Birgid, on the far right, wailed, leaned forward, and slapped the desktop with both palms. Sonja, on her sister's left, whimpered and bent at the waist. Lisa stood next to Sonja. She glanced left at Teresa and grimaced.

"Talk about stern-mode overdrive," she whispered.

"Quiet, Lisa . . . and bend over."

"Yes, sir."

Dylan clamped the board beneath his arm and tucked skirt hems into waistbands. Teresa snorted and put her fists on the desktop beside Lisa's. Hip muscles clenched and four pair of slender ankles writhed. Dylan stood beside his niece's plump cheeks and raised the paddle. Green eyes glowed with unshed tears as she turned to look at him.

"Please, Uncle Dylan, this is so *awful*. Can you not . . . ?"

"Hush, girl, and try to remember my name."

She gasped. "I *meant* Professor! *Please* do not spank me!"

He shook his head and put a hand on her back. She squealed as wood popped tender flesh. He fanned her cheeks nine times more with short, quick smacks that embarrassed more than they stung. She whimpered and reached back to rub when he moved a pace forward and patted Lisa's bottom. He glanced to his left.

"No rubbing, Teresa."

"But Uncle . . . Professor! It is *hurting* and. . . ."

"Teresa Luisa! Both hands on the desk or I'll start over with you."

"All *right*." She slapped oak and glared at him.

Lisa gritted her teeth and stared straight ahead while he spanked her plump curve. She pouted over her shoulder as he took a step and held the board against Sonja's quivery backside.

"*Please*, Professor."

"Be still, Sonja."

The paddle snapped sting into tight roundness and she squealed at each pop. He moved another pace. Birgid puffed and panted as she endured her ten licks, then reached back.

"What are you doing, young lady?"

"It *hurts*, Professor!"

"That *is* the point, Miss. Now put your hand where it belongs."

He went to stand beside Teresa but kept an eye on Birgid. Her arms quivered as she watched him and clasped her hands on the desktop. Teresa moaned and twisted a foot in the air while the paddle smacked. She looked over her shoulder, eyes damp, pleading. He took a deep breath, patted her hip with his left hand, and moved to Lisa. The girl pushed her fanny backward an inch and smirked at him. He glowered and swatted hard. She yelped through the first nine and squealed at the tenth lick.

"Professor!"

"Are you quite finished being impertinent, Lisa?"

"But I *wasn't* being . . . geeze!"

Dylan shook his head and took a step. Sonja's behind dimpled at the sides. He lifted his arm and slapped.

"Ow! Ow! Owee! Nej! Ai! Aieeee!"

She stood straight up and clutched her bottom.

"Bend *over*, Sonja."

"But . . . but it is hurting so hardly!"

"Put your tummy on the desk and grab the other side. That will relax your behind and the spanks won't hurt so much."

"No, Professor, please!"

"*Now*, girl."

He pushed her shoulder and Sonja whimpered as she reached for the far edge. Her knees bent and spread, and a pink flesh fold appeared at the base of her cheeks. Dylan blinked, took a deep breath and kept a palm on her spine as he clapped the rounded fanny. She wailed and kicked but maintained her grip on the desk.

"Much better, Sonja." He took a step. "Birgid, do as your sister did. You're clenching just as hard as she was."

"But, Professor, this will be such a shameful posture! Why must you . . . ?"

"No back talk, young lady, or you'll get extra."

A tear slid down the side of her nose as she glared at him. Her palms squeaked polished oak when she pushed forward, and her thighs quivered as she clamped her legs together, but her little slit peeked at him just the same. He nodded and patted her hip. Birgid blew a noisy breath, then buried her face in outstretched arms and bent her knees. The paddle bounced on rubbery mounds while she squealed. He gave her sore behind a gentle pat and turned to Teresa. She swallowed and grimaced.

"Nuh . . . not so strictly as the last ones?"

"Don't be ridiculous, Teresa . . . your tushy is barely pink."

She gasped at the childish word and a hot blush spread down her neck as she glanced at the amusement in Kate's eyes. A moan gurgled in her throat and she covered her face with both hands. The paddle burned and stung while she kicked. White noise raged in her ears and she heard the sharp claps on Lisa's behind as if from under water. More muffled splats and more yelps from the Swedish girls, and once again she felt Dylan's hand on her back. Teresa sobbed, pushed out with her hips and pleaded silently for him to hurry and finish his horrible task. Warm, smooth wood crashed into the base of her cheeks and she screamed.

"Neee! Aiee! Not! So! *Hard*!"

Her fists pounded oak and she lifted her shoulders, but Dylan pushed down while he spread hot lava across her behind. His warm breath chilled her neck, and she sobbed as he whispered.

"Keep still, sweetie. It's over."

Teresa leaned against the cool oak and wept. Ten quick pistol shots rang out and Lisa shrieked with each smack. Dylan patted her rear and moved on. Lisa turned wet eyes to Teresa, pouted, winked, and then smiled as Dylan doled out the last licks to the twins' tender bottoms. They wailed and squealed, then sobbed as he walked around the desk and studied their flushed faces. He set down the paddle and took a tissue box from a drawer. Quivery hands snatched Kleenex and wiped wetness. He looked at Kate and raised his chin.

"Do you believe justice has been served, officer?"

Four heads turned. Kate lifted both eyebrows and scratched her jaw.

"I'd say so, Professor. I'd better get going."

"One more thing. Stand up, girls. Do you have something to say to the officer?"

They straightened, turned, and muttered variations of *I'm sorry* while Kate nodded.

"It's OK, *ladies*. But stay in your own yard from now on."

Dylan sighed. "I'll walk you out."

He headed for the door. Kate smiled over her shoulder as she led him down the hallway and stopped by the bookcases.

"You haven't lost your knack, Dyllie. Ow!" She scowled and stroked the seat of her tight uniform pants, then grinned and kissed his cheek. "I could arrest you for assaulting an officer, you know."

"Sure you could . . . right after I blister your bottom for felony impudence, *Katey*."

She giggled. "Nuh *uh*. You're not my tutor anymore . . . and besides, Vick takes care of blistering my bottom these days."

Dylan smiled. "I'll bet that's not *all* he takes care of."

"Nope . . . he's pretty good at *that*, too." She grinned. "So when are you coming over for dinner? You've been in town a month."

"Soon, I promise. I'd better get back to my *ladies*."

"OK. You've got some real cuties in there, Professor, so behave yourself." She smirked and then stifled a yelp when he swatted her again. "Geeze, Dyllie . . . how am I supposed to get through my shift if you keep heating up my tushy?"

He scowled, winked, and pinched her nose. "Quite uncomfortably, I imagine, if you keep using that ridiculous nickname. Now go serve and protect."

"Oh, OK. You'll call, right?"

"As soon as I can. Bye, Kate . . . and thanks."

She opened the door and trotted to the squad car parked by the front gate. He sighed and shook his head as he waved, then secured the latch, turned, and strode to the classroom.

⌘

As soon as Dylan left, Teresa yanked up her pants and rubbed hot sting with soft cotton. Lisa shook her head and then twisted her neck to glare at the fiery redness that covered both cheeks. The twins turned their backs to each other and examined the damage, then looked at Lisa's behind.

Birgid frowned. "I think you are having the worst of this punishment, Lisa."

She nodded and rubbed. "Yeah . . . I thought he was kidding at first so I got kinda silly. *Man*, does that burn."

Teresa scowled. "How can you *possibly* think he is kidding?"

Lisa grinned at her. "Oh, come on . . . those first ten were just love taps."

Sonja gasped. "Now it is *you* who is kidding. *All* of these spanks are hurting quite badly."

"OK, OK . . . but you'd better get over it, 'cause he's not done with us yet." Sonja looked at Birgid and whimpered as Lisa turned to Teresa. "Um . . . he didn't say we could pull them up so you might oughta. . . ."

Heels clicked in the hallway and Lisa bit her lip as she stared at the doorway. Teresa snorted and then tugged her panties down. Dylan stalked around the desk and opened the drawer where he kept the paddle. Teresa's heart leapt into her throat when he Dylan took out a black leather sole. It measured four inches wide at the business end, an eighth-inch thick, rigid yet springy. He gripped the heel in his right hand, tapped his left palm, and looked into four pairs of terrified eyes.

"Anything to say, girls?"

"Please not to beat us with *that*, Professor, we. . . ."

Lisa grabbed Birgid's arm. "We really screwed up and we're really sorry and we won't ever do it again. Sir."

Dylan nodded. "I should hope not. That was very embarrassing for me."

"For *you?*" Sonja stomped her foot. "You spanked our naked hind parts before that police person and *you* this embarrassed? And now you will . . . ?"

"Be quiet, Sonja Katrina! You misbehaved at *my* school and that reflects badly on *me*."

"But . . . but. . . ."

New tears flowed from Sonja's eyes as Dylan walked around and took her arm. He held it in a gentle grasp and looked into her eyes.

"And it embarrasses me even further that I have to repeat the lesson you should have learnt two months ago. Your mother entrusted me with your welfare and I intend to earn that trust, even if it means you two can't sit down for a *week*. Now bend over the desk."

"No, *please*, Professor, we never shall have the cigarette so long as we. . . ."

"Hush, Birgid, and do what I told you."

The twins wailed as Dylan pushed them forward.

"Puh . . . please, Professor, not . . . not *hardly*, I beg of you!" Sonja sniffed and turned to him. "Already my backside is burning and. . . ."

"Your backside was burning the first time I punished you for smoking but obviously the fire wasn't hot enough."

Birgid bobbed her head as she twisted her neck. "Truly it *was*, so please do not beat us and we never will. . . ."

"That's enough, young lady. Tummies on the desk, knees bent, relax your bottoms."

The sisters wept and slumped across the oak, their hips an inch apart, firm cheeks rounded and spread. Teresa chewed a knuckle and took deep breaths as she looked into the pale clefts. Dylan leaned over and squeezed the crowns of both bottoms. Satisfied that the redness was superficial, he drew back the sole, flicked his wrist, and swatted Birgid's fanny.

She jerked, then yelped, then wailed as Dylan rained twelve quick slaps across her quivery mounds. He moved his left foot, put his hand on Sonja's back, and did the same to her. Sore bottoms jerked and jumped beneath leathery sting. He alternated sets of a dozen, over and over, while the girls kicked, screeched, and pounded the desk with knees and fists. He held them fast with a forearm across their backs as the wicked sole blurred like a fan blade. When their screeches turned to hoarse shouts, he took their arms and lifted them. They turned, clutched his shirt and sobbed as he caressed shiny, scarlet backsides.

"It's all right now . . . shh. You won't smoke cigarettes ever again, will you?"

"Nuh . . . *nej* . . . no!"

"Nuh . . . not *never.*"

"I think you mean it, so you're my good girls now. Come over here."

Birgid wiped wetness from her face and gasped as he led them behind the desk and sat on the chair. "*No*, Professor, you said we are *good* girls."

He smiled and held up the box so they could grab tissues, then drew them across his thighs. "Of course you are. Don't you want something cool on your sore behinds?"

Sonja swiped tears as she looked back. "You . . . you will be kind to us now?"

"I am always kind to you, Sonja, although you may not realize it at the time. Now relax so I can rub away some of the sting . . . but not all of it . . . because I want you to remember this."

They nodded and wriggled forward while he reached into the drawer for the baby oil. He dribbled a palm full and slicked it over crimson bottoms. Teresa fidgeted as she watched his hand slide across heated flesh, and pouted when his fingertips slipped between quivery cheeks. Lisa coughed and covered her mouth. Teresa looked at her and grimaced when the girl winked. The twins' pitiful sobs changed to throaty moans. Hot blush prickled Teresa's neck as she stared at her uncle and the pert nakedness upon which he was so intent. A droplet of moisture, all unbidden, squeezed between her labia and she blushed even harder.

Dylan glanced at her as he reached his left arm beneath the sisters' bosoms and pushed them back and off his lap. They knelt at his side and waited while he plucked tissue from the box and wiped his hand. He smiled, stood, and pulled them to their feet.

"Go stand in the corners."

The sisters gaped at each other, then nodded to him. Knees quavered as they stumbled away, leaned into the wall on opposite sides of the chalkboard, and sniffled into wet Kleenex. Dylan picked up the sole and looked at the other girls. Teresa gasped and Lisa trembled.

"Sir, I. . . ."

"Uncle Professor, we. . . ."

He snapped the sole against his thigh and scowled. Both girls scrambled to bend over the desk, then looked back at him. He sighed and shook his head.

"What did you think you were *doing?* You don't smoke, *either* of you. Teresa?"

"I . . . I *used* to but I quit, Uncle . . . sir."

"Yes, because it made you sick when you tried it. What were you? Sixteen? That's why I am so put out with you."

"But I did not *inhale* and . . . I will never do it again, I *swear.*"

"I have to make *sure* you don't . . . and Lisa. You know that emphysema runs in your family so why on earth . . . ?"

Lisa whined and twisted her neck. "I . . . I'm *sorry,* Professor, but I was just *flicking* . . . like in the movies, you know? I didn't inhale either, honest!"

He took a deep breath. "All right . . . ten really hard ones, and you had better learn your lesson."

Birgid and Sonja glanced at each other and then looked at Dylan.

Sonja grunted. "But *we* are getting many more than only ten!" She whimpered and turned to face the wall when he glowered.

Teresa groaned as Dylan pushed her forward. Her breasts flattened on the desktop and tiny jolts of electricity tingled her nipples.

She reached out to grab the edge, squeezed her thighs together and hid her eyes in her arms.

Dylan took a step to stand behind Lisa and raised the leather high over her bended bottom. The sole whisked, cracked, and she whimpered at the terrible sting in her right cheek, then yelped through nine more fiery swats. He patted her back and a tremulous sob escaped her throat as she wiped her eyes with a sleeve.

He pressed his palm on Teresa's back and she concentrated on its warmth while fear churned in her tummy. Leather smacked and pain washed her bottom like an acid bath. She kicked, raised her head, and wailed. Nine harsh claps followed, and burned like bee stings. Tears dripped from her eyes, but the shock wore off after a minute, and the bitter hurt softened.

Lisa rubbed her bottom hard as Dylan helped her to stand. Teresa's knees nearly buckled when he pulled her up. She sobbed and leaned against his chest while he hugged them. He gave them Kleenex and they stumbled to the other side of the desk. Lisa sighed when he took her across his lap. Teresa moaned and wriggled her bottom as she bent over his knees. He leaned forward to get the baby oil and Teresa nearly slipped off, but he grabbed her waist and held tight.

His oily hand slicked like a mink glove over her sore behind. Teresa pushed up her hips and then squeaked with pleasure as his fingertips slid along the inside of her cleft. A squirmy, naughty itchiness tormented the wet pink petals between her legs, and she took quick, ragged breaths. His strong hand soothed the burn in her bottom, but lighted a fire of another sort deep in her feminine core.

"Have you two learned anything today?" Dylan's baritone vibrated down to Teresa's toes.

Lisa swallowed hard and nodded. "Yuh . . . yes, sir." She looked at Teresa and blinked. "We . . . we won't play with cigarettes anymore, right?"

Teresa bobbed her head. "Yes. Not anymore will we even *think* about flicking cigarettes." She twisted her neck and looked into Dylan's eyes. "Never, ever, Professor."

He nodded, gave their slippery cheeks a final squeeze, and lifted them off his lap. "Very well. You're my good girls. Now go to your corners."

"But Uncle . . . !" Teresa shut her mouth when Lisa scowled. "Yes, Professor," she whispered.

Lisa turned and walked to the corner by the window. Teresa's loafers scuffed hardwood as she went to lean into the corner by the hallway door. Oil evaporated and chilled her bottom, and the nursery smell mingled with a more adult aroma. Teresa blushed at the scent of her own arousal.

Dylan took a deep breath, let it out, and wiped his hands as he walked over and turned Birgid to face him. He looked to his right. "Come here, Sonja." The girl bit her lip and shuffled past the chalkboard to stand next to her sister. "I will have to call your mother."

"*No!*"

"Professor *please*, you have already. . . ."

"Shh . . . stop that, now. You know I have to . . . but I'll wait until this evening, so I strongly suggest you call her before then and tell her what you did, and what happened to you because of it."

Birgid's lip curled. "She . . . she will be *most* upset that we were smoking."

"She was most upset at the hotel in Bloomington, if you recall . . . but if you're honest and tell her how severely you were punished, perhaps she will refrain from punishing you further."

"You . . . you do not think she will come *here*, do you, Professor?"

"It wouldn't surprise me . . . we're only a few hours' drive from Rochester."

Sonja whimpered. "But perhaps she will not believe that you could be so . . . so *severe* with your punishing."

He shrugged. "I could send her a picture."

Birgid stared at him. "A . . . a photograph? Of . . . of our hind parts?"

"Why not? A picture's worth a thousand words, but we'd better hurry . . . before the redness fades."

Sonja looked over her shoulder. "I do not think this redness *ever* will fade."

"It will . . . and sooner than you think." He opened a lower desk drawer and took out a digital camera. "Turn your backs and look over your shoulders so I can see your faces."

The girls sighed and then twisted around. Sonja took a deep breath.

"You . . . you will send this only to our mother, Professor?"

"Sonja! I'm not a pornographer. Now hold still and try not to smile." The camera clicked. Two oily, crimson behinds glowed in the flash and Dylan nodded. "I'll e-mail this to your mother, then erase it."

Birgid nodded. "She will believe we have been punished severely, I think."

"Yes . . . but I imagine you'll still get a lecture on the evils of tobacco, and I had better not hear that you gave her any backtalk while she delivered it."

Sonja shook her head. "We have learnt to listen to her lectures with no complaining."

"That's good." He glanced at his watch. "It seems our time is up for today. Birgid, you have your assignment for next week. Sonja, um . . . are you reading anything for fun?"

She nodded. "A Tom Clancy novel. It is most exciting."

"Very good. I want a thousand-word book report, and I *mean* a thousand . . . not two thousand or fifteen hundred. All right?"

"Yes, Professor. I understand."

"OK then. Freshen up and get ready to go home."

The twins covered their bottoms as they headed to the bathroom. Dylan turned to Lisa and Teresa, smiled, and crooked a finger. Lisa pouted, stamped her foot, and then ran to him. Teresa bit her lip and followed. Hands clasped at her waist, Lisa stood toe to toe with Dylan and looked up at him.

"Are you gonna take a picture of *our* heinies, Professor?"

She twisted at the waist to show him her bottom. His jaw quivered as he suppressed a smile.

"If you like . . . but it would be the *before* photo." Dylan held out a hand and Teresa took it, but he kept his eyes on Lisa's. "The *after* picture would show your impertinent fanny well and *truly* spanked."

Teresa gasped and clung to his warm palm. Lisa clutched Dylan's arm as she tilted her head and scowled.

"No *way*, Professor. You spanked us enough for one day and we weren't even that bad. Where did you get that nasty leather thing, anyway?"

"Why? Would Mr. Swayne like one, do you think?"

"Not *even* . . . geeze! But I think you oughta take us out for pizza."

Dylan chuckled. Teresa gaped at him, then looked at Lisa.

"What are you *saying*?"

"You know . . . when the going gets tough, the tough get pizza? It's an American proverb." She yelped when Dylan's hand clapped her behind.

"Stop that, Lisa." His smiled as he shook his head. "If impertinence comes in a pill, you must have taken an overdose. Now go to the study and get fresh panties for everyone. The ones you have on are a bit oily."

"OK. *You* want fresh panties, too? Ow! Geeze, Professor!"

She rubbed new sting and winked as she backed away. Teresa stared while the girl skipped out the door and into the hallway. Dylan sighed and wrapped an arm around his niece's waist.

"Are you OK, sweetie?"

"I . . . suppose so."

He patted her slippery cheeks with gentle fingers. "Do you think I was horrible? To spank you so hard?"

Teresa sighed. "Perhaps . . . a little . . . but I am confused."

"Hm? Why is that?"

"Be . . . because you are so stern and strict the one minute, and then after, you make us to feel like . . . like we are your *friends*."

A deep blush burned her face as Dylan hugged her. He cupped her chin, looked into her eyes, and smiled. "When the punishment is over, it's *over*. Besides . . . it's tough to be stern and strict *all* the time."

She stared at him for five seconds, and then grinned. "But you do it so *well*, Herr Professor Uncle."

"Is that so?" He kissed her, spun her around, and tapped her bottom. "Go get cleaned up, young lady."

Teresa giggled and ran out the door.

Chapter 9

RUNAWAY

DYLAN SAT AT his desk in the alcove off the living room and pored over a stack of galley proofs. He jumped when the phone rang, dropped a red pen, and rubbed his eyes. The cordless handset queeped when he thumbed it.

"This is Professor Travis."

"Uncle Dylan?"

He heard the whimper in her voice. "What's wrong, Teresa?"

"Nothing. I . . . I only wanted to say hello."

"Sweetie, it's almost one o'clock. What are you doing up at this hour?"

"I'm sorry, Uncle Dylan, but I . . . I cannot go to bed right now."

"Why not?"

"I . . . I *have* no bed."

He took a deep breath and let it out. "All right . . . I'll play. *Why* do you have no bed?"

"I um . . . Felicia has put me out from the apartment."

"She *what*? I don't believe that for a minute, young lady, so tell me what *really* happened!"

"Please not to yell at me . . . I am sorry, but. . . ."

Her pitiable sob burned his ear. "OK, OK . . . I'm sorry, too. Where are you, sweetie?"

"In . . . in a bar."

He cradled his forehead in a palm. "Have you been drinking?"

"*No*, Uncle Dylan, I . . . merely came here to use the telephone."

"Where is your cell phone?"

"Well . . . I left in a hurry. I had only enough coins to call you."

Dylan sighed and pushed out of the chair. "I'll come and get you. What's the address?"

"I do not know . . . but it is near to your apartment."

"Which one? Davani's?"

"No, the . . . the other one."

"Not Murphy's."

"Yes, that one."

He opened his mouth wide for a second and then swallowed hard. "Teresa, I want you to hang up the phone and walk out the door. There's nothing in there but bikers and drunks this time of night."

"OK. Can I come to your . . . ?"

"Hang up now and *go* . . . I'm almost out the door. Do you hear me, Teresa?"

"Y-yes, sir, I will."

"Now!"

The receiver clicked and he dropped the phone as he raced to the elevator. He pressed the button and the light flickered. His jaw ached as he loped to the stairwell, bounded down five flights, and then ran through the lobby, out the double doors, and down the sidewalk. The green neon sign above Murphy's Tavern winked through a chilly, early morning mist. His slippers flapped concrete and he slowed to a trot, kicked them off, then sprinted in stocking feet. The pub sat on the far corner, across the street.

Teresa waved as she pushed the button for the walk signal. She wore a pink crop-top, cutoff jeans, and dirty-white Reeboks with no socks. Pitted asphalt stung his soles as Dylan ignored the red light and a taxi driver's honk. Teresa's shoulders quaked while he hugged her. A fat, bearded biker in shredded, grimy denim leaned against the wall by the bar entrance and grinned.

"Aw! Ain't that sweet. Daddy done come and got her."

Dylan wheeled and shoved Teresa behind him. She whimpered and wrapped her arms around his waist. He grabbed her wrists and pushed her backward.

"Cross the street *now*, Teresa," he whispered. "Run and don't look back. The apartment is open."

She whimpered and bit a fingertip. The biker shifted his bulk and lumbered toward them. Dylan balanced on the balls of his feet, arms loose, fingers stiff. He watched the man's eyes and waited. The tavern door opened and the thick end of a sawed-off pool cue clacked brickwork. Dylan smiled and nodded.

A tall redheaded Irishman stood in the doorway and looked at Dylan, then grunted and smacked the club in his palm. "What the hell are you doing, Meatball?"

The biker turned and grinned. "Just wanted to say good night to the little girl, that's all."

"Get your ass back inside . . . Keefer's looking for you."

"No shit? He ready to arm wrestle?"

"How the hell should I know? Either get inside or ride on. It's last call."

Teresa grabbed Dylan's arm with both hands as the biker looked at her. His fat, wet lips smacked.

"You sure are cute, little girl. You come back and see Meatball some other time, huh?"

His drunken grin sent a chill up Teresa's spine. He swiveled and rolled toward the door. The man in the doorway gave no ground and Meatball had to squeeze past him. Dylan wrapped an arm around Teresa and nodded to the Irishman.

"Thanks, Murph . . . I owe you one."

He shook his head. "No charge, Professor. Just don't let her come back unless you're with her."

"That's a promise."

Murph waved his bludgeon and the door slammed. The walk light flashed and they crossed the street. Teresa shivered while she clung to Dylan's waist. He bent to retrieve his slippers, tossed them into a trash bin at the lobby door, and then leaned against the wall by the elevator and hugged her.

"You OK, sweetie?"

She looked up at him with lost-puppy-dog eyes. "I am all right, honestly."

"Teresa?"

"Yes, Uncle Dylan?"

"The next time I tell you to run you had damned well better *do* it!" He smacked the seat of her shorts and squeezed.

"Owee! But I . . . I could not leave you to fight that monster *alone*, Uncle Dylan!"

"I had no *intention* of fighting him . . . just keep him interested long enough for you to get going. If you had crossed the street like I *told* you to I would have been ten yards behind you and gaining fast."

"But . . . but you know kem-po or karate or one of those things."

He sighed as the elevator opened. "Only what a college buddy taught me, and it's no good in a street fight. I would have had to kill him to make my point and *then* where would I be?"

"But Uncle Dylan!"

"*Hush.* He didn't touch you, did he?"

"No but. . . ."

"Then I didn't need to kill him . . . so do what I *tell* you next time."

Teresa pouted as they stepped onto the sixth floor. "OK," she whispered.

Dylan shut the apartment door. She kicked off her shoes and then grabbed his sweatshirt sleeve when he tried to make her sit on the sofa. He sighed and took her with him to get a robe from the bedroom closet.

"Do you want hot chocolate, sweetie?"

She nodded as he put her on the sofa, bundled in thick terrycloth. He went behind the bar to fill a mug with milk from a little refrigerator. The microwave beeped as he set the timer. He scritched foil off a bottle of twelve-year-old single-malt, pulled the cork, and poured two fingers into a tumbler. Milk steamed when he took the mug from the oven, spooned in cocoa mix, stirred it, dribbled brandy over the top, and set it back into the microwave for ten seconds.

The scotch warmed his throat as he swallowed half of it. He opened the oven, stirred the mug again, and then picked up the drinks. Teresa stared out the window at the darkness. Dylan put the mug on the coffee table and sat beside her. She looked into his eyes, and then pressed her nose to his chest. He smoothed her hair for half a minute before he lifted her chin.

"It's time to tell me what this is all about."

"I . . . I am *sorry*, Uncle Dylan, I did not *mean* to. . . ." Tears wetted his shirt as she buried her face again. He sighed, turned her around, and put the cup in her hands. She sipped. "This is very good."

"Thank you. Now . . . you said Felicia kicked you out of the . . . ?"

She sobbed and cocoa sloshed the table when she slammed down the mug. "That . . . that horrible *man*, he was going to. . . ."

Dylan hugged her while he rubbed her back. "Hush now. It's OK . . . nothing happened. I won't let anyone hurt you. OK? Sweetie?"

Teresa coughed and swiped a hand across her mouth as she nodded. He yanked a Kleenex from the box on the end table. She blew her nose and then leaned back and tucked her shoulder under his arm. Dylan cleared his throat.

"Why don't we start with an easy one? Like, uh . . . why didn't you wear something warmer when you went out tonight?"

She tossed the damp tissue onto the table and grabbed another. "I . . . I was in a hurry."

"I see . . . and that's why you left your cell phone at home?"

"Yes." She leaned over, picked up the mug and drank. "I had to leave very fast because . . . um . . . Felicia told me to go away."

Dylan bit his lip for a second. "Really? Why did she do that?"

"Um . . . because I asked them to be quiet. So . . . so I could work."

"Uh huh . . . and who is *them*?"

"You know . . . her and that man . . . the Scottish guy."

"The Scottish guy? Haimish McFrazier?"

"Yes. Is that not a stupid name?"

Teresa smiled. Dylan snorted, picked up the whisky glass, and drained it.

"So . . . Dr. McFrazier was at the apartment?" She nodded. "Fel told me she was seeing him. So . . . they came to your apartment and . . . ?"

She licked cocoa off her upper lip. "They . . . they were laughing very loudly in the living room and I could not work. I was merely writing the essay assignment for you, but they were being most obnoxious, so I told . . . asked them to be quiet and Fel is telling me to get lost!"

Dylan puffed his cheeks. "Felicia looked up and said *get lost?* Is that what happened?"

Teresa blinked and swallowed. "Well, she . . . she did not say *exactly* this."

"Oh? What *exactly* did she say?"

"Um . . . she said *go away!* Just like that . . . very nasty."

He nodded, took her empty mug and his glass and went behind the bar. Teresa chewed a fingertip while he cooked more cocoa and poured more whisky.

"So then what? You left the apartment?"

"Yes, of course. I could not stay there after she . . . I think perhaps she was drunk."

"Well . . . that's terrible." He stirred the mug and shook his head. "I'd better have a talk with her."

"No! I mean . . . not tonight. You must give her a chance to cool off."

Dylan's eyes narrowed. He carried fresh drinks and a bar towel to the table. Teresa took the cloth and wiped the spill.

"I am sorry to be so clumsy, Uncle Dylan."

"Don't worry about that. Here. Be careful . . . it's hot. But I think I should call Fel."

"No!" The mug clunked tabletop and steamy cocoa splashed.

"Teresa, for crying out loud!" He leaned over to mop the new spill while he took a deep breath. "She has to know where you are."

Tears slid down her cheeks. "Please don't, Uncle Dylan."

"I'll tell her you're OK, sweetie, that's all."

She whimpered while he retrieved the handset from the entryway floor. Dylan pressed a speed-dial key and Felicia's phone rang four times. He looked down at his asphalt-blackened socks and shook his head while he waited through the voice-mail message.

"This is Dylan. Your little lost lamb is at my apartment and she's fine. I'll put her in the spare bedroom and bring her home tomorrow, so don't worry. Call me when you can. Bye." He switched off the phone and set it on the coffee table. "See? Was that so horrible?"

Teresa pouted, picked up the whisky glass, and dribbled half an ounce into her mug. He gaped.

"What in the world do you think you're doing, young lady?"

"You did not put brandy in this one . . . I was watching you."

She curled her feet beneath the robe while she peered at him over the rim of the mug. He looked at the ceiling and then sat beside her.

"Feel better now?"

"Yes . . . very much. This is good with whisky."

"I'm sure . . . but getting back to what happened . . . you think Fel was drunk?"

"Perhaps. I mean . . . why else would she scream at me like this? And the old man merely sat there and smirked the whole time."

"Sweetie, that *old man* is a year younger than I am."

"Nuh uh! He is like old and wrinkled."

Dylan sighed. "Being around Lisa has really improved your grammar, hasn't it?"

"What do you mean?"

"Never mind. Listen . . . Fel loves you, just like she loved your father and. . . ."

"No! She *hates* me! She would rather be with that . . . that *creep*."

He grabbed her mug, set it on the table and cradled her in his arms. "He is *not* a creep, young lady . . . he's a department head at the university and. . . ."

"I don't care! He . . . he can hardly speak English!"

"What?" Dylan shook his head. "Now you're being silly."

"I am *not*. He is a creep and I hate him!"

"All right, all right . . . you hate him because he has an accent? Or you're mad because Fel has a boyfriend?"

"No! She is mean to me and she made me leave because she hates me and she will rather go to bed with that old man."

Leftover adrenaline from his encounter with the biker burned Dylan's stomach. He gritted his teeth and Teresa gasped when his arm jerked.

"You do *not* talk about Felicia that way, young lady."

She squealed when he picked her up, turned her around, and dropped her across his lap. "*Please*, Uncle Dylan, it is not my fault!"

He pushed terrycloth out of the way. Teresa wailed as he reached around to unzip her shorts, and then tugged them down. Blue bikini panties covered almost half of her firm, round bottom. She yelped when Dylan swatted the plump, bare under curve. He took a deep breath and raised his arm again.

"I don't care *whose* fault it is, you do not . . . speak . . . that . . . way . . . about . . . her!"

His hand clapped hard six times. Teresa squeaked with each slap and reached back to protect her bottom.

"Stop, Uncle Dylan!"

"Move your hand this *instant*."

She moaned and yanked her fist to her mouth as he dragged down her panties.

"Not *naked* . . . please?"

"Quit whining, Teresa."

The cleft contracted to a fine line when she clenched. He spanked hard three times, and then shifted his grip on her waist, shortened his stroke and peppered the tender flesh with short, quick swats. Pent-up ferocity poured into his hand, but he used only his fingers to flick hot sting into her quivery cheeks. Teresa squealed and kicked the sofa cushion.

Dylan jerked when the phone rang, held Teresa tight, and leaned toward the coffee table. She pouted at him and wiped a tear. He grabbed the handset and thumbed a button.

"This is Professor Travis."

"Oh Dylan, thank God!"

"It's OK, Fel. She's right here and she's fine."

"She . . . she just disappeared! I looked all over the building and. . . ."

He cleared his throat while his sister sobbed. "I've got her . . . don't worry."

"But I . . . I was just about to call the *police*."

"Take a deep breath and tell me what happened."

Teresa whimpered and glared at him. He let go of her waist but held her with his elbow while he patted the warm, wriggly behind. Felicia sighed and swallowed hard.

"OK, uh . . . I went to dinner with Mac and we got back about nine-thirty, then we sat in the living room, and . . . I don't know . . . he was kind of playful, and. . . ."

"Oh, really?"

"*No*, Dylan . . . he just did his Humphrey Bogart impression and. . . ."

"Haimish McFrazier does *Bogart*?"

"Well, yeah . . . it's the closest he can get to an American accent."

"I'll have to hear it sometime. Sorry . . . go on."

"So . . . so I'm doing Ingrid's part, and we're laughing so hard we can't stand it, and then all of a sudden there's Teresa, and she just glares at us and tells us to shut the . . . um . . . shut the F word *up*."

He scowled at Teresa and she bit a fingertip. "I *see*. Listen, Fel, can you hold on a minute? I was right in the middle of something."

"Dylan?"

"Don't hang up . . . I'll be right back."

"OK."

Teresa squealed and twisted, but he grabbed her, set the phone down, and raised his arm.

"*What* did I tell you about the F word, Teresa Luisa?"

"Nooo! I . . . aiee! Didn't *mean* to . . . *owee*! It . . . aiee! Just slipped ouuut!"

She howled and kicked while he spanked the same place a dozen times. A bright red handprint glowed at the summit of her right cheek. He flexed the numbness from his palm, picked up the phone, and waited until Teresa's wails diminished.

"Fel?"

"Jesus, Dylan! Why are you so mad?"

"Besides the inexcusable language, she lied to me . . . and you *know* what happens when girls lie to me."

Teresa sobbed and rubbed her fiery bottom. Felicia coughed and cleared her throat.

"Yeah . . . and she should, too."

"So . . . you've been looking for her the past three hours?"

"Well, no . . . I mean . . . after she yelled at us, I told her to go to her room and then spent the next hour apologizing to Mac. He left about eleven and I went and knocked on Teresa's door, but she didn't answer so I got ready for bed."

"I see. Can you hold on one more second?"

"You're not going to spank her again, are you?"

"Not right now. Hold on, OK?"

Teresa clutched his neck when he dropped the phone and rolled her over. She wept into his faded Dodgers sweatshirt while he patted her back and hugged her, then lifted her to stand on shaky legs. Denim shorts fell to the carpet as he stood, untied the robe belt, and slipped it off. Teresa grabbed his arm.

"Uncle Dylan, please?"

He sighed, leaned down, and pushed her tiny panties on top of the shorts. "Go stand in the corner."

"No! You don't *love* me!"

She screeched when he smacked achy bottom flesh.

"*Never* say that to me, Teresa! Go to the corner and I mean right *now*."

He turned her, nudged her with his palm, and she wailed as she slogged across the room. She faced the wall next to the stereo rack, rubbed sting with one hand and wiped tears with the other. Dylan sighed and picked up the phone.

"Sorry, Fel."

"Yeah well, she . . . uh. . . ."

"When did you figure out she was gone?"

"After I talked to her through the bedroom door for ten minutes. I thought she was just being surly. You know how teenage girls are."

"I certainly do."

Felicia scoffed. "What's *that* supposed to mean?"

"One issue at a time, OK? Work with me here."

"Hmph. I was *never* surly." She sighed and Dylan waited. "Well . . . maybe a little. So I finally got the ice pick and jimmied her door lock, and guess what?"

Dylan nodded. "Yeah . . . she got here a little before one. You must have been out looking for her when I called."

"I thought maybe she was hiding down by the pool. I probably should have called you first, but it didn't occur to me she would . . . how did she get there, anyway?"

"She could have walked, I suppose . . . or taken the bus."

"Well . . . I'm glad she's OK."

"Yeah . . . me too."

"But, um . . . Dyllie?"

He grunted. "Yes, *Fleecy?*"

"You . . . you spanked her awful hard."

"She lied to me and tried to blame this on *you.*"

"I know but . . . you're gonna forgive her pretty soon, aren't you?"

"You know I will."

"And you won't make her stand in the corner too long, will you? That's almost worse than getting spanked. I always hated it when you made me. . . ." Felicia coughed. "I *do* love her, Dylan . . . she's Gerhard's daughter and. . . ."

"Shh. I know . . . but I have one question and then I'll let you go to bed."

"OK . . . what?"

"It's a trust fund question. Are you up for it?"

"Geeze, Dylan . . . at this hour?"

"Sorry . . . are you sleeping with Haimish?"

"What?"

He flinched. "It's OK if you are but the trust says you have to maintain. . . ."

Felicia snarled. "I know . . . a wholesome home environment for the little brat. Dammit, Dylan, it's just . . . ooh!"

"Never mind . . . we'll talk about it later."

"We'll talk about it now! Did she tell you we were doing it *here?*"

"Not in so many words, but. . . ."

"Well we're *not.* We go to his lake cottage to fool around, and he won't even *show* me the townhouse because his wife died there. Jesus, Dylan, how could she . . . ?"

"Please, Fel. It's none of my business but I'm stuck in the middle. I've got the purse strings and all the paper work so I have to know. Forgive me?"

He listened to ten seconds of silence while he watched Teresa rub her bottom. Felicia sighed.

"Yeah, I guess so."

"Thanks, honey. You better go to bed."

"Dylan?"

"Hm?"

"I could stay up a while longer if you're going to get the belt out."

"Didn't you say I spanked her too hard?"

"Yeah . . . but that was before I knew what she accused me of."

"I'll bring her home in the morning. We all need some rest."

"That's for sure, but. . . ." Felicia giggled. "I promise not to laugh when she can't sit down for breakfast."

Dylan shook his head. "You'd better not, young lady, or *you* won't be able to either. Now go to bed!"

"Yes, sir." Her grin burned his ear. "'Night, Dyllie."

"Good night, Fleecy."

The phone clicked. Dylan switched it off as Teresa padded across the room to stand in front of him. Her under lip was red with tooth marks.

"Uncle Dylan?"

"What, sweetie?"

"I . . . I am sorry for this little fib I told to you."

"Oh, really? Are you sorry you came out of the corner before I said you could?"

She squealed and her bottom bounced as she ran to stand beside the stereo. "I did not *mean* to, Uncle Dylan! I am being good and I merely forgot, and . . . I am sorry so *please* do not be mad with me, OK?"

Tears slid from her eyes as she blinked at him. Dylan picked up his glass, stood, and swallowed the whisky. She whimpered when he walked over and took her shoulders in his hands.

"Teresa?"

"Ye . . . yes, sir?"

"You've been very naughty, haven't you?"

"*No!* I . . . I was merely upset and I am much better now, honestly, because you have punished me and. . . ."

He squeezed her arms. "Being upset is not an excuse for fibbing, or shouting obscenities, or running away from home, is it?"

"No, I . . . I . . . oh *God*."

She wailed, turned, and collapsed into Dylan's arms. He smiled, picked her up, and carried her to the bedroom. Her head lolled when he laid her on the quilt. He smirked and sat beside her.

"I know you didn't faint so quit pretending." He got up to rummage in a dresser drawer. "Here, sweetie . . . this T-shirt is pretty old but it'll be a good nightgown for you."

He lifted her, tugged off the crop-top, and unfastened a blue satin bra. Tiny lines wrinkled around her eyes and Teresa whimpered.

"Uncle *Dylan*."

"You know better than to play possum with me, young lady." He scooted the bra down her arms and tossed the flimsy garment into a corner.

She clamped both arms across her breasts and curled into a pink, naked ball. Dylan worked the shirt neck over her head. She opened her eyes, pouted, and stuck her hands through the sleeves.

"Uncle Dylan?"

"What?"

"You . . . you are not angry with me, are you?"

"Why would I be angry with you?"

"Because . . . I fibbed and . . . and said a bad word?"

His eyebrow arched and Teresa bit her lip. "I already spanked you for that, and you won't do it anymore, will you?"

"No, Uncle Dylan, but you never said that you will forgive. . . ."

"On the other hand, we *do* need to discuss your running away from home in the middle of the night."

Teresa quivered as she grasped his hand, stunned by his gruff tone, afraid to look at his eyes. "No, we do *not* need to discuss this. Why must you . . . ?"

"I nearly had to kill a drunken barbarian with my bare hands because he wanted to play house with you! What in the name of all that's reasonable were you *thinking*?"

She howled as he dragged her across his lap, yanked up the T-shirt, and leaned across her warm bottom. The nightstand drawer scritched and he took out a bottle of baby oil. Her mouth opened wide while he dribbled half a teaspoonful into his right palm.

"Thank you, Uncle Dylan . . . I *knew* you would not be so cruel to spank me anymore."

"Hush, girl . . . this is for *me*." He rubbed his hands together and then flexed his right wrist.

Teresa gasped. "You cannot be serious! I said I am sorry!"

"And I said *hush* . . . and lie still."

He raised his arm. Teresa clamped her ankles together, mashed her nose into the quilt, and clenched her bottom. Dylan swatted and a moist clap echoed against the ceiling. Teresa squealed as sting lanced through her left cheek and then gasped and clutched the duvet while he spanked oily heat into her behind. He avoided the harsh red smudge on her right hemisphere, but scorched the tender flesh around it.

"Naah! Neiieen! Aiiieee! Daaah! Deh! Dylaaaan!"

Fire blazed across her backside, through her tummy, and up her breasts. She scrabbled to cover the source of the flame but he grabbed her wrists and bit his lip while he showered pain droplets on her bottom. Her moist cleft opened and closed, like a wordless plea for forgiveness, as she bucked on his lap. He leaned back and smacked harder along her squirmy hips to turn her cheeks a uniform, sorrowful scarlet. Finally, he let go of her hands and Teresa sobbed as she wriggled and pounded the quilt with her fists.

"Aiee! Ah! I . . . I am *sorry*, Uncle Dylan, honestly!"

He scooped her up and she squealed when her fanny touched soft cotton sweatpants. She wept into the Dodgers logo and he turned her a little so her sore behind curved away from his thighs.

"Teresa?"

"Hah . . . whah . . . what?"

"Tell me you never will run away again."

"Nah . . . nee . . . no I . . . I will not *never* again, I *swear*."

"And you'll call me before you get so mad at Felicia that you're ready to do something like that?"

"I . . . I . . . I *will*."

"You promise?"

She looked up and Dylan swiped tears with his thumb. "Ye . . . yes, I . . . I promise."

"All right . . . then you're forgiven. But I don't want to hear anymore nonsense about how you hate Felicia's boyfriend, even if he *does* remind you of your father."

"He *doesn't*, he. . . ." She licked her lips.

"Yes, sweetie . . . take away the curly hair and moustache, and Mac would look like your Papa."

"He would *not*."

Dylan shrugged. "Not exactly, but he's too much like Gerhard for you to get along with him."

Teresa puffed air through her lips. "Perhaps . . . and I should not be surprised that she would choose a man so much like Papa. So what can I *do*?"

"Smile and nod, and try to be an adult about it."

"But . . . but . . . could I . . . I mean . . . can I come live with *you*?"

"*What*? You hate your stepmother but you want to live with Herr Professor Uncle?"

"I do *not* hate Felicia and . . . and I really like *you* . . . except when you spank me so cruelly." She reached back to rub harsh sting.

He chuckled and took a jar of cold cream from the drawer. "Don't you think that would happen a lot more often if you lived under my roof?"

Teresa sighed, twisted and settled across his lap. "Of course not . . . because I will always be a good girl." Dylan snickered and she glared at him. "Well I *would* . . . and besides . . . I would make your breakfast and run errands and mend your shirts. . . ."

"I see . . . and when would you do your homework, sweetie?"

"You would *help* me with my homework so I will be a brilliant student and also help *you*."

"I'll think about it." He opened the jar, scooped emollient, and anointed her behind.

"That means *no*, does it not? Mmmm . . . but *that* is feeling much better."

Cool whiteness muddled bitter red and Teresa pushed up her hips to welcome his fingers. He slicked relief across the pain while she moaned and clutched his sweatpants. Pleasure waves swept through her cheeks and sparked between her thighs. Warm electricity tingled his palm as he massaged plump smoothness. He took deep breaths to quiet the pounding in his chest. The cheeks hardened and quivered as she flexed her knees and bit her finger to quench the sweet fire that burned in her core. A hot, delightful tingle flashed up her belly and into her breasts, and she turned to grab his neck.

"Tha . . . thank you, Uncle Dylan," she whispered.

He smiled and tugged the T-shirt over her nakedness. "You're welcome, sweetie."

Her arms trembled when he rolled her onto the bed, spread an afghan over her and then dabbed her face with Kleenex. He dug a T-shirt and a pair of cotton running shorts from a drawer and took them into the bathroom. Water splashed in the tub as he tossed shredded socks in the trash, his sweat suit at the hamper, and then sat on the ledge. He lathered pavement grit from his feet with a bar of Safeguard, but even the soapy odor could not drive her scent from his nostrils.

Teresa curled up and listened to the water run. She caressed her sore, slippery behind, shut her eyes, and felt his warm, hard hand instead of her own. Soft lightning flicked in her vagina and she whimpered as she thrust a finger inside and found the stiff, wet bud. She circled a finger pad, slowly at first, and then quicker as the fire raged, fed by her need and fanned by the heat in her bottom. Bright, sharp tremors rolled down her thighs and up her spine. She trembled, panted, stroked the stiff clitoris, and squealed as an explosion rocked the bed. Damp, shivery aftershocks jolted her as she raised a shaky arm toward the nightstand.

The bathroom door swung open. She gasped, grabbed a tissue and huddled beneath the afghan.

"Sweetie, are you all right?"

"Yuh . . . yes, Uncle Dylan. I am fine."

"I thought I heard you scream."

"No, I . . . I must have fallen asleep and . . . and had a nightmare."

He sat on the bedside and kissed her forehead. "A nightmare?

I'm sorry. Feel better now?"

"Yes, it . . . it was nothing." She bit her lip and wiped dampness with the tissue.

"Good." He smiled. "I'll turn down the other bed so you can get some sleep."

"I want to sleep with *you*."

He took a deep breath. "You know that's not possible, sweetie."

She pouted and rested her chin on this thigh. "Why *not*?"

"Because it *isn't*, that's why."

"That is what you would say to a three-year-old . . . and you *promised* you will not treat me as such."

"Teresa, don't be absurd." He tucked the afghan over her shoulders. "I'll sleep in the other bed if you want."

"No, Uncle Dylan." She tossed off the blanket and climbed on his lap to hug him. "We already will sleep in the same apartment so what is the difference if we are sleeping in the same bed? Who will *know* this?"

"*We* will, that's who . . . now stop being silly and. . . ."

"But I . . . I might have more of these nightmares and you will not want *that*, will you?"

He sighed when she squeezed his neck. "Don't do this, Teresa."

She leaned back and looked into his eyes. "What? I cannot hug you?"

"You can't use a fib to get your own way."

Her stomach churned and a hot blush crept up her neck. "But I *didn't* tell a fib. Why are you *saying* this?"

"We both know why you screamed and it had nothing to do with nightmares. I let you think I believed you, to save you any embarrassment."

"But I *did* . . . it was an *awful* nightmare and . . . and. . . ."

"Shh." He hugged her while she wriggled. "It's perfectly normal and there's nothing to be ashamed of . . . but no one likes to be caught in the act. I only tried to spare your. . . ."

"No!" She pounded his back with a fist. "I . . . I don't know what you mean and I would not *do* that in any case!"

"Teresa, calm down. I said it's all right."

"But it . . . it *was* a nightmare and you are being most horrible to me."

Humiliation scalded her face as she struggled to break free of his arms.

"Teresa Luisa, stop that this *instant*. I blistered your bottom once tonight for lying to me and don't think I won't do it again. Let's just drop it, all right?"

Hot tears coursed down her cheeks while mad butterflies careened about her tummy. "I . . . I am *not* lying."

"All right . . . if that's the way you want it. . . ."

She grunted and pushed against his chest, then went limp as he draped her across his lap. "Uncle Dylan, *please?*"

Hard, bare thighs warmed her tummy. She kicked and squirmed as he tucked her waist into his stomach, and then moaned when he pulled up the T-shirt to once more bare her bottom. Guilt and shame gripped her throat like fists and she gasped short, ragged breaths while her pulse thudded in her ears. A taste like raw parsley dried her mouth.

Dylan slapped the sore, creamy bottom no harder than he would clap a friend's back for a well-played tennis game. Teresa screeched as if a hornet had stung her. He sighed, shook his head, and fanned the shivery mounds with quick, light strokes, just enough to make them jiggle.

Hellish flame covered her cheeks and raged up her spine. She sobbed wordless pleas, promises, and apologies as his brutal blows flogged away her guilt, shame, and remorse. Tears boiled the bitterness from her mouth and she pushed up her bottom, nearer to his hard hand. Hellfire flickered and diminished as warm sting bathed her hips and thighs. She wiped wet eyes with her fingers and then sighed as she collapsed.

He rubbed her cheeks with his right palm and leaned on his left elbow to look into her eyes.

"Sweetie? Do you feel better now?"

"Yeh . . . yes, Uncle Dylan, and I am very sorry I. . . ."

"Shh . . . it's all right . . . I won't ask why I had to spank you because we both know."

She turned and blinked. "You did *not* have to do this and I . . . oh *God*."

"I *said* it's all right so we don't have to talk about it . . . but you won't fib to me anymore, will you?"

"No . . . not *never*."

Sweet relief warmed her breasts as he sat up, turned her around and hugged her.

"That's my good girl. You may sleep in here and I won't be far away. Now hop up so I can turn down the covers."

"Uh . . . Uncle Dylan?"

"What, sweetie?"

"You do not think I . . . I mean. . . ." She sighed as he kissed her cheek.

"I think you're my favorite little girl forever, that's what I think. Now run to the bathroom while I get your bed ready."

She kissed his lips and twisted off his lap. Her water poured into the toilet for a long time, and then she washed, brushed her teeth with a new toothbrush he laid out for her, and opened the door. The quilt and sheet were turned back and the table lamp burned low. She slid under the covers and pulled them to her chin. He came in a minute later, set a glass of water on the nightstand and bent over her.

"Good night, Teresa."

"Good night, Uncle Dylan. I am sorry to be such a. . . ."

"Shh . . . you're forgiven . . . so go to sleep. It's almost three . . . so seven o'clock is going to seem awfully early."

Teresa glared at the clock radio. "Why must we get up this soon, Uncle Dylan?"

"So I can take you home before Fel gets worried. Now go to *sleep*, young lady."

He smiled, kissed her, and switched off the lamp. Teresa pouted as he walked out, and then guzzled half the water. She curled on her side and smiled as she inhaled his scent from the pillows. The clock digits glowed in the darkness and she stared at the boxy red numbers.

Her bottom ached; fatigue gripped every muscle; her eyelids drooped, but she didn't feel sleepy. She sighed and then blinked because the radio looked very odd.

It wasn't a radio at all, but her father's castle, and red flame billowed from the turrets as she cowered on a craggy hillside and watched it burn. She clutched at a ripped and sooty satin gown. Torches glimmered on a dirt road at the bottom of the hill. Angry villagers shouted and snarled as they searched for the King's daughter. She gasped and scrambled upward, through prickly brush and over sharp rocks. Ugly, bearded oafs and screechy, wrinkled viragos climbed after her.

At the top of the hill stood a knight. Torchlight gleamed on his shiny armor and glistened in his blue eyes, for he wore no helmet. He raised a sword and it blazed like a thousand battle lanterns when he bellowed a challenge in an unknown tongue. A white horse reared and stamped the turf beside him. The knight smiled at Teresa and held out a mailed hand. She reached up to take it and suddenly he was astride the magnificent animal and Teresa lay face down across the horse's neck. Her gown split open in back. The knight doffed his glaive and put a gentle palm on her bare bottom to hold her still as the horse's wings spread wide. Terrified villagers screamed and ran down the hill. He shouted a command and his white steed leapt into the sky.

Soft, wild wind caressed her bottom; shiny armor warmed her hip; equine neck muscles rippled beneath her tummy. She sighed and listened to strong wings thrum the night air as they flew toward the rising sun.

Chapter 10

PARTY PLANS

A COOL BREEZE flickered through the window, ruffled the blue muslin curtain Lisa made for the alcove archway, and teased her nose with the scent of fresh donuts. She pressed a hand to her bosom and sighed when the hand beneath her own squeezed plump roundness. Her bare bottom wriggled against hard bare thighs and she blinked to focus. Warm, yellow light glinted past new Venetian blind slats and she gasped as she twisted around to see the clock radio on the other side of the bed.

"Oh *shit*."

Greg coughed and yanked his hand from her breast. "Whah?"

"It's nearly *seven*, for crying out loud! Didn't you set the alarm?"

"Uh . . . yeah . . . I *thought* I did." He sat up, squeezed his eyes tight and then peered at the radio. "Oh shit."

"*Geeze*, Greg . . . you *know* I have to be home before Michael gets up."

Lisa grunted, scrambled off the bed, and shoved muslin aside as she stomped to the bathroom. Greg wiped his mouth, stumbled to his feet and followed her.

"I'm *sorry*, Lisa." He leaned against the doorjamb. "I *did* set it, but um . . . I turned down the radio while I was on the phone yesterday and I guess I forgot to turn it back up."

Water splashed and Lisa snatched tissue from the roll. "That's what I'll tell Michael . . . I'm *sure* he'll be impressed."

Greg mumbled and gathered Lisa's clothes from the secretary desk that served as his bureau while the toilet flushed and water ran in the basin. He shook out wadded denim trousers, a green sleeveless T-shirt and green satin bra, and laid them on the bed, then opened a drawer and grabbed a pair of pink cotton bikini panties. Lisa muttered as she stormed, naked, from the bathroom.

"He's gonna *kill* me."

"Here . . . your other ones spent the night on the floor."

She took the panties and yanked them up her legs. He pulled on a T-shirt-shirt and jeans and stuffed his bare feet into Reebok court shoes, then went to use the toilet.

"Hey . . . it's not all *that* bad," he yelled over the splash.

"Greg! Oh . . . never mind."

"Lisa, knock it off . . . Michael can have his breakfast a half hour late for once." He returned and wrapped his arms around her as she struggled with her bra. "Do you want me to call him?"

Her fingers relaxed and Greg kissed her forehead as he coupled the hooks at her back. She leaned into his chest and pouted.

"He's gonna be mad no matter who calls."

"Let him be mad . . . what's he gonna do? Spank you?"

"Don't you *even* . . . !" She pushed away from him, scrabbled the T-shirt over her head and sat on the bedside to tug on her trousers. "I thought you understood."

His lips fluttered as he let out a long breath. "I'm *trying* to but Jesus, Lisa! This getting up at five so you can run home and poach a couple of eggs for him? And why don't you just *tell* him you're spending the night with . . . ?"

Her heel pounded hardwood. "That's the only thing I *do* for him anymore and I don't want him to *know* yet."

Sobs racked her throat and Greg scowled as he hugged her. "OK, OK . . . it's complicated. Put your shoes on and get your purse . . . and let's hope the Celica starts."

The rusty Toyota growled, sputtered, and then roared. Greg smiled as he squeezed the shift lever, dumped the clutch and screeched out of the parking lot. Lisa wriggled against the shoulder harness and looked at him.

"I'm sorry I was so cranky."

"It's OK. You better call him."

"Yeah."

She pulled out her phone and pressed a speed key, then listened through two rings and a click.

"Michael Swayne."

"Guh . . . good morning, Michael . . . I was just. . . ."

"Lisa? Where *are* you, my dear? Are you all right? Are you lost?"

"I . . . I'm on my way home . . . on, uh . . . Elm, just past Midlands and. . . ."

"Yes, yes . . . I looked for you this morning and saw your bed hadn't been slept in so I was rather worried . . . thought perhaps something had happened to you. Have you had your breakfast?"

"Sir?"

"Breakfast . . . you know . . . food in the morning . . . that sort of thing."

"No, sir . . . but I'll make eggs and toast for you as soon as I get there."

"Hmm . . . well, yes. I did manage to create coffee, of a sort, from this damnable machine . . . but not at all what you coax out of it . . . rather a pale imitation, I'm afraid. When did you say you would be home?"

"About ten minutes . . . and I'll make *good* coffee, OK? Sir?"

"Yes . . . that would be splendid. Is the young man with you?"

"Suh . . . sir?"

"You know who I mean . . . tall . . . thin . . . rather a long nose."

"Yuh . . . yes, sir . . . he's bringing me home."

"I see. Would he care to have breakfast with us, do you think?"

A blush burned Lisa's cheeks and Greg gasped when she stomped both feet on the floorboard.

"Michael! Who's there with *you?*"

"Hm? Only Ms. Trelawny . . . and she's no better with coffee than I am . . . bloody nuisance, these machines."

"You knew where I was all the time, didn't you?"

He chuckled. "I will see you when you get here. By the way . . . you're grounded for the weekend."

"But Michael . . . !"

The phone clicked and went dead. Lisa moaned and shoved it

into her purse. Greg glanced at her as he turned a corner.

"You're busted?"

Lisa nodded. "You are, too."

"Huh?"

"Michael said I'm grounded and you gotta have breakfast with the olds."

"*What?*"

"Uh huh. I should of just told him, I guess."

"You're grounded? But it's Friday . . . Doug and Renée's party is tonight."

"Oh shoot! I forgot about that."

"And I'll have to skip breakfast. I gotta shower before work . . . you wouldn't want your best manager to be stinky, would you?"

She grimaced. "Yeah, right . . . bail on me when I need you the most."

"Oh, for crying out loud."

He pulled into the driveway and stopped next to Beth's Pontiac. Lisa kissed him, long and hard, before she got out and scrabbled a latchkey from her purse. The smell of hot bacon made her tummy growl as she walked through the living room and pushed into the kitchen. Michael sat at the table, his suit jacket draped over the chair back, a newspaper folded in front of him. He looked at Lisa and nodded. Beth forked crispy brown strips from a pan onto a paper towel and smiled.

"Morning, Lisa. Where's Greg?"

"He has to open the store so he went home." She sat next to Michael and held his hand. "Sir?"

"Hmm?"

"I'm really, really sorry and it won't ever happen again."

Michael squeezed her fingers. "What won't? Your stopping out all night without telling me . . . or oversleeping and neglecting your duties?"

"Either! Both! *Neither!* Mi . . . Mr. Swayne, please don't ground me, OK?"

"Would you care for bacon and eggs? It seems Beth *can* cook, after all."

"Michael! I'm too *old* to get grounded and. . . ."

"And old enough to act responsibly regarding the few duties I still require of you . . . or accept the consequences when you don't."

"But I want to go to a. . . ." She whimpered and sat back when he scowled, her arms folded over her bosom.

"You have a class this afternoon, I believe."

"Yeah . . . microeconomics."

"Homework?"

"I already did it."

"What about the college? Have you finished your assignment for Travis?"

"Yes, sir . . . well . . . kinda. I have to type the final draft, but I was gonna do it on Sunday."

"Except for the class this afternoon, you are not to leave the house until Monday . . . and your telephone privileges are suspended until that time as well."

"*Geeze*, Michael!"

"Give me your phone, Lisa. How would you like your eggs prepared?"

Angry breath fluttered her lips as she dug in her purse. "Raw."

Beth squeezed the girl's shoulders. "How about over easy?"

"Yeah, whatever. Michael, I can't *believe* you're gonna. . . ."

He took her cell phone and held up his mug. "And would you *please* show Beth how you make coffee? This is barely palatable."

"Sure but . . . Michael, I really, really. . . ."

"Come on, honey." Beth pulled her from the chair. "Let's fry some eggs."

Lisa dumped coffee into the sink, rinsed the carafe, and refilled the machine while Beth cooked. She fumed and pouted as they put food onto plates. Michael and Beth talked about a property lease while they ate. Lisa chewed in silence. Beth kissed her cheek, Michael patted her shoulder, and they left her to clean the kitchen alone.

She started the dishwasher at eight-thirty, went to her room, and glared at the computer screen while she made changes to the essay she wrote for Dylan. At nine she reached for the phone, jerked her hand back, and then squealed. Her heels pounded the carpet as she stalked to the closet, snatched a uniform, and threw it on the bed. Clothes flew at the hamper when she stripped, and she squealed again when she jumped under the shower stream before it warmed.

"Damn him *anyway!*" She sputtered tepid water between her teeth and washed her face.

Crisp cotton and stiff petticoats rustled as she dressed. At ten o'clock she carried a silver coffee service to the office door, knocked, and entered. Michael looked at her over his reading glasses and then glanced at his watch.

"Thank you, Lisa . . . a bit early, but that's all right."

Beth smiled and straightened a pile of documents. "Thanks, honey."

Lisa set the tray on the coffee table and then stood in front of Michael's desk.

"Sir . . . I don't want to be grounded."

"The subject is closed, Lisa. Now be a dear and pour me a coffee."

"No! Sir."

Her under-lip stuck out half an inch. Michael gaped as she rounded the desk and opened the second drawer from the bottom. She reached inside and pulled out a shiny, double-tailed leather tawse, a wooden paddle half the size of Dylan's, and a whip with a nine-inch handle and eight, two-foot thongs. Her heart thumped as she held the implements out to him.

His chair rolled backward and he shook his head. "This isn't at *all* necessary, so why don't you . . . ?"

"Michael!" Her heel smacked the plastic mat. "Will you quit being so mean and *spank* me?"

Beth chuckled, dropped her pencil and went to sit on the sofa. Michael let out a long breath and pushed to his feet.

"Instead of grounding you, I take it."

"Yeah . . . sir. I wanna go to a party tonight and . . . and. . . ."

"And you'd rather go with a sore bottom than not go at all, is that it?"

"Uh huh . . . but I really *will* learn my lesson, honest, and . . . and I'll tell you where I am from now on and . . . I won't be late anymore, I *swear*."

She set the implements on the desk, closed the drawer with her knee, and clasped her hands at her waist as she bit her lip and blinked sad eyes at him. He folded his arms and looked at Beth. She smirked and poured coffee.

"Whose party is it, honey?"

"Um . . . a couple of Greg's friends . . . they live over in North End . . . in a loft."

"Artsy types, huh?"

"Yeah . . . I guess." She looked at Michael. "So *can* I?"

"Yes . . . but take the Land Rover. I don't want to get a call at midnight that Greg's car has broken down yet again. And whoever is driving . . . no alcohol, and I mean not a drop of *any* sort. Is that clear?"

"Yes, sir. Very clear."

He turned to Beth. "Where are we on setting up the automobile allowance for Mr. Bentley?"

Lisa gasped and Beth shrugged.

"I think I've got it figured out, but Darcy's payroll system is pretty archaic so I might need a couple of pay periods to get it right."

"You're gonna give Greg money for a new car?"

Michael smiled as Lisa grabbed his neck and kissed him.

"Not *give*, my dear . . . it's part of his compensation, and as such is dependent on his performance. But we'd rather our most visible manager drove something more attractive . . . and reliable. Not a word to him until Beth has it in place, though, all right?"

"OK . . . thank you, Mi . . . sir." She let go of his neck and grinned at Beth. "Thanks, Beth."

"Sure . . . and just remember . . . the money is coming out of *your* pocket."

Lisa nodded, looked at Michael, and then at the array of tools on his desk. She grimaced and rubbed her tummy as nasty butterflies awakened inside.

"I . . . I'm ready, sir."

"I would rather not do this, Lisa."

"Me neither . . . so can I go to the party and get grounded *after*?"

Jaw muscles vibrated for a second and then he laughed. "You

never cease to amaze me. Now slip off your knickers and let's get to it."

She pouted and reached under her skirts. "You can't blame me for trying."

"I might have been disappointed if you hadn't."

A hot blush suffused her cheeks as she thumbed her panties down and off, and dropped the warm cotton onto the desk. Michael picked up the whip and untangled the cords. Lisa whimpered and took a step back. His eyebrows arched.

"No?"

"Whuh . . . whatever . . . but . . . um. . . ."

"I did *say* you would go to the party with a sore bottom."

"Yeh . . . yes, sir, but. . . ."

"Oh, very well . . . I spoil you intolerably as it is and I see no reason to change my ways at this late date." He dropped the whip and reached for the tawse. "Bend over the front of the desk and lift your skirts."

"Yes, sir. Thank you, sir."

Her knees quivered while she slowly complied. Petticoats shushed up her thighs and cool air caressed her trembly bottom, still sensitive from Greg's attention the night before. She glared over her shoulder at Beth.

"Don't you have anything better to do?"

The woman swallowed and set down her cup. "Can't think of anything . . . besides . . . I hardly ever get to see your cute little fanny since you went to reform school. Is that paddle rash on your right cheek?"

"Beth!" Lisa jerked her head. "Michael, make her stop."

He cleared his throat and pointed the leather strip. "Did you wish to be next, Ms. Trelawny?"

"No, *sir*, Mr. Swayne."

"Then keep your comments to yourself and get back to work."

Beth sneered and picked up the silver pot. "This is my coffee break so leave me alone. *Sir*."

Michael rolled his eyes and patted Lisa's back. "I'm sorry, my dear. Are you ready?"

"I guess so, but . . . not real hard, *please?*"

"Relax your bottom . . . it only hurts worse if you clench."

"Oh *God.*"

Lisa bent her knees and leaned forward while the nasty, worn-out cliché echoed in her ears. Stiff, sharp leather stung soft, round flesh and she gasped.

She had felt the tawse only once before, when she overfilled the Mercedes tank and gasoline burned the finish. Michael was very upset that she hadn't put the car through the wash immediately, and even more perturbed that he didn't notice the problem for two weeks. That time he scalded her behind with a dozen strokes, each twice as fierce as the one she just felt. Lisa panted and rested her forehead on cool oak. Leather whisked and nipped hard, just beneath the first stripe. She whimpered and wriggled her hips, then bowed her back and waited. The third stroke landed like a bee sting and she pushed up as she yelped.

"Steady, Lisa. Bend down so I can correct you."

"I'm *trying*, Michael, but. . . ."

"Shh . . . no backchat, young lady. You know better."

"But geeze!"

He raised his arm and slapped her squirmy behind. Another pink stripe appeared above the first three, right at the top of her cleft. Lisa squealed and kicked, and then whimpered as she leaned forward. Leather whirred, smacked again, and bright, shimmery pain lanced through her hips. A teardrop welled in her eye and she flicked it away. The strap fell once more and burned the base of her tender behind, just above the tingly orifice that gave her so much pleasure. Lisa shrieked and pounded the carpet with her toe while her anus throbbed. Pain covered her bottom like a fiery hand and heated the moisture between her thighs. She squealed and shuddered as leather clacked and flames raged.

Two minutes, twenty strokes, and a thousand years later, Michael dropped the tawse and gathered the weepy girl into his arms. She trembled, gasped and drenched his shirt with sorrow and perspiration. He held her close and kissed the top of her head.

"There now . . . it's all right."

"Juh . . . *Jesus*, Michael! Thah . . . that really, really *hurts*."

She rubbed enflamed cheeks with both hands as he palmed her chin and kissed wet, pouty lips.

"But you are no longer grounded."

"Yeah well . . . this stupid party better be *worth* it. *God*, that stings."

Michael smiled and unzipped her dress. "I sincerely hope so. Would you like a bit of cold cream?"

"Well *duh*, Michael . . . owee!" She caressed a handprint and blinked through a veil of tears. "Yeh . . . *yes*, sir. Thank you, sir."

"Better. Now lift your arms so I can remove your clothes."

He led her, naked but for bra, stockings, and suspender belt, to the sofa. Beth sidled over so he could sit in the middle and put Lisa across his lap, then she reached into a drawer in the coffee table and handed him a jar. He opened it, scooped white cream, and smoothed it across Lisa's bottom.

Beth pillowed the girl's head on her thigh and smiled. "Your heinie looks like a sunburned zebra."

Lisa looked up and wrinkled her nose. "Michael said to keep your comments to *yourself*."

"Girls!" He shook his head. "That's quite enough."

"Well, she doesn't have to make cracks about my bottom."

"Oooh . . . sorry about the bottom crack, Your Highness."

"Michael!"

"Beth!"

"OK, OK . . . I was just leaving." She smoothed Lisa's hair, then leaned over and kissed Michael's cheek. "I'll run those contracts to Fed Ex."

"Thank you . . . that would be splendid."

Beth scooted off the sofa and grabbed a stack of cardboard envelopes. "See you at D'Antonio's about twelve-thirty?"

"Yes . . . and would you call Schuster to remind him? You know how he is."

"Sure . . . bye, Michael . . . bye, Princess."

Lisa glared at Beth as she shut the door, and then sighed while

Michael massaged creamy relief into her cheeks.

"What's *with* her, anyway?"

"Hm? Beth?"

"Well yeah . . . so sarcastic and everything."

He shrugged. "No more than usual . . . but the two of you don't spend as much time together these days, so perhaps you only notice it more. Lift up a bit . . . there."

"Yeah maybe . . . mmm, that feels wonderful."

His long fingers caressed hot stripes at the base of her bottom and liquid lightning flashed down her thighs. She moaned and wriggled her tummy against hard leg muscles.

"Lisa?"

"Hmm?"

"What are you doing?"

She gasped and looked at him. "Nuh-nothing, Michael."

He patted the slippery mounds and leaned down to kiss her pout. "Go stand in the corner."

"Michael, you can't just. . . ."

"Lisa! You're being punished, not petted. Now do as I said."

"Geeze, Michael!" She snorted and pushed off his lap.

Long minutes ticked by while she fumed and glowered at a book spine. He worked at his desk and pretended to ignore her, but she felt his eyes on her achy, frustrated bottom. Finally, he sighed and leaned back.

"All right . . . come here, Lisa."

She glared and padded across the carpet. He shook out his handkerchief, laid it over his lap, and held out his arms. Her foot slapped the floor and then she huffed, turned and sat.

"Are you gonna be *nice* to me now?"

He smiled. "Are you going to be a good girl and *deserve* it?"

"I'm *always* a good girl . . . after you spank me."

"For an hour or two, at any rate." He held her close while she muttered denials into his chest. "Shh . . . it's only that I don't want you to think I'm rewarding you for bad behavior."

She gasped, and then moaned when his hand slipped between

her thighs and stroked moist, needy lips.

"Muh . . . Michael . . . hah . . . have you been talking to Dylan? Oooh!"

"Of course . . . he *is* a friend, so naturally we. . . ."

"I mean about muh . . . *me*! *God*, Michael!"

Shuddery heat flashed inside her labia and rolled up her belly and breasts. A smooth, gentle fingertip slid inside and coiled delicate circles around the neglected node at the center of Lisa's soul. She gasped and trembled while she clung to his neck. Creamy fire flowed through her bottom as she squirmed against his thighs; the tiny node blazed within; and Lisa quaked like a rag doll shaken by a divine hand.

Soft, eternal minutes later she groaned and looked up. He smiled and kissed her mouth.

"Feeling better?"

"Uh . . . uh *huh*. That was *delicious*, Michael. Thank you."

"And you've already forgotten why you have a sore, bare bottom in the first place, haven't you?"

"Nuh *uh* . . . I didn't! I . . . I was late for work and I got spanked real hard so I don't do it anymore and . . . and then you made me feel better 'cause you *love* me . . . and Professor Dylan is full of sh . . . *stuff*."

Michael laughed and squeezed her. "*That* may be true, but it seems he has brought out the debater in you . . . and I'm not entirely sure how I feel about that."

She grinned and hugged his neck. "You're very happy, 'cause you like smart women."

"Is that so?"

"Uh huh . . . look at Beth."

"Yes, well . . . smart and smart *mouthed* aren't quite the same." Lisa gasped and then smiled when he winked. "All right . . . I'll concede this round. Now go get ready for your class. I have a luncheon meeting to prepare for."

"OK . . . um . . . can I have my phone back?"

"Lisa!"

"What? You *said* I wasn't grounded anymore."

"*May* I have my phone back?"

"Oh, geeze . . . *may* I have my phone back? Please, sir . . . kind, gentle Mr. Swayne, sir . . . ow!"

He chuckled as she leapt off his lap and rubbed the spot he smacked, then he reached into his coat pocket and handed her the little Nokia.

"Will you come home after the party?" Lisa nodded. "Wake me when you get in, all right?"

"Yes, sir." She smiled and leaned over to kiss him. "Thanks, Michael."

She scooped up her shoes and clothes. He sighed and watched her moist red bottom jiggle out the door.

Lisa went to her room, put on shorts and a T-shirt and lay on her bed, the cell phone to her ear.

"Lola's Downtown . . . this is Greg."

"Hello." Her voice husked in a Lauren Bacall imitation. "I have a very serious complaint and I wish to speak to the manager."

He cleared his throat. "I see . . . well, I'm the manager . . . what seems to be the problem, ma'am?"

"These panties I bought at your store . . . they're too tight and I want you to come over here and adjust them for me."

She covered the microphone and giggled when he cleared his throat again.

"That *is* a serious complaint, ma'am . . . and I'll get right on top of the situation . . . as soon as I clear it with my girlfriend."

"Oh, I just bet you will!"

"Hi, Lisa . . . you're kinda perky for somebody who just got grounded."

"Except I talked Michael out of it . . . *and* I got the Rover for us to drive to the party."

"You did? Cool! You want to pick me up at the store around six-thirty?"

"Sure . . . should we have supper first or will they have food?"

"*Lots* of food . . . to go with the wine and beer."

"OK . . . but one of us has to be designated driver."

"Yeah . . . you wanna flip for it?"

"No . . . I'll drive." She sighed, wriggled her sore bottom and scratched her head. "Hey . . . what if I get someone else to drive."

"Like who?"

"Well, there's this girl in my class . . . Dylan's niece . . . and she's only nineteen . . . you think Doug and Renée would mind if we brought her along?"

"I'm sure they wouldn't . . . there's gonna be a ton of people there. But I thought you didn't like her."

"Not at first . . . but she kinda grows on you."

"Has she got a boyfriend? Make it a double date?"

"That's the thing . . . she's from Germany and doesn't know anybody, so I sorta feel sorry for her."

He laughed. "OK, Ms. Compassionate . . . but can she drive? I mean . . . if she's from Germany. . . ."

"They *do* have cars there . . . besides, I've seen her driving Dylan's convertible around."

"All righty, then . . . give her a call. I gotta run . . . busy here today."

"I'll call you later, OK?"

"You got it, boss."

"Greg!"

"Love you! Bye!"

She grunted when the phone clicked, and then grinned as she dug through a folder for the RBC phone list.

"Hello?"

"Hi, is Teresa there?"

"No . . . may I take a message?"

"Yeah, um . . . this is Lisa Carlson . . . I go to school with her."

"Oh sure . . . this is Felicia."

"Hi . . . um . . . so, would it be OK if I call her cell?"

"Certainly . . . do you want the number?"

"No, I got it . . . it's on the list."

"All right . . . her class ended at eleven so she's somewhere between here and campus . . . probably at the mall."

"OK . . . thanks."

"You're welcome . . . nice talking to you, Lisa."

"You too . . . bye."

Lisa thumbed numbers and listened to two rings.

"Hello?"

"Hi, Teresa . . . it's Lisa."

"From the college Lisa?"

"Yeah . . . that one. What's up?"

"Merely shopping . . . why?"

"You want to go to a party tonight?"

"What sort of party?"

"It's in a loft so there'll be lots of cool people. Oh . . . and you get to drive my boss's Land Rover."

"I do? Why is this?"

"Because you don't drink . . . not in public, anyway . . . right?"

Teresa sighed. "I thought America was a civilized nation, but these antiquated alcohol rules . . . *uh*!"

"I know what you mean. So you wanna go?"

"Well . . . I have told Delia and Christa that we would see a movie."

"Oh . . . yeah, um . . . ask them if they want to come too."

"All right . . . I will ask them."

"Great! I've got a class at one, but I'll call you before five with the details, OK?"

"Yes . . . that will be fine."

"See ya, Teresa."

"Goodbye, Lisa."

Teresa thumbed off her phone and carried her bags out the mall door. August heat prickled her skin while she waited beneath an awning. She recognized two other regular passengers and nodded to them. The bus arrived a minute later and she showed the driver her pass as she climbed aboard and then took a seat and settled back.

Delia and Christa started at Red Blossom College in mid-July, too late for summer session at university. When they arrived, all eight seats at RBC were filled, and Teresa almost felt sorry for Uncle Dylan as he tried to teach and manage the class. He used his leather slipper and his paddle, but some days even these were not enough to maintain order amongst his young, excitable students.

The new girls were from Frankfurt, and although older than Teresa, they looked to her for guidance. Teresa and Felicia helped the girls move into an apartment Dylan leased and furnished with essentials for his students. Two weeks later, the Swedish twins left and returned to Uppsala, where their mother had been offered a job as director of medicine at a large hospital. The farewell was tearful, despite their short acquaintance. The strict discipline that the girls endured at the college produced a reflex closeness, similar to that of soldiers in boot camp, and even Ashley and Britney acted sorry to see Birgid and Sonja go.

Uncle Dylan encouraged Teresa to help the new girls adjust to their environment, and let her drive his car to show them around. They enjoyed the rides so much that on their third outing she drove all the way to Des Moines. Her mobile phone rang while they were stuck in rush-hour traffic on the freeway loop and she knew she was in trouble even before she looked at the ID screen. But Uncle Dylan merely told her to come home as soon as she could. When they returned, two hours later, he scolded her for the empty gas tank in the Firebird, out of earshot of the Frankfurt girls and Felicia, and then took them all to dinner at a steakhouse.

The bus stopped at the corner by her apartment complex. Teresa hurried inside, yelled a hello, and dropped the bags on her bed. She grabbed the desk phone, pressed a speed-key and told Delia, in German, about the party. Delia made her wait while she relayed the message to Christa, who grabbed the phone from her cousin.

"*Yes*, we will like to go . . . and speak English or I shall tell the professor."

Teresa laughed. "You wish to put me in trouble?"

"Of course not . . . but I must practice . . . so I may flirt with American boys at this party and . . . oh! How shall we *dress*?"

"As you would for a dance club . . . but not *too* outrageously. Remember where we are, after all."

"But I shall wear the navel ring, do you think?"

"If you like . . . I only warned you that the professor should not see it. He is very unreasonable about the piercing of body parts."

"So you have said . . . and this is most odd . . . that jewelry in a lip or navel is to him barbaric, and yet he will beat his students on their bottoms. Is *that* not barbaric?"

"Yes, but he is a man . . . and men can be *so* illogical."

Christa giggled. "Is this what causes them to be so interesting? When shall we go?"

"Lisa says she will tell me before five o'clock."

"This is most exciting!"

Teresa grinned. "I will call you soon. Bye!"

Knuckles rapped and Teresa's bedroom door opened.

"Hi! How was your class?"

"It was all right . . . but Fel! I shall go to a *party* tonight . . . with some of the girls from college, and I must decide what to wear."

Felicia smiled. "Is that why Lisa called?" Teresa nodded. "What's in these bags?"

"Merely a few accessories and nightgowns . . . it is very warm at night so I bought light cotton ones."

"That's a good idea . . . so tell me about the party."

"I do not know very much . . . only that it is in a loft and cool people will be there, and Lisa's boss has said it is all right for us to go."

"He did? What did Dylan say?"

"I did not tell him yet . . . but Lisa's boss has given her his Land Rover to drive . . . surely he would not do this if it was not all right."

"You'd better ask, anyway."

Teresa sniffed. "Must I also ask *Mac* if I may go to a party?" She stomped over and opened the closet.

"Would you *please* stop doing that?"

"What? Surely *he* must give permission as well!"

Teresa whimpered when Felicia took her arm, turned her around and hugged her.

"I thought we got past all that . . . after the other night."

"Well . . . it *was* kind of Mac to take us to dinner, and I enjoyed our conversation . . . and it truly *is* all right that you are dating him . . . only. . . ."

"Only what, Teresa?"

"He is merely another man who wishes to control my life!"

"No, no, *no* . . . Mac would *never*. . . ." She lifted Teresa's chin and looked into her eyes. "This isn't *about* Mac, is it?"

The girl sighed. "What if Uncle Dylan says I cannot go?"

"Don't you think you should *ask* before you assume the worst?"

"I suppose . . . but what if he is still angry that I ran away?"

"Oh honey . . . you know better than that. He spanked you and that's the end of it . . . unless you do it again, which you won't, right?" Teresa shook her head. "So let's see what you have to wear."

"OK." Teresa took a black silk dress from the rod, stepped back and gazed at her reflection in the full-length mirror. "What about this?"

"I like it . . . but it might be too warm for a summer party."

"Perhaps." She grinned. "But if I wear nothing underneath I shall be quite comfortable."

Felicia gasped and then laughed. "I don't think *that's* a good idea. You're really excited about this, aren't you?"

"Yes. It is my first real party here . . . to meet new people and dance and have fun."

"I know . . . that faculty get-together last week hardly qualifies as a party."

Teresa rolled her eyes. "Why did Uncle Dylan make us go to that?"

"He likes to show us off."

"Do you think so?"

"Of course . . . he wanted everybody to see how spectacular we are."

"Hmph . . . I thought it was only to put me in trouble."

"Yes, well. . . ." Felicia sighed. "You didn't *have* to tell that professor of comparative religion . . . what was it you said?"

"Um . . . all deities are merely sock puppets for whomever is truly in charge."

Felicia giggled. "I thought his eyes were going to pop out."

"They already were near to doing this, because he stared at my bosom *most* intently whilst we were talking."

"I know . . . and it's a good thing Dylan saw that, too, or he would have done more than lecture you on etiquette when we got home."

Teresa scoffed. "He could not have spanked me, in any case . . . because that is a direct quotation from *him*."

"You don't believe that, though . . . do you?"

"No . . . and Uncle Dylan will be very embarrassed when God asks him about it."

Felicia laughed and reached into the closet. "How about this linen skirt with a sleeveless top and that Austrian crystal necklace?"

"Do you think Uncle Dylan will let me stay out later? This midnight curfew seems awfully early."

"If he's OK with the party, it won't hurt to ask."

Teresa picked up the phone and sighed. "I hope he is feeling reasonable today."

Chapter 11

THE PARTY

THE ASSISTANT MANAGER at Lola's Downtown boutique closed a register and handed a bank bag to her very young, very new manager.

Greg smiled. "Thanks, Barbara."

"Pretty good day, huh?"

"I'd say . . . and it's not over yet."

"Almost . . . Friday nights are usually dead. If we have five more sales before closing I'll be surprised."

"Still . . . you guys did really good. Hey, Cindy!"

He waved to a round-faced girl with short, spiky brown hair and three gold rings in her left eyebrow who leaned against the back wall. She turned to look at him.

"Huh?"

"I said . . . good job."

She rolled her eyes and muttered into a cell phone. Barbara laughed.

"Off the clock, ya know?"

"So I see. Tell her thanks for me if she ever comes up for air."

"I'll do that. So you've got big plans for tonight?"

"Kind of . . . you?"

"Just hangin' with the hubby. You want me to open in the morning?"

"Yeah, if you don't mind . . . as a backup. I'll stay 'til closing and you can go home at the usual, but I might not make it right at nine."

Barb laughed. "I understand . . . I was young once, believe it or not."

"Hey, now!" Greg scowled.

She squeezed his hand. "I'm teasing . . . have fun and don't worry about the store."

"So if I show up at noon . . . totally hungover . . . you'll be nice to me?"

"That depends . . . are you mean when you're hungover?"

"I'm not sure . . . haven't had that many hangovers."

"Then I guess we'll find out . . . Sharon was *ugly* after a night on the town."

"You can tell my boss if *I* get ugly, OK?" He grinned.

"Yeah? Which boss? Mr. Swayne . . . or Ms. Carlson?"

He folded his hands and whimpered. "Oh, *please* don't tell Ms. Carlson."

Barb smirked and glanced out the show window. "Well, speak of the devil. . . ."

Greg turned to follow her gaze. A shiny black truck full of young females blocked the alley entrance to the left of the storefront. He sighed.

"In the flesh."

"And lots *of* it . . . did you take your vitamins this morning?"

"Barbara!"

She laughed and pushed him out the door. "Don't forget to do the bank drop."

He winked at her and then strode along the sidewalk. Lisa grinned and leaned toward the curbside window.

"You want a ride, sailor?"

He tucked the cash bag under his arm. "I don't *think* so . . . you look like pirates to me."

Teresa sat in the front passenger seat. She grinned and crooked a finger. "Come with us and we will show you where the buried treasure is."

"Uh huh . . . I'll just bet. You're a gang of cutthroats and I am in mortal danger."

Delia and Christa gaped at each other, and then laughed when Greg jerked the door open and climbed into the back seat beside them. Lisa gunned the engine and sped around two corners. The truck bounced over asphalt mounds and tires screeched as she braked in front of a steel door set into a brick wall. Greg leaned out the window, opened the door with a key, and dropped the bag into a bin. Lisa did the introductions as she drove to his apartment.

ꟾ

The girls sat in the truck, the engine and air conditioner on, and chatted while Greg ran to the apartment and changed clothes. Lisa wore a blue jean miniskirt low on her hips and a bright red scoop-necked crop-top with spaghetti straps. A gold heart with a dozen tiny diamonds hung from a long gold necklace. The heart rested between cupcake breasts and accentuated her cleavage. Teresa's cream linen skirt was brightened by a rolled paisley scarf, knotted at her left hip and slanted down to the right. An emerald cotton blouse, tucked into the skirt waist, accented her green eyes. The sleeveless top was unbuttoned to her breastbone and displayed round, ivory swells, held high by a strapless black bra. A double strand of oval, half-centimeter crystals looped her neck and sparkled against the firm mounds.

Delia's short brown hair was gelled and sprayed into soft points at her forehead and behind her ears. Each ear had eight gold and silver rings in it, and a diamond sparkled in the left side of her nose. She stood two inches shorter than Teresa, and had a more *zoftig* figure. White, even teeth sparkled between full lips when she grinned. Her round, light blue eyes glowed with mischief. Christa was as tall as Teresa but thinner, and had somber gray-green eyes. Light brown hair was clamped above her temples with scarlet clips, and spilled down her neck in soft curls. Three ruby studs adorned each earlobe. Both girls wore sequined halter-tops that held but did little to conceal full breasts, sandals with round two-inch heels, and tight denim jeans. The pants were hemmed just above the ankle, the waists hugged the girls' hips at the chink bone in back, and the crotch laces were tightened to bare their glitter-dusted tummies to within an inch of their shaved mounds of Venus. Jeweled rings glimmered in their navels, a blue stone in Delia's to match her halter-top, and a red one in Christa's to match hers.

Greg sauntered across the parking lot. He wore light gray oversized cargo pants and a green cotton T-shirt that hung halfway down his thighs. Teresa jumped out and climbed into the back seat. Greg smiled and shut her door before he got in the front beside Lisa, then leaned over and kissed her lips.

"Nice um . . . outfit." He stared straight at her bosom, turned, and arched his eyebrows at the girls in the back seat.

"Glad you like it . . . now put your eyeballs back in your head and tell me where we're going."

"Um, sure . . . the breast way . . . I mean the *best* way would be to. . . ."

"Hey!" Lisa giggled and slapped his arm. "Be serious . . . at least until we get there."

"All right . . . go north on Elm."

"Which way is that?"

"Left at the light . . . first star on your right . . . then straight on 'til dawn."

He grinned when she scowled at him.

"Do you want to drive, mister?"

"Why? You're doing fine . . . just keep repeating . . . it's only a movie . . . it's only a movie."

"What is *with* you?"

"Well . . . let's see . . . I'm off work . . . I'm going to a party with my gorgeous, half-naked girlfriend in her ridiculously luxurious SUV. . . ."

"Greg. . . ."

"With three of her half-naked buddies. . . ."

"Greg!"

"All wearing perfume that would turn Jack Nicholson into a slobbering love-slave. . . ."

"*Greg!*"

"Hm?"

"Are you gonna be like this all *night*?"

"What's wrong with being a little jazzed?"

Lisa glanced in the mirror at the smirks on her friends' faces. "OK, but could you try not to be quite so *weird* about it?"

"Weird?" He folded his arms and huffed. "I'm not weird . . . I'm

. . . colorful . . . and witty . . . and, um . . . erudite."

"Erudite, huh? Well, just be careful you don't *erudite* my friends straight back to Germany."

Teresa laughed and leaned forward. "I would never run away. I have met American men in the chat rooms, and none of them are as funny as you."

"Thank you, Teresa." He sneered at Lisa. "See?"

"She meant funny *looking*." Lisa stuck out her tongue and then grinned.

"*No*, I did not mean . . . !"

He pressed a finger to his lips and winked at Teresa. "Pay no attention . . . all the blood rushes to her foot and starves her brain when she drives."

Lisa stomped the accelerator and zipped through a yellow signal. Greg gasped as Teresa jerked backward.

"Yes, I see this!" Teresa snugged her lap belt tighter and Lisa laughed.

"Yeah, well . . . you'd know about blood rushing out of your brain, Mr. Bentley." She glanced at him and her eyelid twitched. "Or is it Mr. Nicholson . . . slobbering love-slave?"

He turned, wrinkled his forehead and let his eyelids droop. "How do I write women?" His voice rasped and curled in his throat. "I think of a man . . . then I take away reason . . . and accountability."

The cousins stared at each other. Lisa giggled. Teresa pounded her temple with a fingertip and squeezed her eyes shut.

"Oh! I know . . . *As Well As It Is?*"

Greg laughed and twisted around to shake her hand. "*As Good As It Gets* . . . I sound just like him, don't I?"

Lisa scoffed. "Not at *all* like Cagney."

Teresa gaped. "But he was pretending to be. . . ."

"She knows . . . she just wants the last line." He glanced forward and patted Lisa's thigh. "Next left . . . where that blue van's turning."

Land Rover tires clicked over cracked asphalt with no curbs, past rows of grimy buildings with plywooded windows. Three blocks into the decrepit neighborhood a high arch spanned a T intersection.

Eight-inch I-beams rose six feet above concrete caissons buried flush with the grade to support a curved latticework of plowshares, harrow disks, saw blades, pipe wrenches, re-bar, stove bolts, and other junk, all rusted, all arc-welded for eternity, or until oxidation reduced them to dust. Beyond the arch there were broad sidewalks alongside smooth tarmac. Late summer sun glowed on blue, green, and yellow walls, once four blocks of warehouses and mills, now apartments, shops, and workrooms. Sodium vapor lamps hung over the street from fluted poles of green-painted iron. Layers of band posters, ads, and lost and found notices were taped six feet up their sides. Cars parked, bumper to bumper, along the curbs. Lisa swung the truck left.

"We'll pay for parking, OK?"

Greg nodded. "Friday night . . . let's hope the lot isn't full."

"Lisa?" Delia leaned forward. "What *is* this place?"

"Teresa didn't show you North End?"

"I did not know it is *here*."

"They've really fixed it up in the past few years and I've only been here a couple of times myself."

She waited at a crosswalk while a gaggle of teenagers ambled toward a computer game shop on the corner opposite the parking garage. Greg twisted around and smiled at Teresa.

"Your uncle never showed it to you . . . but I bet he comes here. There's a basement bar on the other side of the complex where you can get about sixty different kinds of scotch . . . if you can afford eight or ten bucks a shot."

"And how do you know this would impress my uncle?"

"A little bird told me." He smiled and Teresa scowled.

"Lisa!"

"Shut *up*." She yanked the wheel left and stopped beside the ticket kiosk. The window hummed as it lowered and Lisa grabbed a paper slip. "If Uncle Dylan's a friend of Michael's, it pretty much goes without saying that they like the same kind of whisky. I mean . . . that thing with the Guinness and champagne? It's obvious."

"*What* thing with Guinness and champagne?"

Lisa nudged between two other SUVs and shut off the engine, then turned and grinned. "You don't *know* about Guinness and champagne?"

"OK . . . last stop . . . everybody off . . . watch your step!" Greg squeezed out and opened the back door for Teresa. "*Gefährlich, meine Fräulein!*"

Teresa giggled and smoothed her skirt as she sidestepped away from him. "*What* is dangerous, Greg?"

He grinned and followed her. "Scraping somebody's Mercedes with a Land Rover door . . . but I'm tickled to death you understood me. I nearly flunked German in high school."

She coughed to cover a chuckle. "Well yes . . . I can see why."

"Huh?"

"You would never call a friend *Fräulein* . . . a waitress, perhaps, or a shop assistant."

"Oh *man*." He pouted. "What about the accent? Authentic?"

She smiled. "Yes . . . very authentic."

"All righty, then!"

"You sound exactly like an American who nearly flunked German in high school."

"Oh, *geeze* . . . Lisa!"

"What?"

She thumbed the key holder to secure the locks and then followed the Frankfurt girls to the back of the truck.

"Teresa's picking on me 'cause I can't speak German."

"Sometimes I'm not sure *what* language you speak." She grabbed his arm and they headed toward the street.

"So . . . tell me about this Guinness and champagne, Lisa."

They hustled through the crosswalk and into an alley between the computer shop and an aromatherapy boutique.

"I shouldn't, Teresa . . . it's probably not even true. Just a Paul Bunyan story."

Delia wrinkled her nose. "Paul who?"

Teresa nodded. "This is the American tall tale . . . like the Siegfried legends."

Lisa smiled. "Yeah . . . probably just a legend."

"Apocryphal." The girls frowned at Greg. "That's a story that didn't really happen but might have, given the characters."

"See? You don't even speak *English*." Lisa hugged his arm. "So try to concentrate, OK?"

Greg sighed and they ambled through the alleyway, across another street, and then into a maze of potted trees and herb gardens hidden among four-story walls.

"Here we are."

He led them past a half dozen people with lighted cigarettes, through an open doorway and up four flights of wooden stairs. Doors painted in primary colors, some with printed placards, some with hand-drawn logos, lined the hallways at each landing and Teresa pointed.

"Are those apartments?"

"Workrooms . . . or that's all they're supposed to be." Greg waved a hand. "They've got toilets but no kitchens. Doug and Renée have the only residence lease."

Lisa frowned. "How'd they manage that?"

"Renée's family owned this whole block and when they sold it to the city, that was part of the deal for this building."

Delia puffed and tugged up her jeans as they reached the fourth floor. "Why will they do this? Are they such private persons?"

"No, but Doug makes a lot of noise with his metal work, and this way he can go all night if he wants and not worry about bothering the neighbors."

Hard, quick bass and drum throbbed in their soles as they walked forty feet to a half-open door. He grinned at the round face that peered at him, and held out his arms as a tall woman with a loose black ponytail reached out to drag him inside.

"Hi, Renée."

"Hi, yourself!" She looked over his shoulder while she hugged him and beckoned the girls with an empty wine glass. "That's quite a harem you got there, Slim. Come in . . . come in."

Greg stepped back as the girls shuffled through the doorway. "This is Renée . . . this is Lisa and. . . ."

"Oh, God! Lisa!" The woman laughed and threw her arms

around the girl. "I am *so* happy to meet you . . . I was beginning to think you were a figment of his imagination."

He grabbed Lisa's hand and yanked her away. "She is . . . *these* are my real girlfriends . . . all Valkyries from the Fatherland. Teresa . . . Delia . . . and Christa."

Renée chuckled as she hugged them in turn. She cupped Christa's chin and shook her head.

"How did such nice girls get mixed up with a nutcase like Greg, hmm?"

"Um . . . he said there will be a party?"

The woman's eyes widened. "Oh my God . . . you really *are* a Valkyrie. Yes, yes, *yes* . . . there's wine and beer over there." She slung a dolman-sleeved arm to her right. "And food over there." She pointed her empty wine glass left, and then glared at Greg. "And *you*, mister. . . ."

"*What?*"

"Go tell Doug you're here while I talk to your girlfriend." Renée pressed a white envelope into his hand and reached for Lisa, but Greg pulled her away.

"No *way* . . . you are a terrible gossip and will fill her innocent ears with lies and calumny."

Renée cackled. "I'll *find* you, my pretty!" Her empire-waist skirt swirled like a cape as she turned and floated around the corner.

Lisa gaped. "Greg?"

"You can talk to her later . . . but if you think *I'm* weird. . . ." He turned his head and his eye flinched. "Come along, Valkyries . . . *Bier be warten.*"

Teresa laughed and pushed the cousins ahead as they followed Greg to a long table. Six empty wine bottles and a dozen beer cans and bottles stood in rows on its near end. Behind the table were galvanized tubs full of ice, bottles, and cans, backed by stacks of cartons. Printed signs hung from the table and the cartons. They read, "Drink responsibly" . . . "Name your cup" . . . "Never drink and drive" . . . "In vino veritas." Greg held up a finger and one of the two middle-aged women behind the table glanced at him as she drained a Chablis bottle into a plastic cup and handed it to a young man. He dropped two quarters into a thick glass schooner and turned away.

"Hi! Could I see some ID?" Greg opened his wallet and smiled as the woman smirked. "And your entourage?"

"Hm? Oh . . . yeah . . . um. . . ." He looked at Lisa and she frowned as she dug in her purse. "This one's legal . . . the one with green eyes is our designated driver . . . and, um. . . ."

He raised his palms toward the Frankfurt cousins. They grinned and flicked folders from beaded pouches strung over their shoulders. The woman frowned and turned.

"Stella? Are these OK?"

The other woman set two bottles on the table, peered, and shrugged.

"Passports? Sure, Thelma. Just make sure they've got the embossed seal." She looked at the girls. "Long as they're not driving."

Christa shook her head. "No, ma'am . . . we shall not drink and drive."

Stella laughed and reached out to squeeze the girl's arm. "Just checking, sugar. What can I get you?"

"Two of the Burgundy with ice and 7 UP, please."

"You bet . . . what about you?"

Greg looked at Teresa. "What'll it be, Ms. Designated Driver?"

"Um . . . Diet Coke, please."

He nodded. "And two flagons of your finest ale for myself and my lady fair."

Lisa slapped his arm. "Two Miller Lites, please."

"But they've got Harp."

"Yeah, and the last time you drank British beer you passed out."

"Harp's not British . . . it's Irish."

"And you're American . . . so live with it."

He sighed as Thelma chuckled and poured cold, watery beer into cups.

"She's right, sugar . . . that foreign stuff will knock you right on your kiester. You don't want to peak too soon."

"Uh huh." Greg dropped two folded dollars into the schooner.

"Keep that Harp on ice for me, OK?"

The woman grimaced. "Iced Harp? You *are* American, aren't you?"

"Hey, now." He grinned and wrote on his cup with a black marker while Stella ink-stamped their hands with a green mandala, except for Teresa who got a red smiley face.

Christa took the fat pen from him. "This is what means name your cup?"

"Sure . . . so you don't drink somebody's grape Nee-Hi thinking it's your burgundy. I named mine Sir Lancelot."

Lisa sighed and dragged him from the table. "Why didn't you name it *Greg*?"

"What if some *other* Greg has Harp and I drink it by accident? Then I'd be in *big* trouble."

The German girls giggled and followed them toward the music. The loft formed a shallow U, a hundred and fifty feet at its base and eighty feet along each leg. The roof sloped from twelve feet on the outside to twenty feet at the inner walls. White vinyl sheets draped the windows along the legs of the U to block the sun from east and west, and two fans with three-foot vanes, set into the ceiling, pulled air outside and created a pleasant draft. Small metal sculptures sat on plywood cubes by the inside wall, and clothes hung from forms of twisted wire. Lisa caressed a skirt with an asymmetric hem and a free-form batik design.

"Nice. Renée makes these?"

"Yep. Don't you think we ought to at least consider . . . ?"

"Hey! You kids get away from there!"

Greg turned, grinned and then held tight to his cup while huge arms surrounded him. "Hi, Doug . . . watch the brew."

"I'm watching out for the inventory so keep your sticky fingers off it. How you doing, Slim?"

"Not bad, Ace . . . this is Lisa and . . . hey! Put her down before you break something, ya moose!"

Lisa giggled and her sandals scraped hardwood as the man relaxed his bear hug and set her on the floor. He wore denim bib overalls without a shirt, stood six and a half feet tall, and had wide, pink shoulders, a hard, beach-ball stomach, a pleasant, sunburned face, and a broad, white grin.

"Hi, Lisa."

"Hi, Doug. Nice to meet you . . . finally."

"You too . . . you like Renny's clothes?"

"Uh huh. You should talk to Greg about selling them at Lola's."

"Yeah, I heard he got a job . . . finally." Doug winked. "You think he has any pull at those fancy shops?"

"I'd say probably." She winked back and introduced the other girls.

Teresa shook his hand. "Did you make the huge sculpture . . . the arch on the street? It is similar to these small ones."

"Sure did . . . both of them."

"Both?"

"Yeah . . . which way did you come in?"

Greg lifted his cup toward his right shoulder. "The back way."

"Took the scenic route, huh? That's the practice model." Doug jerked his head. "The big one is at the Anderson Parkway entrance."

"That's just for tourists." Greg smirked.

"Yeah, like *Lola's* doesn't make a buck or two off tourists." The man laughed when Greg snarled. "Anyway . . . took me three months to collect all that junk and another two to weld it together, but it paid the rent for a couple of years." He shook his head. "You guys don't want to talk business . . . go on back. The DJ's here and he'll be pissed if nobody dances."

"We're on it, Ace."

Doug stomped toward the door and Greg led the troupe around the corner. Light bars and fat, black speakers ranged along three sides of a forty-foot space. A platform sat against the far wall, loaded with turntables, mixing boards, and amplifiers. A man with spiked, violet hair and a sleeveless blue satin jacket adjusted a rheostat and bounced to the hard rhythm that throbbed from the speakers. Two couples in front of the platform gyrated to the techno mix while a dozen people stood amongst a sundry collection of tables and chairs at the dance floor's edge. Conversation was minimal and shouted.

"What's the envelope for?"

"*What?*"

"The envelope . . . Renée gave you." Lisa pointed to his pocket.

"Oh! Contributions!" He pulled it out and glanced at the back. "Ten bucks each!"

"I don't have that much cash!"

"We'll send them a check! I gotta go to the john!"

"OK!"

Teresa followed him when Delia and Christa dragged Lisa out to dance. Her ears rang as the music faded.

"So . . . Doug and Renée *live* in this place?"

"Sure . . . the kitchen and stuff is on the other side. Oh . . . and be sure to use the bathroom at the far end. The men's room just has this big drain basin full of ice in the floor."

"How strange. So the men merely gather around this and. . . ."

He chuckled. "Yep. They only use it for parties . . . they say."

"But why is there ice?"

"Knocks out the odor . . . *wow* . . . look at all the food. Let's grab some plates on the way back, OK?"

"Yes, it looks very good."

The men's room was a wallboard and two-by-four cubicle set in the corner, with a weathered wood door on swing hinges. Teresa smirked as Greg sauntered inside. She walked by the kitchen, an airy space between two freestanding ten-foot walls, and then past a huge four-poster bed, separated from the rest of the loft by a border of shiny armoires, tall bureaus, and long credenzas. A tile mosaic of white geese on a green pond flanked both sides of the bathroom door, and a sign above read Squatters Only in soldered brass calligraphy. She twisted the knob, found it locked, and stepped back.

"Just a sec!"

"OK . . . there is no hurry."

A toilet flushed and water ran in a basin, then the door swung wide.

"Oh, hi! Um . . . Teresa, right?"

"Yes. Hello, Renée."

"There's somebody I want you to meet. He just got here. I gotta check on the food so you find me, OK?"

Teresa nodded. Five minutes later she looked into the kitchen. A round woman in a white frock and chef's bonnet stirred a five-gallon cauldron on the stovetop. Hot beef, onion, and spice scents filled the air. Renée leaned against the double sink while she talked to a tall man with brown, curly hair clipped short over the ears. He wore dark trousers, loose in the leg but snug at his trim waist, and a billowy peasant shirt in the same dark shade, tucked in. Renée saw her and waved. The man turned and Teresa stifled a gasp when he smiled. He had sapphire eyes, a high forehead, a nose that crooked a bit to the left, and full, moist lips. Renée pointed with her wine glass.

"This is Pieter . . . Teresa, Pieter . . . Pieter, Teresa."

"How do you do?" He bowed and kissed when Teresa held out a hand.

Renée laughed. "I *love* Europeans . . . see you later!"

The woman strode off and Teresa yanked back her hand.

"Oh my *God*."

He scowled. "I did not mean offense . . . only she expects it."

"What?" Teresa looked at her hand. "Oh! No, that is not . . . I must apologize as well. It is merely . . . um. . . ."

"Shall we begin over? My name is Pieter . . . I am from Ljubljana." He bent his neck.

She smiled. "I am Teresa . . . from Hamburg."

"I am happy to meet you, Teresa from Hamburg. Will you like a drink?"

"Yes, thank you. But what is that wonderful aroma?" She looked at the woman in white.

"Swedish meatballs . . . my great-grandma's recipe. They'll be done in a few minutes."

The woman grinned, dipped a tablespoon into the vat, and held it over an open palm. Teresa smiled, blew on the spoon, and sipped. Warm cream, pepper, and nutmeg bathed her tongue and she nodded. Pieter opened his mouth and slurped the rest.

"Mmm . . . truly the nectar of the gods, Sophia."

She dropped the spoon on the counter, grinned, and wiped her hands. "Thanks . . . now get out of here . . . and don't fill up on chips and hot wings or you'll be sorry."

Pieter nodded, winked, and crooked his elbow. Teresa took his arm and they walked toward the bar as she stared at him. He cleared his throat.

"You, uh . . . have we perhaps . . . met . . . before?"

Teresa shook her head and smiled. "I *do* apologize . . . but you look exactly like someone I know."

"Ah! One is always thinking he has the face that is . . . unique . . . but this cannot be true, can it? In so wide a world?"

"I think not." She stared at him. "You were born in Slovenia?"

"No . . . my family were exiled in Italy for many years, but we returned to Ljubljana just before Independence." He picked up a wine bottle and showed it to her. "Is this good, do you think?"

"I am not sure . . . but the California chardonnays seldom disappoint."

"Then we shall have some?"

"No, I . . . I am drinking only soda this evening . . . but you should try it."

"All right." He turned and arched his eyebrows at Thelma.

The woman glanced at the bottle and nodded. "Could I see some ID?"

"Yes, of course." He showed her his passport, then returned it to his breast pocket.

She looked at Teresa. "You want another Diet Coke, sugar?"

"Yes, please." Teresa turned to Pieter. "You have been long in the States?"

"Not so long . . . a month perhaps. My father is agricultural liaison in the city and my cousin lives there also. He was born in this town and knows many people."

"Such as Doug and Renée?"

"Yes . . . they are friends from university." He scowled and then smiled when Thelma stamped his hand. "But you must be here many years to have such a strong American accent."

Thelma set the drinks down. Teresa thanked her and giggled.

"Now you are teasing me."

"Not at all. You sound like the American girls I meet in the city."

Teresa smirked. "If you say . . . oh. Wait." She dug a dollar from her purse and dropped it into the glass. He nodded.

"Thank you . . . I did not know this was customary."

"My American friends did so . . . will you like to meet them?"

"Yes . . . very much."

He took both drinks and again offered his arm. Music pounded louder as they neared the tables. Two plates smeared with hot-wing sauce sat amidst a collection of cups. Greg scowled.

"Hey! Where'd you disappear to? You were supposed to help me feed this crew!"

"Sorry! Greg, this is Pieter! He is from Slovenia!"

"Where?" He grinned and shook Pieter's hand.

"It is northeast of Italy!"

"Oh! Glad to meet you!" He reached out and Lisa turned when he patted her arm. "This is Pieter! Teresa's friend!"

Lisa nodded and then her mouth dropped open. "Oh my *God*." She blinked and took his hand while she stared at Teresa. "Don't you see it?"

Teresa laughed. "Of *course* I see it! Is it not strange?"

Greg pulled Lisa to his side. "*What's* strange? What are you guys talking about?"

Lisa raised her chin but didn't take her eyes off Pieter. "That's *Dylan* . . . Professor Travis . . . except . . . oh, geeze, the girls have *got* to see this."

She wriggled from Greg's grasp and he stared after her as she gyrated through the crowd on the dance floor. Greg puffed his cheeks and turned to Pieter.

"Slovenia, huh?"

Pieter nodded. "You are American?"

Greg blinked and then laughed. "Yeah!"

"Your girlfriend is very pretty!"

"Thanks!"

"May I join your party?"

"I think you already did!" He smiled at Teresa and then yelped when Lisa rammed into him as she tugged the sweaty cousins to the table.

Delia puffed and Christa panted while they guzzled their drinks.

Teresa waited while the girls' eyes focused. They gaped at each other, then squealed.

"Teresa! He is the. . . .!"

"*Where* did you . . . ?"

Pieter laughed and put an arm around Teresa's shoulders. "*Enough* of this joke! Renée says I will meet fun girls here but she does not say the fun shall be on *me!*"

"No, no, *no!*"

Teresa grabbed Pieter's hand and pulled him around the corner. The others followed them to the bar. Two church pews faced each other next to the beer and wine cartons, and Teresa sat down. Lisa and Greg sat across from her and the giggly cousins plopped next to them. Pieter stood and sipped wine, his eyes watchful.

"So . . . this is the next part of the joke?"

Greg leaned forward. "Pieter . . . I've known Lisa a long time and I don't think she's *capable* of a joke like this, and besides. . . ."

"What do you *mean*, not capable? Are you saying I . . . ?"

"Hey, hey, *hey*." He cupped her chin and kissed her lips, then turned to Pieter. "I don't even *know* this guy they say you look like, but I know genuine amazement when I see it, and I guarantee I just saw it."

Delia rubbed her eyes, stood and walked over to Pieter. "You have a Hungarian accent, no?"

He shrugged. "Partly, perhaps. And yours is German . . . Frankfurt, no?"

She giggled and sipped from her cup. "Frankfurt, yes. *Sprechen sie Deutsch?*"

"*Ja . . . und Italienisch und Ungarisch* . . . do you speak Slavic?"

"Um . . . no."

"Then please to tell me . . . in English . . . whom do I resemble?"

"Herr Professor Travis. It is *most* obvious."

The girl stomped back to her seat. Lisa moaned.

"Geeze Louise . . . he even *talks* like the professor . . . except for the accent."

Greg pursed his lips. "Yeah . . . I caught the *whom*." He looked at Teresa. "So *tell* him already!"

"OK! Pieter?" She grabbed his hand and he sat beside her. "You look *exactly* like my uncle . . . an American professor at university. We all . . . the girls. . . ." She glanced around. "We attend his class."

The man nodded and drained his wine. "Then . . . you are not, uh . . . having me on?"

Teresa chuckled. "No . . . but I thought perhaps Uncle Dylan was having *me* on . . . and put on a disguise as his own son."

"His son looks like me?"

"No . . . he *has* no son."

Greg chuckled. "That we know of."

"Knock it off and get me a beer." Lisa thrust her cup at Greg and then turned to Pieter. "You could *be* Dylan . . . thirty years ago. I've seen pictures."

"As Teresa has said . . . this is *most* strange . . . but it may explain why I do not resemble my father."

Christa gasped. "You do not?"

"Everyone says I look like Uncle Vladimir . . . my mother's brother." He winked. "Except for the eye patch and the missing front teeth." Pieter smirked and Greg laughed.

"You want another drink, buddy . . . before you pull our legs anymore?"

Pieter looked at Teresa. "Is the pulling of the leg the same in American as in British?" She nodded. "Then I think I *have* joined with your party." He handed Greg his cup. "Thank you, yes . . . the California chardonnay." Teresa smiled when he turned to her. "And then perhaps we shall dance?"

"That is what we are here for." Teresa kissed his cheek and then blushed when Lisa, Delia, and Christa applauded.

A man in his mid-twenties ambled over and put a hand on Pieter's shoulder. His eyebrow and upper lip sparkled with jewels. "I should have known you'd round up the prettiest girls at the party, bro."

"In truth, they have rounded *me* up." He smiled at Teresa. "This is my cousin Mario."

"Hi! I am Teresa. That is Lisa, Christa, and Delia . . . and that is Greg . . . the tall one by the bar."

"Glad to meet you." Mario grinned and held out a hand when Delia squirmed forward. "You wanna dance?"

"That is what I am here for!" She grabbed his hand, dragged him around the corner, and the others followed.

Music cascaded, pounded, and throbbed while they danced. Plates and cups filled, emptied, disappeared, and then reappeared full. Sweat poured, chilled, evaporated, and Teresa panted as Pieter sat in a chair and she fell onto his lap. Hard-muscled thighs tingled her bottom and she wrapped her arms around his damp neck.

"I must have fresh air!"

"Yes!"

They tromped down the stairs, out the door past a cloud of tobacco smoke and into the urban garden. The fresh air shuddered with drum and bass from the loft above as they wandered a hundred feet and found a bench surrounded by thick mulberries, their roots buried deep beneath brick pavement. Teresa sat, yanked the young man beside her, and tilted her chin. His lips covered hers in a long, sweet, nutmeg-tinged kiss. She caressed the back of his head and his hand stroked her spine, her hip, and then her bottom.

"Oooh . . . Pieter . . . I feel so. . . ." She pushed into his embrace.

"Yes . . . also myself, Teresa. There are no words in any language . . . for how we are feeling." He kissed her again and their tongues played for a long, sultry minute. "But I must tell you. . . ."

She smiled, blinked and focused on his eyes. Wine had melted hard sapphire to watery blue and Teresa giggled.

"What must you tell me, Pieter?"

"Only that I adore your lips . . . and the way you dance . . . and your beautiful eyes . . . and. . . ."

Teresa laughed and pressed a hand to his mouth. "Pieter! You do not need to hand me a *line* . . . I think you are wonderful, as well . . . so just kiss me."

He scowled and squeezed her bottom. "When I am *ready* to do so . . . and do not interrupt me or I will slap your arse."

Hot spasms rocked her breast as he hugged her, and meaningless refusals graveled her throat. "You . . . you *cannot* . . . please?"

She squealed, soft and low, as he pulled up her skirt and caressed the boy-leg briefs that hugged her round behind.

"Yes, Teresa . . . I *will* slap your bottom . . . that is the American word? Bottom? I like this word . . . it is round and soft . . . like the thing itself. And if you behave badly I will slap your bottom."

"But . . . that would be horrible."

Her arms trembled and tightened around his neck. Pieter raised his hand and swatted the deep cleft. She whined and nuzzled his ear while he clapped the lacy mounds a half dozen times, then he smiled as he lifted her chin with his palm and his eyes bored into hers.

"I will not use a *line*, Teresa . . . I merely wish to say that you are the most beautiful girl I have met in this country . . . and you have a most agreeable softness in the behind." His hand drifted down, swatted again and Teresa squeaked. "And most sensitive, as well . . . so please to be still whilst I soothe this pain I have put in your bottom . . . yes?"

"No, *please?*"

She held him close as his hand slipped inside damp lace to caress bare, electrified cheeks.

—⁓—

Greg collapsed into a chair and wiped sweat from his face with a paper napkin. He glanced at his watch and sighed as Lisa plunked onto his lap.

"Hey! It's twelve-fifteen!"

"*So?*"

"Don't give me *so!* You guys have a curfew!"

Lisa leaned back, swiped perspiration from her brow, and screamed. The scream melded in harmony with the music and she grinned as she kissed him.

"You're a pain in the ass!"

"Nice of you to notice!" He squeezed her cheeks. "Where's Teresa?"

She pushed his hand away. "None of your business!"

"What?"

He whacked the seat of her skirt. Lisa screeched and wriggled to her feet.

"I don't *know*, OK? She left about an hour ago! With whatzis-name!"

"That's better!" Greg stood and led her around the corner. "I'll look for Teresa and you go find Christa and Delia, OK?"

Lisa pouted. "But the party just *started*. Don't you wanna stay and dance?"

"You are *so* loaded." He gazed into bleary eyes. "We have to go home *now* . . . or Michael's gonna be mad . . . and Dylan's gonna be mad . . . and *you're* gonna be mad when I spank your bare heinie all the way down the stairs."

"For Christ's sakes, would you lower your voice?"

He grinned and hugged her close. "Time to go, Lisa."

"*God*, you're nasty!"

"What?"

She pouted up at him. "OK! I'll get the girls."

"All righty, then." He kissed her and walked toward the bar.

Damp clothes and sweaty flesh rubbed her as she staggered through the dance floor crowd. She found Delia, tight in Mario's arms.

"We gotta go!"

"No!"

"Yes! *Now*!"

Mario hugged Delia tighter, pressed a card into her hand and kissed her lips. "Call me!"

The girl screeched as Lisa dragged her away and they bounced among hot bodies, grabbed Christa from a red-faced youth with pur-ple hair, and then plunged off the dance floor. Greg smiled as he pushed all three to the pews and made them sit.

"I can't find Teresa . . . do you have her cell number, Lisa?"

"Um . . . yeah . . . at home."

"I have it!"

Christa giggled and grappled with the beaded pouch. Delia caught the tiny phone as it tumbled out. She blinked at the keypad, then thumbed a number and pressed it to her ear. Greg flipped it out of her hand and listened to two rings.

"Hello?"

"Hi, it's Greg. Time to go. Where are you?"

"Greg?"

"Yeah . . . as in Lisa and Greg . . . and Delia and Christa . . . and we gotta go home. So where *are* you?"

"Geeze, Greg . . . you are sounding so forceful."

"Quit giggling and . . . are you drunk?"

Teresa laughed. "No . . . but you are! I am outside with Pieter. Shall I come and get you or shall you come down? We must go home, you know . . . it is late!"

"I oughta blister your . . . we'll come down." He thumbed off the phone and then grinned at the three girls who stared at him. "She's right outside . . . let's go. Oh . . . um . . . thanks."

Christa giggled and took the phone. "You will blister her *what?*" She grinned at Lisa. "Do you *allow* him to blister the behinds of other girls?"

Greg scowled and Lisa laughed as he grabbed sweaty arms and bundled the girls to the door. He looked around and waved. Renée glided alongside, her empty wine glass still in hand.

"Glad you guys could come . . . and Lisa gave me her number so I can dish all the dirt on you."

"You're an evil woman and I love you." Greg kissed her cheek. "But she'd never believe a word of it. Thanks for a great party."

Renée laughed, kissed his lips, and turned away. "Come back when you can stay longer!"

Rough-cut pine three-by-tens trembled as the troupe clambered down the stairs.

"Is there not a lift in this place?"

"Sure there is, Christa . . . but it's only for freight. You're not freight are you?"

"No . . . but you are having a very bad attitude when you are drunken!"

"Yeah?" He opened the door and bowed. "My most abject apologies, Christa . . . we'll leave you here and send Herr Professor Travis to pick you up so you don't have to deal with my bad attitude."

The girl stuck out her tongue and staggered outside. Delia and Lisa laughed as they held onto her arms. She shook them off, ran back to Greg and threw her arms around his neck.

"Whoa! Christa! It's OK . . . I was kidding."

"I know . . . and I love you, Greg."

She sobbed into his chest and Lisa pulled her away.

"Geeze, how much wine did you *have*? Let's find our ride, OK?"

"Yes. We must go to the apartment or Ms. Scott will yell at us."

Greg puffed a breath as Teresa and Pieter sauntered over.

"Hey, guys. Time to call it a night, huh?"

The Slovenian smiled, hugged Teresa's shoulder, and nodded. "For you perhaps . . . but we are not ready to leave. You must get the taxi and I will pay for this. You will see to the girls, Greg? That they shall be safe?" He dug a wad of bills from his pocket and peeled off three twenties. "This will pay for the taxi, I think."

Teresa's heart thumped. "*No*, Pieter . . . I must drive . . . we have agreed."

He bent to kiss her cheek. "But it is early and you need not go home, simply to satisfy this uncle which face you see in me. How will he know, in any case? We shall eat more of these Swedish meatballs, yes? They are most delicious."

"But I promised I would take them. . . ."

Pieter scoffed and yanked her toward the door. Greg's arm flickered and he snatched the man's finger. Pieter quivered and his arm burned as he dropped to his knees. Greg leaned over and pushed.

"Don't mess with my friends, buddy. We're going home . . . and you need to do the same . . . before I mess with *you*."

Lisa grabbed Teresa's arm while Greg clutched Pieter's hand, and the girls hustled into the alleyway. They panted as they reached the streetlights and turned.

"Oh, God!"

"Oh, Teresa!" Christa wept and threw her arms around the girl.

Delia patted their shoulders. "He only *looked* like Herr Uncle . . . but the professor would never. . . ."

"There's Greg . . . let's go."

He panted and wiped his lips as he led the girls over the crosswalk and into the alley on the next block.

"You OK?" Lisa squeezed his arm.

"Yeah . . . just adrenaline, ya know?"

"Greg?"

"Huh?" He turned, slowed his pace and took Teresa's hand.

"Thank you."

He puffed air and leaned against a wall. "It's OK . . . gotta keep track of my designated driver, right?"

She smiled and kissed his cheek. "Perhaps you *are* Sir Lancelot."

"Yeah well. . . ." He winked at Lisa. "A knight's gotta do what a knight's gotta do."

"Uh huh." Lisa looked around. "Just remember *whose* knight you are, OK?"

Christa laughed. "He is *yours* . . . we know this."

Delia sighed and nodded. "Yes . . . but we like it that he is here . . . when we need such. Did you break Pieter's arm when you . . . ?"

"Let's *go*, girls . . . or the real Uncle Dylan is gonna break some fannies."

Heels clattered cobblestone and they neared the end of the alley. The parking lot sign glowed across the street. Lisa gasped and twisted around.

"Greg!"

He turned, grabbed a shirt, dropped, and rolled down the concrete apron while he wrestled. His opponent outweighed him by twenty pounds but gave ground like an amateur and Greg pressed for the pin. A siren squawked and lights strobed. Greg yanked free and leapt to his feet. The squad car angled in and two cops jumped out, side-handled truncheons snug against forearms. Pieter got up and backed away, his hands in the air. One of the cops flanked the two boys while the other walked straight at them.

"Lean on the window and spread 'em!"

Greg turned, slapped his palms on the cool glass above his head and stretched his legs apart. He glanced to his right and hissed through his teeth.

"Hey! Push your feet apart!"

Pieter nodded and complied. The officers looked at each other and shook their heads. The taller one sauntered to the car and sat in the driver's seat. The other walked over, frisked the men and then pressed the truncheon's tip to Greg's back.

"So . . . you guys all done? It's over?"

Greg nodded.

Lisa whimpered. "Don't *hurt* him! Please?"

The officer stepped back, hand on her pistol butt, and peered into the shadows. "Come out where I can see you."

The girls tottered into the light. Lisa and Teresa stared at the pavement. Christa and Delia hugged each other.

Teresa coughed. "Hello, Kate."

"Jesus H. Christ on a Harley . . . Teresa?"

"Yes, ma'am."

Kate laughed. "Are you with these two?" Teresa nodded. "OK . . . hey! You guys look at me." The young men turned. "No more bullshit, right?"

"No."

"No, madam."

"You . . . balloon-pants . . . don't *ever* call me . . . oh for . . . *Teresa?*" Kate rubbed her forehead.

"Yes?"

"Get your ass over here." She glanced at her partner in the vehicle and wrapped an arm around Teresa's shoulder. "Is that Dylan's *son?*"

"I do not think so . . . but there *is* a resemblance, no?"

"Christ almighty, *yes* . . . so what was the fight about?"

"Um . . . he is not so much like Uncle Dylan as he appears. He attacked Greg from behind because he did not want me to go home. Uncle Dylan would *never* do this."

The cop in the car looked up when Kate laughed, long and hard. "No, honey . . . Dylan would never attack a *man* from behind."

Teresa scoffed and pouted. "I know what you are saying . . . and he never would attack a *girl* from behind . . . unless she deserves such."

"Oh, *brother.*" Kate chuckled and squeezed Teresa's arm. "So . . . where did you find this almost Dylan?"

"At a party. He is from Slovenia."

"Yeah? So you guys are headed home?" Teresa nodded hard and

Kate glanced at the other faces. "You haven't been drinking, have you?"

"No, not at all!"

"Then you're the only one in the bunch."

"I am the designated driver."

"OK. I need everybody's name, then you can split."

"All right . . . thank you, Kate. But will you hurry? It is almost one o'clock."

Kate jotted in her notebook. "That's your bedtime, huh?"

"Yes . . . Uncle Dylan extended the curfew . . . but I am afraid we will not be on time in any case."

"Nope . . . doesn't look like it. Who's we?"

"Only the girls . . . Delia and Christa are new, but I think you know Lisa."

"Yeah, I remember." She looked at them and then at Pieter. "What about Mr. Slovenia here?"

"He . . . he was just leaving, I think."

Pieter nodded and brushed dirt from his sleeves. "If I may."

"Sure . . . but I better not see you on the street anymore tonight . . . got it?"

His head bobbed in a quick bow. "I understand."

He looked at Teresa and opened his mouth, then shut it, turned and walked into the alley. Teresa bit her lip and waved. Lisa grabbed her hand.

"Greg's with me, Kate . . . Officer Kate . . . ma'am."

The woman smirked. "Keep *him* off the street too, missy."

"Kate!" The other officer flailed a hand. "We got a B&E over on Claiborne . . . perps are still inside."

"Later, kids."

She jumped in, slammed the door, and tires smoked as the car squealed away.

"Sweet mother of pearl," Greg muttered. He looked at his watch and glanced at the alley. "Shall we go?"

Teresa's arms trembled as she drove toward a booth on the corner. Greg dug a ten from his pocket and Teresa handed him the change as the wooden arm swung up. Christa and Delia sat in the back with Lisa and shivered while they clung to each other. Lisa reached a blanket from the cargo deck and draped it over them.

Delia nodded. "Th-thank you. We are in a world of shit, yes?"

Greg laughed and then clamped his lips together. "Sorry . . . I just didn't expect you to say something like that." He pointed. "Take a right under the arch, Teresa . . . that's it."

The truck crept around the corner and Teresa wiped her forehead.

"Where shall I go first?"

"My apartment, since it's closest . . . then Lisa, I guess. Delia and Christa live over by you, don't they?"

"Very near, yes. Um . . . I must call Felicia so she does not worry."

"No . . . you drive. I'll call her." Lisa took out her phone.

Christa whimpered. "We . . . we must call Ms. Scott also?"

"Take a right at the stop sign," Greg said.

Teresa nodded. "Yes . . . it is past one o'clock."

Delia pouted. "Then she already has called the professor because we are not there."

"Yes . . . but call her anyway or you will be in even more trouble."

The girl nodded and pressed a speed key. Teresa told Lisa her number and Lisa dialed.

Greg jumped out at the corner by his apartment building. Lisa kissed him and then climbed into the front seat. She squeezed Teresa's arm as they stopped in front of Michael's house.

"Call me tomorrow, OK? So I know what I'm in for?"

Teresa nodded. "I will try to explain to him but. . . ."

"Can't be *too* bad . . . it's not like *we* were fighting."

"Yes . . . it could be worse." Teresa giggled. "Good night, Lisa."

"'Night!"

A table lamp burned in the foyer and Lisa switched if off. She removed her sandals and tiptoed upstairs. Michael's bedroom door stood open and she peeked around the jamb. His head lolled against a stack of pillows and a book lay open on his chest. He blinked and looked at her when she sat on the bedside.

"Hello."

"Hi, honey . . . I'm home."

Michael grinned and squeezed her hand. "So I see." He peered over his reading glasses at the clock on the nightstand. "Not *terribly* late. How was your party?"

"It was fun. Where's Beth?"

"At home, I suppose. Or perhaps not . . . she was going out with some friends this evening. Why?"

"I just thought. . . ."

Michael pushed upright. "You thought she had taken up residence?"

"Well, no . . . yeah . . . kind of."

"Don't you think I would tell you of such a drastic change in our living arrangements?"

Lisa sighed. "I guess so." Her sandals fell to the floor and he smirked as she wriggled under the covers. "But it seems like she spends the night a lot."

He hugged her shoulders and kissed her forehead. "Now, now . . . have I not been circumspect regarding how often *you* spend the night other than in your own bed?"

"Umm . . . if that means you knew about it all along and didn't say anything until you had to. . . ."

"Yes . . . that's it exactly."

"Yeah, I guess you were . . . and thanks for not telling Dylan on me."

"I *will* do, if it begins to affect your school work."

"Don't be harsh, OK? I said I'd tell you from now on."

Michael patted her seat and she moaned. "So . . . was the party worth a sore bottom?"

"Uh huh . . . most of it. We kinda had some trouble right at the end. That's how come I'm late . . . and he'll probably give us all a lickin' for it."

"What sort of trouble?"

"Nothing horrible . . . Greg got in a fight with a guy and the police were there but. . . ."

"Lisa!"

"It's *OK* . . . we knew the cop and it wasn't a big deal, but after Teresa talked Dylan into extending our curfew he's not gonna be happy we couldn't even make *that*."

"I expect not. How drunk *was* Greg?"

She scowled. "It wasn't *Greg's* fault. The guy was a jerk, even if he did look like Dylan."

"He did?"

"Uh huh." She yawned, shut her eyes, and snuggled against his shoulder.

"Lisa?"

"Hm?"

"You're falling asleep."

"No I'm not."

"Don't fall asleep in your clothes."

"OK."

He chuckled and pushed off the covers. She whimpered and squirmed, but didn't open her eyes as he undressed her and tucked her into bed beside him.

⁂

Jill's blue BMW sat in front of the building and parked next to it was a red convertible. The girls in the back seat groaned as Teresa stopped beside the BMW and shut off the engine.

"I guess I should not go home right now."

"Perhaps you *should* . . . and we will go with you? We would not like to talk to Professor Uncle at this time."

Teresa snorted and opened her door. "You are *funny*, Christa. We must go in . . . before he sees us and comes out."

They trudged to the entrance and up a flight of stairs. Delia keyed the latch and opened the door. Dylan switched off the TV and rose from the sofa. Jill stood and folded her arms as she walked around a chair.

"Good morning, girls." She looked at her watch, then at Dylan. "You need me for anything?"

"I might. A few more minutes?"

Jill shrugged. "No problem."

He pointed to the sofa and Teresa led the way. The girls sat, clasped their hands and trembled. Dylan took a deep breath.

"I had two phone calls saying you girls missed curfew . . . who wants to tell me why?"

Delia and Christa looked at Teresa. She licked her lips.

"Felicia called you?" He nodded. "Well . . . it is like Lisa said on the phone . . . we had some problems as we were leaving the party."

"What kind of problems?"

"Um . . . Lisa's boyfriend had to fight a very unreasonable young man and so . . . so we were delayed to talk to the police."

"The *police?*"

"Yes but . . . it was only Kate and she. . . ."

"I don't care *who* it was, you shouldn't have. . . ." Jill cleared her throat. He scowled at her then looked at Teresa. "All right . . . go on."

"That . . . that is *all*, Uncle Dylan. We *tried* to be in time and . . . and we called when we had the problem, so *please* don't be angry with us."

He sighed and his lips twisted. "We'll talk about that later . . . but I want to know about the drinking."

"I didn't! Only Diet Coke, I swear!"

"*Somebody* smells like a brewery . . . Delia? Christa?"

They bit their lips and looked at the floor while Teresa stared at them.

"But they were not *driving*, Uncle Dylan."

"They aren't supposed to be *drunk*, Teresa."

"But we are *not*, Herr Professor."

"Only a cup or two of wine."

"Oh, really? Stand up, both of you."

The girls staggered to their feet and Dylan took their hands. "Look at me." He studied their eyes for ten seconds. "Only a little wine, huh?"

"Yeh . . . yes, Professor."

"And . . . also we are very tired."

He shook his head. "Where did you get the pills?"

"We . . . we *have* no pills, only the wine and. . . ."

"Christa! Don't lie to me. How many did you buy?"

"We bought *none* of these and. . . ."

"Give me the rest of them, Christa."

She stamped her foot and sobbed. "*No*, only . . . only the boy *gave* one to us, but we did not *buy* more."

"Are you sure?"

Delia bobbed her head. "It is *truth*, Professor, only this one!"

"All right . . . what was it? Ecstasy?"

The girls nodded and Jill grimaced.

"Should I call the paramedics?"

He shook his head. "I want to keep an eye on them, though." The girls whimpered while he glared. "I'm very disappointed in you two. We had an agreement . . . remember?"

"Yes, but . . . we . . . we are *sorry*, Professor!"

"Wine with meals *only* and no drugs of *any* kind. Do you remember that promise?"

Christa nodded. "But . . . but we *were* eating, Professor, and this boy is *giving* the pill so . . . so we should enjoy more the dancing!"

"Young lady, that is *not* an excuse for breaking your promise and you know I have to punish you." They sobbed and threw their arms around him while they pleaded in two languages. "Go take a shower. Jill, would you see that the water isn't too hot? And make sure they scrub all this glitter junk off. I'll put them in my spare room for tonight."

Jill nodded and crooked a finger. "Come on . . . you heard him."

"You . . . you will not beat us?"

"Not until you sober up. Now go."

The girls looked at each other and ran to the bedroom. Jill followed them in and shut the door. Teresa shook her head.

"I . . . I did not know, Uncle Dylan."

"No . . . and I probably should have told you they had a drug problem." He sat beside her and took her hand. "The reason they're here is because they drink too much, and when they drink they go looking for drugs. Now . . . tell me what happened. Lisa's boyfriend had a fight?"

"Yes . . . Greg . . . and another boy . . . young man." She coughed. "So . . . so you will puh-punish the girls?"

He leaned back. "Yes . . . why did you change the subject?"

"No reason, I only. . . ."

"Did you know this young man?"

"No . . . I . . . we only met him at the party."

"I see. What's his name?"

"Um . . . Pieter . . . something. He is Slovenian."

"Why did Greg get into a fight with him?"

"He . . . he attacked Greg."

"For no reason?"

"Well, he . . . um . . . he would not . . . would not let go of me."

"*Greg* wouldn't?"

"No, the *boy* . . . and Greg made him let go. We . . . we were dancing and Pieter was most . . . most. . . ."

Dylan put an arm around her and hugged. "Taken with you? I
can understand that. And when it was time to go, he didn't want you
to?"

"Yes, and . . . and he looks just like *you*."

"What?"

"Everyone thinks so . . . except Greg because he does not know
you."

"This young man is fifty years old?"

She got up to sit on his lap and wrapped her arms around his
neck. "*No*, Uncle Dylan . . . like you when you were young . . . I mean
. . . not so old as. . . ."

"OK, I get your point." He patted her bottom. "I suppose I should
be flattered."

"Well of *course*. Pieter shall someday be as handsome as you."

He laughed and squeezed her cheeks. "*Now* you're buttering me
up."

"Not a bit . . . his face does not yet have the character of yours."

His left eye flinched and he frowned. "Teresa?"

She noted the change in his voice and leaned back. "Sir?"

"Do I dare ask where your panties are?"

"Oh, God." She wriggled and twisted but he held tight. "They
. . . um . . . I had an accident, Uncle Dylan, and. . . ."

"Don't fib to me, Teresa. There was no accident, was there?"

"There *was* and . . . it was *most* embarrassing when I had to. . . ."

He pressed a finger to her lips. "Don't. You *know* better than to fib and I can see it in your eyes. Were you so impressed with this young man that you gave your panties to *him*?" She pressed her eyes to his shoulder. "Why did you do that, Teresa?"

"I . . . I . . . I don't *know*."

"Was that his reward for good sex?"

"Uncle *Dylan* . . . we . . . we did not *have* sex, only. . . ."

"Only what, sweetie?"

She raised her head and glared at him. "Well it is your fault!"

His eyebrows arched. "Excuse me?"

"Yes, Uncle Dylan . . . if . . . if you were not so handsome and . . . and *sexy* . . . and I happen to meet you thirty years ago and we are making out under the trees it is not *my* fault your hand goes inside my panties and then they are too damp to wear so I must give them to you . . . *him*."

He rubbed his forehead and squinted. "Did *you* take one of those pills?"

Her face reddened and she squealed. "No! I did not do *anything* wrong, and you are being most unreasonable to ask about my underpants in any case!"

"Is that so? Well, in *any* case, you need a reminder not to screech at me."

She yelped when he twisted her around and pressed her onto his lap. "Uncle Dylan, *no*!"

The skirt bunched at her waist and she wailed as his hand collided with bare, sensitive cheeks. Plump mounds quivered and her hips rocked against his thighs. Dylan's familiar, beloved palm swatted hard and fanned the spark lit by Pieter's callow, tentative strokes. Sweet, wet lightning flashed through her vagina and she whined soft, piteous complaints as brilliant tremors swept over her. He held tight to her waist and painted rosy sting across her bottom. She wailed and clamped a hand to her mouth as the climax jolted her. The bedroom door opened and he pulled down Teresa's skirt when Jill peeked out and frowned at him.

"I thought she was the *good* one."

"Never mind the sarcasm. Are they ready?"

She smirked. "Ready for what?"

"Jill!"

"OK, OK . . . yeah, they're ready."

Teresa sat up and wiped her eyes. Jill led Delia and Christa into the living room. Damp hair was combed back, faces were scrubbed and they wore loose, fleecy shorts, oversized T-shirts and sneakers with no socks. Dylan stood and held out his arms. The girls crept toward him. He took their hands and squeezed.

"Look at me." They raised their heads. "How do you feel?"

"We . . . we feel very sorry, Herr Professor."

"Yes, sir . . . and we will not do this again."

He smiled. "I'm glad . . . but what I *meant* was . . . how do you feel physically? Sick to your stomachs? Dizzy?"

Christa shook her head. "No, the wine and the . . . the wine has worn away."

Delia nodded. "We are merely very tired. Can we go to bed *here*?"

"Perhaps." He felt their foreheads with the back of his hand. "You're still warm, though. Jill, would you get the rectal thermometer, please?"

She smiled and turned around as the girls wailed.

"But Professor! This is horrible!"

"*Hush*, Christa. If you don't have a fever you may sleep in your own beds tonight. Otherwise you're coming with me and I'll spank you first thing in the morning."

"You cannot *do* such a. . . ."

"Delia! Stop that right *now*." Jill set a plastic tube, a jar, and a bag of latex gloves on the coffee table. "Thanks. Kneel on the sofa, girls, facing the back."

"But, *sir*, this . . . this will . . . *humiliate* us!"

"No, Christa . . . you humiliated *yourselves* when you broke your promise. Now do as I said."

The girls blushed and knelt on the couch. Teresa stood and chewed a fingertip. Dylan wrapped an arm around her.

"You want to go home, sweetie?"

"Yes . . . I think I. . . ."

"Are you OK to drive?"

She nodded and kissed his cheek. "I am fine, Uncle Dylan. Good night."

Jill opened the door, said good night, and shut it behind her. Teresa took two steps and leaned against the wall. The voices were faint but distinguishable.

"Stop wriggling, Delia."

"But . . . but that is for babies!"

"And spoiled young women who *act* like babies, so be still while I put it in your bottom."

"*Eek!*"

"You . . . you will not spank us if we have no fever?"

"That's *not* what I said, Christa. I *will* spank you, but maybe not first thing in the morning."

Teresa shuddered at the mental image of two grown-up bottoms, bare and vulnerable, open to her uncle's stern gaze. She gasped as electric moisture gathered between her nether lips, then tiptoed down the stairs and ran to the Land Rover. When Teresa got home she found Felicia asleep on the couch, her head pillowed on her arm. Teresa brushed a wisp of hair from her stepmother's mouth. The woman blinked and sat up.

"Hi, honey. Are you OK?"

"Yes. I am sorry to make you worry."

"That's all right. You want some cocoa . . . or something to eat?"

"No, thank you . . . only to go to bed."

"OK. Did you talk to Dylan?"

She nodded. "I think I am not in trouble about the curfew, but the Frankfurt girls are in a world of shit."

Felicia gasped. "Teresa!"

"This is what Delia said . . . I do not know where she heard it."

"Well, don't let Dylan hear it from *either* of you."

"No. Good night, Felicia."

"Why are the other girls in trouble?"

"That is a long story and I will tell you tomorrow." She bent down and kissed the woman's cheek. "Oh . . . has Uncle Dylan ever been to Italy . . . or Slovenia?"

"Slovenia? No . . . he said he went to Rome once. Why?"

"How old was he?"

"I think it was right after he got his bachelor's degree so . . . twenty-one or twenty-two. Why?"

"No reason." Teresa grinned and waved. "'Night, Fel!"

Chapter 12

AFTERMATH

LISA MOANED, ROLLED over, and swiped at the fuzz that covered her tongue. She pushed up on her elbow and looked at the clock, then twisted around and yanked the covers away.

"Oh shit . . . not *again*."

Dressed only in white, microfiber panties, she dropped off the bed and scooped up her clothes. They smelled of beer-sweat and stale perfume. She carried them to the bathroom and dumped them into the hamper, stepped out of her panties, and threw them in. Naked, she leaned over the basin and drank from the tap, then squeezed Crest onto her finger and scrubbed sourness from her mouth. Hangers rattled as she pulled a crisp cotton dress shirt from Michael's closet, buttoned it on, and rolled up the sleeves. She held the rail as she stumbled downstairs, and then peeked into the kitchen. Michael sat at the table with his newspaper and coffee cup. He smiled when she padded toward him.

"Good morning, my dear."

He pushed back his chair and she sat on his lap.

"How come you didn't wake me up?"

"You *did* have rather a long night."

"Yeah . . . but I'm late for work again and my mean old boss is probably gonna ground me."

She cuddled into his chest and Michael hugged her.

"How could he possibly, when you look so adorable?"

"Hmph! I'm a mess, Michael."

He smoothed tousled hair and kissed her forehead. "Don't be silly
. . . there is nothing cuter than a girl in a man's dress shirt."

"You think?" She looked up and smiled. "How's the coffee?"

"Now *that* is a different matter entirely . . . although I seem to
improve with practice. It has gone from barely palatable to almost
drinkable."

"So you think you can talk my boss out of grounding me . . . or
spanking my bottom 'til it looks like a sunburned zebra?"

Michael laughed. "He sounds quite the tyrant. However do you
put up with him?"

"I don't know . . . mostly 'cause I love him . . . and he lets me wear
his shirts."

"*Does* he? That's very generous . . . so perhaps you misspoke
when you called him a mean old boss."

Lisa grinned and kissed his lips. "No way! You oughta see what
he did to my poor heinie yesterday."

"Well, yes . . . I certainly ought. Stand up."

Cotton crinkled as she stood, bunched the shirttail at her waist
and looked over her shoulder. "Told ya."

He leaned forward and caressed the bare cheeks. "Hmm . . . one
might think you had a light spanking yesterday, but one can't be sure."

"Light spanking? It's *purple*."

"Nonsense." Michael traced a pink stripe with his fingertip and
Lisa whimpered at the quivery tingle. "Looks more like you've sat on
a park bench too long and the boards indented your flesh. May I have
my breakfast now?"

He kissed her bottom and she grinned.

"Well, OK . . . since you asked so nice."

Teresa sat up in bed when Felicia knocked and entered.

"Morning! I went to the bakery so there's fresh cinnamon rolls."

"OK . . . what time is it?"

"Almost nine."

She rubbed her eyes and yawned. "I'll be there in a minute."

An electric motor hummed as Teresa brushed her teeth. She slogged into the kitchen and Felicia smiled.

"You look like you're ready to go back to bed, honey."

"No . . . I am all right. Did Uncle Dylan call?"

Felicia shook her head. "I called him. He said you girls had an exciting night."

Teresa shuddered and peeled apart a sticky pastry. "Much *too* exciting. Did he say anything about Delia and Christa?"

"They're in a lot of trouble . . . about the drugs."

"Did they sleep at their own apartment?"

"Yes. He said he thought about taking them to his place but changed his mind."

"Did he say anything about me?"

"He asked if you were all right and I told him you were still asleep. Why? You didn't do anything wrong, did you?"

"No! Only . . . I got home so late."

Felicia squeezed the girl's arm. "Honey, Dylan's not unreasonable. You ran into some trouble you couldn't help, that's all. He understands. Now tell me about this boy."

"Yes, well . . . this *boy* was the cause of most of the trouble."

"Did he give Delia and Christa the drugs?"

"No . . . nothing like that. But he became very attached to me and would not let me leave, so Greg had the fight with him and that is when the police came."

"Uh huh . . . that's pretty much what Dylan said. But he *looked* like Dylan?"

Teresa nodded. "Kate thought he was Dylan's son."

"Who did?"

"The policewoman who is Uncle Dylan's friend."

"Oh . . . Kate, um . . . Hargrove . . . you know her?"

"Yes, she . . . she visited the cottage a few weeks ago and Uncle Dylan introduced us. Do you know her?"

"Not very well . . . I've only met her a couple of times, but Dylan tutored her when she was an undergrad." Felicia grinned. "So is *that* why you asked if Dylan ever went to Slovenia? You thought this boy might be his son?"

"Um . . . perhaps. Pieter was born in Italy . . . but if Uncle Dylan was in Rome whilst in his early twenties, then he would be closer to your age than to mine."

Felicia laughed. "I suppose . . . but I don't think he's the sort to leave unclaimed offspring running around, anyway."

"I do not think so either . . . but the resemblance is what fooled me."

"You aren't the first girl to be fooled by a handsome face. You want coffee?"

"Yes, please." Teresa chewed a cinnamon roll while Felicia poured. "Um . . . did you know Delia and Christa have a drug problem?"

"Uh huh." She put a full cup by Teresa's plate and sat beside her. "Dylan knows *you* aren't into it. That's probably why he didn't bother to tell you."

"He was very cross with them . . . as angry as I ever saw him . . . but even if he blisters their bottoms, do you think this will do any good?"

"I don't know . . . but if nothing else it will convince them that he's serious about keeping them straight and sober."

"I suppose. He has not done this yet?"

Felicia shook her head. "He said he'd go over there at lunchtime."

Teresa swallowed a bite and sipped coffee. "Those poor girls."

"They may wish they had stayed in Germany."

"Perhaps . . . he already has embarrassed them most frightfully."

"The thermometer?" Teresa nodded. "I imagine that was pretty awful." Felicia sighed. "He didn't want to let them into the college because of the drugs."

"Oh? Then why did he do this?"

"I talked him into it."

"Why?"

"I know their parents . . . the girls' mothers are sisters, and they used to work for the same company your Papa did many years ago. We'd see them when we went to Frankfurt. They're nice people and I still consider them friends, but Delia and Christa grew up next door to each other so they've got a long history of getting in trouble together. Greta . . . Christa's mother . . . called me before we left Hamburg and it took me a while to get Dylan to even talk to her."

"But he did?"

"Yes . . . and I'm not exactly in his good graces right now."

"He blames you for this trouble?"

Felicia smiled. "He says he doesn't . . . but I won't be recommending anybody for the college in the near future."

"None with drug problems, in any case." Teresa leaned back. "Still . . . they are my friends, so perhaps I should visit them later."

"That would be sweet . . . and you should take them a present."

"Wine to ease the pain?"

"No, silly." Felicia ran to the bathroom. A white, printed box rattled when she returned and dropped it on the table. "These will help."

Teresa picked up the box and read, then grinned and nodded. "Yes. I believe they will."

The phone rang and Lisa grabbed a handset from the kitchen wall.

"Swayne residence."

"Hello, Lisa. It's Teresa."

"Hi! You OK?"

"Yes . . . I am fine."

"Um . . . that's good. How am I?"

"I do not understand."

"How much trouble am I in?"

"Oh!" Teresa chuckled. "Not so much, I think . . . unless you have done something since last night. Uncle Dylan was most understanding about the lateness."

"You're kidding! *Our* Dylan?"

"Yes, and you need not sound so surprised. Besides, his mind is occupied with the Frankfurt girls and the drugs they took last night."

"Oh my God! So it *wasn't* just the wine?"

"No . . . a boy gave them Ecstasy pills, so with them he was not so understanding."

"I'll bet! That explains all the hugging and mood swings."

"Yes, and Uncle Dylan discovered their condition and. . . ."

Teresa sighed. "Last night he took their temperature . . . in their *bottoms*."

"Oh geeze . . . does Ecstasy give you a fever?"

"I do not know . . . I think it was to embarrass them."

"I'm *sure* . . . that's almost as bad as an enema. He did it in front of you?"

"No . . . I already was embarrassed *for* them, so I left. But I heard their complaining from outside the door."

"Was it before or after he spanked them?"

"Well . . . before . . . because he has not done this yet."

"Yuck! I guess he wants them to sweat, huh?"

"Sweat?"

"You know . . . worry about it . . . imagine the worst."

"Possibly . . . he only said he would not spank them until they are sober."

Lisa chuckled. "Yeah . . . they weren't feeling any pain last night, that's for sure."

"I think not. Um . . . when shall I bring the Land Rover?"

"Sometime before noon if you can. Michael went to the gym and then he's got a meeting, so I was gonna see if Greg wants to have lunch. Hey, why don't you come over about eleven-thirty and we'll both take him to lunch?"

"Thank you, but . . . after last night you may be tired of my company."

"Oh, don't be ridiculous. Besides it's our turn to watch *you* get drunk and silly."

Teresa gasped. "That is a *terrible* idea, after. . . ."

"OK, OK . . . just kidding. But at least a glass of wine where nobody can see you."

"I would not mind *this*."

"Good deal. See you about eleven-thirty?"

"Sure."

Lisa hung up and dialed.

"Hello?"

"Hi . . . is this Lola's Downtown?"

"Um . . . yeah. Uh . . . what can I help you with?"

"Can I speak to Greg?"

"Sure . . . hang on . . . *Greg!*"

She grimaced and shifted the phone to her other ear.

"This is Greg, how can I help you?"

"Tell Cindy not to yell so loud for one thing."

"Hi, Lisa. Sorry about that. I should have sent her home as soon as she came in."

"Yeah? She in a mood?"

Greg chuckled. "Uh huh . . . boyfriend trouble, I think . . . either that or she took a handful of surly pills. How are *you* doing?"

"I'm OK . . . but I passed out about two seconds after I walked in the door last night."

"Oh? So . . . any repercussions over the um. . . ."

"Nope . . . sounds like Uncle Professor's gonna be reasonable for a change. I'll tell you about it at lunch. When can you go?"

"Around one-thirty . . . and I need to take a couple of hours."

"You do, huh? So what's with the long lunch, Mr. Bentley?"

"Well, I came in at nine and I'm closing and . . . now wait a minute, Ms. Carlson. You start micromanaging your best employee and we're gonna have a *long* discussion."

"Oooh . . . it makes me so *hot* when you get all businessy."

He laughed. "This really isn't fair, you know."

"What?"

"That I have an audience and you don't."

"All right, I'll be good. Oh . . . can Teresa join us for lunch?"

"Sure. Tell her I won't try anymore German on her."

"She'll appreciate that, I'm sure. We'll see you around one-thirty."

"Right. Bye . . . love you."

Teresa parked the Land Rover in the driveway at eleven-forty-five, locked it, and rang the front doorbell.

"Hi, Teresa. Oh, thanks." Lisa took the keys and dropped them on the lamp table. "Come on in. We're a little ahead of schedule 'cause Greg can't go until one-thirty."

"That's all right. I had a late breakfast."

"Me too . . . so we can just hang out. You haven't seen the house, have you?"

"No. It's very nice."

"Yeah . . . big, too. Let's go upstairs."

Teresa peeked into the bedrooms on either side of the long hall-way, and Lisa blushed when they got to Michael's room.

"Oops . . . the maid forgot to make the bed this morning."

"But *you* are the. . . ." Teresa gasped when Lisa scowled and pressed a finger to her lips.

"Shh. Don't say anything and maybe my boss won't thrash me."

They laughed as they tossed pillows to the floor and straightened the sheets.

"He is a very violent sleeper, your boss."

"Yeah, it *is* kind of a mess. I think he had company last night."

"Oh, I did not mean to. . . . He is not married?"

"Not officially . . . but sometimes I wonder." They snugged the counterpane over the pillows and Lisa nodded. "That's good. Let's look at the study . . . it's right across the hall."

She opened the door and Teresa walked in. Tall windows all but covered the two outside walls above the back yard. A small desk, leather recliners, and a brocaded chaise sat on deep pile carpet. Teresa ran a hand over the brocade as she wandered to a window.

"A pretty lawn . . . and such a beautiful willow tree."

"I *hate* that tree." Lisa bit her lip.

Teresa gave her a quizzical look, then peered out the window. "It has very slender branches, does it not? Almost like . . . switches?"

"No . . . *exactly* like switches . . . and *man* do they sting." Lisa shuddered, then grinned and jerked her head toward the door. "I'll show you downstairs and we'll get a glass of wine."

"All right." They strolled toward the staircase. "So . . . you were not making a joke? That your boss will thrash you?"

"Well . . . not for an unmade bed." Lisa opened the office door. "Here's the inner sanctum . . . this is where Michael prints his money."

"He prints his . . . but isn't that . . . ?"

"I mean he makes a lot of it."

"Ah . . . yes. This looks just like my father's office in Hamburg."

"I'll bet he was pretty good at making money, too." Tears welled in Teresa's eyes and Lisa patted her arm. "Hey, don't do that . . . um

. . . oh! You see those bookends on the credenza . . . the ones with the brass antelopes? I dropped one once and it punched a hole right through my shoe."

"That's awful! Did it puncture your foot?"

"No . . . but I cussed a blue streak and his lordship is worse than Uncle Dylan when it comes to bad words."

Teresa nodded and pursed her lips. "And . . . and he . . . reacted? The same way Uncle Dylan will react . . . to such language?"

Lisa grinned. "Oh yeah . . . and then some."

She led Teresa into the kitchen, pulled out a bar stool for her, and then took a bottle from the wine cabinet. Teresa coughed.

"Um . . . I think it is a joke but I am not sure. Why do you call him *his lordship?*"

"Picked it up from Beth, I guess." She set the corkscrew and grinned. "We don't call him that to his face 'cause he'd think we're being sarcastic."

"Which you *are*, yes?"

"Absolutely. It fits him, though."

"He is British?"

"As steak and kidney pie!" Lisa grunted and the cork popped. "I'll get some cheese and crackers. You like Monterey Jack?"

"Who?"

"It's a cheese. If you hate it we'll try something else."

"Yes, that will be fine. Lisa?"

"Hm?"

"Can I ask a personal question? And it is not mere curiosity."

Lisa set a box of Triscuits on the bar. "Curiosity's OK . . . from some people. Go ahead."

"You . . . are spanked . . . by Uncle Dylan and your boss, but . . . does Greg also spank you?"

"Uh huh . . . sometimes . . . just for fun."

"For fun? This is *most* perplexing."

Teresa dug crackers from the box and Lisa scowled as she took goblets from a cupboard.

"Hey, now . . . if you're gonna make value judgments. . . ."

"No! I did not mean it is perplexing for *you*, only. . . ."

"Here." Wine gurgled and Lisa pushed a glass across the bar. "You've got something on your mind and this might help you say it."

"Thank you. You really are very kind."

"Oh, geeze . . . just drink." Lisa shook her head, filled her own glass and held it up. "Um . . . *prost?*"

"Yes." Teresa smiled. "*Prost!*"

They clinked glasses and sipped.

"Good, huh?"

"Mmm . . . very. Thank you."

Lisa opened a cheese brick and peeled slices with a wire cutter. "Um . . . so . . . what's perplexing?"

"Oh . . . yes. Well . . . last night, um . . . when I was with that boy. . . ."

"Yeah . . . ?" Lisa piled cheese on a plate and set it beside the crackers.

"He . . . he hit me."

"What? Why didn't you tell . . . ? Oh." Lisa picked up her glass. "You mean he *spanked* you."

"Yes . . . a little . . . and. . . ."

"And you didn't hate it."

Teresa shook her head. "I *liked* it." Lisa walked around the bar and sat. Teresa turned and frowned. "Is that not perplexing? That a stranger will slap my behind and . . . and I enjoy it?"

"Well, first of all . . . Pieter was a stranger, but he was a *familiar* stranger. And I gotta ask *you* a personal question, OK?"

"Of course."

"How many men . . . boys . . . whatever . . . have spanked you?"

"Only Uncle Dylan . . . well, my Papa . . . when I was very little and I threw a chair at his car."

"You *what?* Oh, man! Why did you do that? Do you even remember?"

"Most definitely . . . Papa and Uncle Dylan were waxing the car in the driveway and paying no attention to me and. . . ."

"Wait, wait . . . Uncle Dylan was there? In Germany?"

"Yes, he often came to visit."

"How old were you?"

"Four or five, I suppose."

Lisa nodded. "So they were waxing the car. . . ."

"Well, not so much waxing as drinking beer and talking."

"Now *that* sounds like Dylan."

"What?"

"I couldn't picture Herr Professor waxing a car . . . drinking and talking, now *that* I can imagine." She smiled. "Sorry . . . go on."

Teresa pouted. "Uncle Dylan is a very hard worker and. . . ."

"I *said* I was sorry. So they weren't paying attention to you and. . . ."

"Yes, well . . . you know how children are. I believe I was jealous of the car, so I went upstairs to my room and took my little blue wooden chair and threw it out the window . . . right on top of the Mercedes."

"So you *hit* it?" Teresa nodded. "That's a pretty good throw for a four-year-old."

"My Papa did not think so. I can still hear his feet, pounding up the stairs."

Lisa wiped her lips with a linen napkin. "I'll bet . . . smacked your little tushy good, huh?"

"Perhaps . . . I do not remember. All I remember is his voice . . . not the words, but the strictness in his tone whilst he scolded me."

"Where was Uncle Dylan?"

"Examining the damage to the car, I suppose."

"I doubt that."

"Why?"

"He was probably downstairs, cringing every time your Papa swatted your heinie. I get the feeling he's not into spanking *real* little girls."

Teresa slurped wine and reached for the cheese. "No . . . he has said as much . . . and he has always been kind to me . . . except when he is spanking me himself." She smirked and slid soft whiteness between her lips.

"So when did Uncle Dylan start spanking you? I know it wasn't after you moved here."

"And how do you know *this*?"

"That first day in class." Lisa reached for the bottle. "The way you bent over the desk, like it was perfectly normal."

"I most certainly did *not* . . . I . . . I argued and yelled and. . . ."

Lisa laughed and poured wine. "And took a paddling on your bare fanny the way you always do."

"No I. . . ." Teresa burped, covered her mouth, and blushed. "Pardon me." Lisa smiled and raised her glass, and Teresa giggled as she picked hers up. "You are *so* smart. How many men, or boys, or . . . *whatever* . . . have paddled *your* bare fanny?"

"I'd have to think a minute." She sipped and shook her head. "But we're talking about *you*, remember?"

"All right, then . . . the first time was when Uncle Dylan brought Felicia to meet Papa. He took me to the zoo for my twelfth birthday, and I asked for everything I saw . . . soda, candy-floss, chocolate bars, lemonade. . . ."

"And he gave you everything you wanted."

"Naturally! This is what uncles *do* . . . up to a point." Lisa chuckled and Teresa nodded. "Yes, I pushed him to his limit, and had a tantrum because he would not buy me caramels."

"Caramels?"

Teresa shrugged. "They looked so shiny and sweet in the bag on the kiosk counter, and I wanted them. But he said no so I began to scream and he carried me behind the lavatories and spanked me until I stopped screaming."

Lisa laughed. "And started crying, right?"

"Yes . . . very much so . . . but that was not the worst of it."

"No? What's worse than getting your bare heinie swatted in public?"

"Oh, he *didn't* that time . . . not until I was older." Teresa gulped wine. "He only spanked me on my panties, but he told Papa what happened . . . at dinner that night, right in front of Felicia . . . and I thought I would die of embarrassment."

"Yeah, I can see that. So what did Papa say?"

"Hmph! He merely told Dylan he did the right thing and then sent me to bed."

"Well, *that* was harsh."

"Yes . . . and then the *awful* part happened."

"There's more?" Teresa nodded and Lisa emptied the bottle into her glass. "Well?"

"All the sweets and sodas, they . . . gave me the stomach ache and I did not eat any dinner, so . . . Maria, our housekeeper, she. . . ."

A slow smile brightened Lisa's face as she slid the crackers closer to her friend's hand. "She um . . . helped you go to the bathroom?" Teresa frowned, grabbed a Triscuit and nibbled as she stared straight ahead. Lisa nodded. "With a little nozzle in your bottom?" The girl sighed and Lisa rubbed her back. "So it wasn't your first time for *that*, either."

"No . . . but it . . . it was a most terrible experience."

"What? When you were twelve?"

"No, I mean . . . well yes, but . . . the other day, when Uncle Dylan . . . were you not horrified?"

"Yeah, sure . . . but it worked, didn't it?"

Teresa scowled. "It was *most* effective in releasing. . . ."

"*No*, silly . . . I mean it did what Dylan wanted it to." Lisa smiled and raised her glass. "Made us quit fighting."

"Yes . . . it did *that*, as well." Teresa grinned. "And I hope never to make a friend in such a way again."

"I'll drink to that."

They drained their glasses.

"Is there any more wine?"

"No, and it's probably a good thing . . . otherwise we might start getting personal."

Lisa winked and Teresa blushed.

"I . . . I have never told anyone about this spanking at the zoo or . . . or the enema."

"Then I feel privileged."

"The sign last night is correct."

"Hm? What sign?"

"Behind the bar . . . *in vino veritas*."

"Sounds like Latin. What's it mean?"

"In wine, truth."

"I *guess*. We better have some coffee before we go to lunch, or the truth is we get pulled over by the cops."

Teresa laughed. "And Kate will not come to save us today, because she worked so late last night."

"Was that weird or *what?*" Barstool legs scraped linoleum when Lisa jumped down.

"This woman will think you and I do nothing but get into trouble."

"Kind of goes with the territory when you're a cop . . . always see people at their worst."

"Yes, I suppose . . . so perhaps we will look for her and tell her we are behaving ourselves?"

"Let's think about that . . . when we haven't had quite so much wine."

Teresa smiled and nodded while Lisa filled the coffee maker with Jamaica Blue Mountain.

Greg got into the Land Rover and leaned over to kiss Lisa. She pressed her lips to his for a second, and frowned as he pulled away.

"What?"

He twisted and smiled at Teresa. "Hi! You all right?"

"Yes, thank you. And you?"

"Just great, thanks." He looked at Lisa and shook his head. "I'll drive."

"Greg!"

"Don't Greg *me*, young lady . . . put it in Park and move over." He stepped onto the sidewalk and glared at her.

"I *knew* I should of brushed my teeth," she muttered.

Lisa slammed the gearshift and wriggled across the console. He walked around and got in on the driver's side. She glared straight ahead as he slipped into traffic.

"Um . . . where are we going, Greg? D'Antonio's is back that way."

"I know." He looked in the rearview mirror. "We have to stop at my apartment, Teresa. You don't mind, do you?"

"Of course not."

"Good. You hungry?"

"Not so much."

"How was the wine?"

"It was very good and the Monterey. . . ." Teresa clapped a hand to her mouth and looked at Lisa. "I am sorry."

"It's OK . . . I was already busted." She stared at her boyfriend. "Greg, for crying out loud! We had a little wine before lunch 'cause Teresa can't drink in public and anyway she's *legal* in Germany and. . . ."

"We're not *in* Germany, in case you didn't notice, and after last night. . . ." He grunted, turned into the parking lot at his apartment building and stopped in a space next to the front door. "What were you *thinking?*"

"Jesus Christ, Greg! Why are you being such a . . . a *shit* over a little glass of wine?"

"Because I love you, that's why! We dodged so many bullets last night and you didn't even get in trouble for missing curfew, and then you pull *this?* What if you got rear-ended, huh? Not your fault, but if I can smell it, so can a cop. Let's go upstairs and order a pizza, and then I'll drive you both home."

She stamped the floorboard. "No! I wanna go *out* for lunch." Her eyes pleaded. "Don't be mad, OK? We only had a *little* wine . . . 'cause we were talking, you know? Girl talk? Greg? I *hate* it when you glare like that."

He shook his head. "We go upstairs and have pizza or I drive you home right now. I'll bring the truck to Michael's house when I get off work."

"It was only a glass of wine . . . why are you acting like this?"

"I *told* you. Now. Pizza or home . . . which?"

Lisa growled, looked at Teresa and jumped out of the truck. "Pizza."

Teresa ran after her, through the door and up the stairs.

"Um . . . Lisa? Are you all right?"

"I will be. Follow my lead, OK?"

Greg strode down the hallway and opened the apartment. Lisa dragged Teresa inside and pulled her against the wall. He picked up the phone and waved them toward the sofa. Teresa took a step but Lisa held her arm. Greg scowled at them.

"What do you want on the pizza?"

Lisa sneered. "Smoked eel and fried buffalo tongue."

Teresa covered a smile with her hand. Greg slammed the phone down and stalked toward them.

"I oughta blister your fanny, Lisa."

"No, you oughta quit being such a . . . Greg!"

He snatched her wrist and she squealed as he sat on the couch, tossed her across his lap and smacked the seat of her tight blue shorts. She kicked as he held her waist and rained a dozen more harsh spanks.

"Why are you being such a brat?"

"I'm not! You're . . . ow! Being a jerk! Owee! It was just a glass of . . . *no*! Don't *do* that! Greg!"

A zipper scritched and Lisa wailed as he tugged down her shorts and panties. His arm rose high and Teresa nibbled a fingertip as he slapped bare roundness. Red handprints overlaid pink stripes and Lisa reached back to cover. Greg grabbed her wrist in his left hand and pressed it to his knee while he spanked the jittery, quivery mounds.

"I can't *believe* you'd drink and drive after last night. Are you out of your tiny little mind?"

"Nooo owee not so haaard . . . I'm sorreeee! Don't pleeease?"

"And what's with these belt marks? You *said* you didn't get in trouble."

"I . . . I didn't! That's from yesterday! Owee! 'Cause you didn't set the alarm!"

He flexed his palm and shifted his feet wide, then stood and took her with him. Lisa yelped as he stood her on her feet and whimpered as he hugged her.

"I thought you *talked* Michael out of grounding you."

"Well I . . . *kind* of did. I . . . I traded with him."

"Oh, Lisa, I'm sorry. Why didn't you tell me?"

"I was going to . . . eventually. I just wanted to have fun last night so I didn't see any point in telling you *then*."

"You can be very silly sometimes." He caressed her achy cheeks and kissed her lips. "Now . . . what do you want on the pizza?"

"Eel and buffalo tongue."

"All right, then . . . I'll get the hairbrush."

"Don't be so *mean* to me, and anyway you gotta spank *her*."

"*What?*"

Teresa gasped and cowered against the wall. Lisa shot her a quick wink, then looked up at Greg and pouted.

"Yeah . . . 'cause um . . . she didn't get any wine last night so I gave her just a *little* bit . . . so she wouldn't feel left out and . . . I couldn't let her drink alone, could I? And if *I* have to get spanked so does *she*."

Greg shook his head. "That is the biggest bunch of bull I *ever*. . . ."

"But *Greg* . . . you *can't* spank me anymore, 'cause you already did, and on top of those icky tawse marks . . . so *I'm* not naughty anymore . . . but *she* is."

He glanced at Teresa. Fear and desire smoldered in round, green eyes. Lisa smiled as Greg lifted her chin. He sighed.

"Are you sure about this?"

"Uh huh . . . very sure."

"All right, then . . . go stand in the corner where I can see your naughty bare bottom while I talk to her."

"Nuh *uh*! That's not fair!"

"Teresa can wait . . . if you just *have* to have another spanking."

"All *right* . . . I'm going, OK? *Geeze*, what a grouch."

Lisa held onto her shorts and stumbled to the corner next to the arch. She peered over her shoulder as Greg folded his arms and ambled toward Teresa. The girl chewed a knuckle and pressed her knees together to still the quivery butterflies that fluttered between her tummy and the apex of her thighs. Greg took a deep breath.

"You *know* you aren't supposed to drink wine in this country, don't you?"

Teresa swallowed dryness. "Yes, Greg."

"So you were naughty, weren't you?"

"But Lisa *said* it would be all right and. . . ."

He pressed a finger to her lips. "But you know what a bad girl *she* is . . . so didn't you think she'd get you in trouble?"

"I . . . I . . . perhaps . . . but in any case, you have no *right* to. . . ."

"Spank your bare bottom? That's true . . . so I guess I'll have to call Uncle Dylan, won't I?"

"No! Please do not! Oh, God! Lisa?"

Greg smiled and squeezed her hand. "She can't help you, Sundance."

"*What?*"

"Come on . . . you saw *her* bottom get spanked and now she's going to see *yours*."

"But you are *her* boyfriend so how can you . . . ? No, please?"

Her breasts trembled as he winked and tugged her to the sofa. A thin muslin skirt swirled around smooth bare thighs when she fell across his lap. She stared into Lisa's eyes and whimpered while Greg whisked up the skirt to reveal yellow silk tap pants. The knickers hugged plump mounds and clung deep within the furrow. Lisa's left eyebrow flinched and Teresa whimpered as his fingers slipped into the waistband and tugged the panties down.

A stranger's hand caressed innocent, quivery flesh for the second time in her life, and the second time in two days, and she squirmed against his slender, muscular arm. Hectic butterflies caroused in her tummy, confused by the conflicted emotions that raged in her heart. He wasn't Dylan, or even the faux Dylan, he was Lisa's boyfriend, and yet her bareness, her tender intimacy was disclosed to him, and for what? Must she assuage his anger? Amuse his girlfriend? Seek redemption from the sin of wine?

Sharp sting embraced her bottom and all other matters fell by the wayside. The hard hand clapped again and Teresa squealed. She kicked, wriggled, and screeched, but damp fire sparked in her hind cheeks and dribbled between her thighs. Her arms flailed and she reached back to cover the pain, the shame, the confounded pleasure that a harsh, male palm burned into her nakedness.

"Will you be a good girl now?"

The brisk tenor voice burst in Teresa's ears like a thunderclap.

"Yes . . . Greg."

"All right then."

Strong fingers pulled up her panties and she whimpered when

strong arms lifted her from his lap. Soft muslin caressed warm silk as the skirt fell, and she rubbed her eyes as gentle fingers held shaky arms to steady her. Teresa blinked and gazed into sparkly blue eyes. Lisa smiled at her.

"You OK?"

"Yes . . . are you?" Teresa glanced at the blue shorts, snug around the girl's hips.

"Sure! You ready for lunch?"

"Lisa? Did . . . did you . . . ?" She turned to Greg and glared. "Did you *plan* this?"

He smirked. "I didn't *plan* on spanking two naughty fannies this afternoon, but it seemed like the quickest way to burn the wine out of your systems."

Lisa giggled. "Yeah right . . . I'll just *bet* that's what you were thinking while you smacked our pretty little butts." She yelped when he squeezed her bottom.

"And what were *you* thinking when you ordered me to spank *her*, huh?"

"Yes, I should like to know this as well." Teresa scowled and then gasped when Lisa hugged her.

"I was thinking you really needed it."

"*Why?*"

"Guilt is bad for the digestion . . . everybody knows *that*. Now kiss Greg . . . just a little one . . . and tell him thanks for not making you go to lunch all guilty."

"I most certainly will not!"

"Oh, go ahead . . . he'll feel bad if you don't." A grin lighted Lisa's face as she pushed the girl toward Greg. "Hurry up. I'm *starving*."

Teresa clucked her tongue. "I think you are also insane."

Greg held out his arms. "Certifiable . . . so we better humor her."

"Yes, I suppose." She smiled and stood on tiptoe to press his lips with hers. "Thank you for . . . um . . . ridding me of this guilt, Greg."

"You're more than welcome. Let's go eat."

They sat at a patio table beneath a canvas awning at D'Antonio's and munched breadsticks while they waited for their order.

"So what wholesome and nonalcoholic plans do you girls have for after lunch?"

Lisa wrinkled her nose at him. "We're going to see some sick friends, if it's any of your business."

"Yeah? Who?"

"Delia and Christa."

"You're *kidding*. I didn't think they drank *that* much . . . although they *were* pretty out of it."

"It was not the wine." Teresa leaned over the table. "They took Ecstasy pills."

His eyebrows arched. "*That* explains a lot. Got pretty messed up?"

"Not so much from the drugs, I think, but. . . ." She glanced at Lisa.

"Uncle Dylan found out. He was supposed to go see them at noon."

"Oh boy . . . so it may be more like *injured* friends, huh?" He grimaced when Teresa nodded.

"He is most impatient with people who abuse drugs."

Lisa smirked. "Yeah . . . even worse than some people who get bent out of shape over a little wine."

He took her hand and squeezed. "You just see how bent out of shape I get if *you* ever try that stuff."

"Yeah, yeah." He scowled and squeezed harder. "OK, OK! Geeze, Greg, you know I wouldn't. Anyway, Teresa brought some first-aid for them."

"Not in liquid form, I hope."

"No . . . here comes our food so stop being a dweeb and eat."

Lisa dug into a dish of lasagna while Greg inhaled a crusty meatball sandwich and a pile of roasted potatoes. Teresa took a bite of ravioli, found it hot and delicious, and devoured the rest. Greg pushed his plate away and chuckled.

"Was anybody hungry?"

"Oh, hush." Lisa leaned toward Greg's ear. "Fun spankings do that to people."

He grinned and kissed her. "They're good for all *sorts* of appetites, aren't they?"

Teresa blushed and sipped water. Lisa patted her hand.

"So, um . . . you wanna call the girls and make sure it's OK to come over?"

"Yes. *They* did not get a fun spanking, in the meantime." She dialed her cell phone and waited.

"Hello?"

"Christa?"

"Yes. Hello, Teresa."

"Um . . . the professor has been there today?"

"Oh, God!"

"I . . . I am sorry. Will you like for us to visit, Lisa and I? Only for a little while?"

"No! It is too *horrible* what he. . . ." Sobs and coughs clouded the transmission, and then the girl blew her nose and sighed. "Yes . . . it will be kind of you to come."

"Shall we bring anything? Something to eat or drink?"

"Perhaps Diet Pepsi? We do not wish to walk to the grocery."

"Yes, of course. We will see you soon, all right?"

"All right. Goodbye, Teresa."

The phone queeped and she dropped it next to her plate.

Lisa grabbed her fingers. "Bad, huh?" Teresa nodded. "What are we supposed to bring?"

"Um . . . Diet Pepsi."

"OK . . . and maybe something to go with it."

Greg wiped his mouth. "I should get back to work."

"Yeah." Lisa raised her hand to catch the waiter's eye. "Oh! Are you gonna call Renée? About the clothes?"

"Sure. You think we should carry them?"

"They're really pretty, so I don't know why not."

"Me either. Consignment or outright buy?"

"I'll ask Michael what he thinks . . . and this just became a working lunch, so put it on your expense account."

He grinned. "You make me so *hot* when you get all businessy."

She grabbed his collar and kissed him. "I'll take care of *that* little problem . . . right after work."

"Listen, Ms. Executive . . . there's nothing *little* about this problem, and I'll show you as soon as I get you home."

Lisa giggled. "I'm counting on it. Call me after you close and I'll come over."

"Absolutely." He winked. "And bring some wine."

The waiter offered a tray and Greg clicked a credit card on it.

❧

They carried plastic grocery bags up the stairs and Lisa knocked on the apartment door with her elbow. It opened and an eye peeked out.

"Hi, Delia."

The girl stepped back and let them in. They dropped their load of soda bottles, cookie bags, ice cream tubs, and chocolate bars on the kitchen counter. Christa gaped as she rummaged.

"What is all this?"

Lisa grinned. "CARE packages."

Teresa nodded. "Yes, and we did not bring one thing that is nourishing."

"Ice cream has *some* nourishment," Delia said as she held up a carton of Chunky Monkey.

"Then I guess we should take it back."

Delia scowled and grappled with the plastic seal. "I do not *think* so."

"Here . . . use a knife."

The girls opened four pints of Ben & Jerry's, grabbed spoons, and went into the living room. Cartons passed from hand to hand as sweet, hard cream melted in smiley mouths. Christa and Delia wore their soft shorts and T-shirts from the night before, and leaned on sofa arms with their bottoms perpendicular to the cushions. Lisa and Teresa sat in low-backed armchairs pulled close to the coffee table.

Teresa handed the Cherry Garcia to Delia and took the Brownie Batter. "Um . . . is everything OK?"

Delia shrugged. "It is now."

"But . . . I mean . . . was he very harsh to you?"

"What do you think?" Christa frowned and slammed the Phish Food carton on the table. "Do you know what he *did*?"

Lisa shook her head. "It must have been terrible, Christa."

"Terrible is only where he *started*!" She sobbed into the sofa arm and Lisa knelt by her side.

"Shh . . . you're OK now. It's over. You want to talk about it?"

Christa shook her head and buried her face in Lisa's shoulder. Delia swallowed and took a deep breath.

"He brought lunch . . . sandwiches from the Subway . . . and he was most pleasant while we ate, but then. . . ." She shuddered and jammed her spoon into the ice cream. "We should have known, because he brings Ms. Scott with him."

"Oh, God." Teresa bit her lip and stared at Delia. "Why would he do this?"

"So she will help him to punish us. She is *such* an evil woman!"

"What did she *do*?"

"She . . . she merely *stood* there." Delia pointed to the bedroom. "While he . . . he took us to the bathroom and . . . and said we must take off all of our clothes and then he . . . oh God!"

Teresa knelt to take Delia's hand. "But what did the *professor* do? Tell me . . . it will help to talk, honestly."

"He . . . we were naked and . . . he said we must kneel on the floor . . . and then he . . . he puts a tube and . . . and hot water in my bottom!"

The girl trembled and Teresa grabbed the carton as it fell from her fingers. "I know . . . it was most horrible and it is all right to cry."

"But . . . but that is not *all*, Teresa! He . . . he was looking inside my bottom, and . . . and at my pussy . . . while he does this horrible thing!"

"Yes . . . yes . . . I know . . . it is truly humiliating and. . . ."

Christa jerked away from Lisa and glared at Teresa. "How *can* you know this? Were you there?"

"Hey, now . . . it's OK."

"Let me alone, Lisa! How can you say *anything* when you were not . . . ?"

Lisa held the girl's arms. "We *have* been there, Christa . . . *all* of us. He stuck a nasty, awful tube in my bottom and Teresa's, too."

Delia gasped and looked at Teresa. "Is this so?"

"Yes . . . most definitely."

"But why?"

"Because Lisa behaved horribly to me when I was the new girl." She winked and Lisa smirked.

"*No*, it was because Teresa tried to pick a fight with me *twice* her first day at school and got us in trouble."

"Pay no attention to her . . . it is the ice cream talking. But in any case, that is why we were concerned for you."

"So . . . so you *knew* he would do this to us?"

"No, but I am not surprised. He hates drugs very much."

Christa sighed. "Yes . . . he said this to us . . . many times."

Delia whimpered. "He says the enema is to wash out the drugs we took."

"He told *us* it was to wash out the lies."

"You *lied* to him, Lisa?"

"Well, yeah . . . after he paddled us for yelling at each other, we got into it *again*."

Teresa nodded. "And then we made up a story . . . merely to avoid another spanking."

"But he was standing right outside and heard the whole thing."

"That was not very smart," Delia said.

"Neither was taking those. . . ." Lisa stopped when Teresa scowled. "No . . . I guess it wasn't."

"So, um. . . ." Teresa cleared her throat. "He made you have the enema before he spanked you?"

"Yes, and then. . . ." Delia rolled onto her tummy and tugged her shorts down. "Look!"

Lotion glistened on the girl's striped and swollen bottom. Lisa grimaced and looked into Christa's eyes.

"I'm sorry . . . really . . . 'cause I've been *there*, too."

Christa shivered, twisted, and pushed up her hips so Lisa could fold the pants off puffy, shiny cheeks. "You . . . have had such as this?"

"Yeah . . . not from him, but I hated it when my Dad used to. . . ."

Lisa swallowed hard and turned her head. "I think it's time for the stuff."

"Yes . . . yes, of course." Teresa dug the box from her purse and opened packets.

Lisa stroked tender flesh along Christa's right hip as she looked at Delia's sore bottom. "It was a belt, wasn't it?" Delia nodded. "And he made you lie down on the bed while he whipped you with it."

Christa sighed while Lisa's soft fingers soothed her. "How do you know this?"

"These blue dots . . . that's where the little holes in the end of the belt kind of pinch the skin and leave a mark. Do you guys have twin beds?"

"Yes. You have not seen the bedroom?"

"No . . . but you were on his right and Delia was on his left . . . and Herr Uncle stood right in between and spanked you with his belt."

"You can tell this from these marks?"

"Uh huh . . . the end hit Delia on the left hip and you on the right. If you'd been side by side they'd be on the same one."

"Yes, that is correct."

"Where was Ms. Scott?"

Christa sneered. "She was kneeling by the bed table and holding our hands."

Delia whimpered. "Yes, and she . . . she tells us it will soon be over . . . but it was *not* soon over!"

"I believe it." Lisa turned. Teresa peeled tape from a soft plastic compress and gave it to her. "These are for headaches but I bet they work pretty good on other kinds of aches. Hang on a second." She reached to the lamp table, grabbed a handful of Kleenex, and gave some to Teresa. "I'll be gentle but we need a dry place or the pads won't stick, OK?"

The girls cringed as soft tissue dabbed away slickness. Lisa smoothed a pad over Christa's right cheek. She moaned as chemical iciness flowed into her bottom. Delia wriggled her hips.

"Me too?"

Teresa smiled. "Of course."

She pressed a bandage onto plump redness and Delia squeaked.

"Oh! *Oh*! That is almost as good as Chunky Monkey!"

Lisa laughed as she put the second bandage on Christa's bottom. "So? What do you think? Headache better?"

Christa smiled as she hugged Lisa's neck. "Yes, thank you."

"Don't thank *me*. This was Teresa's idea."

"Not really . . . my stepmother gave them to me. She knows her brother very well."

"So *one* member of the family is not so cruel." Delia reached for the ice cream.

Lisa handed her the carton. "Two, Delia . . . what about Teresa?"

"Oh . . . yes, of course." She nodded and looked at Teresa. "I do not mean to insult your family . . . only. . . ."

"That's all right . . . I understand."

Christa palmed the bandages and sighed. "He did hug us afterwards . . . while we were crying . . . and we cried for a *very* long time."

"That's the least he could do."

"And he was most generous with the lotion." Delia smirked. "Especially when Ms. Scott left and he. . . ."

"Delia!" Christa glared at her sister.

Lisa coughed to cover a gasp. Teresa blinked, and then her eyes widened when Christa's face turned as red as her bottom. The girl pulled up her shorts and grabbed the Phish Food.

"So, um . . . you never tried Ecstasy, Teresa?"

"No, I . . . I get into enough trouble merely with wine."

"But I thought you did not drink wine."

"That's not *quite* true." Lisa grinned and Teresa stuck out her tongue. "She just tries real hard not to get caught."

"Yes, and you were *so* helpful, Lisa . . . with your wine-sniffing boyfriend."

Christa smiled. "Greg? What happened?"

"Well, we had only a *little* merlot before lunch. . . ."

"About half a bottle each. . . ."

"And Greg of all persons smells this on Lisa's breath. . . ."

"And he threw a fit! I couldn't believe it!"

Delia took the spoon out of her mouth and gaped. "He was

angry because you drank wine?"

"Yeah, he went on and on. . . ." Lisa frowned and dropped her voice an octave. "After last night how could you drink and drive and blah blah blah!"

Teresa giggled. "Yes, and then he spanked her." She bit her lip when Lisa huffed and glared. "Sorry."

"Yeah, well, you should be."

"So show us," Delia said.

Lisa shook her head. "I'd be too embarrassed."

"But we have seen your behind . . . in class . . . so what is there to be ashamed of?"

"The fact that it's white as a sheet compared to yours."

Christa frowned. "Oh, *please*? I would like to see how the tall, strong boyfriend spanks."

"OK . . . but Teresa has to, too."

Delia gasped. "He spanked her also?"

"So you *do* allow him to spank other girls." Christa grinned.

Lisa's nose wrinkled. "Not as a general rule . . . but it seemed like a good idea at the time." She stood and unzipped, then turned and pulled her pants down. "Teresa?"

"Oh, very well." She twisted around, lifted the skirt and slipped down her knickers.

"Are you *sure* he spanked you, Teresa?"

"Yes, Delia . . . but that was over two hours ago."

"Then he was not very angry about the wine. But why do you not have the stripes as Lisa does?"

"Oh . . . those." Lisa blushed. "That's from a tawse and Greg doesn't have one . . . that I know of."

Teresa giggled and pulled up her pants. Christa shook her head. "Then who *did* this?"

Delia nodded. "And what is this *tawse*?"

Lisa knelt on the floor and dug a spoon into Cherry Garcia. "It's kind of a short belt. Michael used it on me yesterday because I overslept."

"Who is Michael?"

"My boss."

"Your *boss* will punish you also?" Delia blew a long breath when Lisa nodded. "Then perhaps we are lucky to have only the professor."

Christa gasped. "*I* do not feel so lucky."

"Perhaps . . . but we are lucky to have friends who will bring us cold treats for our mouths and our hurtful bottoms, yes?"

"I cannot argue with this." Christa raised her carton. "We thank you . . . and hope we never will have to do the same for you."

Teresa and Lisa smiled and returned the salute.

Chapter 13

THE PERFECT STORM

HUMID, SULTRY AUGUST melted away and the university summer session ended. Dylan flew to Boston, gave the girls a two-week holiday from Red Blossom College, and scheduled their next class for the Wednesday afternoon before fall semester began.

Teresa smelled rain when she stepped off the bus, and low, gray clouds hung in the sky above her exactly the way bricks don't. A warm September breeze ruffled her hair as she walked to the cottage and opened the gate. Only a few late blossoms drooped from the vines and a trace of honeysuckle fragrance teased her nostrils. She slipped her key into the latch and pushed. The door squeaked against its jamb and swung open. Two overhead lamps brightened the entryway, and the smell of old books was strong enough to touch. Lisa waved at her when she entered the schoolroom.

"Hi, Lisa." Teresa dropped her bag next to a worktable and looked at the big desk. "The professor is not here?"

Ashley turned. "He's in the study."

"The door's been shut ever since we came in," Britney said.

Delia nodded and rattled a question in German. Teresa shook your head.

"No, I have *not* seen Pieter, and speak English, understand?"

"*Ja, verstehen!*" The girl grinned.

"Knock it off, Delia." Teresa rolled her eyes.

"But *we* did." Christa leaned on her palm and smirked.

"You did what?"

"Saw Pieter."

"Oh?" Teresa smoothed her skirt and sat. "Where?"

"At a bar downtown . . . last Saturday."

"Did he see *you*?"

Christa nodded. "He would not speak to us, but Mario wished to sell us more . . . products."

"Christa!"

"Teresa! We did not *buy* them, you know. You are such a worrier."

Lisa cleared her throat and sat up straight. Chairs squeaked, books thumped and pages rustled as Dylan strode through the door. He leaned against the front of the desk and smiled.

"I hope everyone had a pleasant holiday." Heads bobbed. "Excellent . . . but I seem to be missing a few assignments. Lisa?"

"Sir?"

"Is your computer broken?"

She sighed. "No, sir. I um . . . I'll e-mail it tonight, I promise."

"Very well. Delia? Christa?"

"Yes, Professor, we also will do this."

"Teresa?"

"But I *sent* it, Unc . . . Professor!"

"I know . . . but I want you to rewrite it."

Teresa gaped. "But . . . but. . . ."

He held up a hand. "There's no point in arguing . . . I won't accept a paper you threw together in twenty minutes. Britney?"

"Oh, God."

"I see you catch my drift." The girl nodded. "Very good. Ashley? Thank you for sending your assignment on time. I found it . . . interesting." She nodded and bit her lip while the others stared at her. Dylan walked behind the desk, removed his suit jacket and hung it on the chair. "In an obviously misguided attempt to give you a rest before the new semester begins, I made those assignments as easy as I could without actually doing them for you. They would have cost you no more than three or four hours of your two weeks off, and yet you . . . *most* of you . . . decided that a last summer fling was more important than your homework . . . and that makes me very unhappy."

"But Professor, I'm almost done with it and. . . ."

"That's enough, Lisa." He walked to the window and opened the blinds. "I want those essays by tomorrow . . . and they had better be exceptional. All right . . . open your grammar books to the section on prepositions."

The clock on the wall clicked off a tedious half hour and Teresa's eyelids sagged. Distant thunder rumbled as flashes illuminated the horizon. Clouds roiled and a wind gust rattled the casements. Water drops smudged dust as they slid down the panes.

"Teresa!"

She gasped and sat up straight. "Sir?"

"What do we never end a sentence with?"

"A . . . a preposition, sir."

"And what did I just do, Teresa?"

"You . . . you *shouted* at me." She blushed when he grinned and the other girls laughed.

"Yes, I believe I did that as well. It must be time for a break. Ten minutes, girls . . . and let's stay inside today, shall we?"

Chair legs scritched hardwood and light, woolen skirts bounced out the door. Dylan went to the study and the girls gathered in the kitchen. Delia slurped from a short, brown bottle.

"Mmm . . . this is good. You should try one, Lisa."

"Nah . . . they're mostly milk and sugar, with a little coffee for flavor." Lisa rummaged in the refrigerator. "I don't see any Mountain Dew."

"That is like *so* midwestern." Britney clicked the plastic collar off a chilled frappuccino.

"I don't like sugar in my coffee, Valley girl."

"Orange County is nowhere *near* the Valley."

"Oh sorry . . . *Disneyland* girl. Didn't recognize you without your mouse ears."

Britney's eyes flashed. "So how was the tractor pull, *farm girl?*"

Lisa took a step but Teresa grabbed her arm.

"Here, Lisa . . . have a Pepsi. We do *not* need a fight . . . we are in enough trouble already."

She took the bottle and turned away. "Yeah, all except Ashley."

Ashley grinned. "Well, thanks just all to pieces, honey child."

"Eat dirt and die, OK?"

"Lisa, don't *do* that." Teresa put a hand over the upraised middle finger.

Britney and Ashley moved shoulder-to-shoulder and glared. Teresa sighed and stood next to the little blonde. Thunder boomed in the distance and the air crackled with tension. Delia coughed and sidestepped in front of Lisa to reach the refrigerator.

"So, uh . . . perhaps it was not a good idea to spend these two weeks goofing up?" Delia opened a water bottle.

"Goofing *off*, Delia." Lisa stepped back. "Probably not . . . but it sure was nice to hang out at the lake and do nothing."

Teresa nodded. "Do you really have this essay almost done?"

Lisa arched her eyebrows. "Define *almost done*."

"That is what I thought. A paragraph perhaps?"

"Almost." Lisa grinned and Teresa rolled her eyes.

Christa sighed. "I have not started, but it is only one letter grade if it is late, and it *is* an easy assignment." She looked at Teresa. "Why is Professor Uncle in such a bad temper? Did he not take a holiday?"

"Yes . . . he was ten days in Boston, but I think no amount of vacation will keep him from a bad temper when we do not do the homework."

Delia frowned. "Why will someone holiday in Boston? For the historic monuments?"

Teresa shrugged. "Perhaps . . . or the sailing," She smiled. "I should not say but . . . also his girlfriend is living there . . . I think."

Britney smirked. "You *think*?"

"I am not positive . . . he says he goes for research at the university library, but Felicia has given me hints that he visits someone."

"So why do you think it's a girlfriend?"

"Only from the knowing looks she makes when he talks about the city."

"Hmm. . . ." Ashley shook her head. "I'm trying to picture Professor Travesty's girlfriend."

Lisa pursed her lips. "Let's see . . . a lot younger than him . . . real pretty . . . good figure but not too heavy on top . . . perfect grammar . . . round butt with big red handprints on it. . . ."

The girls laughed while Lisa grinned. Christa looked at Britney.

"Did you have fun on your trip to California?"

"It was OK. We drove down to the beach at Oceanside every day."

"How far is that?"

"Half an hour or so . . . depends on traffic on the 5."

"So you are like us . . . going to the beach instead of writing the essay?"

Britney looked at Ashley. The girl sniffed, threw away her bottle and they both left the kitchen. Lisa blinked.

"*That* was weird."

Christa frowned. "Did I say something wrong? I only wished to show interest."

Teresa patted the girl's arm. "It was a good try but I think they are determined to be hostile today."

Lisa grunted. "You can say that again."

"Yes, but *you* did not need to react so strongly."

"Oh yeah?" Lisa smirked and bumped Teresa with her hip. "So you're the reaction police now, huh?"

"Do not *start* something, farm girl." Teresa bumped back and Lisa stumbled sideways.

"Hey, pick on somebody your own size or my boyfriend will. . . ." She clapped a hand over her grin and backed away as Teresa stalked toward her.

Dylan's voice echoed through the hallway. "All right, everyone. Break's over."

"Whew! Saved by the bell."

Lisa squealed when Teresa laughed and pushed her out of the kitchen.

⁂

The oaken edge bit his thighs as Dylan leaned against the desk and crossed his arms. "The penalty for late assignments is usually one letter grade per day." The girls frowned at each other. "But that's for a *usual* assignment in the *usual* timeframe." Frowns turned to grimaces as he walked around the desk and opened a drawer. "This was neither . . . it was a piece of cake with *twice* the time allotted . . . and failure to complete it indicates nothing but laziness. That stops as of *now*."

Moans and whines filled the room. Lisa raised a hand.

"Puh-Professor, you're not gonna. . . ."

"I most certainly *am*, Ms. Carlson. Now stand up . . . all of you except Ashley."

Lisa grumbled and stood. Teresa's knees quivered as she pushed back the chair. Delia and Christa sighed and got up. Britney glared at him from her seat in the last row.

"Britney? Did you not understand what I said?"

She jerked to her feet. "This isn't fair 'cause you never *told* us. . . ."

"Hush, Britney."

Lightning split the western sky, low and close. Thunder cracked and tapered to a rumble as Dylan took two leather soles from the drawer. One was plain, black, and familiar, the other new, different, and frightful. It had a dozen eighth-inch holes drilled through the center of its wider end in the shape of an X.

Delia and Christa stood at the two front tables, Teresa and Lisa behind them. Britney sniffled and stared at Lisa's back. Ashley sat in her chair behind Teresa and sucked a lacquered thumbnail. Dylan smacked his desktop with the familiar sole. The slap echoed in the girl's ears, louder than the thunderclap, as he walked toward them.

"Clear everything from your tables, step around to the front and bend over." Petulant whiffs and whines assailed his ears and he waited while the girls fumbled books, papers, and pencils into satchels. "Raise your skirts."

Five pair of sensible shoes shuffled the floor. Five pair of damp, angry eyes peered at him over quivery shoulders. Five light wool skirts slid up smooth thighs. Five bottoms wriggled and clenched. Dylan sighed.

"Delia, *what* are you wearing?"

She blinked. "It is called a thong panty, Herr Professor."

"I know what it's *called*, young lady. Is it authorized school wear?"

"I . . . I have no other which is clean."

"Then I'll give you a reminder to do your laundry more often."

Plump, bare buttocks squirmed around lacy thong. "I . . . I am *sorry*, Herr Professor."

"Yes, I'm sure you are."

He tucked the sole under his arm, leaned over, and tugged the garment down her legs. She whimpered and bit a knuckle, then stepped out of the panty. He dropped it into her satchel and stepped back.

"Twenty strokes for the assignment and five for the dress code violation."

"But *sir*, I. . . ."

"Hush, girl. Teresa?"

She turned to look into his eyes. "Yes, sir?"

"Would you please bring Delia proper panties from the cupboard?"

"Yes, sir."

Teresa's skirt slithered down and she clutched at the butterflies in her tummy as she hurried out of the classroom. Rain spattered the roof and blood pounded her ears. She stopped and turned at the door to look back. Delia grimaced and stared straight ahead, her face flushed and damp. She writhed on the table while Dylan smacked her bottom. Teresa chewed a pinky finger and watched the leather rise and fall as she backed toward the study.

She bumped the desk and the iMac screen flickered and focused on an open web page. Teresa glanced at it and then listened to sharp splats and girlish yelps while she searched for panties. The plastic wrapper cooled her sweaty palms and she pressed it to her forehead as she read the text on the screen. She gasped and went back to the classroom.

"Stand up, Delia."

Dylan glanced at her as Teresa tiptoed through the door. She bit her lip, set the package on Delia's table and then stood in front of her own. Delia sobbed, pushed herself upright, and turned to him. Her bottom glowed red, with curvy scarlet lines where the edge of the sole bit tender flesh. Teresa stared at the sore behind and a tight thrill shot through her tummy and into her throat. She felt Dylan's eyes, whirled around, bent, and lifted her skirt.

Delia hiccupped and rubbed hot sting. "I . . . I . . . I am very sorry, Herr Professor."

"I know, Delia. You're a good girl. Now go stand in the corner by the cloakroom."

"But *Professor*, I . . . yes, sir."

He tucked her skirt hem into its waistband, patted her arm and she shuffled toward the chalkboard. A jolt of lightning flickered and thunder boomed overhead. Gusty rain clicked window glass. Christa whimpered and looked back at him when Dylan took a step and stood behind her.

"Twenty strokes for the missed assignment."

"Please not to spank *hard?*"

She whimpered when he thumbed down tight cotton and her bottom wriggled. Pale cheeks flushed pink at the first leathery swat, and their color deepened to coral as he spanked. She pleaded and apologized in a mix of German and English while her right foot pounded the floor. He patted her back and she wiped tears as she stood and turned.

"I trust you've learned your lesson, Christa."

"*Ja*, Herr Professor, *ich* . . . I will do these assignments in time, I *promise*."

"That's a good girl. Stand next to Delia."

A tiny squeal escaped her lips as he tucked her skirt in, then she went to lean against the wall. Lisa stared at him over her shoulder. He stepped between the tables and she pouted when he pulled her panties down.

"I'm *sorry*, Professor."

"I want the assignment e-mailed by midnight tonight or this will happen again tomorrow morning. Is that clear?"

"But Professor!"

"You *said* it was nearly finished so that won't be a problem, will it?"

"Nuh-no, sir."

He raised the sole high and slapped hard. Rain splashed a liquid melody on the roof and thunder rumbled the bass line beneath sharp claps. Lisa screeched, squirmed and pounded the table while her behind turned red and then crimson.

"Stand up, Lisa."

Both hands rubbed fiery tenderness as she rose. "*Geeze*, Dylan . . . I . . . I mean Professor, that really, really . . . why so *hard*?"

"The other girls didn't whine like this."

"'Cause their butts weren't *smoking* when you got done!"

"Perhaps you feel it more keenly because you know better than to blow off assignments."

"Yeah right." She wiped a tear. "Can I go to the corner now?"

Dylan tucked in her skirt and slapped her bottom with his fingers. "Yes, you *may*."

"Professor!" Lisa grunted and stomped away.

"Right next to Christa and no rubbing, young lady."

"Yes, *sir*."

Manic butterflies raged in Teresa's tummy when he stepped toward her. Cold blue eyes bored into her soul and opened wellsprings of guilt.

"Uncle . . . sir, I . . . I really *am* sorry."

"Did you truly imagine I would accept that drivel you sent me?"

"But I . . . I was going to do another, honestly! To . . . to make up for it, only I had to. . . ."

"Teresa! Whatever you're about to say is either an excuse or a fib, and I don't want to hear either."

She sobbed and bit a finger as he yanked her panties to her knees. His accusation echoed in her ears and tears clouded her eyes as she stared straight ahead. Leather burned her behind even worse than the wooden paddle. The shock spread across her cheeks rather than into the tissue, and set fire to nerves that the sole didn't touch. She yelped when the second stroke fell, and the sting redoubled.

Ashley hid her mouth with a hand but Teresa saw the smile in her eyes. She clenched her teeth and moaned through ten sharp licks. At the thirteenth, she squealed; at the fifteenth she screeched; at the twentieth, she kicked and screeched. Red, crackly flames shot through her bottom as Dylan lifted her. A warm, wet curtain parted and she gazed into soft, sapphire eyes. He held her close while she rubbed sore flesh with one hand and clutched his arm with the other. She took a deep breath and swallowed hard.

"I . . . I am *sorry*, Uncle . . . sir . . . *Professor*."

"Shh . . . it's all right, Teresa. You were about to fib to me so I had to spank you very hard . . . but it's over. You're a good girl now, aren't you?" She nodded and wiped tears on his shirt. He smiled and patted blazing cheeks. "We *do* have Kleenex, Teresa."

"Suh-sorry."

He grabbed tissues and pressed them into her hand. She blew her nose and dabbed her eyes while he led her to stand next to Lisa. The girl looked at Teresa and bit her lip while Dylan tucked Teresa's skirt in. A windblast quivered windowpanes and leaked through to cool her bottom. Rain fell in sheets and the back garden glimmered with deep puddles. Teresa leaned her forehead against the wall and sighed as Dylan turned.

"Britney?"

"Sir?"

"Why did you not send me your assignment?"

"I . . . I forgot. Sir."

"You forgot to do it, or you forgot to send it?"

"I . . . didn't do it."

"Didn't you? Or did you know better than to send me a plagiarized essay?"

"Oh *God*."

Britney looked at Ashley and the girl slumped in her chair. Britney straightened and cleared her throat.

"I . . . I was going to do a *real* one tomorrow, I swear! I *told* her it was wrong."

Ashley shrieked. "Damn it, Brit!"

Dylan glared. "Keep *still*, Ashley. I'll deal with you in a moment."

"But I. . . ."

"Be *quiet*." He pointed a finger and Ashley covered her face with her hands. "Britney?"

"S-sir?"

"I will assume you did no assignment at all."

She bit her lip and nodded. "OK . . . um . . . thank you. Sir."

Britney bent over the table, raised her skirt and pushed out her small round bottom. He lowered her panties and stepped back. The cheeks glowed a deep tan. A band of lighter skin curved about her waist and a pale arrowhead pointed downward just above her chink bone. Dylan raised the sole and painted a harsh patina of dull red over the tan with strict, unhurried swats. Britney yelped, squealed, and sobbed, but held tight to the table. When the last spank cracked hard across the narrow cleft, she jerked upright and grasped her behind in both hands as she danced away the sting.

"It's all right now." Dylan hugged her and tucked in her skirt. "Get some Kleenex and go to the corner."

"Y-yes, sir. I . . . I won't ever do it again."

"Of course you won't. You're a good girl. Go on now."

She walked stiff-legged away and Dylan looked at Ashley's tense, ruddy face. He shook his head, turned and walked to the front of the room.

"All right . . . I want all of you to bend over my desk."

"Professor, you *can't* be. . . ."

"For Christ's *sakes*, Professor, you. . . ."

"Uncle Dylan, you have *already*. . . ."

"Hush! And do what I told you."

He took the baby oil bottle from the drawer. The girls moaned and scowled as they shuffled over to offer him their bottoms.

"Real cute, Professor," Lisa muttered as she leaned on the desktop.

"Don't be impertinent, young lady."

Dylan tipped the bottle into his palm and spread cool slickness over red behinds. The girls sighed and wriggled while he soothed their torment and awakened warm, quivery desires. He smiled as he caressed five sore bottoms, and then started again at the head of the line and rubbed a few drops more onto the crimson curls left by the sole's edge. Delia squeaked when he patted her slippery cheeks.

"Put your knickers on, Miss . . . the *proper* ones."

"Yes, sir." She grabbed the packet off her desk, ripped it open, and sighed as she stepped into demure underpants and pulled her skirt down.

He wiped his hands on a tissue and nodded. "All right . . . panties up and straighten your skirts, then return to your seats."

Lisa pouted at him. "Cah . . . *may* we have some pillows, Professor?"

"Yes, you may."

"Thank you, sir." She smirked and stepped backward. "That's very kind of you, sir, to let us sit on soft pillows after you scorched our. . . ."

She turned and dashed away when Dylan reached for the sole. He shook his head and returned the bottle to the drawer. The room grew silent except for the wind's howl and the rain's clatter. Lisa returned with a stack of throw pillows and passed them around. The girls sighed as they wriggled on soft foam. Dylan cleared his throat.

"Ashley?"

"Sir?" she whispered.

"Come here, please."

"*Why?* What did I *do?*"

"Don't speak to me like that. Come here."

Lightning flashed and thunder roared. Ashley trembled and trudged to the desk.

"But I didn't *do* anything."

He took her hand and turned her toward the class. She whimpered and stamped her foot. Dylan scowled.

"Tell them, Ashley."

"But I didn't. . . ."

"I said *tell* them."

"*Professor.*"

Her whine arpeggioed to a wail as he bent her under his left arm. The wail quavered as Dylan whisked up the skirt and slapped her panties hard a dozen times. Shameful tears pooled sad, hazel eyes when he set her down and made her face the class.

"*Now*, young lady."

"But I . . . I. . . ."

"Tell them or I'll spank you until you *do* and then punish you afterward."

"No I . . . *OK*." She puffed and swallowed, then took a breath. "I . . . I copied my essay off a web site, OK?"

"You rotten little brat." Lisa clamped her jaws when Dylan glared.

"What is that called, Ashley?"

"It . . . it's . . . I don't *know*."

Dylan shook his head. "Class?"

"Plagiarism," four voices chorused.

Ashley sobbed into her hands. "I . . . I'm *sorry*."

"You know I should expel you immediately, don't you?"

She gaped, then grabbed tight to his shirt and wept into his chest. "No, *please*? If . . . if you . . . if I . . . *no!*"

He sighed and patted her back. "If I *do*, you go right back to California . . . to Uncle Mike and Aunt Gloria."

Her sobs deepened and she wagged her head like a mare beset by a fly swarm. "Yuh . . . you *can't*! They . . . they're like . . . *Neanderthals*."

"All right, then. If you take your punishment like a good girl, you may stay."

"Yes! *God* yes! Spank me, I don't care, just don't . . . oh *God*."

Dylan's eyebrows arched as Ashley lifted her skirt, yanked down her panties and bent over the desk.

"No, Ashley. Remove *all* your clothes."

She jerked upright and stared at him. "You . . . you're not *serious* . . . not *naked*, it . . . that's *horrible* and . . . and it's not *fair*."

"Neither is stealing. Do you want to remain in this school or not?"

"Yeah but . . . *Jesus*, Professor, I . . . oh shit." She clapped a hand to her mouth when his frown darkened. "I mean *shoot*, but . . . but do they have to *watch*?"

"You watched *them* get spanked."

Teresa puffed. "And you found it *most* amusing."

"That will *do*, young lady." He glared and Teresa bit her lip, then he turned and tapped the desktop with his knuckle. "Put your clothes right here."

"But Professor!"

"Don't make me tell you again."

Tears dripped as Ashley turned toward the chalkboard and fumbled with buttons. She grunted, tugged off her blouse and tie, and dropped them on the desk. Her eyes pleaded but he only frowned as she reached back to grasp her bra strap. Numb fingers refused to cooperate and Dylan unhooked it, slid it down her arms and tossed it beside the blouse. She hugged pear-shaped breasts with her right arm while she unzipped her skirt. It floated to the floor and she whimpered as she bent to pick it up. Dylan nodded.

"Shoes and socks, too."

"No, *please?*"

He scowled and she sobbed. Brown loafers clunked hardwood and water streamed from her eyes as she tugged off white anklets. She stood straight and looked at him over her shoulder, then moaned as she pushed her panties down and off. An arm covered her nipples and she cupped a hand at the apex of her thighs to hide the tiny sliver of bikini-waxed hair and the tight lips beneath. Dylan turned her to the class.

"Ashley has something she wants to say."

She blinked away hot, sorrowful tears. "*What?*"

"Apologize for your arrogance and tell them why you're going to be spanked. Go on."

"I . . . I *can't.*" She wept into his arm.

"Don't make this any worse than it has to be."

"But Professor, I. . . ."

His palm cracked her behind. "*Do* it, Ashley."

"Ow! OK! Jesus Chr . . . naaah!"

The palm landed again and she sidled away as she reached back to rub. He glared and she covered herself once more before she looked at her classmates. Her breasts trembled when she took a deep, quivery breath.

"I . . . uh . . . I copied that essay, OK? And . . . and I'm really sorry, and I'm sorry I acted so . . . like I was all over it when I wasn't, and um. . . ."

"And you're sorry you appeared so pleased while the other girls were being spanked?"

"Uh huh . . . yeah." Ashley looked at Teresa. "I didn't mean to . . . you know . . . be so . . . so . . . um . . . I'm sorry?"

Teresa nodded and looked at Dylan. He picked up the perforated sole and Ashley wailed. Thunder crashed and rolled as he dragged his chair in front of the desk, sat, and pulled the naked girl across his lap. Christa gasped and chewed an index finger. Delia licked her lips, glanced at the ceiling, and then focused on Ashley's slender bottom. Lisa coughed into a hand and leaned forward. Britney wiped her eyes with her fingers and turned to the window. Electric bolts, like white scars on a black face, lanced through the clouds. Teresa squeezed her thighs together and watched the holey sole rise above vulnerable flesh. Dylan's lips compressed when he slapped. Tender cheeks bounced and the report echoed like a gunshot.

"Neeeaaah!"

Ashley kicked as a pink oval, scored with an X of tiny, white pips, appeared on her right cheek. She jerked back a hand to cover the pain but he grabbed her wrist and held it while he paddled the soft bottom. The pale X's glowed red, then crimson. Ashley screamed curses, then promises, and then wordless pleas as leather burned away her crime. Thunderclaps rumbled beneath her shrieks. Smooth mounds clenched, writhed, and turned to a bright-red sea, dotted with scarlet archipelagos. Sobs rasped her throat as Dylan lifted and turned her onto his lap.

"It's all right, Ashley."

Her arms trembled around his neck while tears drenched his collar and soft heat warmed his thighs. He stroked her hair, looked at Britney, then at the Kleenex box. Britney chewed her lip, stumbled to the desk, pulled tissues, and pressed them into her cousin's hand. Ashley wiped her eyes and nose, and Dylan smiled at Britney. She whimpered and returned to her chair.

Lightning flashed and a boom, not thunder, shook the cottage. Ashley dug her nails into Dylan's back as the lights flickered and died. His scalp tingled and he blinked while his eyes adjusted to the gloom.

"Don't worry, girls . . . the power's gone, that's all. Lightning must have hit the transformer." He hugged Ashley hard and patted her back. "Teresa, can you see to get to the kitchen?"

"Yes, I think so."

"Good . . . you and Lisa go look in the cupboard above the sink. The step stool is in the corner, behind the table. Be very careful when you climb up."

"I will . . . but what shall I look for?"

"There's a battery lantern, boxes of candles, and a weather radio.

The matches are in the bottom drawer next to the refrigerator. All right?"

"OK."

"And be careful . . . there's no hurry."

Two gray shadows crept to the door. Ashley whimpered and wriggled on his lap. He shushed her and kissed her forehead.

"Britney, will you get Ashley's clothes, please?"

"Yeah, sure."

The girl stood and shuffled forward. Lightning flared and illuminated the room for an instant. Thunder boomed and even more intense darkness followed. Dylan forced a smile into his voice.

"Missed us again, girls. Go ahead, Britney . . . Ashley's freezing."

"OK."

Wind slung rain at the cottage as Britney ran to grab the clothes. Ashley lifted her chin and whispered into Dylan's ear.

"I'm not cold, Professor . . . it's kinda cozy here."

"Shh."

Britney stumbled against his shoulder. "I got them, Professor."

"Good girl." He grunted and stood. Ashley whimpered when he set her on her feet. "Help her dress, will you?"

Ashley pouted as Britney led her behind the desk. Hundred-year-old walls groaned in the harsh wind. Hail clinked the roof and clattered the windowpanes.

A yellow circle of light danced into the classroom. Lisa led the way and Teresa dropped her armload onto the desk. Shadows writhed in the lantern's spill. Teresa scrabbled cellophane off a box of tapers and struck a match. Sulfur and smoke wrinkled her nose as she lighted candles. Lisa held a cell phone to her ear as she twisted candle bases into pop bottles half-filled with water and passed them around. She sighed and put down the phone, switched off the lantern and winked.

"Just like Christmas, huh, Professor?"

"Indeed . . . but please be careful, girls. Hot wax can be very painful."

Christa giggled. "Is your fire insurance paid, Professor?"

"I certainly hope so."

He sat on the desktop and twisted a knob on the brown plastic radio. It crackled and hissed while Delia and Christa dragged chairs into a semicircle in front of him. He bit his lip and nudged the tuning knob, then patted their arms when Ashley and Britney leaned on either side of him. The radio speaker hummed.

" . . . with heavy rain, frequent lightning, and the . . . *click* . . . *shhk* . . . of straight line winds in excess of eighty miles an hour. Once again, this is a severe thunderstorm warning and tornado watch. Travelers in the vicinity of . . . *scritch click pop* . . . are advised to use extreme caution due to possible flooded road conditions. Flash flood watches are in effect for the following counties. . . ."

Dylan smiled. "Class dismissed."

Lisa laughed. "Yeah right, Professor . . . you're gonna send us out in *that*?"

He sighed. "I suppose not, but I'll have to stack you like cordwood in the Firebird if I drive you home."

Teresa scowled. "I do not *think* so, Uncle Dylan. The top has leaks everywhere when you are driving in the rain."

"Geeze, Teresa." Lisa winked. "Don't you know *anything* about men? You might as well insult his mother as diss his car."

"But I only. . . ."

"All right, all right." Dylan grinned at his niece. "The Firebird stays in the garage . . . but I still have to get you all home, so what's our alternative? I don't want you standing at the bus stop."

"Wouldn't do any good, Uncle Professor."

"Why is that, Lisa?"

"I called the bus line. The streets are flooded downtown so they quit running."

He nodded. "If it's *that* bad the Firebird would be useless. Would Mr. Swayne help out? He's got that Land Rover."

"Sure . . . except he's in Chicago and the Rover's in the shop."

"Felicia could bring her car, Uncle Dylan."

"Maybe . . . I wonder if the taxis are still. . . ."

The radio blared a two-tone alarm. "The National Weather Service has now issued a tornado *warning* . . . I repeat . . . a tornado *warning*. Funnel clouds are reported in the vicinity of. . . ."

Two sirens shrieked a continuous blast, one close by, one farther off, and Dylan jumped to his feet.

"In the bathroom *now*! Take the candles . . . just the lighted ones. Move!"

The girls scurried to pick up the jerry-rigged holders. Lisa grabbed the radio and the lantern and led the way. Dylan shut the blinds, scooped up the rest of the candles, and followed, his sweat cold on forehead and upper lip. He dumped everything onto the cloakroom floor and reached through blind slats to open the casement window an inch, then peered into the bathroom. The girls huddled around the basin counter, their faces red with candle glow. He nodded.

"Good evacuation drill, girls. Everyone gets an A."

He went back and propped the cloakroom door open an inch with a rubber doorstop. Lisa grinned when he walked in.

"So if we all get an A, does that mean we don't have to do those essays?"

"Hm?" He grabbed a towel to mop his forehead. "Oh . . . I suppose not. I'll um . . . just make the next assignment more challenging."

Teresa sneered. "Thank you so *much*, Lisa."

"Oh shut up . . . he was gonna do that anyway."

Dylan looked around. "Is everyone all right? Ashley? You're a little pale. Why don't you sit down?"

"What . . . what are the sirens for?"

"That's the . . . warning signal. It means there's a tornado in the area."

"Oh, God!"

She leaned against the wall and slid down. Britney and Christa grabbed her arms and eased her to the floor. Delia bit her lip and tiptoed over to Dylan.

"A . . . a tornado will come to this house?"

He hugged her and kissed her forehead. "No, Delia. Red Blossom College has a very strict *no tornado* rule. This is only a precaution. Why don't you gather up the extra candles and put them on the shelves with the towels?"

"OK, Professor."

"I wish those sirens would shut the hell up."

"So do I, Britney." Dylan took a deep breath. "Meanwhile, everyone sit down and relax."

"Um . . . Uncle Professor, we only got the one stool and this floor's not real good for bottoms that just got spanked as hard as ours did."

"All right, Lisa, I'll get the pillows. I need to open a window on the other side of the house anyway."

"OK . . . you do that and I'll get the pillows."

"Lisa, I'd rather. . . ."

"Oh go on . . . if the twister hits us, it hits us."

"Very well, but hurry . . . and close the door behind you when you come back in."

Dylan kicked away the doorstop and ran to open the bedroom window while Lisa gathered pillows, then he went to the kitchen and stuffed a plastic garbage bag with bottled water, crackers, and fruit. A wind gust shook the house and he jumped when Lisa tapped his shoulder.

"Can I have a soda?"

"Lisa!"

"*May* I have a soda?"

"I *told* you to get back in the bathroom!"

She opened the refrigerator and loaded her arms with bottles. "Don't forget Mountain Dew next time you go shopping, OK?"

"Young lady, you are in *so* much trouble."

"That bag looks heavy. You want some help?"

He opened his mouth and then shut it when thunder cracked. Lisa's teeth sparkled in the darkness. Dylan sighed and followed her out of the kitchen. She opened the cloakroom door and waited while he passed, then propped it open as he had done. The girls sat on pillows against the walls. Ashley lay on her side, her head on Britney's thigh. Delia jumped to her feet as Dylan set down the bag.

"Professor, I must use the toilet."

"Oh, um . . . I suppose we could all wait in the cloakroom while you. . . ."

Lisa snickered as she stacked soda bottles next to the candles. "Just *go*, Delia. Shut your eyes and pretend you're in the girl's room at school."

"Yes but. . . ." She looked at Dylan and giggled. "This is nothing *you* have not seen, Professor Uncle."

He sighed and shook his head. "Go ahead, Delia. I'll turn around . . . for appearances sake if nothing else."

"Here." Lisa grinned and handed her an aerosol can.

"But it is not *that* sort of. . . ."

"Just in case."

Dylan turned his back and grabbed Lisa's arm. "*Now*, young lady, just what in the name of . . . ?"

She stood on tiptoe and kissed his cheek. "You're taking this *way* too seriously, Uncle Professor. I've been through a million of these. It's gonna be OK, I promise."

"I wish you'd tell that to whomever is blasting those sirens."

"The radio said there were three touch downs right in a row out in Glen Fields, and the storm is headed this way."

"Oh boy."

The toilet flushed and Dylan turned. Teresa walked over and took his hand.

"Are you all right, Uncle Dylan? We were worried about you."

"You too? Don't you girls know it's not polite to be calmer than the man in charge?"

Lisa chuckled. "Is that in the rule book?"

"It *will* be as soon as I. . . ."

"Uncle Dylan, I think you should talk to Ashley. You are certainly calmer than *she*."

He smirked. "Thanks for the ego boost, sweetie. Oh, I brought food if anyone's hungry."

"What a calm thing to do, Uncle Professor."

"Lisa, you're going to be *really* calm when I. . . ."

"Yes, sir, sorry, sir . . . now *go*."

Dylan crouched in front of Ashley and then sat cross-legged on the floor. She jerked away when he reached out.

"What's the matter? Don't you feel well?"

"I'm fine."

"We're all scared, and that's OK."

She glared at him. "I said I'm *fine*."

"Are you still mad at me?" He shook his head when she sat up and pouted. "I know I was very strict with you, but I had to teach you a. . . ."

"It's not *that*, I just. . . ."

"What then?"

"You . . . you didn't . . . *you* know . . . take care of me . . . after . . . like you did the other girls, and . . . and you spanked me a lot harder than *them*."

"But the lights went out and. . . ." He took a breath and nodded. "That wasn't fair, was it? Would it be all right if I take care of you now?"

Thunder exploded above the house and wind whistled through the open window. Ashley threw her arms around Dylan's neck.

"I . . . I *am* scared . . . a little," she whispered.

He hugged her and stroked her neck. "We don't see many tornadoes where we're from, do we?"

"Just on TV." She smiled when he chuckled.

"Very true. Maybe this is what we both need." She sat back and rose to her knees. "Britney, there's a bottle of lotion on the shelf . . . if you can find it. It's Bvlgari Petits et Mamans, spelled. . . ."

Britney grinned. "Babies and mothers . . . you've got a pretty good accent, Professor. I'll get it."

"Excellent . . . thank you."

Ashley stretched across his splayed thighs and he lifted her skirt. Redness glowed beneath snug white cotton. He slipped the panties down and Britney handed him a bottle. Flowery sweetness filled the air when he dribbled lotion. Ashley whimpered as he slicked relief across tight, bright redness, and then moaned while his fingers soothed and caressed.

Teresa and Lisa sat side by side against the opposite wall and ate apples. Lisa got up and threw her core into the trash, glanced at Ashley's behind as she washed her hands and went back to her pillow. She leaned close to Teresa's ear.

"Not any worse than ours."

"Really?" Teresa rose, repeated Lisa's drill, and then whispered.

"You're right . . . except for the little red dots."

"Why do you think he was he trying to paddle *our* fannies off?" Lisa rose to her knees, rucked her skirt, thumbed her panties down and peered over her shoulder. "I've had worse, but not with just twenty licks. Let's see yours."

Wool rustled and Teresa turned as she bared her bottom. "It looks more painful than it feels, however."

"Yeah, but that's not saying much." She glanced at Delia and Christa, who sat across the room next to the shower stall, munched pears, and watched Dylan tend to Ashley. "How come he didn't spank the German girls that hard . . . I mean the *other* German girls?"

"I knew what you meant, American girl." Teresa smiled and pulled up her pants. "I hate to say this, but I think he expects more of us than of them . . . or the California girls."

"Yeah . . . you're probably right." Lisa grimaced as she snugged tight cotton over oily, swollen cheeks. "And it's too late to dumb down and lower his expectations, huh?"

Teresa covered her mouth and giggled. "If we try this, our present soreness will only be a sampling of what is to come."

"We're too smart for our own good."

"I have heard this phrase but did not know its true meaning until now."

Dylan replaced Ashley's clothes and patted the seat of her skirt. She pushed backward and smiled as he hugged her.

"Better?"

She nodded, and then jumped when thunder crashed. "Yeah. Thanks, Professor Uncle . . . I mean. . . ."

"That's all right. No reason you shouldn't call me that . . . everyone else seems to. Now get some water and something to. . . ." He blinked and looked up. "Do you hear that?"

Britney bit a finger and shook her head. "What is it?"

"Nothing . . . no sirens." He whirled around. "Lisa, turn up the radio."

Lisa shook her head. "I've been listening. They lifted the warning but the watch is still in effect."

"*Drat.* All right. Does anyone have a cell phone?" Purses rattled and six hands held out phones. "Lisa, I *told* you . . . just get the pillows."

"But I had to bring the *essentials*, Professor Uncle."

"All right, all right . . . did everyone call home? Teresa?"

"Yes. Felicia is downstairs with Mrs. Fredericks and they will go to the basement of the corner church if the tornado comes."

"And Britney called her mom, in case this makes the news back home."

He patted Ashley's knee. "Good job. Christa?"

"We have also called home, Professor."

"I won't even ask *you*."

Lisa grinned. "My dad said to say hi, and Beth will call Michael in Chicago."

"I'd better call Jill, then."

"Felicia has called her. Would you like a soda, Uncle Dylan?"

He scratched his head. "Sure. Why not?"

"I'll get you a whisky if you want."

"Lisa!"

"OK, OK . . . just a suggestion."

Teresa opened a 7 UP bottle, dropped her pillow next to him, and sat down. "Now that we are all calm and everyone is safe, we should talk."

"Hm? About what?" He drank as she cuddled into his arm.

"Oh . . . about things . . . places . . . Boston, perhaps."

He looked around. All the girls sat within two feet of him. "Well, *this* is interesting."

"Very cozy, don't you think? And we shall be here a while, so you may as well talk."

"Oh, really?"

Delia giggled. "Yes . . . tell us about Boston."

"Well, let's see . . . it's a major port on the eastern seaboard, renowned for it's fine restaurants and theaters as well as. . . ."

Lisa grunted. "You're stonewalling, Professor Dylan. Now just relax and *tell* us."

"Tell you *what*?"

"About your *girlfriend*. Lisa says she has a flat chest."

"Ashley!" Lisa grinned and slapped the girl's arm.

"What *are* you on about? Who's been telling you . . . ? Teresa!"

"Well, you *are* very mysterious, Uncle Dylan, and if you *will* be so, then you merely leave us to guess."

"Oh, for crying out loud. It's not a secret, but it's also none of your business, young lady." Teresa pouted and hung her head. "All right, all right . . . don't *do* that. Her name is Gwen . . . she's divorced . . . we've known each other about fifteen years . . . she works for an insurance company . . . and she has quite a *full* chest, thank you very much."

"And a nice round bottom?"

"Lisa Marie!"

"*OK* . . . so where did you meet her?"

"How old is she?"

"Does she have kids?"

"What does she look like?"

"Do you have a photograph?"

"Whoa, whoa, *wait*. If I'm going to get the third degree, maybe I *will* have a whisky." Lisa jumped to her feet. "But I'll go and. . . ."

"No! Sir . . . we've got you right where we want you."

She ran to the door.

"The liquor cabinet key's in the. . . ."

"I know!"

"Desk drawer." He sighed and looked at Teresa. "*When* did I lose control, sweetie?"

She giggled and hugged his arm. "As soon as you said *class dismissed* . . . but we will give it back, after the emergency has passed. Now . . . about Gwen . . . does she come from a large family?"

Thunder cracked and rumbled. Ashley got up to use the toilet. Dylan turned, leaned against the wall, and wondered if one bottle of single-malt scotch would get him through the dark and stormy night.

※

End of Volume 3